DEATHTRIPPING

COLLECTED HORROR STORIES

ANDERSEN PRUNTY

GRINDHOUSE PRESS

Deathtripping: Collected Horror Stories
Grindhouse Press # 067
ISBN-13: 978-1-941918-74-6

Published by Grindhouse Press
PO Box 521
Dayton, Ohio 45401

DEATHTRIPPING

Also by Andersen Prunty

Neon Dies At Dawn
We Don't Talk About Her
Irrationalia
Failure As a Way of Life
Kill Your Neighbor
This Town Needs a Monster
Squirm With Me
Creep House: Horror Stories
Sociopaths In Love
The Warm Glow of Happy Homes
Bury the Children in the Yard: Horror Stories
Satanic Summer
Fill the Grand Canyon and Live Forever
Pray You Die Alone: Horror Stories
Sunruined: Horror Stories
The Driver's Guide to Hitting Pedestrians
Hi I'm a Social Disease: Horror Stories
Fuckness
The Sorrow King
Slag Attack
My Fake War
The Beard
Zerostrata
Jack and Mr. Grin
The Overwhelming Urge

To Carrie,

You are the FIRST person I would have chosen to be stuck in the apocalypse with. Thank you for not eating me.

CONTENTS

ROOM 19

SHE MOVED INTO Room 29. That was the one right over mine. I wish she had moved somewhere else.

The first time I saw her, I was coming home from the store, a bottle of whiskey wrapped in a paper bag clutched in my right hand. She had three cardboard boxes in front of her and was bent over one of them, lifting it. Dirty strawberry hair hung over the right side of her face so my gaze drifted lower to the skin between her blue stockings and thin yellow sundress. I tried not to let it stop me but I had to stare. She finally hoisted the box up against her chest and turned, startled, to see me standing only a couple of feet away.

"I'd like to help you," I said. "But I can't . . . I just can't."

"Yeah," she said in little more than a resigned whisper. Her face was thin and pretty. Everyone was thin these days but most people who were left weren't very pretty. She turned her back to me and started into the shell of the building.

I stood there until she disappeared into the darkness. There hadn't been a door since before I moved in. I took a deep breath and looked up at the ashy gray sky. I couldn't remember the last time I'd seen the sun. I couldn't remember the last time I'd seen a pretty face. Once I was sure I wouldn't run into her again, I went into the building and into my room, Room 19.

I walked through the trash strewn about the floor, flipped the television on, and sat down on the wasted, moldy couch. I put the bottle, still in the bag, on the saggy upright cardboard box that served as an end table. Upstairs, I heard her clunk the box down on the floor. Static flickered across the television. There weren't any stations. Electricity, for now. Electricity was useless. It would keep the refrigerator running but there wasn't anything to put in it. It would keep the television going but there wasn't anything to watch. It would keep the lights on but, Christ, who wanted to see?

I heard her shuffling back down the hall, just outside my door, to get another box. Three boxes was pretty impressive. That was a lot of stuff to own. No one owned anything anymore. Things were just status symbols anyway and now there wasn't anyone to impress. She was probably wondering why I wouldn't help her. Or maybe she wasn't. One tended not to wonder about much. We'd seen it all. All of our nightmares had blazed to life right in front of us so if a stranger didn't offer to help you carry a few boxes, well, she was probably just thankful I didn't drag her into the building and have my way with her. Because I could have. The law was too busy to concern itself with something like rape.

The truth was that I was afraid to go toward the back of the building. And you had to go to the back to get to the stairs. The landlord, Mr. Grangely, lived back there. Until the girl showed up, I was the only other person in the building. He didn't charge rent but if you died in his building he would cook you up and eat you. Sometimes I think he helped that death along. I never went near him by choice.

I looked at the unwrapped bottle.

The screams were coming on. I could feel them way down in my guts. My ma used to say that was a demon. She said it explained the way I acted much of the time. I didn't believe in demons. I thought Ma was full of shit, rest her soul.

I knew what happened if I didn't let the screams out. I had to. It was like a release valve. But it was going to be embarrassing now. Now that there was someone besides a cannibal to hear me. What would she think? Did it matter what she thought? Probably not.

The screams came on all of a sudden. I dug my fingernails into the arms of the chair, reached down deep past my diaphragm and dragged the first scream out. It was long and brutal and painful. Twelve more followed it. I screamed until I could taste blood in the back of my mouth. Then, with sweaty, shaky hands, I opened the bottle, tossing the bag and the cap on the floor, and dumped the first swallow into my mouth.

Ah, the numbing fire.

There was a knock on the door.

I didn't say anything. My voice was gone. The screams always stole my voice, not that it usually mattered.

"Are you all right?"

I took another slug of the whiskey and doubled over, resisting the urge to run to the door and throw it open. But I didn't because I knew it could only end in pain.

"You okay in there?"

She twisted the knob but it was locked. When sharing the house with a cannibal of questionable ethics, one does not leave the door unlocked.

"I'm right upstairs if you need anything, kay?"

Then she was shuffling away, back that dark hall toward the stink of Grangely's room and up those rickety stairs. Right above me. I heard her moving around. Opening boxes. I sat in the chair, drinking and watching static until night fell.

I must have dozed off or passed out in the chair. When I came to I could hear her crying upstairs. It was so loud it sounded almost like she had her face pressed to the floor. It was the most melancholy sound I'd ever heard. I must have still been half asleep because I imagined her tears seeping through the floorboards, falling through the rancid stale air like drops of seawater, hitting me in the face, trickling into my mouth. I drifted back off, my belly full of whiskey, sadness, and longing.

The next morning I woke up stiff and sweaty. The days were like this. Most of them were cold but there were these occasional sticky, humid days. I didn't know what season it was. I'd had a calendar once but lost it and then stopped caring. I stood up, stretched, went into a corner and pissed. You get used to the smell. The whiskey bottle was empty. I don't know why I didn't just piss in the whiskey bottles. Whiskey in. Whiskey out. Now I'd have to go to the store. I suppose I could just clean the store out but going there gave a sense of routine and normalcy to the day.

I opened the door and saw her standing with her back to it on the other side of the hall. She was looking at the wall of little metal mailboxes. Most of their doors were hanging from the hinges or torn off completely. I quickly shut my door and imagined her turning around. Then I heard her going away. I opened the door again and stepped out, looking at the mailboxes. I looked at the one for 29.

She'd added her name to it. Blue marker on a piece of masking tape. Anita Marvel, it said. I ran my fingertips over the tape and thought about that tiny expanse of pale skin above her stockings. I could still smell the fumes from the marker. I thought about my dead wife and my dead kids and wondered if I could ever feel that way about another person. I didn't know.

I came back from the store and hoped to run into her again but she wasn't anywhere to be seen. Her room was silent above me. Sometime in the afternoon I had another bout of the screams and started drinking shortly thereafter. Night fell and I heard Grangely leave the building on one of his excursions. Hunting. That's why he was so fat. He went into the city at least once a week and returned with fresh feral children, wild animals, whatever he could catch and cut down in the dark back alleys of the city. They were always dead when he brought them back. I don't think I could have stood it if they were still alive. What he did was ghoulish enough without having to listen to some poor innocent struggle as he took them out of this rotten world.

The girl, Anita, began moving around shortly after he left. She walked back and forth across the floor. It squeaked and wobbled. What was there to walk back and forth to? What reason was there to even move? I thought about going up to her room, knocking on her door, introducing myself, but I was pretty sure I was too drunk to stand up. After a long while I heard her settle down and begin that weeping again. Some people scream. Some people weep. The sound of her weeping made me sad but there was something about it more human and beautiful than I had heard in a very long time.

The days and nights continued like this. She became part of the routine, as unchanging as the cloud-covered sky. But I never forgot about her. I longed for her. That became a constant too. That became part of the routine. I watched her check her mail each morning, always in that dingy yellow sundress and blue stockings. She never received anything. I listened to her pace and cry at night. I thought about going up there all the time. I should have. At the very least, she needed warned about Grangely. She needed to know what it was he did, what would become of her if she happened to die here.

I never went.

One evening, something banged against my door and I snapped out of my drowse. My hands had gone numb and I thought I was blind in my left eye. I flexed my hands and blinked. I stood up and went to the door. I opened it but there wasn't anyone or anything there. I thought Grangely had accidentally bumped into it on his way out. But I could hear him at the back of the hall. I looked at him. He was down on all fours, sniffing. I looked down. If he was sniffing the floor there was a good chance something was there. Something was. A thin trail of blood.

Anita was my first thought. Grangely and I were accounted for. The blood trail led outside. I turned to face Grangely. "Get back in your room, Fatass." There wasn't any need to shout. No noise. No other people.

He stood up. He was a large man, tall and robust in a skeletal age.

"You don't boss me," he said. "I'm the fuckin landlord."

"I know what you do. If I wanted, I could tell someone. There aren't any landlords anymore. There aren't any titles anymore. Just people."

"You'll fuckin get yours." We stared at each other for a few uncomfortable seconds before he turned and went back toward his room, slamming his door shut behind him.

I turned back toward the opening of the building, staring out at the dark, milky night. I didn't see her. The trail of blood was thin at first and then, by the time I had reached the curb, it had tapered off into sporadic splashes. I didn't want to venture out any farther. Not at night. I thought about yelling for her but I couldn't bring myself to do it. She didn't even know me. I looked back down at the final splash of blood. I'd never be able to find her that way.

I looked into the surrounding darkness and took a deep breath. Loss was nothing new. I wasn't even close to her. If I started grieving for people I didn't know then I had a whole life of grief in front of me. Every day people died. Every day people disappeared.

I went back into the building. Back into my room. Despite having drunk an entire bottle of whiskey, unconsciousness wouldn't come back. I began to wish I had stockpiled it so I would have something else to dive into.

I had never experienced the night like this before. It was maddening. I sat in the chair, watching the static and listening to hear if she ever came back. Toward dawn the electricity started flickering and I knew this was the beginning of the end. Not that it mattered to me anyway. I hadn't allowed myself to become reliant on any of the appliances. I only kept the television on because I thought I should use something.

Once it was full-on morning, I went to the store to get some more whiskey. I almost passed out on the way there. How was it that I could stay up all night and now that the air was bright I felt like I would fall asleep if I shut my eyes? I was so tired I felt sick.

I made it back to the building, put the whiskey on the cardboard end table, and screamed myself to sleep.

She was the first thing I thought about when I woke up. I had to do it. I had to go up to her room to see if she was okay. I took a slug of the whiskey to fortify my nerves and began the long walk down the hall and toward the stairs. The stink, as I drew closer to Grangely's, was increasingly nauseating. It was one thing to be a fucking cannibal but you'd think he'd clean up after himself. He didn't have to be so unashamed about it.

I climbed the dark and rickety staircase, waiting for my foot to drop through one of the boards, until I reached the second floor.

Down the hall to Room 29.

The door was ajar. I pushed it inward. It smelled like flowers and meat inside. Something light and pretty over something black and rotten. I didn't want to snoop but, well, there wasn't anything better to do. My conscience wasn't what it used to be. Besides, it didn't look like there were a lot of things to snoop through anyway.

The three boxes she had brought with her were turned on their sides on the floor at the bottom of the far wall. Notebooks were lined up on top of them. They looked swollen and puffy like they had been left out in the rain. Her room had a bed and I wondered how many people had died in it. On top of the bed sat another notebook. It was the old kind of composition book with the black and white, vaguely bovine, pattern.

I really shouldn't have.

But I had to. Because there wasn't anything else to do and, I rationalized with myself, if she never came back, this would be a way to remember her. I imagined what I was about to go through was a journal. How could the pages of a journal live if no one ever reads them? I knew it was more than that. I knew I was going to read it because I wanted her. I wanted to possess some small part of her and if I was too much a coward to try and get inside her physically then this was how I'd do it mentally.

I opened up the notebook.

I expected to see the hasty scrawl of handwriting. That's what a journal was, wasn't it? That's not what I saw at all. It was an oblong, crusty, crimson-black mass. It looked like a scab. I flipped the pages with a mixture of disgust and intrigue. More of the same. One per page. I closed the notebook and went over to the other notebooks arranged on the boxes. The first two I opened were empty. Perhaps those were for the future. But the rest of them were filled with more of the same. Scabs. I was sure of it. These were diaries of scabs. I ran my fingers over them. The ones on the boxes were drier, older. Bits of them had flaked off and were smashed between the pages. Some of them came away on my fingertip. I stuck it in my mouth. It tasted like blood, come back to life on my tongue. I put the diary I presently held back on the cardboard box and arranged them as they were originally, neat and orderly. Then I went back to the bed and flipped through that one. This must be the latest one. The scabs inside this one seemed fresher, hanging on to the blue-lined pages with more intensity.

I sat down on the bed and continued to flip through it, running my fingers over them and wondering what the point of this was. Really, what was the point of anything anymore?

I thought of her melancholy weeping. Was that what it sounded like when she cut herself? Did she do that to let some of the pain out? I had dreamed about reading her diary and possessing a little of what was inside of her but this was greater than I could ever have imagined. I probably stayed in her room for two hours. Then my insides were crying to pour out so I left the diary where I had found it, went back down to my room, released myself to the screams, and drank myself into a coma.

When I woke up it was dark and all the electricity had gone. That made it official, I guessed. The end was here.

The next two days continued like all the ones before it only now I spent a bit of time in Anita's room, lost in her diaries and wondering if she would ever come back. Then, after being gone for four days, she did.

Unfortunately, I was busy looking through her diary when she entered the room. A rare thunderstorm was upon us, turning the dim afternoon nearly nighttime black. She startled me but I immediately realized I had been caught.

"What are you doing?" she said.

I held up the diary. "Looking through this."

Her left arm was missing below the elbow. A yellowish bandage covered the stump.

"What happened to your arm?"

"You know . . . You know what I've been doing up here, don't you?"

"I think I do."

"I cut myself too deep. I had to go look for help. I don't want to die, you know? It just feels like something I have to do." She paused and held her right arm up to her chest. "Like your screaming."

"Yes."

It was then I decided I was going to kill her. She had crossed the room and was arranging her past diaries. Her dirty sundress was up above her blue stockings again and it was then I decided everything was hopeless. I would kill her and keep her for my own because I couldn't stand the thought of that beast Grangely gnawing on her. Her being in the apartment was something. She was the promise. The promise of everything missing. I would kill her and then I would kill myself. I realized I would never see her in anything but that yellow sundress and blue stockings, the screams would never go away, the electricity would never come back, the whiskey would run out, and the sun was never going to show its face again. I had already done some very bad things and the dead world was rotting around me.

I turned my attention back to the diary I held in my hand.

"You shouldn't just read people's diaries right in front of them," she said.

"I know." I closed it and stared out the darkened window at the nothing darkness outside. "I came up here to warn you."

"Warn me? You didn't need a reason to come up here. I'm surprised it took you this long. What were you going to warn me about?"

"Grangely."

"Who's that?" she whispered from behind me.

"The landlord."

"The landlord?"

"Yes, he lives downstairs."

"No one lives downstairs except you."

I laughed. "You've had to have seen him. The fat guy. The one who smells so bad. Anyway, when the tenants die, he eats them. And he makes excursions out into the city at night. He brings back all kinds of things."

"Things? Like people?"

"Yeah. Sometimes."

"That's horrible. That's how I lost my sister. At least, that's what everybody suspects."

I felt her weight on the other side of the bed. I thought about turning around but didn't want to spoil everything. I could imagine her hot breath on the back of my neck. It had been so long since I had felt anything like that. Would I actually get to possess her?

"That's a shame," I said.

"It is. She used to go to this little corner store for candy. She went there just about every day. Usually she took a grownup along with her but you know how candy is . . . It's like an addiction after a while. Somebody got her. Apparently, he got quite a few people. He was keeping them in a deep freezer of the store's cellar. He would keep them there and go back every day, eating little pieces of them, cooking them on a portable grill in the store's office. They sifted through the ash and found Sis's earrings."

She said that and I had an image of the cellar. The owners had lived above the store and had apparently used the cellar for their own storage. They had died a long time ago.

"Guess he's shit out of luck now that the electricity's finally gone," she said.

"Yeah," I mouthed but my throat had closed up.

She leaned over me and I felt her hot breath on the back of my neck and cold steel pressed to the front. I looked down and saw the handle. It was the kind of straight razor no one had used in a very long time, even before the end of the world.

"I always wondered why you were always screaming until I saw that. We've been looking for you for a very long time. You know, most everybody else has really come together. I've seen people do things I didn't know they were capable of. Good things."

"You can kill me," I said. "I deserve it." What else could I say? This would be the best way to go. Visions of lynch mobs filled my head. There was no point in fighting back. Even if she was a one-armed girl.

"I'm not going to do that. We can use you."

Outside, I noticed lights from a car. I still wasn't entirely sure of all the things I had done but I knew they were bad and I knew it was me who had done them. Within the next few seconds the room was swarming with people, most of them tired and hungry and hostile. They were not very gentle with me.

They brought me to a hospital. It's a hospital for some, a laboratory for others, and a prison to many. They never told me anything directly but, since I was now human waste, they talked about me like I wasn't there so I heard a lot of things. They had discovered the nature of the plague. They thought they were close to figuring out how to reverse it. It was the only way. To reverse it. To regrow what had rotted on our insides. No one used the word soul. I was recruited.

I've become an experiment. I sit writing this with a third hand growing out of my forehead. It's all a sick joke. They wanted to see if I could develop my dexterity with this new hand. I wanted to ask about Anita. I wanted to ask if she still kept her scab diary. I wanted to ask them if any of them knew why she kept that diary in the first place ... You have to admire the human spirit—we'll continue building things just so someone else can watch them fall. I wish I could put the pen down and run my fingertips over Anita's scabs because that was what we were leaving behind and that was what we were working so hard to build. Bloody crusts over wounds.

I haven't seen her again.

Now I sit here and keep my own diary, written in the pus from a hundred different infections.

SUNRUINED

1.
Sunlight

THE CALIFORNIA SUNLIGHT pouring in through the windows seemed meaningless. Paul Ward listened to the voice squawking on the other end of the phone. The voice belonged to his sister, Dorie, and it struggled to sound sympathetic but it came out all wrong because sympathy did not suit its owner. When Dorie stopped talking, Paul hung up the phone, not fully aware of everything she had said. He found a chair and sat down, his legs weak. His father had died—three months after his mother. The official diagnosis had been inoperable cancer but Paul figured it could just as well have been loneliness and sorrow. Tomorrow, he would have to catch a plane to Ohio.

He sat in the chair, sunlight all around him, his hopelessness struggling to drink it up and turn it black.

2.
Dorie

Early spring outside. Cold, but not the bitter Ohio winter cold.

After the funeral, Paul followed Dorie back to the their childhood home on Birch Street. Now they stood in the living room that nobody lived in anymore. The house was completely empty. Paul hadn't seen Dorie since his mother's funeral. Even though that was only three months ago, she looked like she had aged ten years.

Always a severe tight-faced woman, her hair had gone even grayer, the circles under her intense, probing eyes were even darker.

She passed him a manila envelope. It wasn't until she used her left hand, drawing his attention to it, that he was reminded of the fact she only had three fingers. Her pinky and ring fingers were missing and she had a burn scar extending halfway up to her elbow. He couldn't remember exactly what had happened. Some kind of accident. He was only about four or five at the time. Dorie was ten years older than him.

"There is the will and the check for half of the auction earnings," she said, her voice robotic, harsh.

"You sold everything, didn't you?"

"He had been in the hospital for the last two months. The doctors knew he wouldn't be coming home. Stop pretending you would have been interested in any of it."

"It was just an observation."

"I never could figure out why you hated them so much."

"I never hated them. I just . . . had a separate life to live. That's all."

Outside, the rain spattered against the windows.

"Selling the house?" he asked.

"Yes. You'll get half."

Then he asked a question he had never asked before even though he had always wondered what the answer would be. He pointed to the small bedroom in the back of the house and said, "Why didn't anyone ever use that room?"

"Mother never told you?"

"She wasn't as close to me as she was to you."

"That was going to be the nursery for their first born. He never made it home from the hospital and they just left it empty as a sort of . . . memorial."

"Did you ever think Mom and Dad were a little bit odd?"

"I'm not getting into this with you, Paul. Let them rest. You can stop slandering them now. Have a good time in California."

And then she turned and left, heading out into the tempestuous weather.

3.

A Memory

Paul had *looked into* the room before but he couldn't remember ever *being in* the room and he only really remembered looking into it the one time.

He had been seven. Just old enough to have some really vivid, terrifying nightmares he always remembered in their entirety. After one of these nightmares, in the middle of the night, he got out of bed and went to his parents' room. They were not in their bed. He thought this was strange because they always went to bed at the same time as the children. Once they said it was bedtime then the only sound in the house came from Dorie's radio inanely spewing out Top 40 hits. Thinking about Dorie listening to that kind of stuff now made him smile a little bit on the inside—imagining something within her being soothed by all that was common and shallow.

He had wandered through the darkened house, gently calling for his parents. They were not in any room. That left only the empty room to be searched. He had no idea why the room remained empty. He hadn't really thought about it. He just kind of assumed their family didn't really need the extra space. Nevertheless, the room had always given him the creeps and he was afraid to go all the way in.

He approached the room and cracked the door.

He looked in.

He did not see his parents in the room. He could hardly see anything. The room was too bright. He didn't know why his parents would leave the lights on in an empty room all night, especially since his father, with stringent frugality, faithfully turned off *every* light in the house when they went to bed.

He closed the door and went back upstairs to his parents' bedroom, still having no idea where they were. He was a little bit frightened but not terrified because he didn't think anything that bad could ever really happen to his parents. He crawled into their bed, waiting for them, thinking of where they might be. Maybe just to a neighbor's. Maybe they were in the basement for some reason or the other. That was probably it. He hadn't checked the basement. Or maybe they had been in that awful empty room and he just hadn't seen them because it was too bright. It had to be something like that.

Paul had fallen asleep before his parents came to bed.

Upon waking he found himself in his own bed and knew it was

his parents who put him there.

4.

The Empty Room

Now it was the middle of the night many years later and Paul left his hotel on Main Street, getting in his car to drive back to his parents' house and not having the slightest idea as to why he was doing this. Thick black clouds obliterated the moon and he kept the heat cranked up in his car, driving through the streets of the town and remembering why he hated his parents so much. Most people would have said it was because they had put him in rehab when he was seventeen for what they had seen as alcoholism and what he had seen as being a teenager. True, this had wiped out his last year of high school and stigmatized him beyond belief but he didn't think that was the reason he hated them. And he *did* hate them. He had lied to Dorie earlier. But he thought it was for a completely different reason than forced rehab.

He hated them because he never really felt loved. It was that simple. Maybe it was juvenile. Maybe it was self-pity. Maybe it was even untrue. But he didn't think so. His parents had always seemed pre-occupied. Like there was something more immediate and more important than he and Dorie. He had always been a sensitive person. He felt things. He felt things when they were there and he felt the absence of things when they were not there.

Reaching the house, he had no problem gaining admittance—he still had the key on his keychain from his teenage years. He opened the door and walked into the empty house, the ghosts of distant years pressing down on his shoulders. He didn't bother shutting the front door all the way. He didn't think he would be there very long. He wasn't even sure exactly why he had come.

Only he was. He was sure. He was going to look in the empty room. He was going to look in there just to convince himself it was a normal room, just like every other room. And then he was going to leave. He was going to leave feeling like some grand secret had been lifted from his brain and then he was going to catch the first plane back to California and put this whole godforsaken past behind him.

It was ridiculous, he knew, but his heart quickened as he reached the door to the empty room. This was not a big deal. This was not as traumatic as losing his parents should have been but he felt a greater surge of emotion as he clutched the cool doorknob in his hand. Sure, open up the door, see the darkened empty room, erase every childhood fear he had about this room and then go back home to begin forgetting and forgiving because, really, he thought those things would have to be synonymous to him. Forgiving. Forgetting. When all was forgotten, all would be forgiven.

He turned the knob and swung the door inward.

Light stung his eyes.

His heart hammered in his chest as he tried to discern the source of all that fantastic light.

It came from the window.

Sunlight. And now that he stood there in the room, it didn't seem that bright at all. Just odd. For sunlight to be pouring in through a window after midnight. That had to be impossible. Impossible, yes, but it felt kind of nice.

Very nice.

Exquisite.

Yes. That was how he thought of it. Exquisite. He stood there in the sunlight pouring in through the window. The same sunlight that had poured in through the same window for many many years and he saw it radiate off his skin, sneak in through his skin, lifting his mood, lightening his memories, erasing sadness.

The sunlight had meaning again. A burst of meaning, shooting through him, creating a curious, revelatory sensation that made him feel like he could create or destroy anything he wanted to.

And then he was gone. No longer standing in the empty room.

5.

The Land of Laughing Children

And no longer looking at the exquisite sunlight.

The sunlight was gone entirely, replaced with illumination that was somehow more eerie. It was like the wan light afforded by an eclipse or perhaps that found on a clear night with a full moon.

He didn't know exactly what he was looking at. In front of him, towering over him, was a mansion. It was a prototypical mansion, very Italianate and symmetrical, with eight white plaster columns supporting a second story balcony. He had no desire to go into the mansion. For some reason, he knew what he would find in there. A lot of old furniture covered with sheets. Dusty mirrors that turned every image spectral.

To his left dripped a huge weeping willow tree. To his right, a gnarled live oak twisted out its branches, nearly parallel with the ground. Farther off to his left was either the ocean or a lake. Whatever it was it did not wave or even lap at the shore and it seemed to loom with its deep cobalt blue depths slightly above the ground he stood on, threatening to wash over him and consume him and everything in his surroundings at any moment.

Yet, the feeling he had felt back in the empty room remained. He felt like he walked in some kind of revelatory vision, one that he seemed entirely cognizant of at the time, like when you're having a dream and you know that you are dreaming and you do not want the dream to end. From somewhere, behind the house possibly, he heard the sound of children laughing.

A boy popped out from underneath the willow tree. Paul quickly took him in. The first thing he thought was that the boy looked Amish. His brown hair was cropped in a strange fashion and he wore heavy black clothes over a dirty white shirt. Then Paul noticed the boy's bare feet. They seemed too large and the nails were long.

"Can't catch me!" the boy said and took off running to the right of the mansion.

Paul thought he *could* catch him. He took off running after the boy, suddenly aware of the cool, soft grass on his feet that were also bare.

He chased the boy around the house and came to a stop.

There were other boys there. And they all looked just like this first one. Paul started to count and stopped when he got to ten. There were more than that.

Paul's good feeling went away. He didn't know exactly why except that something just didn't seem right anymore. Something didn't seem right and it didn't seem good.

"Wanna play ball?" a boy at the front of the pack said.

"I don't think I do," Paul said, already backing away. Maybe if he could just get to the front of the mansion then he could find that beam of perfect light and go back into the empty room because even that place, that place and all of its silent, inherent scariness, was better than this place.

"I think you do," the boy said and hurled something that was not a ball at Paul's head.

The rock struck him above the right eye and consciousness swam around him, a grim nausea tickling the back of his brain.

He turned to run.

Another rock caught him in the back of his head and sent him to the ground.

The children were upon him and he kicked, trying to scoot along on the grass, trying to get away, finding it absurd that he was being beaten by a group of children. Quickly, they bound his arms and his legs with a thick rope. Then they hoisted him up and carried him.

Paul screamed.

It was the first time in his life he had ever screamed.

Looking up at the black, moonless sky, he screamed and screamed, the sound of his voice feeling like the only power he had.

The boys put him down on a wooden slab. It was a table of sorts. A fire crackled somewhere beside him but the boys wouldn't let him turn his bloodied head. Instead they held it straight, so that he stared forward.

Sitting at the head of the table, looking at him with only a vague sense of familiarity, were his mother and father.

Suddenly, things made sense to him. They made sense and he put things together in his head but he couldn't blurt them out fast enough.

No. His parents had never loved him.

And he thought he knew what had taken Dorie's fingers.

Thought he knew how she had come about the burns.

And he thought he knew why she was able to love their parents and he was not.

She had understood.

She understood about the first born. About the first born being the only real child his parents had ever wanted and when that first born child had died, a part of his parents had died too because they realized something about mortality and then maybe somehow they found this place that allowed them to escape mortality and, feeling the boys' hands on his body, Paul knew they had come here again and again. Here, to this place where the first child would always live. Where he would always be born into perfection.

Again and again.

These were the children his parents had loved.

And why not? Paul thought. They would never get old. They would grow to whatever age his parents wanted them to grow to and then they would stop and they would never die. They would never hate. They would only love. Unconditionally. Regardless of what the parents wanted them to do.

Paul started to say something to his parents, sitting there with their cold eyes measuring him, but he was yanked up by the throat and carried over to the crackling fire.

Dorie had gotten out. Somehow, she had escaped this fate. But Dorie had always been the strong one and, as the first of the flames licked his bare feet, Paul knew he would never feel the sunlight again.

BLACK ROSITA'S MAN

THE HILLS WERE dark and the hills were mean. But, the rumor went, give Alistair Doos a guitar and things would lighten up a little bit. Judging by the crowd that turned out at the Downtrod Inn, he could make things lighten up a whole lot.

It was the crowd there on that Saturday night that amazed Nathan East. The music was expectedly astounding, but he had heard most of that from recordings. All the recordings took place in this same location—the Downtrod Inn, Sawmill, Ohio. Nathan looked at the crowd around him. He had hoped to be pressed against the stage but even halfway back in this tiny bar was a great place to be. People were packed in from the stage back to the actual bar and, beyond that, out the front door. If anybody wanted to sit and drink they had to do it out on the porch.

Looking around, it was easy for Nathan to divide the locals from the people like him—country blues fans whose curiosity finally got the best of them. It surprised him how many of the people there were white and how many of them looked like they should be listening to something a little more hip. When you're great, Nathan thought, it doesn't matter what type of music you play, your audience is diverse, to say the least. It was true, Alistair Doos wasn't one of the first blues musicians. At something like 70 he was too young for that, but he was certainly one of the best, if not *the* best. Nathan skeptically told himself that probably wasn't true. He wondered how many great musicians went unrecorded or, in a more hateful time, were completely excluded from the music world.

The main thing Nathan thought about was that he was here now.

He had braved the state routes and the back country roads, gravel or dirt in many cases, to come and stand here in this tiny, white paint-peeling bar and watch a genius at work. Here in one of the poorest regions of Ohio. Here on a mountain, the summer spice fresh outside and the cheap draft beer as fresh as it got on the inside. Here, with people slowly nodding their heads or grinding their hips on every side of him. He was here. He was watching his favorite musician doing his thing on stage, completely alone. Just Doos, an acoustic guitar and a sliding steel.

Part of Alistair Doos' popularity, without a doubt, was the sheer mystery surrounding his life. There were two or three really great books about Doos, one written by a man named Jack Napier, Nathan's colleague back in New York, but all of them were spun from the stories of relatives and acquaintances. Doos had never allowed an interview in his life. At the time when Doos would have granted an interview, nobody was asking and now, he simply wouldn't talk to people. Nathan thought it probably wasn't so much a Salingeresque retreat from fame as it was a simple, Bartlebylike, "I prefer not to." Nathan also gleaned from his readings that it was impossible for Doos not to be very wary of the human race.

Doos was born into the most abject poverty in Mississippi in a shack close to the river in a place that didn't have a name. His father ran out on the family that included Doos, his mother, three brothers, and five sisters. Mrs. Doos dragged the family north to Ohio where she'd heard people were a little friendlier to black folk. She had heard wrong. The Doos family lost two children to murder and three of the five sisters were raped before they turned eighteen. Mrs. Doos died young, presumably killed by stress, and the children went their separate ways. But Alistair stayed in Sawmill because of a woman ten years his elder. The woman's name was Rosita Johnson.

Rosita was able to make some cash as a laundress and her job was enough to support Doos in his drinking and music endeavors. According to the folks in the town, they had never seen two happier people. When Alistair wasn't playing his music, they were running around the town, drinking and making friends. And whenever Rosita could get the time off, she and Alistair traveled, Doos playing in whatever clubs would have him. There were rumors of a contract and then the bottom dropped out for blues. Alistair and Rosita looked around and found an America that was now heavy into jazz.

But this didn't discourage Alistair, he was still able to make some cash playing locally and Rosita put in some extra hours at the laundry. Then the bottom dropped out for Alistair and the lovely Rosita.

A crazed preacher from the town proper decided to turn Alistair and Rosita into a moral lesson. The preacher, William Kerch, said a lot of things about them that didn't make any sense like—"The colored folks shouldn't be given the power to run around this town acting the way they do." But the thing he said that people listened to was, "It's a sin for them two coloreds to be livin like they do." By that he meant unmarried. So the Reverend Kerch assembled a lynch mob and went up to the house of Alistair Doos and Rosita Johnson. He fired one shot into each of them as they slept and had his goons haul them out and string them up by their necks from a tree. As the mob stole back into the night, Kerch whispered into the small space between their dangling bodies, "I hope you both rot in hell."

The town was slightly perplexed but, in Sawmill, Ohio in the '40s, popular entertainment rated a great deal lower than old time religion. So they kept their mouths shut. The one thing the townsfolk decided on was that it was more likely Rosita Johnson was living in hell than Alistair Doos because, two weeks later, Doos walked into Hinkle's Grocery and bought the same things he'd bought since old Hinkle could remember: a fifth of whiskey, a carton of unfiltered Camels, a loaf of bread, a jar of peanut butter, and a jar of apple butter. When he checked out he told old Hinkle, "Reverend said I should rot in hell. The way I figger, this here place's as close a man can get." Hinkle didn't take that to mean his grocery store.

For the next thirty years, Alistair would make the same trip and buy the same things. No one ever talked to him or went to his house because they were, quite simply, terrified as hell. The first year or so, he would occasionally enter the town sporting a garish white face and wearing a blond wig. On these occasions he'd say things to Hinkle like, "Just tryin to fit in." It was this white face that earned him the title, "The Ghoul from the Holler." Rumors had it Reverend Kerch had got so freaked out that he skipped the state of Ohio completely.

After that first year, Doos never said anything. Old man Hinkle would say things to him and he would occasionally laugh, flashing a bone white smile, but he never said any words.

Then, in the early '90s he showed up at the Downtrod Inn, looking not much older than he had when the place was still called the Lookout. He played to a bar littered with five people. The reception was as grand as five people could give. Even though racial attitudes hadn't changed a whole lot, the old drunks could still appreciate virtuoso guitar picking. Doos came back every night, except for Sundays, and played. It was always the same. He carried his tattered black guitar case up to the stage and placed it by the scuffed brown chair. Then he walked over to the right of the stage and ascended the three steps. He sat down. He opened the case. He slid his belt buckle around to his hip, put the sliding steel over his left ring finger, picked up the guitar, and let go. Sometimes he would play for fifteen minutes and sometimes he would play for three hours, never cracking a smile, never talking to anyone. When he was finished, he left by the exit behind the stage.

Slowly, the audience grew. They liked his stuff and some of the really old people thought his name sounded familiar but couldn't remember hearing anything by him. Eventually, a recording crew turned up. They showed Doos a contract. He signed it without reading it and began playing his set.

The only song he played consistently every night was "Black Rosita's Man." He seemed to add new verses all the time and Nathan must have heard about fifty versions of this song.

Nathan stood there, completely unaware he was sweating profusely, and listened to the magic coming from Doos' mouth and fingers. And visually, it came from his eyes. Nathan felt like Doos must make eye contact with virtually every audience member—extended eye contact. It was like he played and sang almost absently while his eyes searched and probed. When Doos' near yellowish gaze fell on Nathan, he started wheezing. Nathan imagined that was what an asthma attack felt like. Clamps wrapped around his lungs. And that gaze was impossible to look away from. That gaze made Nathan think there was something about Alistair Doos no one really knew about.

What happened to Jack?

There was a depth, a dimension there, Nathan thought, most people only dream about.

And that's why they were all there. The locals were pale dirty ghosts scattered lazily around the back of the bar. The newcomers were early arrivals, filling the floor in front of the stage. Nathan knew something he thought none of them did. He knew where Doos lived.

Seeking out Doos' house had been the furthest thing from Nathan's mind when he had come down here. A naïve part of his intellect had told him he respected the old man's privacy too much for that. Something happened amidst the thumping of Doos' dusty shoe against the floor and the dry molasses moan of his voice and the steel chime of his thick fingernails picking the guitar. A feeling overwhelmed Nathan. It was a weird and beautiful feeling, filled with deep mystery. It was a feeling he hadn't felt since the summer when he was sixteen and the only black girl in the small town of Oracle, Kentucky, had introduced him to the magic of the moon and sex, the smell of clove cigarettes and the blues. She had taught him to love the blues and then taught him to feel the blues when she ran off with a musician from Cincinnati. But most of all, Nathan remembered the good feelings. The feeling a new world had opened up. Doos' gaze fell upon him and whined, "Follow me," and Nathan knew when Doos walked out that back door, he would be behind him.

That stare, that *feeling* was dangerous. He thought of other things, sliding steel liquid thoughts. Like where was Jack Napier? He had disappeared was all, Nathan told himself—*convinced* himself. Jack had come to Sawmill, intensely scrutinized a man living out life exactly the way he wanted to, nothing but solitude and music, and had decided to follow suit. Maybe Jack was holed up in some other small town, writing the Great American Novel he'd always talked about. The royalties from the Doos biography and the jazz textbook he'd sold a year earlier would certainly allow him to do that. It was Jack who had told Nathan where Doos lived but he didn't mention anything spectacular about it.

"The man goes inside. He comes out the next day to play," Jack had said. And yet this exercise in banality was something Nathan would have to observe for himself because he was here and he was alive and he was listening to that old man wail and he was looking into those eyes and he was so . . . *alive*, drunk off the moon and the smell of clove cigarettes and the blues the blues the blues.

Doos wound up his set, nodded his head in thanks, and folded up camp. There was no hope of getting past the crowd and following Doos out the back door. By the time Nathan squeezed past the lingering patrons and found his way out the front door, cutting quickly around the building, there was no trace of Doos.

You don't need to follow him, Nathan thought. *You know where it is.*

Nathan remembered that conversation, his last, with Jack very clearly.

"There's an opening in the woods behind the bar. Follow that and, after it starts to get really bushy, just try to stay as straight as you can. My guess is old Doos walks that path every night and then shoots off in some slight other direction so no particular path gets worn down. Keep going straight until you reach the clearing. It's a long way."

Then Jack had said: "I know I can trust you with this, Nathan." That was one of the only times he could remember Jack ever using his name in conversation.

Was there something panicked in that last conversation? Was there any hint Jack was going to disappear off the fucking planet?

Nathan's mind raced, emotions chasing themselves in circles.

He hasn't been gone that long, he told himself. And no, Nathan knew Jack and he hadn't sounded panicked in the least. He had sounded completely blissful. Nathan remembered, after getting off the phone with him, he had thought Jack sounded like someone who'd had a near death experience or found God or . . . or something else. Something that meant much more to a staunch atheist like Jack.

Cars were parked four rows deep behind the Downtrod Inn and Nathan wormed his way in between. The moon was a night away from being full and Nathan's vision was greatly helped by its purplish glow. He found the opening in the woods after only a minute's search. Once inside, he knew he would be away from the moon's nurturing glow. His vision reached no more than a couple of feet into the woods but he could sense its secret world. The insects with their secret language chirped and hummed, scurrying. He could smell the damp wood, resting up for another day of growth, however slight. And he could smell the sweet decay of the leaves, layered on the ground from a hundred sad and magical autumns.

He took a deep breath and began walking. He listened for the sound of the man in front of him but didn't hear so much as a broken twig or the soft swish of a leafy branch. No amount of paranoia could stop him, Nathan knew.

This world was far removed from his apartment in New York. There were no blaring horns or screeching trains or squealing cars or sirens and, perhaps most unsettling, there were no people. The woods were like nothing and everything, timeless.

More to keep himself company than anything else, Nathan began playing Alistair Doos' music in his head. The time flew by as quickly as it had at the bar.

Soon he reached the dead end.

"Keep walking straight," Jack had said.

Where are you, Jack? Nathan asked himself and the question was followed by that night's "Black Rosita's Man," still fresh in his head; there to comfort him, to ward away paranoia. *Follow me.* To guide him into something he hadn't felt in a long time.

The terrain rose uphill a little more, but Doos' music was there in his head, biology's iPod, to carry him on. Fallen sticks barked his shins, thin limbs scratched at his cheeks. That music, thick and sweet.

And there it was. Gleaming as white as the teeth in Doos' head, his house sat humbly in a large grassy circle.

Nathan stayed at the perimeter of the woods. The whole clearing seemed to glow, the moon reflecting off the house. The bargain iPod had turned itself off and Nathan tried to concentrate on what his next move would be.

Okay, you've seen it. You can go home now.

"The man goes inside. He comes out the next day to play." *There's nothing to see, right?*

Except it seemed Doos hadn't just gone inside.

What happened to you out here, Jack?

Nathan heard the slow refrain of "Black Rosita's Man" coming from somewhere in that illuminated circle. It sounded almost too clear to be coming from within the house but Nathan couldn't see a trace of Doos.

He moved slowly to his right, crouching down into some of the smaller foliage. He continued moving cautiously and the music got closer. The night was almost chilly. Nathan found himself drawn to this sound, feeling brief flickers of warmth in his stomach. Nathan wanted to feel wrapped in it like he had back in the sweaty bar, like he had in the arms of the girl who'd graciously taken his virginity. He continued to move to his right.

Nathan found out why he had come.

The secret that lay behind Doos' slightly hooded eyes unfolded itself right there in front of him. It had all the elements of a completely fucked up dream but Nathan felt the warmth of the music and the chill of the night and he knew it was really happening.

Doos sat on a chair, plucking and singing away. He sang to a small tombstone at his feet. Nathan knew if he could read the tombstone it would say, "Rosita Johnson." The grass on top of the grave quivered. The air around Nathan was changing. It felt like the moments before a thunderstorm when the wind kicks up and the temperature is a schizophrenic swirl.

Doos played on.

Nathan couldn't tell if what he saw next was some sort of ghost or the real thing but there was Rosita Johnson, slowly taking form on top of her grave. She wasn't coming out of it the way zombies did in the movies. She was slowly becoming more . . . substantial, thicker, more *there*. And then, Nathan would have had to touch her to be a hundred percent certain, she *was* there.

She was Doos' music made flesh. All the beauty. All the pain. Nathan knew this was what Doos lived for. This was why he still played music. It wasn't for those adoring faces at the Downtrod Inn. It wasn't to be known as the best at anything. It was for love. For the love of Rosita Johnson.

He put down the guitar in the open case beside his chair.

What the fuck was Jack talking about? There's nothing to see! *What the hell* was *this?*

Doos laughed. A sweet sound, rich and loud.

"I missed you, old girl," he said.

It was Rosita's turn to laugh, shrill but filled with joy—"I missed *you*, old man," as though they had said this countless times before.

They embraced, turning in circles under the moonlight. Doos picked her up, cradling her in his arms.

Nathan turned to run. Not out of fear but out of guilt. He felt like he shouldn't have, no, he felt like it wasn't his *right*, to see what he had just seen. He tried running but his heartbeat slowed and thickened in his chest and his legs rubberbanded him to the ground.

He threw his head wildly up at the moon. The moon mocked him and he lowered his head to see a hundred other leering moons coming toward him from the dark mass of the forest.

Some of them were faces he recognized from the bar. And in the front, grinning wildly, was a face Nathan knew very well.

"Jack?"

"I found it, Nathan," Jack said. His blondish hair was longer than Nathan remembered, hanging almost down to his shoulder.

All those moons were coming closer.

"I swear I didn't tell anybody else, Jack." Why was he suddenly so afraid of Jack?

The eyes, Nathan thought. They contained a touch of Doos.

"Now you've found it, too," Jack said.

Jack put his hands on Nathan's sweaty face and turned it around, back toward the house. The rest of the people moved in tightly, forming a crescent around him.

Nathan's muscles, already stiff with fear, tightened even more.

Another moon face was quickly constructing a makeshift gallows from a tree beside Doos' house, behind the tombstone.

Doos and Rosita were dancing off to the gallows' right, singing a mock jazz duet.

"*We're gonna live for eternity,*" Doos sang.

"*Just you n me,*" Rosita sang.

"Bay-*beee,*" they sang together.

Nathan shivered violently. He heard his teeth clacking in his head like some form of mad music behind the lovers' duet.

Jack pulled him up by one of his arms. The crescent moved in on him, lifting him up, carrying him toward the gallows.

"The mystery is darkening," Jack said.

"*I told you that sky was filled with holes,*" Rosita sang.

"*Don't waste yer breath on me, I'm out collectin souls,*" Doos half-sang, half-laughed.

The mob carried Nathan past the tombstone and he noticed it said, "Rosita Doos," not "Rosita Johnson."

"*Why don't we get married, baby?*" Doos.

"*Just you n me . . .*" Rosita.

The noose over the branch creaked.

"None of us should have done this, Nathan," Jack said.

"No," Nathan didn't know if he was protesting or agreeing. He screamed. He heard his scream rolling over those hills.

"Kerch will take care of you."

The Reverend Kerch placed the noose around Nathan's neck.

Doos laughed and began strumming, "Black Rosita's Man."

The crowd stepped away.

Nathan dropped.

He felt his neck snap and he felt the red shivers of pain bursting in his skull and he waited, but he didn't feel death. He felt fire. But it was just a feeling and he opened his eyes and everything he saw was hallucination red.

The hands tore away the clothes from his body.

The teeth bore down on him and he could hear the punctures more than feel them.

He looked down and Doos' mouth was clamped on his left wrist, Rosita's on his right.

"Let these two be joined!" the Reverend Kerch shouted. "Let these two be joined!"

The next night, Nathan looked at the fresh faces that had come to the Downtrod Inn. He was pressed back against the bar. He turned and looked toward Doos' eyes but those eyes didn't meet his. They looked at the sea below the stage, searching. Outside, the moon was full. The faint smell of cloves drifted in from outside, drowning out the sweat and the beer smells. And, in the slow coursing of his veins, Nathan felt the blues.

THE NIGHT THE MOON MADE A SOUND

WALT FERRYMAN WOKE up around five in the evening. There wasn't a need to put on his clothes since he'd apparently fallen asleep in them. He sat on the edge of his small single-sized bed without head or footboard, rubbed his rough hands together between his knees, and surveyed the chaos of the house in the dying sunlight. "House" really wasn't the right word for it. "Room" best described it. From where he sat on the bed, he could see the entire place, even the bathroom, its door wide open just three feet from the foot of his bed. He smiled slightly to himself, deciding the situation was too sad to warrant a chuckle. *That's right*, he remembered, *I had to go to the bathroom to puke before I went to bed.* Otherwise, he would have been too terrified to leave the door open. He knew that the squeaky things could only get through if the door was open. Even if it was just a crack. But the alcohol had taken the squeaky things to sleep with him.

Had there been blood in the puke?

You bet. He knew without looking. It was the same as his shit. The blood seemed to be coming from all of his major orifices these days.

He bent down to grab his dusty brown work boots from underneath the bed, only slightly expecting a squeaky thing to graze his fingertips. When his hand hit nothing but cobwebby air, he realized he was still wearing his boots. And, best of all, his hand came away unscathed. He stood up and arched his back, crossing the littered floor to the kitchen area at the front of the room. Grabbing a speckled glass from the sink and some milk from the refrigerator, he filled the glass half full. Then he reached under the sink for the bottle of grape Mad Dog and poured that in with the milk. He turned a burner on atop the gas range, pulled a crumpled Pall Mall from his shirt pocket, placed it between his dry lips and lowered his head to the burner, inhaling greedily like he was sucking liquid through a straw. The first smoke of the day filled his lungs and he took the glass in his hand, relishing its coolness. He leaned against the counter and looked through the partially raised and seriously askew yellowed blinds at the steaming paper mill across the street.

He had stopped noticing the stink of it a long time ago.

Now he smelled different things. Unseen things. Unseen things that smelled like meaty decay. He smelled these odors on the breath of the squeaky things, pressing down on his chest and smiling down at him while he slept, leaving before he could open his eyes.

He took another drag from his cigarette and downed the glass. He was a firm believer in the hair of the dog. If he was a believer in doctors, or if he had the money to go see one, the doctor could have told him he was rotting from the inside and nothing could put him back together again. The milk and cheap wine hit his stomach, sending up a squall of pain from his gut and a peaceful white cloud in his head. Could the doctors tell him about the squeaky things?

"Gahdamn," he mumbled, raking a large hand across the grit of dried sweat on his face. With his callused middle finger, he scraped some sleep from his eyes.

He thought about cleaning up the room and decided he'd rather take a walk in the bloody diarrhea of the sunset first. He knew he could clean the room, make it spotless, and it would be a mirror image of its current disheveled state come tomorrow. *That's the nature of life*, he thought. Every day was like being raped up the ass with a hot poker prick. Anger surged up through him, coming from some great nowhere. He turned and threw the glass toward the back of the room where it shattered, not nearly loud enough, against the wall. He would be gone by the time Ms. Davenport came over to ask him what the heck he was doing over here.

Sometimes it took this anger to get him moving. He dropped his cigarette into a coffee cup in the sink and headed out into the evening.

The coastal evening was usually, by turns, balmy or cold. Sometimes, like tonight, it was both. There was warmth in the air, a summer kind of smell pervaded by the ubiquitous odor of the sea's brine. Yet, from within that comforting balm came a stabbing wind that made Walt think of the scary isolation deep out in the ocean, miles away from safety. It was an abstract notion. He had never been out to sea. He was, in fact, terrified to step foot into the ocean. He imagined all those hard-shelled squeaky things, rolling under the unfeeling water, waiting for the meat to come. But Walt liked to go sit on the benches that sank into the sand on the beach. He liked to feel the sun at his back and wish he lived in the West, where the sun could scorch his eyes before drowning itself in the Pacific only to be resurrected as a ghostly moon. Maybe after scorching his eyes it would melt his brain. Melt it clean away until it ran out of his ears.

Walt also liked the company of Janey, who was six.

Walking down Factory Road toward the beach, past the flumpingly noisy paper mill, he wondered if the factories contained thinking men who operated unthinking machines or if the machines had turned the men into mindless drones. He thought about his callused hands and melting intestines and wondered if he still had a brain. Maybe so, he thought. But what was the use of a brain if he tried to shoot it out every night? What was the use of a brain if it couldn't tell him the squeaky things didn't exist?

He hoped Janey would be there.

It took him about twenty minutes to get down to the beach and when he did, the sun was gone. All the gold had left the beach and the ocean and everything around it was twilit and spectral. The sun had taken its heat with it and there was now only the persistent, unrelenting wind and the crash of the gray waves, each one slightly colder than the last, Walt was sure.

No Janey.

Not yet, anyway.

He sat down on a bench and lit up a cigarette. It took him a couple of tries to get it lit all the way. He finally got it by cupping his hand over the flame and hunching down until his head was nearly buried between his knees. He pulled his thin jacket around him, crossed his legs and sat back on the bench, lost in his thoughts. His thoughts mostly consisted of thinking about not thinking.

The sky darkened like beaten flesh. The ocean, darkening with the sky, went from the color of ash to the color of oil. His cigarette burnt itself out in the yellowed tips of his fingers and he didn't bother tossing it off to the side.

The sand crunched behind him and he turned to his left.

"Hi there," Janey said.

"Whoa, ya scared me." Janey wore a plastic gray and white wolf mask. "I thought it was a . . ."

"Wolf, huh?" Janey said before growling at him.

Besides the mask, Janey wore a blue dress and no shoes. The mask was new to Walt, but the blue dress and absence of shoes were constants.

"How ya doin?"

"Great!"

"Ain't ya cold?"

"Why should I be cold, Mr. Silly?"

"It's windy and . . . *cold*."

"I guess I can't feel it. Feels good to me." She spread her arms out and ran in a tight circle around the sand, making a sound like she was enjoying a fine summer day.

"Hey, Mr. Silly," she said. "You know what I am?"

"A big bumblebee?"

"No, silly, a wolf." She growled again. "Know what?"

"Whut?"

"I'm six."

"*Really?*"

"Honest." She growled and moved closer to Walt. "You smell funny."

"Jeez, that ain't a nice thing to say."

"You smell like the poison."

He chuckled. "Yeah, girly, guess I prob'ly do." He reached out to pat the top of her sandy brown hair and quickly withdrew his hand.

He had touched her once before, helping her up after she had fallen down in the sand, and it had sent a wave of nausea through him with enough strength to make him run to the water's edge and vomit until it felt like the next thing to come up would be his stomach.

There had been something else, too. Something besides the nausea. There had been an image. But it was too fleeting to tell what it was.

"That's okay," she said. "My dad drank the poison sometimes too. But I don't think he drank it quite as much as you do. And I don't think it was the same kind of poison."

"He stop drinkin it?" He tried to make visual contact with the sparkling blue eyes behind the mask but she looked up at the sky.

"I dunno," she said.

"Why'nt ya know?"

"I don't see him much anymore. Boy, the moon sure is big."

Walt looked up at the sky. "It sure is," he said. "Why'nt ya see your dad much? Don't he live with you and your mom?"

"He lives with my mom, but I think he's getting ready to move out."

"Don't you live with em? Your mom and dad?"

Janey skipped off into the darkness and then skipped back. "Sometimes, I guess."

"Whaddya mean, 'sometimes'?"

"Well, sometimes, I'm in the house. I can see Mom and Dad, but I don't think they can see me." Janey growled and raised her right hand like an injurious paw.

"Why'nt ya think they can see ya?"

"Cause, that's why I think Dad's leavin Mom. He always cries and talks about how much he misses me. I keep wantin to tell him that I'm right there. But he's a big sillyhead. He can't hear me."

Clarity wasn't something Walt really thought too much about. Most of his life had been spent trying to dull that clarity a little bit. But, that night, talking to Janey, he felt completely invaded with clarity. It wasn't something he welcomed. No, it was like a knife to the back, something cold and real and very much there.

On previous visits, Walt had thought of Janey as an adventurous girl with slightly irresponsible parents. Now he saw her as something else. Like maybe there was something she was trying to tell him but couldn't because . . .

Because she doesn't know what happened herself.

Maybe there was some other way of finding out.

The time you touched her.

That nauseous feeling and that other thing. Something indescribable. A vision. Was it a vision?

No. No. Just a flash of red. Something else. Something sickening. The squeaky things.

That blade of clarity again, running down his back right alongside his spine. He pulled his jacket around himself and that's when he first heard the moon make a sound. Walt looked up at its unwavering, luminous placidity. There it was again. A low, slobbery sound like a dog that wants in some place and presses its muzzle to the crack in the door, slowly panting a pant infused with just enough brainless desperation for you to feel sorry for it.

"Shit," Walt thought, maybe even mumbled, and dropped a hand across his face.

He took out another cigarette and lit up. The wind had died down and it was a little easier this time.

Janey, who had been lightly skipping around the bench, trying to capture Walt's attention, stopped and tapped him on the shoulder with a small finger. Walt flinched.

"Christ, don't do that!"

"Did I scare ya?"

"No." *It's that feeling,* he thought. "Yeah, maybe a little. Old man like me. You gotta be careful. Heart could pop like a firecracker."

"Bam!" Janey shouted.

"Yeah. *Bam's* right."

There was a trace of that feeling when Janey had tapped him on the shoulder. Of course, it was very brief contact and he felt it through two shirts and a jacket. When he had helped her up, he had pulled her up by her sweaty little hand.

"You wanna take a walk, Mr. Silly?"

"Not just yet. You let me set here for a minute or two. Finish this here smoke."

"You really shouldn't smoke. Mom says it'll give ya cancer."

"She's right, of course. I find it enjoyable. I don't really care bout cancer."

"If you get cancer, you'll die."

"Only if God wants me to. Some people live with cancer all their life. Sometimes, the cancer just up and goes someplace else."

"I don't think you got cancer yet. But I think you're sick."

"Me too, Janey. Me too. I think I'm pretty bad sick."

"I hope you don't die."

"We all die someday. Got to. It's God's will."

"Why do you think God does that?"

"Don't rightly know, I guess. Maybe he needs the comp'ny."

"May*be,*" Janey laughed. "Seems kinda mean."

"Maybe. At least there ain't so many people to deal with."

"You think it's scary to be dead?"

"Don't rightly know. Guess it would be if there wun't no one there with ya. Like if ya just died and *poof,* that was it, you was all alone."

Again, the knife of clarity entered his skin, snaking in at the base of his skull.

The moon made another sound. There was no mistaking this with the sound of the ocean.

"Yeah. I get lonely sometimes," Janey said.

"Me, too."

He tossed the cigarette out toward the water and hopped up. He took off his jacket and tossed it onto the empty bench.

"You ever play Tag, Janey?"

"Of course, big silly." She reached out and smacked his forearm. "Tag! You're it!"

He winced. He felt a squeaky thing take off up his arm. He looked for it but it was gone. Janey took off running in the darkness. A vision rushed through Walt's head. He tried to retain the vision as he took off racing after Janey. It was hard to run on the sand, a task he hadn't tried since he was a kid. In his head, he saw an empty street filled with ominous black snake alleyways.

He wouldn't have reached her to tag her if she hadn't doubled back toward him, trying to jaunt past.

"Bench is base!" she called. But not before Walt could loop out one of his long arms and tap her on the forearm. The squeaky things raced up his back on dagger legs.

"Yer it," he wheezed, attempting to run off into the darkness from which Janey had come. There was another vision, this one a little longer, a little clearer. And again there was the sickening nausea, screaming through his head and guts, threatening to drop him to his knees.

Squeaky things. Bad visions. Nausea. Why the hell was he doing this?

In this vision, Walt saw a low black car. It was a model that he didn't recognize. The car was an older one, but maintained perfectly. *Restored*, he thought as Janey crept up behind him and smacked the back of his dangling hand, sending a horde of squeaky things shooting up his pantlegs.

"You're it!" she shouted. Then: "You shoulda touched base."

He coughed, nearly falling to his knees. The sensations were harder to deal with when they came back to back like that, almost overlapping.

Walt felt his stomach come up and managed to suppress it back down, swallowing the puke before he tasted it.

He looked up at the moon. More than whimpering, it howled

softly.

The vision was this time accompanied by a marrow-scraping feeling of panic. It felt like *him* standing on that curb and watching the restored car, but he knew it was Janey. The visions were seen through Janey's eyes, or had been so far. The car door opened and a hand reached out. Walt turned to run, as Janey in the vision, as himself there on the beach.

Janey circled around him, knowing he couldn't catch her on his own. He reached out and tagged her elbow, giving it a little squeeze in the process. The feeling, the vision that accompanied it was so strong he couldn't even yell, "You're it!"

A squeaky thing, he was sure, sliced at the back of his neck.

The moon howled, a deep guttural sound blossoming into something nearly metallic.

He went down on one knee, vomiting into the sand before collapsing onto his back.

In the vision he, as Janey, turned to run from the man getting out of the car but there was another man, a thicker man, standing right behind her, waiting. Something went over her head, turning the world to black. From inside the blackness came spinning thoughts of panic and doom. There was an impact, something blunt hitting her head and Walt came out of her head. No longer Janey in the vision, he became some omniscient eye—maybe a ladybug on the ceiling of the car, maybe a bird perched on the trunk, staring intently through the tint of the windows. What he saw was shocking. It brought on another wave of nausea. He turned his head and vomited down the side of his face.

The people in the car with Janey weren't exactly human. They weren't like anything Walt had ever seen. Boil-covered skin stretched too tightly over the expansive bones of their faces. Their eyes were too clear, too liquid to really be eyes. And when they stuck their reptilian tongues out to lick their thin lips, their teeth were large and sharp and yellow. And then he saw the squeaky things. Images lent to the sounds that had infected him since childhood. Something like bloated cockroaches with legs that were too thin and antennae that were too long, fat swollen sacs sagging behind their mid-sections. They came out of the men's mouths, crawled from the cuffs of their suits, swarmed over Janey.

"Oh God," Walt whispered to himself as he heard their thirsty suckling.

He looked up at the moon. It seemed whiter now than it had earlier. He thought it seemed, somehow, angry. The sand felt like a welcomed mattress beneath him.

Janey moved closer to him, her wolf mask eclipsing the moon.

"I guess Tag's over, huh, you big sillyhead?"

"I tried, girly-girl. I tried."

"C'mon. I'll help ya up. You remember that time you helped me up?"

"Don't recall." He stuck out his hand, bracing himself.

Janey wrapped her little hand around his big hand.

The moon screamed bloody murder.

Nausea gnawed at Walt's soul but blossomed into a kind of ecstatic knowledge. He had the answer now.

He got to his feet, the latest vision burning just behind his eyes.

He saw Janey from above. She lay on the ground and from the impossible cant of her head and limbs, her overall *deflatedness*, he knew she was dead. And then, spilling over the vision was the blood and the squeaky things—all over Janey, all over the trees surrounding her, all over the fallen leaves on some unknown forest floor.

"That was real fun, Mr. Silly," she said. "I guess I better go now."

Walt stood silently and watched as the little girl walked toward the ocean, toward her lonely purgatory. He watched as the water crept up to her waist. He watched as she became somehow less substantial.

"Janey!" Walt called.

She stopped and turned her wolf face toward him.

"You want some comp'ny?" he shouted, already walking toward the ocean.

She stood still until he reached her. "You know where we're going?" she asked.

"Nope. I got a question for ya, though. You ever hear of the squeaky things?"

She looked at him, the moon lighting off the blue of her eyes. He saw something like a flash of recognition. Maybe it was a look of fear.

"They any squeaky things where we're goin?"

"No," Janey said, shaking her wolf mask from side to side.

"Then I'm all fer it."

"You'll be my company."

"That's right," Walt said, waiting for the ocean to rise up through his nose and suffocate the squeaky things away.

Together, they walked out into the ocean, toward a moon that had never been quieter.

THE LIBRARY OF TRESPASS

YOU GET EVERYTHING upstairs?" Leggy asked.

"Yep," Dump replied, tucking his feather duster into his belt. "You get everything down here?"

"Just about. You wanna help me with the library?"

"Guess so."

The auto parts factory shutting down two months ago put a lot of people out of work. Since there wasn't a lot of other work to be had, a lot of people, people like Dump and Leggy, found themselves taking jobs they wouldn't normally take. Like housekeeping. Never, at any time in either of their lives, did Dump or Leggy think they would find themselves as maids.

"Too bad the old bitch ain't here today," Leggy said, strolling across the wood floor of the living room toward the glass doors of the library on his overly long legs. Dump guessed that was probably how he got the nickname. Practically no torso and legs like two skinny trees.

"Why's that?" Dump asked. He liked to work much better when the "client" wasn't there. That way he didn't feel watched.

"Old whore usually tips pretty good."

"I guess," Dump said. Dump was a very squat man, shaped somewhat like a dumpster, and when he worked up a sweat his stink really broke open. Even he was aware of it. He couldn't imagine what other people thought. To be surrounded by that pungent, wet dog kind of smell wafting out of him regardless of how often he bathed.

"What?" Leggy said. "You couldn't use a few extra bucks. Usually enough for a six pack, at least."

"Yeah. You're right. Maybe she'll tip us more next time." Truthfully, he didn't care. He was comfortable around Leggy. If Ms. Blanchette wasn't there, that was just one less person to be around. One less person to smell his stink or look at his repellant physique.

Dump watched as Leggy, reaching the library doors, depressed the silver, antique-looking lever. A blossom of sweat had started just below the 'Happy Housekeepers' logo on his shirt.

"Maybe we shouldn't," Dump said.

Leggy, hand resting on the door lever, turned and fixed Dump with a ferocious stare. His perm had worked itself up into a frenzy and sat above those hateful looking blue eyes with a wild intensity. Leggy took his hand off the knob and twisted the waxed tips of his gray-brown handlebar mustache.

"Why the hell shouldn't we?"

"I don't know . . ." Dump looked at the ground, rubbed his greasy chin with his hand, the other hand fumbling with his utility belt loaded with bottles and rags and the feather duster. The feather duster was perhaps the most emasculating part about the job.

"You tell me not to do something I'd goddamn like to know why not."

"It's just . . . When she's here she always tells us not to go in there."

Leggy made an exasperated sigh, throwing up his arms. "Dump-o. Know what?"

"What?"

"The bitch ain't here."

"I know."

"So, if the bitch ain't gonna be here, then we're gonna do what our contract tells us to do. Which is clean everywhere in the house unless otherwise specified by the client. Well, the client ain't here to specify us not to clean in there."

Dump shuffled nervously on his thick legs, admiring the job Leggy had done on the wooden floor.

"Stop bein a fuckin candyass, Dumpy."

"Whatever."

Leggy moved closer to him.

"Look, Dump—what does Miss What's-her-face call that room?"

"The Library."

"Yeah. Of course she calls it the library." He screwed up his face and started mocking Ms. Blanchette. "'Don't go in the library.'

'Never mind the library.' 'The library's okay. Just leave it.' 'I'll get the library myself.'" He slackened his face, pulled an engraved silver flask from his jeans pocket and took a swallow. The crazy light in his eyes intensified and, after capping the flask and putting it back, he gave a couple of frisky upward tugs on his mustache. "So what *is* a library?"

Dump knew what Leggy was fishing for. Knew that was probably his whole reason for wanting to get in there in the first place. "It's a place that lets you borrow books."

"Right, my man. A library is most definitely a place that lets you borrow books. So, I guess since Miss Drycunt ain't here to give us her little tip, we might just have to borrow one of her precious books."

Dump didn't really want any part in thievery. He hated this job, hated the people he worked for, every bit as much as Leggy did, but he didn't think that gave him the right to take things from them.

"Now," Leggy said. "You gonna help me clean up in there or not?"

"I think I'm just gonna go wait in the truck."

"Aw, shit, man. You know you wanna get in there too. I mean, I ain't ever had the urge to read a goddamn thing in my life but something so shut up like that, something I ain't *supposed* to touch, well, that makes me awful eager for some fuckin learnin. Don't it you?"

Leggy had finally hit upon something that struck a chord with Dump. He had, on a number of occasions, wondered what was in that room. Maybe it was a collection of old pornography. He'd heard that some rich fucks collected that kind of thing although he didn't really see what a bunch of old shit could have that *Hustler* didn't, except the girls didn't shave their pussies back then.

Leggy could tell Dump was now interested. He turned back to the glass doors. "So you go ahead and sit out in that hot ass truck if you don't want to do what our contract states but if you want to do a good job you'll follow me on in here."

He pressed the handle down and it didn't move. "Locked," he said. "No bother. A lock ain't never stopped me before."

Dump's heart jumped around a little bit. He half-expected Leggy to take out one of the windows. Instead, he pulled a thin pick from his pocket and jabbed it into the keyhole, moving it around until he heard a click.

"Now," he said, "I ask you: if these books is so important then why the fuck don't she get a better lock?"

Dump couldn't answer him. He was sweating again. He came up behind Leggy just as the taller man swung the French doors outward.

"You smell like a fuckin outhouse," Leggy said.

"Sorry."

They entered the library together. It smelled like the one library Dump had ever been in. It was cooler than the rest of the house.

"Feels nice in here," Leggy said. "Why do those old shits always keep it so fuckin warm all the time?"

"Don't know," Dump said, eager to get his hands on one of the fat volumes lining the room.

He pulled one down. Nothing was written on the spine. Dump thought that was kind of odd. Most books, even old ones, usually had the title of the book or the author or *some*thing on the spine. Looking around, he noticed none of these did. But they *were* arranged, if in an unconventional manner.

The room was your standard rectangular room, probably intended to be a dining room until this book-acquiring addict had taken it over and made it into something else. There was a window at the front of the house and to the left of the French doors. Except for these areas of glass (concealed with dark wooden blinds) the walls were lined floor to ceiling with books. It looked like the "arrangement" began in the far right corner of the room. The first volume there was white. While the other books varied in thickness they were all of uniform height. And they seemed to follow the color spectrum, more colors than Dump had ever imagined. Starting with that white book they darkened through every variant of every primary color until they reached a black book, located at the bottom of the wall facing them. The one with the windows that, had the blind been drawn up, would look out over the front yard.

Dump was eager to see what the book contained. Something nondescript like this was almost sure to contain pornography.

He opened it right up to the middle.

And was greatly disappointed. No gaping spread-legged poses. No emotionless couplings. Just a picture of a small block-like building, kind of gray in color, surrounded by a blue sky and resting on what looked like desert ground. Silently, he flipped through some more of the book. More of the same. Pictures of landscapes, sculptures, mountains, appliances. Every image seemed slightly familiar and slightly alien at the same time. Maybe it was just because, put in the context of a book, something bound between two covers and lovingly photographed, it made the ordinary seem like something else.

He glanced up at Leggy. Leggy had that angry look in his eyes. He shoved the book he had been leafing through up on a shelf and pulled out another one.

"What'd yours have in it?" Dump asked.

"Fuckin just pitchers of shit."

"Yeah, that's what mine is."

"This is gotta be some kinda joke or somethin."

"Maybe she's a photographer."

"Naw. Photographers got those special pitcher albums. Kinda like binders or somethin."

"Maybe she had these made special."

"Maybe she's just a crazy old cunt. Besides, some of these pitchers ain't right. I mean, you'd need some kinda Hollywood effects for some of this shit. Look here . . ." Leggy crossed the room with a couple strides of his long legs and showed Dump a picture in one of the books, this one a light purple color.

The book showed a tree but it was all wrong. The roots were scraping at the sky and the leaves were down at the bottom. Another one showed some kind of flying device he had never seen before. It looked like one of those old round metal trashcans turned on its side with giant, papery moth wings.

"See," Leggy said. "Don't make no sense."

"Maybe it makes sense to Miss Blanchette."

"I tell you what: these books make me mad." Leggy put the book back on the shelf and took a quick swig from his flask. "But I'm takin one anyway."

"I don't think that's such a good idea," Dump said.

"Why the fuck not?"

"Well, it's stealing, for one thing. And, besides, what would be the point? You can't read it. Don't think you could sell it."

"Maybe they're real rare. I bet I could get somebody to put it on the computer."

"I say we just put em back and get the hell out."

"I say we help ourselves."

Dump replaced his book on the shelf and Leggy put his hand on the black one.

"I wouldn't take that one," Dump said.

"Fuck not?"

"She'd stand more of a chance of missing the first one or the last one but half of these are so close in color they almost look the same." And it was true. If you stood far enough away, you probably wouldn't be able to tell they were individual volumes.

"Guess you're right." Leggy's hand bounced to his left and landed on an espresso brown one. "This one'll do." He slid the thin hardcover book into the front of his pants and pulled his shirt, two maids in dresses emblazoned above the left breast pocket, over it. "Ready?"

"As I'll ever be."

They collected their things and headed out to the truck, locking the door behind them and stowing the key on a narrow ledge running just under the roof of the porch. Dump glanced at his watch. Just now four o'clock. They were finished early and he guessed that made it an okay day. As always, they would fudge their timesheets, probably putting down that they were out at five, and that almost made up for losing out on the tip.

"You wanna come back to my place, hang out for a bit?" Leggy asked.

Dump didn't really want to do that. He was kind of mad at Leggy but the alternative was to go back to his crappy apartment and listen to the wild children on one side of him yell and scream and the wild newlyweds on the other side of him fight for a few hours and then fuck each other's brains out for about ten minutes before they started fighting again. At least, he figured, Leggy would have some booze.

"Sure," Dump said, rolling the window down on the old truck as they wound out of Ms. Blanchette's neighborhood.

Somehow, Leggy had managed to save enough money to buy a couple of acres out in the country. Of course, that took all of his savings and the only thing he could afford to put on the land was a trailer. A *used* trailer at that. But out so far from the town limits nobody really gave a damn how it looked. Leggy didn't mind a little rust. As long as the inside was dry in the rain and warm in the winter.

Once at the trailer, they left their cleaning supplies to go inside and start in on some grape Mad Dog and a case of Natty Light. Leggy had a big-screen TV and a satellite hookup and Dump watched a baseball pre-game. The Reds were playing the Pirates and he thought to himself what a godawful boring sport baseball was. Leggy continued to occupy himself with the dark brown book.

Leggy, entering the first stages of drunkenness, had started to repeat himself. "This book makes me real mad."

"Why?" Dump said, polishing off the last of the Mad Dog and cracking open another beer, a happy haze finally starting in his brain.

"I dunno. I guess books just make me mad. I don't see no point in em."

"Yeah. I guess."

"I mean, when you go to school they always tell you how you should read read read . . . Well, I been outta school a long time and I can't see where readin benefits nobody. Too much like work. And this here book. I don't understand. I don't think it's one of them photography books cause their ain't no captions or credits or nothin."

All in all, Dump was getting pretty fucking tired of hearing about the book.

"If you hate it so much why you keep lookin at it?"

"Cause I don't get it. There must be somethin special about it."

"Why you say that?" Dump downed his beer in three large gulps. Leggy's trailer was kind of warm and he could tell his stink had busted open again.

"Cause she had it all locked up. Had all of em locked up."

"I guess. Not many people lock up books, do they?"

"None that I know of. Of course, most people I know only own the Bible."

"The bestselling book of all time."

"The biggest piece of shit of all of them."

"Ain't never read it."

"Christ. You stink to high heaven."

"Sorry."

"Let's go out to the dirt pile. Let this place air out some."

"Game's gettin ready to start."

"You hate baseball."

"Guess you're right about that."

Dump stood up from the raggedy brown chair he had chosen to pollute, a little wobbly at first. Leggy crossed the small trailer and went into the back. Dump figured he was just going to use the bathroom but when he came back into the living room he was carrying his shotgun.

"What's with the gun?" Dump asked.

"I'm gonna have me some fun with this book."

"Gonna shoot it?"

"Damn right I'm gonna shoot it."

"Cool." Dump no longer gave a damn about the moral implications of stealing something Ms. Blanchette undoubtedly treasured.

Together, Leggy carrying the book and the shotgun, Dump carrying the half-empty case of beer, they went out to the dirt mound, which was pretty much just that—a big mound of dirt, about six feet high and fifteen feet long. Neither of them really knew why it was there and neither of them really cared. They both liked to come out and fire off Leggy's arsenal from time to time and the dirt mound made a most excellent backstop.

Leggy opened the book up and placed it into some loose dirt on the mound.

"I'll fire one and then you can fire one, kay?"

"Sure." Dump cracked open another beer. He was about ready to piss his pants and wished he had used the toilet before coming out.

Leggy counted off about twenty paces and smiled. Some of the wax had sweated out of his mustache and it drooped a little bit. "Fuckin book." He pulled the trigger and Dump watched as bits of paper flew up from the book as the buckshot ripped into it. Leggy yipped and raised the rifle up in the air. Score one for the illiterates, Dump thought, and then said, "My turn."

"Get it right in the middle and we'll split that fucker in half," Leggy said.

"I'll try." When Dump looked through the sight, he saw two books and decided to aim for the one on the left.

The deafening roar of the shotgun threatened to split his skull but the effect was satisfying. The book didn't come completely apart but a large hole had opened in the middle.

Dump handed the gun back to Leggy. "You gonna give it another go?"

Leggy was now so drunk he had to hold his left eye open. He chose to do this with the end of the gun while he patted himself down with his free hand. "Shit," he said. "I didn't bring no more shells."

Dump staggered up to the mound, pulling his penis out of his dirty jeans. Once he got within pissing distance, he let go with a stream of rancid urine. It soaked the pages of the book.

"Shit, man," Leggy said. "I can smell that all the way back here. Don't make me blow your dick off." He aimed the unloaded gun at

Dump. It still made Dump nervous.

They took the rest of the beer and the gun into the trailer and waited for dark. Destroying the book seemed to have taken both of their minds off it. They watched the baseball game, drank more, and played some cards. Eventually, after all the beer was gone, Dump decided he wanted to go back to the apartment. The truck was a company truck both of them used to do most of their driving. As long as it showed back up at Leggy's house in the morning to pick him up, he didn't really care where it went.

Leggy had fallen into something like a stupor on the couch. Dump didn't know how but he knew Leggy would be just as well-coiffed and crazy-eyed at nine o'clock in the morning as he had been earlier. Dump would be dragging. He didn't like to get this drunk through the week, on work nights, but sometimes there just wasn't anything else to do.

As he walked toward the truck, something caught his eye. Movement. Over by the dirt mound. His first crazy thought was that fucking book had some kind of tracking device in it and now the police had come to claim it. He thought about just hightailing it to the truck and driving away as fast as possible but he was too drunk to follow what could be considered the path of reason.

Drawing closer to the dirt pile, he saw the book had fallen down off its little ledge of soil.

And it seemed to be crossing the ground on its own.

Dump stopped there. That was some freaky shit. If the book was crawling now, he didn't want to be anywhere near it.

Then he noticed the book wasn't moving on its own. It was . . . *attached* to a figure.

Dump's heart began a hard thud in his weighty chest.

He moved closer to the book. The reason he couldn't see the figure so well at first was because it was covered in blood.

Now he was maybe ten feet away. He didn't know if he should move any closer to the figure, mainly because of the sheer oddity of the situation. But what harm could it do? It seemed to be pulling itself along the ground. And he had to know who it was. Because if his suspicions were correct then he would have to seriously reevaluate his reality.

The figure let out a garbled wheeze.

Besides, Dump thought, moving closer, what if this person needs help? He couldn't just turn and leave them. He wouldn't do that to anyone.

Now he was only a couple of steps away, looking down at the shattered and bloody face of Ms. Blanchette. Her body was riddled with buckshot. She reached toward him. Dump thought of something like a nuclear bomb, opening up some other world, ripping everyone up, turning them all into a shadow of this mutilated Ms. Blanchette.

"You don't know what you've done," she said. "You have to stop him." Her head dropped down, nearly hitting the grass.

"Stop who?" Dump asked.

"*Him.*"

"I think maybe I need to get you to a hospital." He said this knowing that a hospital wouldn't do any good. No doctor was good enough to patch up all those holes. And how would he explain this to the hospital staff? True, maybe they had shot her but she was a *book* when they shot her. Just a fucking book.

"Close it," she coughed up at him, dying madness in her eyes. "Please, let me die at home. Close it."

Dump reached down. The hole was open as far as it could be. He didn't see how it was possible, didn't know how she would fit in the book, but he closed it anyway. And Ms. Blanchette was gone. He held the book in his right hand, not minding that there wasn't much of it to hold or that he had urinated on it only a couple of hours ago. It deserved better than to just be buried in a pile of dirt. Standing there, he realized he could very well be holding some kind of apocalypse.

He started back toward the trailer. He would have to wake Leggy up and tell him about this. He didn't know how he would take it. Since he hadn't actually *seen* Ms. Blanchette, half-in and half-out of the book, he probably wouldn't believe him at all.

Dump opened the door to the trailer.

Leggy was not at all how he had left him.

He was changed.

His legs were still very long but he had more of them. They bent from his torso, all six of them, like the fattest spider legs Dump had ever seen. His eyes had changed. They were silvery and slanted, reaching back nearly to his ears. And now his handlebar mustache was curved downward and looked more like fangs.

In front of him was the black book. The bastard had taken it after all. Had probably, in fact, known about the import of those books far longer than he had let on. For all Dump knew—and judging by what he now witnessed—Leggy wasn't human at all.

Briefly, watching this weird spiderthing in front of him, Dump thought back over all the years he had known Leggy. Curiously, he found himself thinking about all the stuff Leggy *hadn't* told him. He could spout philosophies, ideas, and opinions but he never talked about the good old days, the school days, the teenage years—the things most of their blue collar ilk talked about.

"Leggy," Dump said. He wished he had his gun. He wouldn't hesitate to put some bullets into this snarling thing in front of him.

Leggy didn't seem to hear Dump. He looked at the open book beneath him and Dump's eyes strayed in the same direction. The picture there was spread across two pages and looked very dark. Dump thought he saw other things, things like Leggy and some maybe even worse, flit across the pages. Leggy lowered his head and began squirming into the book. Shocked, Dump looked on, not knowing what else to do. He dropped the book he held in his hand onto the couch, picked up the shotgun that had been drunkenly tossed aside and went toward the back of the trailer.

In Leggy's bedroom was a strange smell. One Dump did not like at all. It was far worse than Dump usually smelled, even on his worst day. And there were pictures plastered on all the walls. Alien pictures. Pictures of things Dump could easily imagine existing in the pages of Ms. Blanchette's library. For all Dump knew, these pictures could have come from the books *in* Ms. Blanchette's library.

Dump rummaged through drawers until he found what he was looking for. The bright red plastic shells. He split the gun and put in two shells, heading back to the living room. Just as he entered, he saw the last of Leggy, heading into the black book, a toothed tail dragging along the worn down carpet.

Dump didn't hesitate. Maybe he had had enough of this world. Maybe he just couldn't stand the thought of that spider creature being loosed on some other world. Maybe it was the guilt at having aided in the theft and destruction of the other book. Maybe he had always hated Leggy. Picking up that other book and holding it in his free hand, Dump jumped into the black book after Leggy, having no idea what he would find on the other side.

MAY TO MAY

ZENA RADO KNOCKED on the door and waited. She slid the key into the lock and opened the door. This was always the part she found most thrilling. The rest of it was exciting in a different way. The excitement of discovery. Like the kind an archaeologist on a dig might have. The initial discovery—unearthing—of the way these people lived was a shot of pure adrenaline.

Sometimes there wasn't anything at all. Sometimes the house was simply empty. As it really should be. Nothing except an old scrap of paper or toothpick shoved into the back corner of a kitchen drawer. But this was rare. Most people left something behind.

A few of the tenants had been hoarders. This, other than the obsessiveness of their condition, offered little clue as to any specific personality. It was just the compulsive acquisition, almost randomly, of stuff. The only thing their hoarding really said about them was that they were consumers, and possibly more sentimental than most. Or they were just lazy. Most people in our modern world were consumers. The only real difference between a hoarder and the rest was how one curates and displays her acquisitions.

More often than not, she found the perfect balance of things taken and things left behind. This helped her form a far more accurate life of the tenant who'd lived at 523 Glowers Pike, Twin Springs, Ohio 45---.

Alan Beaumont was an example of this type of person.

Zena had to check the lease in her hand to make sure she had his name right. Even though she'd opened his checks for the past twelve months, the name had eluded her.

She stepped into the dining room through the door in the carport and breathed in the familiar musty, earthy smell. One of the tenants had complained about a mold problem a few years back and they'd had to take care of that. Like everything her parents did with their rental properties, it was done cheaply and half-assed. Sometimes a tenant would manage to successfully tamp down that smell that made Zena think of a grave but it inevitably came back. It wasn't an odor she would describe as a stench. She found it pleasing, comforting, woodsy.

Everything was in her parents' name. Zena handled things while they wintered in the Florida Keys. Their winters were getting longer and longer. And why not? They were getting older and, having lived most of her life here in Twin Springs, Zena had heard many people refer to the "damp chill" that seemed to hang around nine months out of the year. Maybe it was because of all the old growth trees or maybe it was because of the creek. "Shady" and "dripping" were two adjectives that came to mind when Zena thought about the Springs.

"Mr. Beaumont?" she called.

No answer.

"Hello. Is anybody here?"

No answer.

There was a certain protocol she followed. She didn't know if it was necessarily legal or not but she figured she could do pretty much anything within reason. Anything that wasn't completely out of line. She was not the landlord, after all. Merely the flaky art school graduate daughter, offering to pitch in and help in exchange for a free ride through life. Little more than an office assistant. Sounded good to her.

A rectangular black wooden table dominated the dining room. Probably a four- or, at best, six-seater. There were no chairs. A couple of dead plants cancerously blighted a wrought iron stand. The floor and everything else was gritty with dust.

She had not always been so brazen about entering the house. Her parents owned many houses throughout the town and surrounding farm country and this was the only one she would ever enter like this. She had been working for her parents since shortly after graduating a prestigious private art school in New England. The school was very similar to Twins Springs' own Shrine College, the place that, she guessed, really put it on the map. Shrine College was why many people knew the town of Twin Springs when there probably wasn't really any reason for them to.

That was ten years ago.

No one had rented this for more than thirteen months at a time. And it was always May to May. Which meant that it sat vacant for eleven months out of the year. It was something she and her parents never even really thought about anymore. Her father had drawn up a contract from May 1st one year through May 30th the following, the rent was twice what it was for any of their other properties, and it was always taken. Twin Springs was a highly sought-after area. The school system was good. Crime was low. There were things to do and restaurants to eat in. It was a welcome liberal enclave in a mostly conservative part of the state. "For Sale" signs rarely lasted more than a month and she had placed rent signs in yards and turned around in an hour to remove them because the property had been taken that quickly. Now, with the internet, she barely needed to put out signs.

Not so with 523 Glowers.

Her father told her it had been like this for as long as he could remember. One year he'd put a sign in the yard that said FREE RENT with his phone number beneath it. He left it up for eleven months and didn't receive a single call. Until late April. Zena was too young to remember it but that was the year that writer guy had lived there. Holger Something-or-the-other. Twin Springs was an artsy, literate place. There were probably many people living here over the years who fancied themselves writers but this guy had actually had some stuff published. Zena couldn't remember any of the titles. It was trashy, Stephen King-type stuff she'd never really been interested in. The guy disappearing off the face of the planet without a trace didn't even make his name more known. JD Salinger was just a reclusive asshole and that only helped his popularity. Not poor Holger Writer Guy, though. Maybe it was just the difference between timeless literature and sensationalistic pulp. Hell, maybe it had been a pen name. When her father informed Holger the free rent only applied through April, he said the guy seemed unaware and offered to come in and pay all thirteen months up front.

So she knew, if it was beyond May 31st and she entered the house, she would be alone.

Only she never really felt alone.

At first she'd been terrified of finding someone dead but that hadn't happened either.

She was not aware of anyone dying in the house. So she hesitated to think the presence she felt was a ghost. It was probably just her imagination.

Now she stood in the library. That's what it looked like Alan Beaumont had used it for, anyway. Some people liked to use it for a study or guest bedroom. One family had even used it as the playroom. It had a large window in one wall and a door that let in as much light as the shady backyard would allow. The door opened to the back patio, if it could really be called that. It was a thing of bizarre . . . not beauty, exactly . . . Existence, maybe. She had no idea who created the patio but it looked like he'd had a bunch of spare bricks and got drunk with his friends while they placed them on the ground. The bricks mostly touched each other. It didn't look like any mortar had been used and they weren't at all even. While they may have been drunk when they laid the patio, she had to think that being drunk post-construction was a bad and possibly dangerous idea. So, yes, it was bizarre the patio even existed. Why spend time on something that looked like that? Why not scrap it and hire a professional?

A desk was pushed against the door. She would never know if it was so he could enjoy the view or if he was trying to keep something out. The window had what looked like a large dreamcatcher hanging from it with a sachet of something fastened to it. She sniffed the sachet. It smelled dry and dusty with maybe an underlying odor of rotting flowers.

She performed a quick survey of the bookshelves. Since no one had ever left behind anything like a computer or laptop or smart phone or even a diary, the bookshelves were often the best way to figure out what went on in some of these people's heads. Mr. Beaumont had seemed to like books on various religions with an emphasis on the occult. Or maybe those were the books he was least interested in. Maybe those were the ones he cared so little about that he left them behind.

She looked at his agreement again to see if it listed an occupation or an employer. She raised her eyebrows. It was like Mr. Beaumont knew his renting this house was in no way contingent to his employment.

EMPLOYER: FUCK ALL GODS
ADDRESS: 123 Anywhere Street
          Anyplace, Ohio 66666
PHONE: 1-800-BUTTSEX

She wondered if her parents kept any of the previous tenants' agreements on file. If so, it could make for some amusing reading.

In the middle of the room was a small, uncomfortable looking futon couch. Zena immediately thought of it as a bachelor's couch. There was a single book on the couch. It was called *The Book of Lies* by someone named Aleister Crowley. Zena thought the name sounded familiar although it carried a vaguely negative connotation. She thought about taking it since it seemed like this might possibly be the last thing Mr. Beaumont had read before he left. But she figured there would be plenty of time for that. If people didn't clean out this house before vacating it, they never came back for their stuff. Everything in here was now Zena's responsibility to get rid of. This had happened plenty of times before. Her parents had once tried to simply open the doors and have an estate sale, perfectly willing to let everything go for free, but no one showed up. Even when Zena listed shit on eBay, it sat there for an inordinately long time before selling. Nowadays, she was more inclined to pay junk men to just come and remove everything.

She left the library behind, moving back through the dining room and turning left into the narrow kitchen, making another left into the living room. More dust. A faint odor of incense. A couch. A couple of chairs. A low coffee table. A couple more dead plants. No television. No stereo. No DVDs or CDs or records. Not that there was any need for physical media anymore. All one needed was an internet connection to stream everything from space. She imagined every work of art that had ever been created orbiting the earth like an asteroid belt.

She walked through the living room, turned right into a short hallway, and entered the kitchen. She now looked through the kitchen and into the dining room. Sometimes different perspectives provided fresh insights to things. But she didn't have any revelations. She opened up some cabinets and drawers. All silverware, plates, and cups seemed to be left here. A coffeemaker and grinder were plugged into the wall but she was sure the power had been turned off, probably as of this morning. She opened the refrigerator, figuring she should probably remove any food that might have or would potentially go bad. There was a half-empty glass bottle of water with a rubber pop-top and an unopened bottle of Stone IPA. She'd probably take that back and put it in her own refrigerator.

The freezer contained three empty ice cube trays and a yellowed letter, still kind of cool to the touch, that read: REMEMBER TO GIVE BACK.

Cryptic, maybe. Or maybe just a simple reminder.

She walked down the hallway, stopping at the bathroom on the right just long enough to throw back the shower curtain and lift the toilet seat to make sure nothing too organic had been left behind. She'd have to remember to wash her hands when she got back to the office.

She glanced into the bedroom at the end of the hall but it was completely empty.

The smaller bedroom across the hallway contained a bed with messed up covers and a chest of drawers.

She wondered why Beaumont would have chosen the smaller bedroom and reminded herself he might not have been the only person living here, even though his was the only name on the agreement. Maybe he'd actually spent most of his nights in the larger bedroom and decided to take that stuff with him because it was newer or more expensive or more comfortable. Or maybe he had preferred this bedroom because of the large window looking out into the backyard and the thick woods beyond. It was a good view. There were no curtains hanging on the window and she wondered if Mr. Beaumont had ever put any up.

She watched two squirrels fucking in the yard. In the distance, a cat hunkered in the tall grass, hiding in the shadow of the woods, ready to spring into action.

In his closet she found that Mr. Beaumont preferred mostly khaki pants and blue jeans with a number of black shirts, one light blue oxford, and a clown costume. This was more creepy than hilarious and she tried to convince herself it was probably a Halloween costume. Still, she pulled it out and inspected it for blood, rips, anything. Nothing. Not really a surprise.

She went through the chest, expecting to find socks and underwear and t-shirts since most of the clothes seemed to be left behind. The only thing she found was an eight-inch black dildo in the middle drawer.

She closed the drawer, embarrassed.

Why was she embarrassed?

She didn't know. Now that she thought about it, it seemed irrational.

There's no one here with you.
You're all alone.
All alone.

With her hand on the dusty chest of drawers, she stared almost longingly into the woods across the yard. They seemed darker and more foreboding than the woods closer to town. A person could get lost in these woods.

The squirrels had finished fucking.

A third squirrel came up and began fucking the squirrel that had been on the bottom.

It made Zena think of a rabbity guy in a porno waiting his turn.

The cat sprang out from the woods and attacked the now idle squirrel.

All four animals made panicked squeals and dispersed.

There was an explosion of bird sounds. The birds were still there, watching.

Maybe it was all the animals making Zena feel watched.

But an animal was not a person. An animal could react to something she did, but it had no way of recounting her actions. Beyond the animals, there was the other natural world—the trees, the weeds, the sky—that never reacted to something a human did. Not consciously anyway. Not by choice.

Zena realized she was wet.

You're all alone.

She wondered if she was ever alone. Sometimes she felt like she had to do things to prove she was alone. To prove there was not always a reaction to her actions. To prove this to herself. This sensation of being watched was really just ego, she thought.

She slowly lay down on the bed, watching the early afternoon make the green backyard glow.

She shucked down her pants and underwear and ran her fingertips over herself, spreading her labia. The cat was back, spotting her, casually licking its paw. Not judging her. Zena scooted to the edge of the bed, her pants still around her ankles. The chest was close enough for her to reach forward and open the drawer, pull out the dildo.

She didn't know if it had been cleaned since its last use. She didn't know how many times or on how many people it had been used.

She didn't care.

She leaned back.

The cat was gone.

She stared at the ceiling and slowly slid the dildo inside of her, as deep as it would go. She looked at the shadows gathering in the corners of the room and closed her eyes and created a shadow within herself. When she thought about who she pictured on top of her, she wasn't surprised to think it was probably Alan Beaumont, even though she had no idea what he looked like. A stranger thought—that this was his big black mummified cock she had so deep inside her. That turned her on more than it disgusted her.

On the way out, she threw the dildo in one of the trashcans outside. It was now a talisman of her guilt. She hadn't used one of those in a really long time. She'd forgotten how pleasurable it could be. In many respects, it was the perfect man. The house was only a ten-minute walk from the office so she hadn't bothered driving. She walked slowly, as if in a daze.

She thought about stopping off at her house before going to the office. She should probably wash her hands and change her underwear.

THE MAN WITH THE FACE LIKE A BRUISE

E LI," SHE WHISPERED into his ear.
Nothing.

She shifted in the bed, turning over to face him.

"Elijah?"

He only whimpered and turned away from her. She leaned her head over top of his, feeling the heat coming off his face. She pushed her lips into the stubble that grew from his jaw line, sliding her tongue between her lips, pressing it against the stubble, running it up the sleep greasy sheen of his cheek until she could taste the tear that had trickled from one of his closed eyes.

"Eli?" she whispered again.

Still nothing.

She rolled back over, pulled the sheet up to her chin, and closed her eyes against the dawn.

After the blueness had left the room, replaced with a yellow that was harsher and fuller of sun, Eli woke up. Maya was lying next to him, already awake. He reached over, beneath the sheet, pulled down a little lower now, and ran his hand up her silk smooth thigh.

"Morning, Sweetness," he mumbled through drymouth.

"You were whimpering again." She didn't even look at him, just kept staring up at the ceiling.

"Was I?"

"Actually crying this time."

"Did I wake you?"

"No, I was already awake."

He rolled over and nibbled her ear.

"Look, Eli, is there something you need to tell me?"

"About what?"

"It's not like you, that's all. The whimpering. The crying. I want you to tell me what the hell's the matter with you."

Eli leaned across the bed, over Maya and her fabulous heat, to grab his cigarettes and lighter from the nightstand. He brought himself back over to his side and propped the pillow up against the headboard, shook out a cigarette and lit it. Through the thin, twirling veil of gray smoke, he looked at their small apartment. They had something good. He liked what they had created over the past year. They never argued. They didn't really have any worries and, until this past month or so, they had had some really great sex. Eli didn't want to lose any of that.

Maya sighed into the heavy yellowness of the room.

"Are you going to tell me?" she said.

Eli took another drag and crushed the cigarette out.

"Yeah, I'll tell you."

Sometimes, when everything was blue, Elijah didn't just see what was in front of him. There was something else. It was like the air around him was too thin or something. Almost like he could see through it. And it wasn't just his sight that was affected. He heard things too, when everything was blue.

It started right before Eileen and Cynthia died. The week before, to be exact. June 15. More than two years ago. Two years and one week ago.

Dawn in the bedroom of their new house in the suburbs and Elijah had woken up and looked around the room. The blue filled the room and inside the blue, Elijah saw the swirling shapes. He got out of bed and walked into the middle of the room, deeper into the blue, Eileen sleeping soundly, Cynthia still tucked away in her room with the Dr. Seuss murals painted on the walls.

The blue wasn't like any other color Elijah had ever seen. It almost seemed like calling it blue was to do it some sort of injustice. It couldn't be categorized like that. It was the blue of a hundred different skies. The blue of Heaven, perhaps.

Elijah stood in the middle of the room, shivering cold and still sweaty—clammy. He felt the blue moving all around him. He felt it brush up against his ear and whisper something no more intelligible than the wind. Sitting down, he marveled at the way the blue could coil itself up before slowly, hypnotically unfurling. He admired the color and the sheer mystery of it.

Over the next week, his feelings changed.

The blue continued to visit him, gaining in intensity.

Three days after the first, Elijah noticed there were people in the blue. Spirits maybe. Ghosts. Who knew? He wasn't sure he *wanted* to know. By the end of that fourth day, he could make out some of the faces in the blue. There must have been hundreds. All surfacing through the blue before receding.

Before the sun ate the blue that day, he saw the face like a bruise. That was when he knew everything wasn't going to be okay.

On the fifth day, there were fewer faces.

On the sixth day, even fewer.

On the seventh day, the day of Eileen and Cynthia's death, the only face remaining was the one that looked like a bruise. That was when Elijah assumed the man with the face like a bruise had somehow consumed the other faces. Maybe he would have opened it up to speculation, something to ponder, to think about, maybe even ask somebody about, if it weren't for the car crash that took Eileen and Cynthia that night.

The grief in and of itself was crippling and then there were all the legal ramifications on top of that, the people in suits telling him his time for grieving was over, and the blue was gone anyway so there wasn't really anything to think about.

A little more than a year later he met Maya and his grief was replaced with love. Although the love was somewhat tainted with guilt. So much guilt, in fact, that Elijah could never really bring himself to tell Maya about the previous loves of his life. Initially, he told himself he was just waiting for the right time. Eventually, he convinced himself there wasn't a right time. He had waited too long. To tell her now would surely cost him the relationship.

But the blue had come back—and the man with the face like a bruise—and Maya had heard him crying and whimpering names, fragments. Enough to make her suspicious. That, on top of the impotence and the despondency, was sure to ruin everything he and Maya had.

Neither one of them had gotten out of bed to open the windows or turn on the air conditioner and Maya lay beside Elijah, the tears coming out of her eyes mingling with the sheen of sweat on her cheeks.

She brushed the moisture off with the back of an already moist hand and reached over to the nightstand to get a cigarette. He had never seen her smoke. She seemed like a different woman as she greedily lit the cigarette. She inhaled the cigarette and coughed up a combination of tears, phlegm, and smoke. She sat up, keeping the sheet pulled to just above her breasts.

"I thought," she said, "that you had found someone else. I thought those were the names you were saying. Some whore at the office you were fucking."

"I would never do anything like that to you." He put his hand on her thigh, ran it up to the crease between where her leg met her pubis.

"I thought that was the whole reason why you couldn't . . . you know."

"I would never cheat on you. You know that . . . *don't* you?"

She shook her head. "It happens."

There was a moment of awkward silence. Maya's crying increased. Unable to finish the cigarette, she crushed it out. Elijah moved his hand onto the soft mound of her sex. "It happens," she mumbled again through a thick mouth. He brushed his hand over her clitoris and then stopped, bringing his hand quickly away.

"I need to go," he said.

"Don't go," Maya cried.

"I have to work. I need to go."

He dressed in a hurry and left the apartment, slamming the door on his way out.

Once in the car, he knew he wasn't going to work. He was too angry. He didn't exactly know why. He sat in the hot car, sweat rolling down his face, shaking with anger. Slowly, he composed himself enough to pull away from the curb and take the twisted mess inside his head with him.

Stopping at the liquor store, he bought a bottle of Jim Beam and continued on to the Moston Memorial Gardens. There, he would be able to sit. To contemplate. Sort some things out.

He opened the Jim Beam as soon as he got out to the car and was nearly drunk by the time he got to the cemetery. He pulled the car up near Eileen and Cynthia's gravesites and stumbled across the freshly manicured lawn until he reached their tombstones. Once there, he sat down in between them, the bottle between his legs.

It was then he decided to sort some things out, to try and figure out why he was so goddamn enraged.

The most obvious fact was that this was the two-year anniversary of their deaths. The grief and anger had never really relented since he had received the call at home to come to the hospital and identify the bodies. The grief, he knew, would have to subside on its own. It would never go away completely. He didn't expect, didn't even really *want*, that to happen. The grief was like a memory. To remove the grief, he would have to take away all the memories of them. He didn't want that. Memories were the only things he had left.

The rage, though. That was something different altogether. It was something he hadn't expected and, once upon him, couldn't figure out how to get rid of. Entangling himself in hostile relationships with virtually everyone he knew didn't seem to do the trick. That merely rendered him isolated and friendless. It wasn't just the world he was mad at. It was Eileen, too. If she had been more alert, maybe, or a better driver, then none of it would have happened. He knew that was ludicrous, of course, but knowing it didn't stop the feelings and the thoughts rushing through his head. Knowing it almost made it worse, turning the whole situation into some all-consuming paradox.

God was at fault too, naturally. Elijah had never been a very religious person but he wouldn't have considered himself an atheist until that day. A god that would kill a beautiful, successful woman in the prime of her life and an innocent child wasn't a god worth believing in. A god that would force him to suffer as much as he had after their deaths was a god that was better off dead.

Completely drunk at this point and watching the thunderheads gather up their black dresses of grief and march toward the graveyard, he realized there was a new dimension to his anger and he finally figured it out.

Maya was cheating on him.

The signs were there, he had merely refused to acknowledge them. But now that he did, now that he told himself she was cheating on him, the pieces fell into place.

It started with the way she was acting this morning. How she had told him affairs happened. It wasn't even the way she said it, "It happens," it was the way she completely broke down after he had told her he wasn't cheating on her. Like, after her suspicions were denied, she was the guilty one. It would be completely like Maya to fuck someone to get even with him.

Then Elijah remembered something else. Actually, it was some*one* else. All last week, about the same time everything became blue again, Elijah had seen the same man coming from the direction of their apartment building. In a small town like Moston, it wasn't unusual to see the same faces over and over again, but he hadn't seen this man until last week and he never saw him at any other time.

Elijah remembered touching Maya this morning and how unresponsive she was.

Well, he thought. There's only one way to prove it.

With that, he stood up, guzzled down the rest of the bourbon, pulled some flowers away from a neighboring grave and put them into the empty bottle, setting it down in between the graves as a small reminder he was there.

On his way back into town he drove straight through the storm. By the time he reached the apartment the storm had subsided and the air around him resonated with the ozone blue of sun trying to break through dark clouds. He did the best parking job he could muster, nearly popping the tire as the car flew up onto the curb. It didn't matter. He didn't plan on being there for very long anyway.

He knew what he expected to find and, at this point, a scary thought, it was almost what he *wanted* to find. He wondered if they would actually be fucking or maybe Maya was now feeling guilty and blowing the guy off. Whoever the creep was, Elijah felt certain he would try and get a little something from her before saying his goodbye.

Elijah threw open the door from the street and bounded up the stairs.

Would they even bother locking the doors?

He had his key ready but, turning the knob, discovered he didn't even need it. Hell, the anticipation of getting caught had to be half the thrill of it.

One could not see the front door from the bed. It was one of the small touches that made the apartment feel a little less like an efficiency.

Elijah grabbed the aluminum Louisville Slugger he kept propped against the door in case of intruders. It had never really occurred to him before that was probably the worst place he could have kept it if anyone wanted to break in. It would be like arming the criminal. Of course, there was a gun in the bedside table. He anticipated Maya going for that if he didn't act quickly enough. Elijah hated guns. He had no intention of trying to go after it himself.

As he rounded the corner, his mind took a quick snapshot of what was happening on the bed before he moved in to put a stop to it.

Maya was lying back, her eyes closed, her ass supported by the edge of the bed. Her sundress was pushed up to her waist and there was a man's head between her legs, his hands wrapped around her hips, one of her legs thrown over his right shoulder.

Elijah moved in quickly, taking a firm grip on the bat's friction tape and hoisting it above his head. Maya must have heard him. She opened her mouth, trying to say something, but it wouldn't come out before the bat smashed across the man's upper back, the fat of it landing on his left shoulder, the very tip of it connecting with Maya's right leg.

The man let out a pitiful groan as he fell to the floor, struggling to turn over onto his back and identify his assailant. Elijah was on him, pressing the bat down against his throat so he couldn't yell. He needed this to be as subdued as possible because this wasn't the end. The more he thought about it, the more gruesome he wanted it to be.

"Everyone needs to shut the fuck up," Elijah said calmly. "If anyone decides to cry out or yell for help then I'm swinging the bat again. And this time I'll hit something more vital."

"Eli . . ." Maya said.

Elijah put more weight on the bat and watched the man's face turn purple.

"I think you should be quiet, Maya," he said. "Now, we're all going down to the car. If we pass anyone and you try and say something to them, I'll beat you both to death before any help can arrive. When we get down to the car, you are going to get in the driver's seat, Maya. Do you understand that?"

She nodded her head.

"Good," Elijah said. "Loverboy here is going to get in the passenger seat and I'm going to sit in back. We're driving to Keifer Road, where it meets Salton Lane. Do you know where that is, Maya?"

She nodded her head again. Her mouth was pulled tight and she was trembling, exactly what Elijah wanted to see. Her hands were gripped tight over her knee, already swollen and purple.

"Do you think you're going to have trouble walking?" Elijah asked her.

She nodded her head.

"If you fall down, then I'm taking this bat through loverboy's head, do you understand?"

She nodded.

"Are you going to fall down?"

She shook her head.

"Good. Let's go. Maya, you first. Loverboy second."

Elijah pulled the bat away from the guy's neck and stood up, backing away from the small battery scene. The man still had his shirt on but now the back of the shirt contained a lump that looked something like a football. He had absolutely no use of his left arm and Elijah found the way he had to struggle to stand up quite comical. He chuckled a little.

This was definitely the guy Elijah had seen on the street in front of their apartment. They must have had some way of seeing Elijah coming so they could get him out of there in time. For some reason, this infuriated Elijah even more. The fact Maya didn't feel the need to be even more discrete about her affair. The fact neighbors had to have seen this man come into the apartment, never at the same time as Elijah. Elijah wondered if any of the neighbors had heard them fucking, heard the headboard beating against the wall. Surely they must have.

Maya limped slowly to the door, bracing herself on whatever objects she could find along the wall. Elijah didn't enjoy watching her as much. It had never really been his intention to hurt Maya. When Elijah looked at the man he saw the man with the face like a bruise. Not really, only symbolically. Just as the man with the face like a bruise had somehow taken everyone he had loved away from him before, so this man had come along two years later and done the same. But the man with a face like a bruise was only a spirit, quite possibly a metaphysical hallucination, impossible to destroy. In this man, Maya's nameless lover, Elijah had a very palpable target for his revenge. Elijah reached out and jabbed the man's swollen shoulder with the end of the bat, watching the cords in the man's neck draw tight as he stifled a wince.

They made their way down to the car, Elijah standing outside until he saw that Maya and her lover were in their assigned positions. Still cautious, he slid into the back seat, maintaining a firm grip on the baseball bat. After sitting down, vigilantly leaning forward, there was an awkward pause in the rhythm.

"Start the car," he barked at Maya.

"I don't know if I can use the gas pedal," she said.

"You don't need your leg to use it, just your foot. Now start the fucking car."

She did as she was told. Music from the Birthday Party filled the car, Nick Cave's hooting and barking, along with the churning and screeching of the guitar, matching what Elijah felt in his head. Maya's hand instinctively reached out to turn the volume down until she thought better of it. Elijah realized he was still in control of the situation.

The storm had now passed completely and the late afternoon was sparkling and humid.

"Roll down your window!" Elijah shouted over the music.

Maya rolled down the window.

She pulled away from the curb and started down the road, where Main Street turned into the Pike. From there they would hit Keifer and be just about where Elijah needed them to be.

Elijah sat in the back seat, studying them—the tense musculature of their necks, the way their shoulders seemed all drawn up. He basked in it. He basked in what he had planned, never once thinking anything would stop it from going off.

But he didn't want to end anything without getting some answers first. Eileen and Cynthia had taken the open book with them, leaving Elijah to write up his own conclusions and close the book. It was something he didn't ever think he would be capable of doing. Of course, with their situation he had no control over it. He had simply decided it was the man with the face like a bruise and had spent the next two years of his life searching that man out. He wasn't going to let that happen again. He had the man with the face like a bruise right here in front of him and he wasn't going to let him get away.

Elijah slid the bat in between the two front seats and started ramming the stereo violently until it cracked, splintered, and the music went away.

"So, Maya, you never properly introduced me to loverboy here. I mean, in a round about way, I guess we were quite intimate but, shucks, I don't even know his name."

"Hunter," she said.

"Last name?"

"Green."

"Hunter Green? Sounds like a fucking golf course. So, Maya, how old a man is Hunter?"

"Twenty-three."

"Oh. Robbing the cradle a bit? Well, that's all fine, I guess I'm pretty much past my prime anyway. By the way, how big is Hunter's cock, Maya?"

She was silent.

Elijah quickly flicked the barrel of the bat to his right, smacking Hunter on the side of the head, just hard enough to stun him and make a satisfying sound.

"I never measured."

"But surely you have an idea. Erect? What, both hands plus the head? Then some, maybe . . ."

"Nine inches."

"Hunter, does Maya give good head? I mean, is it up to your standards? I always found it pretty good, except that she could never really go all the way with it. You know, she could never get it all the way in without gagging."

Hunter stared dazedly ahead. "She's good," he said through clenched teeth.

"That's pretty vague there, Hunter. I mean, if you're nine inches then you have something on me so I know she wasn't able to get it all the way in."

"She tried."

"Well, sometimes that's the best you can ask for, I guess. Did you like the taste of her pussy? I ask this because I noticed you kind of feasting on it when I came home today."

"Yes."

"On a scale of one to ten?"

"Eight."

"Have you tasted a lot of pussy?"

"A few."

"So have you ever tasted a ten?"

"Yes."

"Who was she?"

"Lorna Brett. My sophomore year."

"So you like the young pussy?"

"I guess."

"Maya, did you let him fuck you in the ass? Did you fuck her in the ass, Hunter?"

"Once."

"How was it?"

"Good."

"Not great?"

"It was good."

"She never let me fuck her in the ass. Not that I really tried all that much but variety's the spice of life, you know. It would have been something different, in between all those affairs with girls from the office. Right, Maya?"

"I'm sorry." She was crying, wiping the tears from her eyes.

"Doesn't feel good to have your life, your *secret* life all exposed like this, does it? I mean, my secret life, hell, it only involved me but yours was a little, I don't know, des*truc*tive maybe. Is that the right word for it?"

No one answered Elijah, there were a few seconds of silence, the car flapping along the ill-maintained road.

"So, did you ever come in her face, Hunter?" Elijah quickly pointed off to his right and said, "You're about to miss the turn, hon." Maya whipped the car onto Salton Lane. Elijah lost his balance momentarily but quickly found it again. "Because, you know, I always kind of wanted to but I could never really muster up the courage to ask her. I guess it's just one of those things you either have to be asked to do or you just gotta do at the spur of the moment. So, what about it, Hunt?"

"No."

"Same reasons? I mean, you wanted to, right? When she's having an orgasm, you can't look at those perfect little lips and not have the thought of coming onto them cross your mind."

"Yes, I wanted to."

"Okay, slow down a little bit. Stop at this bend."

But she didn't stop at the bend. She didn't even make it to the bend. Just before the road broke swiftly to the left, Maya cut the wheel to her right and the car rolled off the road and into a ditch. She wasn't going very fast and there wasn't really any damage, but everyone in the car was thrown around.

Elijah could tell what her intention was. Her intention was to wreck the car in such a way that he would not be able to open his door. Instead, all the doors were free to be opened. The front of the car had merely run into some small trees at the edge of the woods.

Before Elijah could get his bearings, Maya had already opened her door and took off limping into the woods on the other side of the road. But Maya wasn't really his main concern. Elijah's main concern was the man in the front seat struggling with his door, trying to assemble some kind of propulsive rhythm with the one side of his body that worked.

Elijah beat him out of the car, baseball bat in hand.

Hunter opened his door, oblivious to Elijah standing outside of the car, and slid his legs out until they found the ground. Elijah, looking at Hunter's stretched out legs, swung the heavy bat across the man's knees. He was pretty sure at least one of them shattered. Elijah swung the bat three more times, the sound of connection becoming a little pulpier with each swing. Once he was certain Hunter was no longer mobile, he grabbed him and dragged him outside of the car.

Elijah was pleased to see Hunter was now suffering from hysterics. With his good arm, the man groped for Elijah's pants leg.

"Please," he sobbed. "I'll do anything you want me to do. Just let me go. Please."

Elijah squatted down next to Hunter.

"There is something you could do for me."

"Anything." Tears streamed down Hunter's straining face.

"Okay. I want you to look at that big sycamore. You can see how large it is. How it sticks up a little bit higher than the rest of the trees. Do you see it over there?"

Hunter nodded his head.

"Two years ago. Two years ago today, actually, my wife was driving a car that smashed into that tree. My daughter was also in the car. Did you know that sometimes God kills people?"

Hunter nodded his head again.

"Have you ever lost somebody that you loved more than anything?"

"My mother," Hunter blurted out, sticky spit stretching between his lips as he spoke.

"I'm sorry to hear that," Elijah said. "So what did she die of?"

"Cancer."

"Oh, so you knew she was going to die?"

Hunter nodded.

"Do you know what it's like to lose someone suddenly? You wake up one morning and you're this person and before you go to sleep that night, supposing you *can* actually go to sleep, you find out you're someone else entirely. And sometimes, you find you don't really like the person you've become."

Elijah paused, looking at the sycamore, how it seemed to stretch toward the road, looking for victims. Below him, Hunter continued to whimper.

"Do you believe in God?" Elijah asked him.

"Yes," Hunter said without delay.

"That's good," Elijah said. "Now I'm going to give you a reason why you really shouldn't."

Elijah stood back up and stooped into the car, leaning across the front seats to pluck the keys from the ignition. He walked up the small but steep slope of the ditch until he got to the trunk of the car. He put the key into the lock and opened the trunk. Looking at the assorted contents of the trunk, Elijah crazily thought all trunks must look like they belonged to a serial killer—ropes, tarps, a flashlight, the tire iron, the jack and other random debris, all of which could be construed as sinister.

He grabbed a few of the bungee ropes, with each end being a steel s-shaped hook, a pair of pliers and a length of chain. He didn't even know why the chain was in there.

He carefully but quickly descended the slope until he reached Hunter.

"I thought you said you were going to let me go!" Hunter screamed.

Elijah furiously kicked at the man's head. "I never said any such thing."

As he went to Hunter's feet, the man thrashed around, screaming frantically, but it did no use. His legs were shattered and immovable from the knees down. Elijah took the bungee cords and wrapped them tightly around his legs, just below his swollen knees, taking the rope around and then through the circle created by doing that. He took the pliers and squeezed each of the s-hooks shut so they couldn't dislodge themselves from one another, leaving one of them open.

With the chain slung over his shoulder, he grabbed the cords like a handle and pulled Hunter behind him. Going up the slope was the roughest part and Hunter screamed exceptionally loud as the asphalt scraped at his back when they reached the road.

Elijah remembered what the length of chain was from. It was

from the dog he and Eileen and Cynthia had had. Before he sold the house and got rid of it. The dog's name was Night. The chain was used in the backyard, part of the dog's runner that gave him free range of the yard while still being restrained.

Hunter fingered the clamp at the end of the chain, opening it and closing it around the end link of the chain so that it made a giant loop. He was oblivious to Hunter's panicked screams. Or maybe the screams were fuel.

He eyed one of the sycamore's thick branches hanging low over the road. Elijah threw one half of the looped chain over the branch, bringing it down and through the other half he held in his hand. Releasing that end, he pulled on the other side until the chain was secure around the branch. The ellipse of the chain now dangled just above his head.

Elijah went back to Hunter and dragged him toward the branch. Hunter screamed and twisted, trying to get away from Elijah, his fingers clawing at the asphalt until the ends of them were turned into bloody rags.

Elijah hoisted him up from the bungee cord bundle around his knees and raised him above his head. He was glad Hunter was not a fat man. Hunter swung his one good arm fiercely, raising it up and ramming Elijah in the groin. Elijah winced and briefly let go of the cords, sending Hunter to the asphalt on the top of his head. Hunter tried to slither away in some kind of hideously modified army crawl. Elijah took a deep breath and kicked at Hunter's good elbow until his torso was flush against the asphalt.

Snatching the heavy pliers from his back pocket, Elijah brought them down continuously on Hunter's arm until he was pretty sure he wouldn't be able to move it anymore.

Elijah dragged Hunter back over to the tree, again hoisting him up, happy and disappointed at the same time that some of the fight seemed to have left Hunter. Elijah pulled Hunter up until his head was even with Elijah's knees and stuck the open s-hook through one of the links in the chain, fastening the hook shut with the pliers.

By that point, Hunter had stopped struggling. Suspended there, his eyes rolled back in his head, drool came out of his mouth, running over his cheeks and pooling in his eye sockets before melding with his sweat-matted hair. Elijah retreated to the car, shutting the trunk and the other doors before sliding into the driver's seat.

The car started without a problem. Elijah gunned the ignition until the tires found traction and allowed him to strainingly back out of the ditch. He continued to back the car up the road, to allow for acceleration. He checked the rearview mirror to make sure another car wasn't coming along to ruin everything.

Suddenly, his breathing got caught up in his throat. His stiff, adrenaline-filled body was reduced to a shivering mass.

His face.

His face was the color of a bruise, dark blue swirling into black.

He gunned the accelerator, ripping his eyes from the mirror and watching the speedometer as it climbed.

The car hit the swinging Hunter and continued off the other side of the road, into the woods, crashing into a number of the trees.

Elijah sat in the car, all too quiet after the deafening crash, listening to the hissing of the engine, the quiet tinkling of glass dripping from the windshield and onto the dash. He felt blood running down his face. There were many other parts of his body he couldn't feel at all.

Slowly, he slid out of the door, dragging a bloody arm across his face to stop the blood running into his eyes. Walking toward the road, he kept his eyes on Hunter. Or what was left of Hunter. The car had ripped him in half and what hung from the branch looked like a pair of pants spilling some type of intestinal gore. Below Hunter, the road was covered in a pool of dark blood.

Elijah stood there, not knowing what to do.

Something hit him in the head and knocked him to the ground.

He stared up at the darkening sky.

Then he saw Maya, standing over top of him.

She was crying. She held a large rock with two hands.

"My God, look at you," she said. "What's wrong with your face?"

"He found me, Maya."

"Who found you, Elijah?"

"*He* did."

"I never knew you were so fucking miserable."

"Sometimes it happens, Maya. It happens."

Elijah closed his eyes.

Maya sat down on his torso and looked at him, her tears dripping down onto his face like a bruise. She raised the rock up above her head and brought it down on that face until it went away, becoming something else.

RAYLES

THEY STACKED THE skulls on the south side of the tracks. They didn't know what else to do with them.

Nissa grimaced with the weight of the skull-laden bag slung over her left shoulder. Sarot had an easier time dealing with his. Sarot was Nissa's younger brother. Younger but stronger. Dressed in dirty gray rags, Nissa set her heavy canvas bag down and gestured for Sarot to do the same.

"Why are we holding up?!" he shouted. The train, Rayles, circled the town constantly and, here, so close to it, normal conversation was impossible. Everything was a shout.

"We should rest for a few minutes before going up! It's a long climb!" Nissa shouted back.

She looked across the town. The sad, depressing town, cloaked in perpetual gloom, the huge and angry black train circling it, surrounding it, the engine car always chasing the caboose, separated only by inches. Since the train never stopped, it made escape impossible.

Impossible, maybe, but tonight escape was exactly what Nissa and Sarot intended to do. These last two bags of skulls, these were their tools. They had practiced for this night. All they had to do was carry the skulls to the top of the mountain—the same ritual that had been performed for years—and then . . . Well, that was the mystery. They didn't know what came after that. No one did. Except maybe Rayles.

Sarot cleared his throat. He was an exceptionally serious and morose boy even for a town that turned out hardly anything except serious and morose boys. "Why hasn't anyone just built a ladder or something like that to get out?!" Still the shouting. It added a sort of jocularity to a very serious question.

Nissa looked guiltily at the ground. She should have told him the whole story. She should have told him the whole story a long time ago. Now, it was too late. And she would have to shout the whole thing anyway. The story was far too serious to even attempt conveyance by shouting.

"It wouldn't work!" she yelled.

"Why not?!"

"It just . . . wouldn't work, okay?!"

"Okay, but I don't understand why!"

"Sometimes it's best not to understand why!"

Indeed, that was the truest thing she had said to the boy since he was born. She didn't think he needed to understand why everything had dried up. Why there were hardly any people left in the town. Why they had been here for so long, since birth, held prisoner. Why the people in town didn't look the way they used to. Why they were now gray, some of them mutated so much they could be considered human only by the broadest of standards. It was solidarity, Nissa thought. Any human, no matter how monstrous, was better than that thing circling them, trapping them.

And no, she didn't really think he needed to know about Rayles. How the train was more an extension of the conductor than a piece of machinery.

He had once innocently asked her what kind of cargo the train carried and why it never seemed to go anywhere except in circles. She couldn't remember how she had skirted the question but she had.

"We should start up now," Nissa said loudly, tired of shouting.

"Huh?!" Sarot blared.

Nissa pointed up to the top of the mountain of skulls sweeping toward them from the train. "We should go now!"

"Oh! Okay!"

Nissa repositioned her bag of skulls, now shifting it back to the other shoulder, and led the way. It had not been their turn to climb the mountain for six months. Last time, it had taken just over an hour. Nissa wondered how many skulls had been added by the other townsfolk during those months.

They had to tread very carefully. One wrong step and the whole mountain of skulls could come tumbling down. Then the townsfolk would have to spend days rebuilding it. To do so could, quite possibly, attract the attention of Rayles himself. Although there had never been so much as a story about Rayles leaving the engine to come down to the town, she didn't want to think about the further horrors awaiting them if that actually happened.

She was amazed how the skulls had stayed this way, the pile growing larger and larger, over the years. Perhaps Rayles was merely toying with them. Maybe he was too busy tending to his other duties to care. Maybe he didn't think the townsfolk would be around long enough for the mountain to become a threat. Or maybe something even worse waited for them on the other side. That thought had crossed her mind quite a lot over the past few months, ever since learning she and Sarot would be the ones to attempt this feat.

Poor Sarot. If his life ended tonight, he would never know the story behind his death. But Nissa would. It was a story she knew all too well. It had been told to her in the cradle and she had heard it at least weekly until her mother had met her end trying to escape the snaking iron and steel that was Rayles.

Sarot had asked about ladders. He should have asked his father. His father who, as one of the strongest men in town, had been elected to hold the mammoth ladder while the women tried to climb it.

The women were the first to be consumed in the blaze. Rayles' cars growing orange-hot before the fire erupted from the windows, turning the wood ladder to cinder and teaching a valuable lesson to the townsfolk.

They were no longer here by choice.

Nissa remembered her father's weeping, his blackened arms and singed eyebrows. It wasn't long after that he died. And Nissa, only twelve, had become something of a mother to Sarot.

Rayles was born in a day when humans had godlike abilities. They erected cities and castles. They invented flight. They invented industry and commerce. And the only thing Rayles had wanted was a perfect little town. So he had made Uroboros. Gleaming silver and loaded with cargo, it circled three miles of lush land.

Sometimes Nissa wondered what the town had been like before the decay, when it still had a name. When people dreamt things and those dreams came true. Hadn't this town once been the dream of Rayles? She saw signs of that old life—the houses built along the perimeter of the town, along the tracks, because Rayles used to bring them something other than misery. And people had flocked to the once green valley where there was no want for anything. Food, shelter, warmth, beauty, leisure, a good sex life—it was all brought by the man who had built the gleaming silver train and promised people that, in his town, people's dreams would always have a home.

But Rayles got sick. Apparently, he was not godlike enough to avoid illness. Only he wouldn't die, he couldn't, because his dream was immortality. Immortality and the train he had made.

Deals with the devil were mentioned. The rumor was that Rayles would be able to live eternally if he agreed to carry the souls of the damned on his train. Hell, it seemed, was full.

Townspeople noted the changes in Rayles and in the train itself. Rayles grew gaunt. His eyes grew yellow. His hair grew long and gray, trailing out behind him. Not that anyone could get that close a look.

The train stopped stopping. Not only that, it seemed to go faster and faster. It made people dizzy just to look at it. It became black with soot because it never stopped to be washed.

And there were the faces.

That was the most shocking change of all.

The cargo.

These were not the goods and services Rayles once delivered.

Through the windows of the cars, the townspeople could see the faces of the damned, staring out from the grimed over windows, longing for anywhere other than the inside of that train. Sometimes there were screams. Screams of such volume that they rivaled the rumbling, jangling sound of the train itself. And the whistle changed too, sounding very much like a scream itself. Nearly every minute, it loosed one of its shrieks.

Nissa was conscious of all this as they neared the top of the skulls.

The engine car went past and she swore she heard Rayles laughing from inside.

Did he know? she wondered. Did he know what they had planned?

The skulls were those of friends and family, neighbors. Some of them had died trying to escape. Some of them had died trying to reclaim the world beyond Rayles' tyranny. For some, that world was a green memory. For others, it was a dream, something unseen by any eye other than the mind's.

Nissa liked the idea of using the skulls to escape. It would be like using Rayles' victims against him. His very evil would be his downfall and her loved ones and acquaintances could experience a small scrap of revenge.

At the top, she cautiously unslung her pack and said, "Careful now!" to Sarot. It was a little less deafening here at the top of the mountain of skulls.

She began placing the skulls so they were every-other-one with the previous layer.

"I'm scared!" Sarot said.

"You should be scared!" she said, not comforting him at all. There wouldn't be any sense in filling the boy with false hope. Not at this point.

After emptying her bag, she gestured for his. He placed it gently down on the skulls and opened it up. She took them out one by one, hoping it would give them the leverage they needed. She wanted to be able to see what lay on the other side of Rayles. Hopefully, the mountain would be high enough to clear the train when they tried to jump it. She knew it would be a long fall down the other side but she felt like maybe a twisted ankle was worth it. A broken leg and fractured skull would have been worth it. Together, the brother and sister had worked on their jumping skills and now, staring at the width of the train from this vantage point, she didn't think they would have a problem clearing it.

A giddy excitement pounded in her chest. She wanted to be done with it. She wanted to taste freedom and get out of all this deafening gloom. Every second of hesitation was another link on their chain. Only, as she stared out at the impregnable blackness, she wasn't so sure of herself. She didn't know if she wanted to make the jump not knowing what was out there.

No.

They had to.

This was what they came for.

But she wasn't going to risk Sarot. She couldn't do that. How could she be sure there was anything out there at all? It had been a long time since Rayles had closed his town against the rest of the world.

Turning toward Sarot, she grabbed his shoulders.

"Listen to me," she said loudly. "You need to stay here. If there's something better out there then I'll come back for you and the rest of the townsfolk. If I don't come back . . . *make sure no one else attempts to escape.* Do you understand?"

The engine sped past again. She figured she had only a couple of minutes until he was all the way across town. His whistle shrieked.

Sarot wiped tears from his eyes and shouted, "But I wanna come too!"

"You can't," she said. "But I have to go quickly. Remember, tell the townsfolk what I said. Learn to make this your home. A better home."

The boy nodded.

She hugged him, felt his bony chest press against her. She released him and went into her crouch. She took a deep breath and sprang out into the night, sailing over Rayles.

She hit the rocky ground on the other side, crying out in pain as her knee buckled and her hip shattered. She managed to pull herself up on one leg, wincing at the explosions of hurt and the sight in front of her.

The world.

The world beyond Rayles.

The stink of death raped her nostrils.

Smoke and fire.

The world gone bad.

The whole sick world sprawled out dead before her.

And there were . . . *things* out there. Dead things, snarling as they rooted through ashes, rose from the dust, smelled the fresh meat and came toward her.

Desperately, she looked back toward Rayles. The engine was charging around the last turn.

The whistle shrieked and she saw the look of hurt in the dead things' eyes. But it wasn't enough to stop them. The scent of fresh meat—fresh, *obtainable* meat—was too strong. They scrabbled toward her, closing in from around her.

Nissa saw Rayles, reaching his long frail arms from the engine, trying to grab her, trying to save her.

But he was too old and too tired and the dead things were so hungry.

THE MAN WHO HATED STEPHEN KING

MARISKA FOUND HERSELF in the small town of Twin Springs. It had happened more than a few times in the nearly three decades since the disappearance of her father. And why not? It was a quaint town. Charming. It was someplace that would seem almost at home in a Bradbury story. Maybe even a Stephen King story. Hell, maybe that was even more appropriate. There was more a sense of '60s counterculture and baby boomers living out their golden years than Norman Rockwell American pie-ism, now that she thought about it. But that name—Stephen King—she didn't like to think about it. She'd never read one of his books and probably never would. She wasn't really much of a reader anyway. Her father had hated Stephen King far more passionately than he hated most things.

She had come to Twin Springs for the fall street fair but had apparently missed it by a week. She wasn't really sure how that had happened. The town was currently no busier than it was on any other gorgeous Saturday in early October and signs for the fair were still posted here and there.

She paid for her small black coffee at the tiny, dirty café and contemplated dropping into the used bookstore next to it, but that made her gag a little. The only reason she would have gone in was to see if they had any of her father's books on the shelf. She wondered if bookstores still even had horror sections. Then she remembered that this particular bookstore—Thing Books, here for as long as she could remember—had called it 'terror,' not horror. Her father had dragged her in here countless times and then he'd stopped. In retrospect, he'd probably been banned. He had a tendency to be goading and cantankerous, especially when he left the house.

She pulled her knit cap down over her ears, extracted her

electronic cigarette from her coat pocket and took a long and satis-fying hit. Not as satisfying as the real thing, she was sure, but using it made her feel less like an addict.

Addiction was a family curse.

An older couple passed her and said 'hi.' She nodded and tried her best to smile. She moved in the direction of the state park and it didn't occur to her what she was doing until she stood at the trail-head taking a warming sip of her coffee, another hit from her fake cigarette, and staring at the beauty of leaves that had not yet dropped.

She was subconsciously moving in the opposite direction of *the house*. The house where her father had disappeared from on a bitter cold winter night nearly thirty years ago. Although she always had to wonder if he'd disappeared *from* the house or *into* the house.

It was a ridiculous thought, she knew.

She decided to catch the last hour or so of daylight and drift into the woods. She told herself these were not the same woods looming behind that house. After all, there was the whole town separating them. But they probably wrapped around. They probably *were* the same woods.

But they didn't feel the same. These were somehow thinner, sparser. They let more of the good sunlight through. Maybe there were fewer pines or something. Maybe they just grew from soil that wasn't blighted and cursed.

Now Mariska found herself wanting something even stronger than an actual tobacco cigarette. Maybe a joint. She didn't even know where that thought came from. She'd never really liked pot and the last time she'd smoked it was probably five years ago when she had dated a guy roughly the same age she was now. He'd been going through something of a mid-life crisis. He smoked pot, listened to Nirvana on vinyl, and wore old school Doc Martens. After she dumped him she'd referred to him as Mr. Nineties around her friends.

She wandered deeper into the woods until she came to the town's namesake, Twin Springs. It was an odd name, she guessed, since it really appeared to be one creek. Enough so that a lot of people re-ferred to it as Twin Springs Creek, which seemed somehow redun-dant. Maybe, somewhere, there were two springs joining to form this creek. She didn't know. She wasn't much on research. Sometimes knowing the way things worked destroyed the mystery. She preferred to look at the single creek rushing through the gorge and imagine the interplay between two streams of water. Two things with completely different origins combining into one seamless whole.

She breathed the late afternoon air, crisp, full of clean water, damp bark, and earth.

If she was going to go by the house—and she knew she would—she needed the fortification.

She finished off her coffee and chucked the cup off the ledge and into the creek.

Holger Blackwell bought all of Stephen King's books as they came out, read them, and burned them. Tonight's offering was going to be *It*. It was a good night for it. For *It*. Early February and the fire looked hungry.

Her father had seemed to be in a bad mood all night. He'd sat in his shabby chair and chuffed his way through the last few pages of the book while Mariska sat in front of the television and watched *Strawberry Shortcake*. She knew she was lucky to have a VCR. She was the only one of her friends at school who had one. Of course, she only had one here, at her dad's. Her mom liked to say her dad used it as a babysitter but her mom liked to make everything her dad did sound bad. In retrospect, Mariska realized the only reason she was probably able to come to her dad's was because her mom wanted to go on dates or maybe just have the night alone.

Holger closed the book and placed it on the coffee table.

"Why's it so big?" Mariska's books were a fraction of this size.

"Who knows? It could have probably been half that long."

Holger's latest book, the one that would turn out to be his last, was called *The Jackthief*, and it was nearly as long. Only his book had only ever been a Tor paperback so it didn't have the mass of King's hardcover. And it was only so bulky because the print and spacing were larger. *The Jackthief* had never even been picked up by the Book of the Month Club so it would, alas, never see a hardcover release, not even a poorly printed, not-quite-full-size shabby one. And, technically, it wasn't his *final* book, but it was the last one published while he was alive. Mariska's mother had unearthed a partially finished manuscript of a book called *The One Who Creeps* and bestowed it upon Mariska because, well, Holger didn't have anything else to leave behind. Mariska had never read it, had never read any of her father's books. It seemed weird and invasive and she was pretty sure it would end up making her dislike him. An odd man named Gregory

Seymour had contacted her when she was in her mid-twenties, asking her about her dad's books, which had all gone out of print. He said he'd like to do limited editions of them and she said, "Tell me where to sign." The partial manuscript of *The One Who Creeps* came up and Seymour said he knew a really good author who could do a bang up job of completing it. Mariska didn't even ask who it was, just said, "Yeah, sure," and asked how much this gig paid. Seymour said he was struggling, the whole book industry was doing poorly, and the most he could offer at this time was five thousand dollars. The contract arrived two days later along with the check. Mariska signed away the rights to all of Holger's books, put the contract on top of the partial manuscript, put it all in a large bubble mailer and washed her hands of the whole writing business. She was young, after all, and five thousand dollars could be a decent down payment on a house or nearly a year's worth of rent. That wasn't exactly what it went for, but it did allow her to have a really exciting, if not completely memorable, few months.

Mariska sat on her knees in front of the coffee table, rubbing the glossy back cover of the book.

"Is he a rock star, too?" she asked. "Is that why he's playing the guitar?"

"He's playing the guitar because he wants you to know he's rich enough to indulge any interest he has."

"Is that bad?"

"I don't know."

Holger rarely spoke to Mariska like a child so she only grasped a little of what he meant. Maybe he was hoping she would remember what he said and the meaning would color itself in as she got older. Maybe that had been the case.

He picked the book back up, riffled the pages and made an exasperated sigh. He looked exhausted. He only ever wore black. Tonight he wore a thick black sweater over his customary black work shirt and corduroys. This made his whiskered chin, the circles under his eyes, and the lines in his face look even darker than they actually were.

"What happened to his beard?" she asked. "I liked his beard."

"He's all yuppified now. You want to look like your target audience and those college hippies have all grown up."

"Are yuppies bad people?"

"They're monsters."

An author photo of Holger Blackwell had never appeared in or on one of his books. Mariska had once thought maybe it was because there wasn't anyone to take one, then she'd thought her dad just didn't want an author photo or that if someone saw a photo of him they wouldn't buy the book. Her dad looked scary. She didn't think that at the time, but looking back through her mother's photo albums at the younger Holger Blackwell—always in black, never smiling, looking at the person holding the camera like he wanted to eat them—she thought maybe that was the case. That notion didn't drop until she got older and realized the world—especially women— loved evil men.

Holger stood up and opened the door to the fireplace. This was at least the third such offering she'd witnessed.

"Mom says it's wrong to burn books."

"I'm the child of Nazis," Holger said and chucked the book into the fire.

Mariska paused her video and stood watching the fire, taking her father's pinky finger in her little hand.

One thing Mariska had learned was that books didn't really burn well. They curled up at the edges. They blackened. Her father had to jab it with the poker several times and Mariska had completely lost interest and gone back to *Strawberry Shortcake* before it completed its transformation into ash.

Holger placed the poker back in its stand, closed the fireplace door, dusted his hands, and said, "Well, it's time to get back to work."

A period of furious activity usually followed one of the burnings. It never really occurred to Mariska that when her father left her there in front of the television, when he went through the kitchen and the dining room and into his office, that he was sitting at his desk to work on *The One Who Creeps*.

She fell asleep on the floor in front of the television.

She dreamed she was outside, in the woods behind the house. She was freezing cold. The woods around her were frozen but the leaves were still on the trees. They were frosted over with ice and it made her think of a moth's wings. She could sense someplace warm and moved toward it. A stabbing wind rolled through the woods and the frozen trees creaked and moaned like they'd been frozen forever. She reached what she thought was the back door to her house but when she got closer to it she realized it was the door to a giant fireplace and assumed this was the warm place she sought. Drawing even closer, she saw her father beside the door. Children were lined up behind him and he casually plucked the first in line and tossed it into the house, into the roaring fire. He spotted Mariska and a bolt of fear seized her. Her father said in a voice that didn't sound at all like his own, "Don't be afraid. Take your place at the back of the line." She obediently did so. She thought it would be awful, standing at the back of the line and waiting her turn to be burned alive, even though, at this rate, it looked like it would take her father ten or fifteen minutes to get to her. But the girl next to her in line was friendly looking and a little bit fat. Mariska asked her if she ever watched *Strawberry Shortcake* and the girl said, "All the time!" and they began excitedly talking about that and the dream dissipated and Mariska woke up to credits rolling up the television screen and the room seemed too bright because no one had turned off the lights and she was freezing because the door was open and an icy wind had sucked all the fire's warmth from the room and the fire itself was only a bed of winking orange coals.

She stood up and walked over to the door.

"Dad?" she called out into the darkness. Sometimes, no matter how cold it was, he would go outside to smoke. Sometimes he smoked cigarettes that came in a red and white package and sometimes he rolled his own and sometimes he smoked a fat, smelly cigar.

When he didn't answer, she shut the door.

She locked it because that was what her mother told her she should always do when shutting the door to her house. Mariska walked through the kitchen and into the dining room. The light from her father's office was on and the door was open. She had never seen this door closed unless he wasn't in it, which he usually was. He didn't care about being bothered, but he didn't want anyone going through his stuff when he wasn't there. Mariska understood. She didn't like it when people played with her toys either.

His shoulders were slumped over the desk and he pecked slowly on his typewriter that she thought was the exact same color as her nipples.

"Sweetie?" he said without turning his head.

"I had a dream."

"Were you in your room?"

"No. On the floor."

"You shouldn't fall asleep on the floor."

She noticed a bottle of something the color of apple juice. This bottle looked fancier and was made from glass.

"Do you need me to tuck you in?" he said. He sounded ready to fall asleep himself.

"I'm thirsty." She now stood right beside him.

"Do you need me to get you some water?"

"What's that?" she pointed at the bottle.

He laughed a little. "That's bourbon, sweetie. It probably wouldn't make you less thirsty."

He offered her the bottle.

She brought it to her lips and recoiled at the smell. She handed it back.

She pointed at his nipple-colored typewriter and said, "Can I play on the typewriter?"

"Sure," he said. "This one's electric. See how it plugs into the wall? Do you want to play on this or the old typewriter?"

He pointed to one of the bookcases lining the walls. There was something that looked like the skeleton of what he currently pecked away at. She also thought it looked like it was made from coal.

She touched the electric typewriter and said, "This one."

"Okay. Maybe I need to stop vacuuming my brain for a minute anyway."

Her father never said he was writing. He was either "working" or "vacuuming his brain." He pushed back his chair, stood up, and stretched, the bones in his body making soft popping noises.

He put a couple of pillows in the chair, lifted her up, placed her down, and scooted the chair toward the desk.

"Remember," he said, "writing is the worst job in the world."

"I want a new one."

"Huh?"

"New paper."

"Oh. Of course. Collaboration is for the weak and simple minded."

He stripped out the piece of paper with his words on it and rolled a new one in.

"Have at it," he said.

She pecked out a few letters, hit the space bar, and pecked out the same letters because she liked them. He grabbed the key to one of his desk drawers from the top of the desk and dipped it into a little amber bottle. He quickly sniffed the key and put the bottle back into his pocket.

"Was that medicine?" She continued to peck at the keyboard, already feeling herself getting tired of it.

"Something like that." He grabbed the bottle of bourbon and sat down in the comfortable chair beside the desk. "Sometimes this makes me sleepy." He held the bottle up and took a slug. "And the other stuff wakes me up."

"If I had that medicine, I bet I wouldn't even *have* to take naps."

"And you probably wouldn't fall asleep in the middle of the floor."

She was now completely uninterested in the typewriter. She turned to face him.

"Can we go look at the trees?" she asked.

"Why would you want to do that?"

She told him about her dream.

"We'll have to get you bundled up."

"Aren't you gonna read what I wrote?"

"Oh, of course. I wasn't sure if it was ready yet."

"It is. It's really good."

He leaned over the desk and read aloud. "Yog yog yog yog yog."

She started laughing. She didn't exactly know how to pronounce what she'd written and liked the way it sounded coming out of her father's mouth, like the sound a frog would make.

"That's really great. Very Lovecraftian." He placed a hand over the top of her head.

"Not the brain sucker!" she squealed.

He flexed his hand. "I think it's starving to death."

They crunched across the backyard. She wore her snow boots, her father's big wool coat, and one of his knit stocking caps.

"Aren't you cold?" she asked.

"I think the air feels nice."

The woods seemed a lot farther away in the winter than they did in the summer. When they reached the woods, he scooped her up and rested her on his hip.

"Is this okay or do we need to go into them?" he asked.

She studied the trees closely. There were maybe a few dead leaves clinging here and there to the ones that didn't have needles like a Christmas tree. But they were mostly bare.

"See," her dad said, "it was just a dream."

They turned and walked back to the house. The lights from the living room and her dad's office were still on, producing a warm glow. The back door was shut tight and, hopefully, not locked. She'd forgotten to tell him about the open door.

"Did you leave the door open earlier?" she asked.

"No. Why?"

"It was open when I woke up."

"Are you sure that wasn't just part of the dream?"

She looked back toward the woods. She couldn't see them at all now. They were just a gray mass in the distance. They hadn't been full of leaves. How could she be sure of anything?

"I don't know," she sighed.

When she looked toward the house, she focused on the windows that didn't have light in them. She thought she saw shapes moving around in those dark rooms. Quick moving liquid shadows. They made her scared. Or maybe it was what her mom called anxious. Her mom had said that was like being scared when there wasn't really anything to be scared of.

"Will you read what I typed again?" she asked her father.

"Sure. When we get back inside. Okay?"

"I mean now. You remember, don't you?"

She thought it would make her laugh if she heard him say it again. It would make her less scared. Less anxious.

"*Yog,*" he croaked.

She started laughing and wrapped her arms around his bony shoulders.

"*Yog yog yog.*"

They stamped their feet and walked into the house where the fire was now completely dead.

He made her some hot chocolate and sipped bourbon. They watched *Strawberry Shortcake* until her head started to droop and then he picked her up and carried her into her bedroom.

"Are you going back to work?"

"Yeah, honey, I have to. Night night."

He gave her a peck on the forehead and disappeared into the yellow light of the hallway.

It was the last time she ever saw him.

Mariska had bypassed her car in town, deciding to take the ten-minute walk. She wasn't really much of an outdoors person. She felt like it would be better if she saw the house unencumbered by her car. She could linger. It was a good time for lingering. Probably not for much longer. The last few nights had been below freezing. Soon the town would be naked and cold, but she would be very far away from it. Although, she knew she'd probably be back.

The house was at the end of Spring Street, facing it, sitting low across a fairly large lawn. When her father lived there, when she used to visit him on the weekends, a series of three or four towering pine trees had stood behind the ugly guardrail. Those trees were gone now. They had been gone the last time too. The long gravel driveway was off a road farther down, so that the address was not actually Spring Street. She tried to remember what it was. Something Pike, maybe. She'd always used her mother's address as her own.

She stopped at the guardrail at the end of the road, almost close enough for her knees to touch its cold surface.

She stared at the house, at the couple windows that were lit up. Of course the light that came from windows was hardly ever a soft yellow anymore. Now it always seemed sterile—clear or bluish.

She never found out what happened to her father. She didn't think she wanted to find out. The thing that would have been best for him and probably the hardest for her to take was if he had just decided he'd had enough of his current life and left. If that were the case—and she really doubted it was—some part of her hoped he would make contact with her before he died. She had no clue what they would possibly say to one another. She didn't think she'd ever really known him very well and she was now very very far away from being daddy's little girl. But she had always felt close to him. Still did.

The door to the carport at the top of the driveway opened and her heart sped up like she'd been caught doing something she wasn't supposed to be doing.

A man walked out under the carport and lit a cigarette. He glanced at her but didn't make any gesture of acknowledgement. A woman who looked a little younger stepped out behind him and did the same. He said something to the woman that Mariska couldn't hear and they smiled and laughed. The woman playfully, almost se-ductively, punched him on the arm. They looked happy. Mariska knew she needed to go. She could already feel the house's power reaching for her. The memory of something frozen almost perfectly in time. The lure of contentment. The feeling of contentment would always be followed by the world crumbling beneath her feet.

THE DUST SEASON

THE CARAVAN MOVED from east to west. One of the last genuine freak shows, the campers and trucks rattled through the dust. That was about the only thing Bradley could remember. The dust. It felt like they were following some eternal drought across the continent. Everywhere, there was dust.

Through the bars of his trailer, at a gas station, Bradley watched the feet shift through the film. He couldn't bring himself to raise his head and look at the faces that belonged to those shuffling feet. The faces seemed too sad. This was the bad time of year when the dust mixed with the humidity and formed some kind of airborne mud that filled the lungs. But, even though it was everywhere, the dust was the least of Bradley's worries.

Something terrible had happened.

Flashes of it came to him, as flitting as his geological location. He went to sleep thinking Georgia, Georgia, Georgia, we're in Georgia and it would be Mississippi when he came to. And with the waking, there was the surging electric blue pain, an afterimage left like a tear-soaked postcard in his memory.

It's a job, he told himself. Just like any other job. Think of it as a demotion, that's all.

No. No. It was more than that. Although he had no idea in what capacity, what area he had worked in before, he was well aware of who he was now.

The attractions had their own separate booths, small places made hastily from garish, crudely painted plywood and pressed board. Nowhere near as alluring as the banners that adorned the outside of the tent. Bradley's booth stank. It smelled like raw sewage, mildew, and rotting meat.

Helton was about ready to let the first group in. The grating sound of Helton's voice as he shouted promises at the undoubtedly small crowd sent more memories shredding through Bradley.

Helton—the tiny, hideous leader. Substantially under five feet tall, with pale skin that looked like it had been painted on with a sponge, Bradley knew Helton had something to do with his demotion.

Bradley cringed. Helton's voice, augmented through a cheap megaphone, made his insides squirm.

"Ladies and gentleman! Prepare yourselves for spectacles that can't be seen anywhere else. No sir. Rest assured that this is the only place where you will see a real, live giant. That's right, he stands through these doors, waiting to meet your gaze. But it gets stranger than that. Mr. Magneto will show you how he can hang from a steel beam with nothing but the magnetic force of his skin. We have a man with gills. A man who can lift barbells with his tongue. And tonight, making her first appearance—the Painted Lady! Watch her get another flesh piercing tattoo right in front of your very eyes . . ."

More memories. More excruciating than the first ones. Longer in length.

The Painted Lady hadn't always been the Painted Lady. She used to be Elastica, Queen of Bending. Unlike a lot of the other freaks, being the Queen of Bending didn't involve any physical deformity or mutilation. Bradley knew her as Eliza, the Hideous Leader's wife. But Bradley didn't let that stop him. When Eliza beckoned, Bradley answered. Each time they met, whether they slept together or not, was heaven for Bradley—

He remembered now. He'd been the psychic, more of a money-raiser than a freakish attraction

—and there were occasions when he really did have the gift. That's one of the reasons he enjoyed being with Eliza, her mind was so open and easy to enter. He stared into her eyes, crawled into her mind, and started opening doors. He felt like they had created a dark and secret world between them. They talked about running away. When we get to California, they agreed. Before the sideshow doubled back.

They were in this mental dreamland, hiding in the blackly magical woods of Louisiana behind that night's encampment. Before either of them could run off, the Hideous Leader, Strong Arm, and The Lift were upon them.

Helton's small white hands glowed in the dark and gripped Bradley's wrist, squeezing impossibly tight.

Strong Arm guffawed. "We thought you'd see us comin, future boy."

They were both dragged out into the pool of light created by the circle of campers and trucks. The other freaks wandered out of their temporary homes, the only ones they knew. It was rare that they got to watch a show themselves.

Between the three of them, they had Eliza stripped bare in no time. She tried to struggle, tried to fall down, but they kept standing her upright. Mr. Fish, the man with gills, doubled as the resident tattoo artist. At that hour, he was a very drunk tattoo artist. The Hideous Leader shaved Eliza's head and pubis, savagely dragging the razor along until too much hair got caught up in it. Then he simply rubbed the blade against the moist grass and went back to work. Eliza screamed when the needle went in at her crown. Helton barked around his cigar, "Go deep with em. We don't want none of em wearin off."

Eliza continued to scream. It wasn't long before other onlookers were invited to join in the tattooing. A few of the men squabbled over her breasts and between her legs. Every few minutes, the Hideous Leader threw a bucket of cold water on Eliza to rinse the blood away and keep her in a state of semi-consciousness.

Bradley had stayed tapped into her secret place during the whole ordeal. What he saw, he guessed, was Eliza's life flashing before her eyes. All of that hitting him at once was overwhelming. And over top of that, like a burning blanket, was the pain. Although her skin went numb to the physical pain relatively quickly, the mental anguish was soul draining and constant.

Bradley's memory faded out as his mind had wanted to that night.

The Hideous Leader droned on: "That's right. Just last week, she was the Human Scab, but here she is in her full, multicolored regalia. But that's not all—the Strongest Man in the World, Siamese Twins, the *real* Elephant Man and, this one, folks . . . this one I'm gonna bring out first . . . Now, it's kind of an experiment so I want you to make him feel really welcome. Ladies and gentlemen—I give you the Quarter Man."

The yellow bug-swamped light hit Bradley. He swooned, stuck

out his arms to brace himself from the fall and—

When they were finished with Eliza they took her out and threw her into the dust. Bradley quickly learned what they meant to do with him. Struggle was useless. His breath came in harsh, ragged bursts. They threw him to the ground and tied his wrists and ankles to tent stakes. The Hideous Leader made sure to sharpen the knives by his ear, digging his little knees into Bradley's back. Helton started on his backside, just below the buttocks, and removed each of Bradley's legs. Mercifully, he was unconscious when they cauterized the wound, despite the Hideous Leader's attempts to revive him.

—and realized that there was no fall to brace. His hands were now his feet. His feet and legs were somewhere else altogether.

He looked out at those blank faces, wondering how he was still alive. Not for long, he thought. He could feel and smell the blackish-yellow tentacles of infection, working their way up his spinal column.

And from another booth came faint glimpses of the secret place, ruinous now, so much gray dust, filled with a sense of dread. When they covered her body with tattoos, they made sure to leave a few blank spaces. Tonight, the first one would be filled. By the time they got to the last one, the freak show would need another quarter man or, perhaps, a quarter woman.

THE JACKTHIEF

OLETTA GOOM WOKE up on the morning of October 31st and went into the baby's room, knowing exactly what she would find.

Emptiness.

The crib stood in the middle of the room, white cotton blankets piled up against one side. Outside, the wind, turned cold with the season, spat at the house and invaded the open window. Oletta grabbed the worn wooden rail of the crib with a bony hand and cried, her tears running down her wrinkled face and falling onto the cotton sheet that still smelled faintly of Jacquelyn. "Jack," Oletta had called her.

But now Jack was gone.

Just like all of the girls that had come before her. And it was always on this day, the first birthday, Halloween, that the Jackthief came and took them away. Now she would have to wait another year before going into the haunted woods to claim her prize.

Unless she could find out where the Jackthief took the babies. Unless she could get this one back.

Oletta had been several years younger when she had retreated to her house in the woods. Perhaps it was more of a shack, but it served the purposes of shelter and warmth just fine and that was all she needed now. Shelter and warmth. Maybe it wasn't all she *wanted*, but it was all she needed, along with a little food every now and then.

What Oletta wanted more than anything was a baby. She was not a young woman anymore, twenty years past childbearing age, but that desire had never left her. It was only since the death of her husband that she realized it was an impossibility. Before, she had always prayed for a miracle. Maybe, she had thought, God would fix whatever was broken inside of her and she would finally get pregnant. But it was never meant to be.

So her husband had died and she had moved to the woods feeling like, if she was going to be alone, she was going to do it right.

But moving to the woods proved to be the source of more joy and sorrow than she would ever know.

It was there she met the Jackthief. There, during the strangest of circumstances.

Summer was buried, Halloween standing atop it like a cold gray tombstone, and Oletta didn't see how she was going to spend a winter alone in the tiny shack. She figured her best days were well behind her and there weren't going to be any good ones ahead. She found a length of strong rope in the old woodshed. She was going to take the rope out into the woods, find a good sturdy branch, and hang herself. She didn't plan on learning how to do it proper. If she had to dangle for a while, choking on her own windpipe, then she just figured that would be penance for the awesome sin she was about to undertake.

After a brief survey, she found a branch that would do the trick. The rope was slung around her neck to give her frail arms the strength to carry an old wooden ladder. It was a gray day. The clouds were bloated black-gray, threatening rain. Maybe, if it rained, it would help weigh down her body.

It took about a half an hour to make sure everything was in place. She figured the knot was strong enough to do the trick. Climbing to the top of the ladder, the fiber of the rope scratchy around her neck, the sky rumbled a hungry growl and she hoped it would drown out the sound of her strangling to death.

Standing at the top of the ladder, she wondered if she was doing the right thing. But this wasn't a spontaneous decision. It was something she had thought about for a very long time. This was the only way out. The lonely days had become unendurable and she was too proud to be stuck in this constant state of self-pity.

The sky screamed.

Oletta took a deep breath and kicked the ladder away.

She dropped. The rope tightened around her neck.

And then broke.

She fell to the ground, lightning streaked across the sky, fat cold drops of rain hammered down, and her life changed forever.

On the other side of the tree she had tried to use to kill herself, she heard a baby crying. Oletta unfastened the rope from around her neck, not believing what it was she thought she heard. Nursing a twisted ankle, she trudged through the dead leaves, turned soggy, until she found the source of the crying.

When she saw the baby, swaddled in black cloth, at the base of the tree, her face split and her tears mingled with the beating rain. Stooping down, she picked up the baby and took it back to the house, wanting to get it out of the rain, wanting to get it into the warmth.

Sometimes, Oletta knew, when a person wanted something so much, it was not necessary to question the source. It was not necessary to question the truth or validity behind that desire. A Christian wanted a God to save her and an afterlife to house her soul when she dies. The Christian does not question these things, she believes them and calls that belief faith. So Oletta believed in her new baby maybe not so much as born but given to her on this Halloween day.

She took it home with her. First she named her Jacquelyn and called her Jack. She loved Jack. She fed her and sang to her and talked to her and cared for her and took her everywhere she went. She even took her into the town to buy food and clothes, not caring if the folk talked and wondered. They would, Oletta knew, come up with their own reasons why she now had a baby and those reasons could not come even remotely close to the fantastic truth.

For exactly one year, Oletta was the mother of a beautiful baby.

On Jack's first birthday, Oletta opened the door to her room and discovered the baby gone, the bedroom window open, a cold wind blowing in. The following year, she searched for baby Jack. Searched and mourned because she knew the baby was gone.

That was the worst year of Oletta's life, having had something and then lost it. Each day was worse than the one before. Her life had become a spiraling black nightmare as she wondered about who would steal the only thing she had ever wanted. She never found the Jackthief but she had a picture of him in her mind.

The Jackthief was carved from wood and bone. He traveled by moonlight and drank the sorrow of others. He was drawn to this sorrow and, drunk off it, had to create more. Oletta knew the Jackthief had always been there. He was the one who had snapped the rope when the only thing she wanted to do was snap her neck. He did it because she had not suffered enough. She was a well of suffering and the Jackthief had not drunk the last of that well. So he had let her love the baby for a year. And just as quickly, he had taken it away. Now he surrounded her in the woods, watching her, mocking her silently as she searched and searched.

A year later, she found baby Jack in the same place she had found her two years earlier. The baby was the same size as the very first time Oletta found her and she had a distinct feeling of falling back two years in time. But, once again, the sorrow had lifted. She had her baby. Maybe the circumstances were not normal. Maybe they weren't even believable, but it was nice to hold Jack in her arms once again and feel a year of sadness melt away.

Over the next two years, the cycle repeated itself.

Always from Halloween to Halloween. One year of joy. One of sorrow. One a trick. The other, of course, a treat.

After losing Jack again, Oletta did not search for her.

She sat in her house and waited, her mind expanding out into that depressed madness, knowing her time would come again. Yet knowing that did not make it easier. The only thing she could think of was the year after that, when she would have to go without the baby again. The Trickyear. And, after all, wasn't the point of having a baby to watch it grow? To shape it and give it a good life? To see what kind of adult it became?

That year, Oletta decided she was not going to go without Jack again.

On October 31st, when she found Jack under the tree, Oletta said to her, "I'm never letting you go. If he takes you again, I will find you." And she took the baby back home and they had another good year—the Treatyear—but now the time had come again and Oletta stood in an empty room, surrounded by nightmares.

That morning, she left the house in search of the Jackthief, knowing he was out there, somewhere. She was not going to go back home until she found the baby. For days, she wandered deeper into the woods, the noose of cold and hunger wrapping around her neck.

Madness rats nibbled at her brain. She followed the Jackthief. She followed his scent. He smelled like wax and fallen leaves. He smelled like memories. Some nights, she thought she heard the baby crying. Some nights, she thought she heard the Jackthief laughing.

She became hungry and confused, knowing she was too far from her house to ever get back. The sorrow was black and swollen in her mind. She let it grow, knowing that the greater the sorrow, the more likely she was to see the Jackthief. And then she could take her baby back.

On the night of her death, before the Jackthief came and took the sorrow away for good, Oletta couldn't open her eyes. She couldn't see the Jackthief. But she thought she could open her eyes far enough to see the little black bundle he held in his arms. She pawed at the blankets, wanting to touch Jack's soft baby skin one last time but the thing inside the blankets was not Jack.

It was carved from wood and bone.

It smelled like burning wax and dead leaves.

And when it opened its mouth, it didn't want milk, it wanted to drink sorrow and a whole life filled with longing. And when it satiated itself on those things, it laughed, and moved onto the next person in the next town.

THE SMOKE OF SAMUEL

DECAYED LEAVES DROPPING from a tree, the memories swirl back into the autumn of her mind as she sits thinking.

She slowly surveys the room. It truly is picturesque in its decay. Easels burdened with blank gray canvases surround the middle of the room like dark monks preparing for séance. Stacks of books, magazines, photos, and old drawings are limp heaps in the corners. Two stark gray filing cabinets are locked against the wall to her left. The walls are bare, absent of pictures, no life clinging to them. Dust is the only substance that clings to anything. Dirt dust, incense dust, dead cancer cigarette dust. Dust is death, she thinks, we rise and fall into dust.

After nearly a week, they had finally moved all their stuff into the sizable but dilapidating house. Samuel Bean, secretly tortured artist and alleged master of mayhem, disturbance, and vandalism at Raven Creek High School was finally settling down at the ripe old age of twenty. Married to the former Gina Blanc, aspiring dancer and general wallflower of Raven Creek High School, they made a good couple. She appealed to Samuel's quiet, artistic side, while responding well to his exuberant energy in bed.

Most of Samuel's stuff had been haphazardly sorted into the upstairs studio. His boxes of books covered the vast wooden floor, canvas-burdened easels standing erect on its surface. He left the middle of the studio open so Gina could practice her dance. Samuel enjoyed watching her. He enjoyed watching her thin, well-defined muscles rippling beneath tights or, sometimes, nothing at all. She seemed to float around the room. The silent beauty of a butterfly pleasing his eyes and sinking further into his heart.

After they had been there for a few months and were somewhat practiced about coexisting with one another, Samuel decided to sit down and begin painting again. He was mad to get back to it. The art had been eating away at him.

Once he began painting he felt somewhat out of practice. It seemed that everything he started ended up looking like something else or something that resembled excrement. Searching for a reason, he came across the only explanation he could think of.

The pain was gone.

All of his works had been driven by pain. Pain and ugliness. Gray death, black suns. There was no happiness inside of Samuel Bean.

A testament to Samuel's artistic rendering of pain was Gina's refusal when he had asked to paint her naked. "I'm sorry, Samuel. I really mean no offense. You just . . . well, you have a way of making things look, uh, *ugly*." She quickly reached out to catch his plummeting ego, "I'm not saying it's not good. It's brilliant, it really is. It's beautiful in its own way. But I really just don't want my feelings to be hurt."

Samuel, looking at things objectively, understood what she meant. He still argued to do it, mainly because he thought it would be a huge turn on, but she was unwavering in her stance.

Gina's observations had been something that Samuel had lived with ever since he had started showing his paintings to her. Continually, it popped up in criticisms of his work, if it was a criticism at all. Samuel had never really stopped to figure out why his art was so 'ugly.' To him, it was the only thing he knew, what he'd been raised with.

Samuel had grown up, most of his young life, in Louisville. The worst parts of Louisville. The parts that nobody ever thinks of when they think of Kentucky because pictures of the slums and the factories didn't make it into the travel brochures. There were no horses for miles and you'd have to walk through an ocean of concrete to get to the nearest mountain.

His family had moved to Raven Creek at the beginning of his freshman year. Raven Creek was a small town where everyone had pretty much the same income, but Samuel seemed to bear the stigma of living in the absolute *worst* house in it. The feeling of being the only poor person in town was coupled and tripled with the facts that he was not athletically inclined in the least and he was relatively bright.

During high school, he was the daily subject of beatings, taunting, and general disdain directed in his favor. He was once shoved into a ditch and called "nigger," even though his skin was quite pale. Samuel guessed that the fine rednecks of Raven Creek, Kay-Why, population 512, had never even *seen* a black person outside of the television, which made the KKK carvings in the school desks pretty much irrelevant.

He became involved with Gina his junior year, bringing her into his dull realm of pain. Her first taste of that, other than the rumors, was reaped when he had tied her up. Before him, nobody even knew who she was. With him, she enjoyed wide fame under such names as: poor white trash, bitch, slut, whore, freak, as well as many others that were much less pertinent to either her gender or socioeconomic status.

So, after graduation, Samuel and Gina moved as far away from picturesque little Raven Creek as they could while still remaining in the beautiful blue mountains of Kentucky.

Still traipsing in the midst of his funk and wallowing in self-pity, Samuel sat himself in front of the only window in his studio. In the mist of a gray morning, through the window, across the river behind their house, Samuel found his muse. His ugly, decaying, wasted muse. A river mill of some sort that had slowly devolved into an industrial wasteland unveiled itself in all its desolate grandeur.

Positioned between two objects of sheer beauty, the river and the lush green hills drifting steeply upward to meet the sky, the mill sat like Satan ready to be cast out of heaven. Lifeless smokestacks rose, brown brick streaked with black stains, to probe the surrounding magnificence. The mill seemed immense in its horizontal gray-brown-black structure, a line of shattered windows sitting on top of its 'X'-shaped steel supports. It looked like someone was trying to smudge it out of existence.

This is it! Samuel thought, excitedly grabbing his sketch pad that had sat beside him ever since his slump began.

He didn't know where to start. It was all so voluptuously ugly!

Once started, Samuel realized he wouldn't be able to quit until it was finished.

At first, Gina brought him coffee and ran to the discount tobacco store to get him Sampoerna clove cigarettes, happy to see him working on his ugly art again. Then her visits became less frequent, punctuated with grumbling complaints. His body, which should have been aching with unnoticed nicotine, caffeine, and general sustenance withdrawal was fueled by the painting. Eventually, Gina would only come up to practice her dance and, without speaking to him, storm out of the studio, slamming the door.

When too tired to stand up or move his arms, Samuel collapsed onto the floor, waking to the developing painting before him. A beard burst through the smooth skin of his face. New smells from various areas on his body reached his nose. He was thankful there was a toilet on the same floor.

When it was light, he could not stop staring at the vast industry, trying to capture and detail every last trace of ugliness. By no means was it a photorealist piece, but there was some nuance forever jumping out at him. Something he had to incorporate somehow. When it was dark, he couldn't stop thinking about it while he applied layer after layer of thick oils. The scenes that must have been played out there! The horrors that no doubt lurked in the minds of some of the extinct employees. The pain that seemed to surround the mill, envelop it in bleeding red. The stink of those who had, for whatever period of time, become machines or parts of the machine, fighting to keep themselves and their families alive.

Eventually, Samuel reached a point that would have been called finished if it would have been any other subject, but there was something he felt was missing. It wasn't one single thing. It was the feeling, the mood. His painting just didn't seem to encompass *everything*.

Maybe, Samuel thought, *the shading needs altered.* He covered other miscellaneous canvases with various shades of gray. He mixed every degree of black and white, trying to achieve the perfect value and failing each time.

Samuel fell to merely sitting in front of the window and staring at the damned thing. What the hell *was* it!? What could he not reach out and grasp with his mind? What, dear fucking Watson, was *missing*? What detail? What one little thing? No, it wasn't any single aspect, it was an *aura*. Not a single facet, it couldn't be given a term, it was simply something all-encompassing that would make the entire thing work. Yes, but what *was* that aura, that feel, that mood?

Finally, it hit Samuel. The *inside*. He'd never seen the inside of any factory or mill. Maybe the interior was the final veil of sadness.

Maybe it was the clarity of a tear, cutting through the years of dust. Even though he wasn't painting the inside, he felt as though that would be the key. Samuel was certain, certain that all the answers to his consternation lie inside the sadness beast, the breeder of pain and death.

Maybe the workers, the people who *ran* the dead blemish were the Devil and *they* had been cast out.

Quickly, Samuel Bean formed a mental game plan. Tonight, he would rest. Tomorrow morning he would wake up and go to the mill to snoop around and get inside if he possibly could.

Samuel slept. The first night he had even resigned himself to a full night of sleep and he was plagued with a single dream—

He's almost done but he can't get off the floor. Why won't his body move? Deep blazing fire climbing the walls throwing violent light on the circle of easels shifting into hooded Druidic specters moving closer and closer to him horrible chants exiting their bodies through the dim openings in their cloaks like a bunch of dead air a song of dead air a symphony of morose sepulchral breath moving closer and closer so slow but never ceasing no hope of ceasing and the fire not spreading but becoming more alive and violent eating walls eating souls making those insane visionary easel monks more acute more pronounced as they advance and slowly pulling back their cloaks revealing what is inside so ambiguous so bright like the sun at noon on the summer solstice not even seeing everything in front of him and not even seeing What? *he screams* What is it? *What!*

And then the sound of being sucked through a void and thrust into that comfortably dark room.

Samuel spent the rest of the night in a very welcome, very deep, undisturbed sleep.

The next morning Samuel went into the bathroom to shave and take a shower. It felt like a great cleansing to remove his black beard, wash the grease and dust from his long dark hair, and peel back the second skin of grime that had formed over him. Pulling his hair back into a ponytail and donning some clean clothes, he went downstairs feeling fresh and new.

The morning was bright and crisp. Gina greeted him with a fresh pot of coffee and a hot breakfast of sausage and gravy and eggs in the sunwashed kitchen. The first cigarette of the day was strong.

"Good morning," Gina said, eagerly setting the table in one of Samuel's flannel button-down shirts and her simple white under-wear.

"Good morning, honey. Breakfast smells great."

"Are you finished with the painting?" she asked.

"Almost, Gina baby. Almost."

He went on to explain his plans about going into the mill.

"When can I see it?"

"Soon. I promise. Soon. I don't know how long it'll take me to put the finishing touches on it but I know, I *know* it's almost there."

Gina noticed the fire dancing in his eyes. It was a fire she had not seen in a very long time. As the water and razor had cleansed his outside, she knew the fire was doing the same to his insides.

Samuel devoured the breakfast. It filled him up fast. He ate it all, regardless. After slurping down some milk to nourish his aching, calcium-deprived bones, he stood up and said, "Well, I'm going to the mill."

"Wait a second and I'll come with you," Gina said, already walking toward the bedroom to fetch some pants.

"No, honey, I'd . . . rather go alone."

A look of hurt pride flooded her sparkling blue eyes.

"No offense. It's just, well, since I feel kind of close to the painting, I'd rather go alone. I won't be gone long. Promise. I just wanna poke around on the inside some, that's all."

"Okay. I understand." Samuel admired her deep reservation.

He quickly kissed her on the cheek and left.

Samuel stared at the padlocked garage-type door with growing anger. He picked up a couple of large rocks and hurled them at the rusty iron. There was no way he was going to get this far and then be locked out of the one thing that had become his life for nearly a month. The front of the mill dropped off into the river, making the broken windows there impossible to enter. The back of it was stuck into the mountain. Swearing under his breath, he continued to hurl stones at the unfeeling steel.

"Why won't you let me in!" he shouted and then thought, *Christ, I'm acting as if this thing were human.*

A voice shouted from behind him, "Hey!"

Samuel turned, half expecting to see a wonderful peace officer standing there with his little shiny badge in his little blue suit. Instead, it was a slight man in dirty navy-colored coveralls, supporting himself against the handle of a wide broom. "Hey," he repeated, moving closer to Samuel, his right hand swishing the broom forward while the other hand braced his back as he crept along in the gravel. "Yuh-yuh-you wuh-wuh-want in there?"

The man was very close to Samuel now. Samuel noticed that his left eye blinked rapidly open and closed while his right eye stared forward, occasionally shooting off to catch some movement in the woods beside them.

"I guess I want in there almost more than anything right now," Samuel told the man.

"Huh-huh-who are you?" the man stuttered.

"Samuel Bean," he said, extending his hand. "And you?"

"Kuh-Kuh-Kent MMMMMMurr," he spat out, switching the broom to his left hand and holding out his right. "Huh-huh-Who suh-suh-sent you?" Both eyes were now open wide, boring into Samuel.

"Who sent me? Whaddya mean?" Samuel asked and then realized that he didn't want to wait through the man stammering out an explanation. "Well, nobody, I guess. I'm doing a painting. Just decided to come down and check it out. So, you can get me in?"

"Sure can," Kent Murr spat out and began walking outrageously slow toward the padlocked door. Samuel followed him, anxiety like lighter fluid on the flames of his anger.

After what seemed like an hour, Murr finally reached the door. He leaned his broom against the dirty brick of the outside, hunched down, and seized the lock in shaky hands. After several attempts at trying to line the key up with the slit in the lock, Samuel grabbed the tiny key ring with this one single key on it and pushed it in.

Murr began stammering as Samuel jiggled the key around until he heard a click. "Luh-luh-live uh-uh-up yonder in da da woods . . ."

Samuel pulled the heavy door up.

"She died in there," Murr said with no stammer. "Still in there," he added, deftly seizing the key from the lock and moving away.

When Samuel turned to watch him go, Murr was already a few yards away. "Duh-duh-don't ferget to cuh-cuh-close up," the man called from over his shoulder, raising his right hand in a wave of departure.

"Fucking nut," Samuel muttered before entering the factory.

Inside seemed impossibly cold. Inside seemed impossibly damp. Inside seemed impossibly dark and dirty. Samuel decided he preferred the outside, but his fascination and curiosity pushed him farther in.

Samuel, having felt as clean as a newborn less than an hour before, automatically felt grimy and dirty. Shattered bricks, cinders, and shredded shingling littered the floor with copious amounts of animal excrement dropped from various dwellers of the dark. Spider webs clung to every possible corner. There didn't seem to be any opening anywhere. Samuel began to feel very claustrophobic even though the inside of this manufactured manufacturing beast was huge. The darkness and filth were oppressive.

'She died in there,' Samuel mused the words of Kent Murr. *What the hell is that supposed to mean?* Who *died in here? Careful, man, you'll spook yourself out. Try not to think about it. Think of Gina. Sweet Gina.* 'She died in there. Still in there.' *What the hell!?* Who.

Samuel pulled a tiny toylike flashlight, the only thing he'd had, from his pocket and shuffled deeper into the darkness. His beam of light fell on rows of antiquated machines of mass production. They were set in rows. He marveled at the exact design of each row and how every machine in that row looked the same. They'd even aged the same way, the spiders spinning their overtly similar webs, the bats shitting the same piles of shit in the same exact spots. And he moved along the ends of these rows, not wanting to get in between the machines, afraid they may start up and devour him.

Samuel was drinking the darkness, the clotted textures, moving farther and farther back into the old factory.

Something caught his eye.

A light.

Farther back in the factory a light was on.

Samuel paused. It wasn't fear really. He had to devise a plan for he was certain about proceeding to the very place that light was on. Probably, he reasoned, it was just something the creepy Kent Murr had concocted because an old factory wasn't really abandoned if there were still lights on in it, was it? Maybe it served as some sort of makeshift hideout for a group of kids or some bums that had grown tired of riding the rails. Samuel figured he would just stick to the truth. He was a painter. He had to know what this place looked like on the inside. Kent Murr had let him in. No harm to anyone. He would just turn and walk away.

As he drew closer to the light, he had no real use for his weak flashlight. It was a fluorescent light and he saw now that it was coming from a room. What he'd seen from way back there was just the doorway. The door wasn't even open. All that light was pouring from the window of the door. Samuel could see flowers on the wall in there.

The closer he got the more clearly he could see but the scene got farther from his understanding. He'd never seen anything like it so he had to put it together piece by piece.

Okay. It had once been somebody's office but it was now devoid of any real office qualities except for the huge wooden desk in the middle of the floor. A naked body adorned the surface of the desk. Flowers were scattered all over the floor, climbing the walls, outlining the body on the desk.

Samuel opened the door, greeted with the scent of the flowers. It smelled like walking in the hills after a spring rain.

Samuel stared at the figure, a beautiful female figure. She was young and quite voluptuous in her nudity, though lifeless. He noticed her eyes; large, gray, staring into the bright fluorescent above the desk. Her skin was smooth and gray, but so beautiful, so many shades and values. Her hair was jet black, cascading in soft rolling waves over her shoulders.

"My daughter," a voice said from the darkness behind Samuel.

His heart pounded. He froze with confusion and, yes, now fear. Being in the bright room had caused him to lose whatever night vision he'd gained and the darkest of dark greeted him as he turned to face the voice. Samuel placed the voice as Kent Murr's.

Murr stepped into the bright light and Samuel realized that he was much thinner and paler than he had at first thought. From behind his back Murr pulled a bouquet of red roses that the lighting turned nearly violet. He picked up the oldest-looking bouquet of flowers at the foot of the body, pulled them up to discard them on the floor, and put the new bouquet in their place.

"The prettiest things grow wild up there. In the hills."

"They're all very beautiful." Samuel made it a point to stay at least arm's length from Murr. Samuel realized that Murr no longer stuttered and his eyes were perfectly normal, sedately hooded at that. He couldn't help looking away from Murr to drink in the sight of the body on the desk.

"She's not dead," Murr said, placing a hand on her foot. "Touch her. You'll see."

Samuel reached out and touched her forearm. Although she wasn't as warm as a living human body, she wasn't completely without temperature. And her skin felt very pliant, like one of the petals on the flowers surrounding her.

"Unbelievable," Samuel whispered. "Why is she in here?"

"Oh, she was dead once. When I found her. She can't go out in the real world."

A slight moan escaped the body. A very low, sensuous moan. Her eyes blinked once.

"Sometimes she gets hungry."

Murr unbuttoned the right cuff of his coveralls. The wrist was purple, mangled and scarred. With his left hand, Murr pulled a small knife from his pocket and made a very surface incision on his wrist. He let the blood drip over her lips and chin before lowering his wrist and letting her hungrily suckle. When he pulled his wrist away, her tongue snaked down over her chin, licking it clean, leaving it glistening with her saliva.

"I know what you thought, out there," he motioned toward the front of the factory. "You thought I was the village idiot. Hopefully everyone does. When Linda was alive, I was the proudest father in the world. Mr. Bean, you don't know how much I loved Linda. No, it was nothing sick. I wanted all the best for her and was able to provide it. I wish I could have done more. She always came to me with all of her problems. I listened attentively, trying to offer suggestions. Just trying to help. Then I began to fool myself when she stopped coming to me. 'She's too young to have serious problems,' I told myself. There's nothing wrong. She's just growing up. It was all lies. Still, I don't know what pulsed inside her brain. I don't know what happened to her. What led to her death."

Murr walked around behind the desk. Tears rolled silently down his cheeks.

"My daughter," he stroked her hair with his hand. "Exactly as I found her. I had to rob her grave to put her back, but she's still beautiful."

Samuel knew that Murr was trying his best to sound casual and poetic even though the tremor in his voice was threatening to throw him into incomprehensible sobs.

"I ran this place. I owned this place. She was only seventeen. I don't know why she was down here. I don't know if I really want to know. But one or more of those vile mindless beasts that sold their lives to this stinking death hole murdered her. Maybe she did ask for it. Maybe she was that kind of girl. She was never easy. But *this*. Nothing justifies this."

Awkward under standard social interactions, Samuel was entirely without words.

"I'm sorry," Murr said, breaking down. "Is this . . . is this what you wanted to know?"

"This is, uh, more tragic than anything I could have ever imagined. I'm very sorry."

Samuel extended his hand and entwined his fingers with Murr's thin and trembling fingers over Linda's body. Not only was Samuel no longer afraid of Murr, he wanted him to feel every bit of sympathy he was able to give.

"Well," Murr began, "I suppose you got things you gotta get back to."

Samuel took his cue to leave.

"Thank you for letting me in, Mr. Murr," Samuel said and left.

Once outside, Samuel felt drained and sensuously dirty. He started home toward Gina, wanting only one thing—beautiful, seventeen-year-old, dead Linda Murr.

Gina greeted Samuel at the door, practically yanking him inside. After shutting the door, she quickly unfastened his pants and had them down to his knees. Her hands were all over him—her lips, her tongue—and nothing was happening.

Samuel's mind was back in the industry. The face of Linda Murr as she licked her father's blood from her lips. So beautiful in her death.

She *was* death.

She was darkness.

She was loneliness.

She was the muse.

And by the time Samuel started getting excited, Gina was frustrated.

"I need to finish the painting," Samuel said.

"It's been almost a month," she was nearly crying. "We haven't even been married a year and you've already stopped fucking me!"

In his studio, Samuel couldn't concentrate enough to paint. He was planning his next visit to the industry where the heart of the painting, alive in death, breathed and throbbed beneath the surface of his fingertips.

Samuel spent the next few hours smoking cigarette after cigarette, gazing between his now lifeless canvas and the dark expanse out his window, listening to Gina bang from room to room in the house, slamming every door as violently hard as possible. Eventually she burst through the door to the studio.

She stalked toward him so fast he nearly fell out of his chair. She had suitcases in her hands.

"You call this working?" She walked over to the painting. "Yeah, that's beautiful. Really fucking brilliant. I can't even tell what the fuck it is. That must mean it's really good, huh? Wait, though, it needs something." She coughed and spit onto the painting. She was crying, shaking, near hysterical with anger. "I'm going to stay with my parents for a while. Maybe you can call me when you grow a personality or a cock. Really, either one would do at this point." Then she stormed out, slamming the door hard enough to put a crack down the middle of it.

Samuel felt numb.

He spent the rest of the evening drinking beer and Jack Daniel's, winding up at the industry. This time the door wasn't locked. No flashlight now and his mind was as dark and cloudy as the inside of this place.

And he found himself at her altar, his hands running over that smooth skin, color rising in her cheeks as she pulled him to her, their lips meeting.

Linda's hands were all over him and she tasted like the sweet decay of dead roses. Samuel gasped for breath as she pulled her lips away and slid them down his neck. Samuel couldn't open his eyes. He grew weaker with each breath he took. Feverishly, he continued to move his hands over her body, feeling the heat between her legs, the hardness of her ribs, the soft heft of her breasts, and the slow, increasingly strong beat of her heart.

Sliding into darkness, Samuel heard her voice, seductive and cold—"Mmm . . . I could get drunk off his blood. You bring the best flowers at night, Daddy"—and the last thing Samuel saw through the doors of light that were flying open in his mind was Gina's tear-streaked face.

Gina and her father have finished loading all of her stuff into the moving van. She sticks a stick of Samuel's opium incense between the floorboards, lighting it and one of his clove cigarettes with the same match. She looks at his painting on an easel positioned in front of the window. She's never liked his paintings but when they first met he seemed to handle her with the same passion and care as he did those horrid canvases. As she looks out the window she sees the mill sitting like a cancer on the hill. Black smoke pours from one of the hideous brown smokestacks.

That's odd, she thinks. She figures a homeless guy has probably found a furnace and started a fire in it.

"Gina, honey, it's all packed!" her father calls up the stairway.

"Coming, Dad!" she calls back.

Gina crushes the clove on the floor and leaves the incense burning as she crosses the room and closes the door on the smoke of Samuel.

MARKET ADJUSTMENT

1.

New York—October 28, 1929

A HOTDOG, MISTER?"

"Got any money?"

Myron Barnes patted his tattered overcoat, knowing he didn't have any money. He caught the vendor's eye and tossed his hands out to the side. "I ain't had no money for days. Thought I might find somethin." Myron turned away. "I understand. You got a business you're tryin to run."

"Hold up now. I think I can spare one."

Myron turned back around to face him. Their eyes stayed locked and the vendor's motions were mechanical, assembling and wrapping the hotdog, handing it across the cart to Myron.

"Jeez, thanks, mister. When I make my fortune I'll make sure to pay you. Consider this a loan." He held up the hotdog before taking a big hungry bite of it.

"I wouldn't count on that. Don't think nobody's makin money today. Head down to Wall Street, you'll see a whole lotta panic. That is . . . unless you got somewhere else to go."

"I think you and me both know I don't."

"Enjoy. I think a whole lotta people's about to join you."

Myron turned his back on the vendor with a dismissive wave. He took another bite of the hotdog and headed toward Wall Street. The vendor's words stung him. Had it become that obvious he lived on the street?

Luckily, Myron thought, he still had his youth and some vestige of his looks. Maybe it was just his eyes. Somehow he was able to compel people to do things for him. Maybe they just saw poverty and desperation. So, yeah, he lived on the street, but it wasn't hard to find some girl to take him in for the night. More often than not, he had a place to sleep. And he had the Enclave.

He crouched down in front of a sewer grate and took one last, longing look at the remainder of the hotdog before dropping it down. He rose and wiped his hands on his filthy pants, his stomach now gurgling pleasantly as it broke down the food.

He breathed in the crisp October air and turned onto Wall Street.

It was choked with panic. People shouting in disbelief, running hands through their hair, and clutching their pockets like something could reach in and take whatever was left right out. A palpable buzz binding everyone together.

Who were these captains of industry?

Materialistic money worshippers, Myron thought. No one knew which gods they worshipped anymore so these people had chosen to worship their bank accounts. They had built a house of cards and now, watching a man's hat fly off as he kicked the tires of a nearby Nash with great fury, that house of cards had fallen. This was the aftermath.

Myron did his best not to smile. Not that anyone would have noticed.

Join me, he thought. Join me here at the bottom of the world.

A rain of glass exploded from above, followed by a heavy wooden office chair. The crowd gathered on the sidewalk backed out into the street and craned their heads upward.

A collective gasp. A man flying through the air, framed against the gorgeous blue sky, his jacket and pants flapping as he clawed at the empty space around him.

He hit the ground in an explosion of bone fragments and gore. Myron crossed his arms to shield his eyes. A woman to his right screamed. An eyeball had slapped against the lapel of her jacket, and she did a weird little dance as it sluggishly slid down before plopping onto the greasy asphalt.

Myron felt blood spattered against his palms. He held his hands out in front of him to examine them, the gesture of begging all too familiar.

A hundred-dollar bill rested wetly in each palm.

He casually wrapped his hands around the bills and slid them into each of his pants pockets before disappearing down the nearest alley.

2.

The grimy alley smelled like piss. Behind him, savage screams and squealing tires. It was like a switch had been thrown and every siren in the city now roared around him. He looked up at the endless blue sky. A thick black cloud drifted over, sealing the entire financial district in shades of gray and black. No more blue sky.

Toward the end of the alley, he saw what he was hoping to see. A service entrance door. A place for the dirty people to enter. A place for the under people. A man staggered out of the door. He wasn't an under person. He wore a dark pin-striped suit and looked slightly disheveled. He turned to his right, toward the hungry throng out on Wall Street and, noticing Myron, said, "Hey! Hey, buddy!" He threw out his right arm and grabbed Myron's left, jostling it. Then he retracted his hand and wiped it on the thigh of his trousers.

"I ain't your buddy," Myron said.

This didn't seem to faze the man. He blinked his eyes and shook his head. "No hard feelings, buddy. Times are tough for everyone. You know, I got a boat. Docked in the harbor. It's a fine boat. The *Black Swan.* You wanna see my boat?"

"I don't think I got time. I gotta get inside and do some things."

The guy chuffed and straightened his lapels. Myron wondered if maybe he was drunk.

"Fuck man. I'm gonna go get on my boat and sail it to . . . hell, anywhere but here. Then I'm gonna come back and everything's gonna be over." The man pulled a flask from his pocket and un-screwed the top, belting it back and answering Myron's question. "This shit's gonna blow over." He brandished the still open flask at Myron. "Just you wait and see. But it's gonna get real ugly before it does."

Myron nodded and made for the door. The guy moved to stand in his way. Myron grabbed the flask and threw it toward the far end of the alley. It clanged as it skidded down the asphalt and the man ran after it. Myron opened the service entrance door and walked into the Chambers National Bank building.

3.

Not surprisingly, he didn't run into any service workers as he took the stairs down to the basement. On the whole, they tended to be smarter than the people whose toilets they cleaned. They had probably taken off at the first sign of trouble. Sick kids. Sick relatives. Funerals. Viewings. Not feeling well. Appointment. The excuses were endless.

Once in the basement, he went immediately to the fuse box. It didn't take him long to find what he was looking for. The fuses for the forty-third floor. He wondered briefly why the building was named after the Chambers National Bank when they only occupied part of one floor. He hoped this was the floor he needed. That was where the checks had been addressed to, and later not addressed to.

Be best if it's done in the dark. Mama Hodap's voice, sweet as sugar, rolled around in his head.

Unscrewing the fuses, he thought about the two hundred dollars in his pockets and wondered if that would have changed anything.

Maybe some things were inevitable. Maybe everyone built his own house of cards. He unscrewed the final fuse and, because he was alone and because he didn't think anyone would hear him, he screamed.

He quit when he tasted blood on the back of his tongue.

4.

He took the stairs back up to the lobby. He supposed he could have taken the elevator all the way up to 43 but he didn't want to go up there as an under man. He wanted to go up there the same as everybody else. In the brightly lighted, scrubbed clean lobby he looked toward the elevator and decided he wanted to look outside again. He had been told this was going to be a monumental day and he wanted to see just how monumental it was to be.

For him, he knew it was going to be huge. But what about for everyone else?

He wandered over to the front of the lobby. It was hard to look casual. Through the glass he saw the storm-dimmed street.

There were even more people out there now.

The man who had been kicking his car was still kicking his car. His shoe had deteriorated, his foot a red pulp.

A crowd of people stood around the remains of the jumper. The ambulance and police had arrived and were busy trying to shoo some enterprising dogs away. The medics looked at the remains like it was a very complicated puzzle. People parted quickly as a car came roaring down the street and continued out of Myron's view.

Myron watched with interest. Their god was dead, at least temporarily, and it would take them a while before they learned to move on. Maybe they would look for a new god. Mama Hodap had introduced him to a couple of new gods and told him about a whole lot more.

Did he believe in them?

Sure. Mama was an under person. She had no reason to lie. Did he *worship* them? Well, he didn't think he'd ever worship a god again.

He moved toward the elevator so he didn't rouse any suspicion from the dumpy receptionist sitting wide-eyed behind the gleaming counter. He made eye contact with her and nodded. She was lost to the brisk voice of the broadcaster on the radio.

The broadcaster was talking crash.

He was talking bad times.

He was talking depression.

Myron pressed the up button and the elevator opened immediately. He stepped inside and hit the button for 43. He took a deep and shaky breath and ran his hand through his greasy hair. Sometimes to get to the very bottom of things you had to go to the top.

Breathing in the greasy mechanical air of the elevator, he thought about Melinda and Joanie. It had been nearly a year since they had lost their house. But even after that, he had still had *them*. He had still had his family. Six months ago he lost Melinda to TB in a government funded hospital for the poor. Less than a month later he had lost little Joanie to pneumonia. He had been alone and on the street ever since. Even when he went to bed with another woman it was only for the comfort of a bed and a roof over his head. He thought Melinda would understand. Sometime after losing Joanie, he had searched desperately for a purpose since his American dream had become a very cruel nightmare. Those other women, the lifestyle of a carefree tramp, quickly wore on him. Their beds of sweat and perfume, their need and greed and desperation and loneliness could not help him find his purpose.

He blinked the bad memories away before they could sting his eyes with tears and the elevator opened onto a darkened floor.

Before he found his purpose, he'd found the Enclave. And the Enclave had introduced him to Mama Hodap. And she had given him his purpose.

And now the days were getting shorter, and the nights were getting longer, and the god of the new world was dying right in front of him.

5.

He stepped into the wide hallway and left all shreds of a rational world behind.

He didn't mind. It was rationality, cold and clinical, that had gotten him where he was, which was nowhere.

6.

And maybe this was nowhere. *The* Nowhere.

Residual light from the window to his left illuminated the hallway. The elevator closed behind him, sealing him from any impulse to turn back. He knew he could just hit the down button and he also knew he wouldn't be able to live with himself if he did that. He couldn't let the rest of the Enclave down.

A shape moaned to his right and Myron looked down to focus on it.

A man dragged himself along the floor. He wore a dark suit. It was rumpled and torn. His face was swollen and bloodstained. The left leg of his trousers had been ripped away and his leg was severed at the knee. Blood trailed away into the murk behind him.

Myron covered his mouth and fought the urge to throw up. He had prepared himself for this. The black woman in the sewers beneath Harlem had touched him. Mama Hodap. She had looked into him. Amidst thick incense smoke in an unused utility room, Mama held his hand. Alternately grim and smiling, she had gently folded her hands over his and, in those brief moments, Myron had seen things he begged Mama to take back.

No, sir. She shook her head. *Can't unshow somethin already been showed.*

And he knew she was right.

She had prepared him for this.

The man on the floor grunted as he took another great heave

forward.

Why didn't Myron help him? How *could* he help him? This man was one of the fallen. There would be no rising.

The man pulled himself along until he reached the elevator. Myron continued to watch him. The man seemed to notice Myron for the first time. "Hey, mister?" Down there in the alley he was buddy. Apparently he was mister up here. The man on the floor gagged and strings of blood ran from his mouth. "Think you can help me with the elevator?" He wiped blood from his mouth with the back of his hand and then held it up to the button to demonstrate how he couldn't reach it.

Myron took a couple of steps toward the button and reached over the man to press it.

"Ah, jeez, thanks a lot, mister."

The elevator opened. The man pulled himself halfway in. Before he could make it all the way, the doors shut on his waist, paused, and once again retracted. The man grunted and tried to pull himself faster. Myron reached down to push the man. He didn't know if he wanted to help or if he just wanted the man's blood on his hands.

Myron got him all the way into the elevator and said, "Let this man take my place in the world." With a smirk, he backed away from the elevator.

"What's that . . ." the man said before the elevator swallowed him.

7.

Now Myron was again left with the meager daylight bleeding into the hallway. Double doors stood at the end opposite the window. He walked toward them, breathing deeply and evenly. From behind the doors he heard glass shattering and people screaming.

CHAMBERS NATIONAL BANK

The name was branded across both doors in the same stylized pattern embossed on the monthly bills he had received. He ran his fingertips across the lettering. While Mama had tried to mentally prepare him for this, he didn't know how one could ever really be prepared for what was about to happen.

This is just a smokescreen. She smiled that gentle smile, put her warm brown hand over his. He would have believed anything she told him. *Him and his like are just takin advantage of the chaos. They serve other gods.*

Oh, they might worship money but you can't serve money. So I feel it's only fair I let you borrow a couple of my gods: Papa Legba and Baron La Croix. They'll need off'rins like any self-respectin deity. And, of course, you don't gotta worship em, you just gotta believe in em.

Myron had offered the remainder of the hotdog to Papa Legba. The only thing he had left was the money. He pulled the still damp bills from his pockets and placed them in front of the door. He heard a piercing scream and repetitive thump.

"For you, Baron La Croix."

He looked at the bills lying on the floor, expecting them to disappear or something. They didn't. But the blood did. One minute it was there and the next minute the hundred-dollar bills looked like they had come fresh from the treasury. Myron picked them up and put them back into his pockets. He stood up and tried the knob on the right. The door wouldn't budge. Already knowing the outcome, he tried the door on his left.

Papa Legba opens doors.

What if these weren't the doors he was supposed to open? Would Papa only do something once? Or would he open many doors if Myron asked him to? Better play it safe.

Myron thought he could handle these himself. He went back down the hall about halfway until he came to an emergency station, complete with a fire hose and an ax. He smashed out the glass and grabbed the ax. He held it with both hands, felt its heft, the smooth wood against his palms. Wasting no more time, he stalked to the locked office doors and began smashing at them. All he had to do was bust them a couple of times at the latches and the doors swung open.

8.

As he walked through the doors, another lobby surrounded him. Much like the one on the first floor, only on a smaller scale. A woman lay bound to the receptionist's desk. Her mouth was gagged with dark cloth. She stared crazy eyed at Myron as she struggled against the ropes. Two very large and very black dogs flanked either side of the desk. They growled at Myron. Lean muscles rippled through their haunches.

He heard a man's gruff voice say, "Stay." Then he felt something smack against his head and everything went a little darker than it already was.

9.

It took his eyes a few moments to adjust to the dusky room. His wrists were tied together over his head. He was suspended from the ceiling, his legs bound at the ankles. The room was a very spacious office, fit for the bank president.

The shelves were in disarray, many of them pulled down altogether. A behemoth desk lay toppled on its side. He hung in front of a row of windows. A cold, damp breeze blew in through the ones that had been shattered.

Four people stood watching him from the other side of the room, slightly to the left of the devastated desk. Two younger men who looked eager and willing to begin their climb up the corporate ladder, a slim blond woman and a stocky, gray-haired man holding a severed lower leg around the ankle.

"I'm looking for Robert Chambers."

The older man barked at him, "Shut the fuck up!" The two goonish men smirked.

Was *this* Robert Chambers, the bank president? It almost had to be. If so, this was the man responsible for foreclosing on his home. This man was partly responsible for the swirling chaos and panic raging through the streets outside.

"Are *you* Robert Chambers?"

"I told you to shut the fuck up!" He turned to the goon on his right. "I thought we had him out of the way but I guess we forgot to do something about that mouth."

"If you're Robert Chambers, I have a message for you from Patrice Hodap . . ."

In his right hand, he held a stack of papers. He brandished them at Myron.

"I don't know who the fuck that is!"

"You know you're a murderer."

The man stomped up and down like a child throwing a tantrum. "Fuck! Fuck! Fuck! Fuck you! I don't have to listen to you or any other piece of trash from the street."

"I ain't from the street, Mr. Chambers. I'm from a place even farther below."

"I don't care where the fuck you come from." Chambers took a few steps toward him. "I'll cut you loose and you can go back to eating rats in the sewer with that nigger bitch. You have no part in this."

"I'm afraid I do." Myron spit at Chambers, saliva spraying the front of his suit.

Chambers turned his back on Myron and began walking toward the other side of the room.

"Steiner!" Chambers shouted. One of the younger men snapped to attention. "Take these certificates and feed them to this stupid fuck."

"But what if he tries to bite me, sir?"

Chambers drew back the lower leg and smacked Steiner on the shoulder. "You want to join him?"

Steiner took the stock certificates and approached Myron. He struggled against his bonds. He wasn't going to give them the satisfaction of screaming. He made eye contact with Steiner.

"Listen to me," Steiner said. "I'm going to shove these into your mouth and if you make one attempt to bite me you're going out the window. Understand?"

Myron shook his head.

"He's going to bite me! I know it! I can see it in his eyes!"

"If he bites you, we'll break out his teeth and shove them up his prick."

"Open up," Steiner said.

Myron opened his mouth. As Steiner crumpled up the first certificate and pressed it against Myron's lips, Myron gnashed his teeth. Steiner drew back his fist and punched him in the mouth. Myron felt teeth shatter. Steiner shook his hand with pain, dropping the certificate to the floor. It was probably the first time he'd ever hit anyone.

"Lora! Front and center," Chambers barked.

The blond woman approached Chambers. The other man stood to his left, beside a thick-looking door. Myron wondered if it was some kind of safe. It looked like it was made from wood but it could have been lined with steel, for all Myron knew.

Steiner took the first certificate and shoved it into Myron's mouth. Myron gagged and spit the crumpled certificate and some blood back into Steiner's face.

"Little fucker," Steiner said. He bent down and removed a very expensive brown leather shoe.

From the other side of the office, Chambers said, "I need

servicing."

He unzipped his trousers and let them drop to the floor. His erection was enormous.

"No," Lora said.

"What do you mean, 'No'?"

"I won't do it."

"Think about what you're saying. Out there," he gestured to the windows with the leg, "people are going out of their heads because they've lost everything they had. Now I'm offering you whatever it takes to get you down on your knees. How much?"

Steiner balled up another certificate and shoved it into Myron's mouth. This time he took his shoe and crammed the paper to the back of Myron's throat. Myron gagged but the shoe forced his gorge back down and then he had to fight to swallow the paper so he wouldn't choke on it. The aged paper worked its way down his throat. He coughed. Steiner had another certificate ready, shoving it in. It seemed like he'd hit some sort of groove. Myron tasted the old water flavor of the paper, blood, bile, street grime and shoe polish.

"This much?" Chambers produced a stack of bills from the inside pocket of his blazer. He peeled off a couple and threw them in Lora's face.

"I won't."

"This much?" He threw a couple more bills at her.

"This much?" He ground a wad into her face.

Myron wondered why she stood there and took this. Why didn't she turn and run? Why hadn't she run a while ago when Chambers had undoubtedly blown some kind of gasket? Maybe this wasn't abnormal. Maybe he always acted like this.

He dropped the entire stack on the floor in front of her.

"Still no?"

"Never."

"Fuck it. Money's worthless anyway."

Chambers kicked the stack away and it exploded in a greenish flutter. He set the severed leg onto the floor. He ripped off his jacket and his shirt, finished stripping off his pants, standing stocky and naked. Through Myron's watery eyes, he looked like a predatory animal. Chambers picked the leg back up.

"Todd!"

"Yes, sir!" the remaining man bellowed.

"Shit on this stack of money."

"Yes, sir!"

Todd came out of his stoic stupor to walk over, drop his pants, and squat over the stack of loose bills.

"I'll just take what I want," Chambers said.

Myron choked down another certificate and coughed, "Lora!"

The woman turned to him as though she hadn't even realized there was anyone else in the room until now.

"Run!"

"I can't. The dogs." She stood there whimpering, looking down at Todd and the stack of money with disgust, bringing her arms instinctively over her chest.

Was she just hoping the madness would suddenly end?

Chambers snapped out with the leg and caught her on the side of the head with a meaty *thunk*. Lora fell to her right, bloody hair sticking to her face. Myron didn't know if the blood came from her or the leg.

He couldn't watch this. He had to do something. He pulled his knees up to his chest and savagely kicked out at Steiner as he reached toward him with another certificate. He planted the kick squarely in Steiner's chest. He staggered backward, caught himself, and was on Myron in a second, catching him across the face with the hard sole of his shoe. Myron went dizzy with the bolt of pain and the violent swinging of the rope. He wondered what he was suspended from. How easy it would be to break.

He heard fabric rip and Lora scream.

The office smelled like shit and vomit and blood. And beneath it all, the smell of old money and endless comfort.

He swung around, staring out over the city through the busted window and now back into the office. His eyes quickly followed the twisting rope to a vent in the ceiling. Steiner's shoe met his nose this time. He heard it pop and saw flashes of purple. Heard Lora savagely slapping at Chambers, saying, "No, no, no." Chambers laughing—lecherous and guttural. Myron threw himself toward the open window.

"Crazy fucker's trying to go out!" Steiner shouted. He sounded terrified or ecstatic.

Myron thought maybe the vent gave a little bit. He timed his next push for when Steiner came at him with the shoe again. It met him on the ear with a buzzing roar and he threw himself out the window, felt the air kiss his sweaty skin, heard a crumbling and a clanking and started his descent.

On the way down, he tried to think about nothing at all.

10.

He hit the cement and everything fractured and exploded before it imploded upon itself. He felt twisted up and inside out but surprisingly whole. He opened his eyes to stare up at a black sky streaked with lightning and pissing down rain.

If you ask the Baron to cause the death of another, you be prepared to pay. But just know—he is the master of death and it's only he can take you there. So you make sure to pray for him to keep your heart beating and leave him out of that other man's business. That other man's for human hands. You and me and everyone else.

Myron took a breath of the soggy air and felt his heart pound into life.

How many times would he be able to defy death?

He stood up, expecting to see a crowd of gawkers.

He didn't.

11.

What he saw—what he *could* see—was much worse. This was the world of his vision. This was the world Mama Hodap had shown him. This was not the world he had left behind. Only maybe it was that world, perverted and decayed.

This was still Wall Street. The buildings were still there but they were in shambles, crumbling ruins. Every building except for the Chambers Building. If anything, it was even taller than before and now it looked more like a tower than a building. For a moment, Myron thought it was glowing. Several torches were stood up along the side of the road, almost like primitive streetlamps, their flames guttering against the rain. Naked corpses were stacked on the sidewalks to either side of the road. Men, women, children, animals. All stripped and thrown there like garbage, in various states of decay. Now was not the time to mourn them. He had other things to do. He had a purpose and now that purpose was renewed. Mama Hodap had felt it when she had touched him. She had said he was the one. She had said he had been brought to her. He had been chosen. He had not found them. They had found him. For the first time since entering the sewers, he was able to understand what she meant.

He didn't put himself together and stand up after falling forty-three floors for nothing.

He tried to shake the vision from his head. It didn't do any good. It was no longer just a vision. It was very real, slouching in front of him. The torches still burned. The bodies were still there. The rain continued to pour. Lightning continued to flash. He was in the belly of chaos. He was in the middle of Wall Street, adjusted to fit this savage world.

He turned toward the Chambers building.

This time he was going to enter through the front door.

He had encountered Chambers. He was still alive. He still had his dignity. He was still an under man, still a resident down there at the bottom of the world. But he was not unequal. He knew that now.

As he drew closer to the building he saw that it wasn't made of brick and concrete like most buildings. Not anymore. Bones—gray, white, and black—made up the intricate framework. It was covered in a luminous membrane. The glowing, oozing tower contrasted against the black sky. He reached out to grab what may have been a handle or maybe just a jaw bone when the door opened to receive him.

He passed through it into the cramped, humid lobby.

12.

The door shut behind him and Myron knew he wouldn't be going back out that way even if he wanted to. He turned to survey the lobby area. It was arranged much the same as the old lobby area. The receptionist's desk was made up of various bones. These bones, enmeshed with the membrane and bone meal, made up the interior walls, as well. They made him think of fossils covered in semen. The membrane coated everything with that glow. It *had* to be glowing. He didn't see any other sources of light. The floor was some kind of black dirt or more bone meal. Maybe the ashes of the dead.

In front of him, the floor was moving, opening up.

He stood rooted in place, staring at the disturbance.

A pair of little hands reached up through the ashy floor, followed by a mostly familiar face.

Joanie.

He breathed the name aloud. *"Joanie."*

This was Joanie after death. Gray and rotten but still mostly intact. She hadn't really been dead very long. He reached out to help pull her from the ground. He took her hand and pulled gently. He could feel the bone separating from the joint and shuddered with the thought of the arm coming off in his hand. He released her.

"Joanie," he said again.

"Daddy." Her vocal cords didn't work very well. The muscles of her mouth were mostly rotten. Dirt and insects filled her throat. It didn't sound like Joanie at all.

She pulled herself the rest of the way out. Black dirt caked her deteriorated clothes. He wanted to hug her but fought the urge. What good would it do? This wasn't his Joanie. He knew that. It would be impossible for his Joanie to be here. He imagined hugging her and having her fall to pieces in his arms just like she had died under his watch. He fought the crippling wave of grief and guilt threatening to pull him down.

"Follow me," Joanie said.

She turned to his left, walking with a quick, jerking shamble. She disappeared through a man-size opening shaped like a vagina. He followed her, pushing the thickly dripping membrane aside, the thick lips of the vagina painting him in the substance.

Once through the opening, he found himself in a claustrophobic chamber even more sickeningly humid than the lobby. It breathed around him. Slowly. A sleep breath.

"Joanie?"

"Up here, Daddy!"

He looked up. A deep shaft ascended up through the building. Perhaps this was the elevator at one point. It didn't make any sense. The shaft was lined with what looked like circular bones, monstrous ribcages. He grabbed the first rung and began climbing.

His new body felt strong and powerful. Up to the task or merely equipped to take him to some awful end.

He knew where he was going.

All the way to the top.

Somewhere along the way, he lost sight of Joanie. But he figured he didn't lose sight of her. She was probably never there in the first place.

He climbed the rungs smoothly and as quickly as he could.

The shaft continued to ooze and breathe around him.

On the way, he thought about the path that had brought him

here.

13.

Shortly after the death of his family, Myron turned his back on the homeless shelters and the free government care that went along with them. As far as he was concerned, the only thing they had succeeded in doing was killing Melinda and Joanie. In the shelters and on the streets, he had heard whisperings of all kinds of things. It wouldn't do to go out looking for a job because a storm was brewing and the factories weren't hiring anyone and would probably be shutting down shortly. You could move out west but work was just as scarce out there and they paid slave wages for brutal days of backbreaking labor. None of that mattered to Myron. With his family gone, he didn't have anyone to work for anyway.

But Myron had kept his ears open. Eventually, rooting through a trash can behind a diner in Hell's Kitchen, he found Kevin Pierce. Pierce told him about a group of people who lived in the sewers and the subways. The Enclave, Pierce called them. Myron spent the day with Pierce. He was hungry and dirty just like everyone he knew. But he seemed calm. Toward the end of the day, Myron thought he had it figured out.

"You ain't searchin," he said to Pierce.

"Whaddya mean?"

"Well, ever'body else's lost ever'thin but they're tryin to get it back. They're all bunched up and anxious."

Pierce threw back his head and laughed, scratching the thick beard on his neck.

Then he told Myron about the Enclave.

And Mama Hodap.

Myron, who didn't have anything else to search for, followed Pierce down.

So Myron went below and embraced what he knew he had always been. An under man.

He was introduced to Mama Hodap and she told him what he needed to do. He didn't disagree with her.

She was the closest thing the Enclave had to a spiritual leader. Or any kind of leader. She took him to that disused utility room. She filled it with incense smoke and laughter and a sense of life Myron hadn't felt in a very long time. Meeting her for the first time, he had been nervous. All the nervousness melted away when he looked into her soulful eyes and felt her calming touch. She had told him how he could be one of them.

You gotta contribute fore you can partake.

And she had told him what he needed to do. He was skeptical at first. He no longer took anything at face value.

She had given him a vision and the vision had become a kind of truth in his heart and he hadn't doubted her since.

Even now, climbing up this abstract elevator shaft, climbing to a fate that might very well be his death, he didn't doubt Mama Hodap. She spoke from an under place and that place held a lot more truth than the offices situated quietly in the tops of skyscrapers.

14.

He reached the top of the membranous shaft and crawled out. He hadn't noticed any other openings along the way. It was designed to take him to this place. It was designed to take all visitors to this place.

But what was this place?

He emerged into a low, narrow hallway. He stayed on his hands and knees. There wasn't any room for him to stand. There were no windows in this nightmare hallway. The only light came from the glow of that mucous substance. Toward the end of the hallway, he searched for an entrance to Chambers. He saw something that looked like an anus at the far end. That was probably it. He crawled along thinking he should be exhausted after his climb but he wasn't. He still felt strong. He still felt powerful and he wondered if this was from the gods Mama Hodap had equipped him with or if it was from the woman herself. Or maybe it was something that came from inside him. Maybe his instinct for revenge and survival was stronger than he had given himself credit for.

Drawing closer to the anus door, he noticed the awful stench seeping from it. It wasn't completely unexpected. When he thought of sliding through it, he gagged. He raised himself into a crouch and placed his hands palms together before inserting them into the center of the anus. He took a deep breath, closed his eyes and sprang forward, hoping the sphincter wouldn't constrict and trap him.

Finally thankful for the membrane coating him, he slid through effortlessly and ended up in a warped version of the previous Chambers reception area.

The same woman was still strapped to the receptionist desk.

Her skin was now a ghostly gray. Her clothes had been stripped off. Her sizable breasts fell to her sides. The ax he had used to chop down the door was stuck into her chest. Her dead eyes were frozen wide open with terror and a black tongue lolled from her mouth. Her legs were spread wide, dried blood crusting her sex. Myron's stomach sank. It was the ax. He felt partly responsible for this. But he wasn't the one who held the ax. He wasn't the one who had plunged it down into the innocent's chest.

Chambers was.

Would he still be in his office?

He turned to face the door, ready to make his final drive.

It wasn't going to be that easy.

The door was guarded. Two men, maybe Steiner and Todd, with the heads of the dogs, watched Myron. The one on the left growled at him. The one on the right dropped to his hands and knees, his lean thigh muscles flexing.

Papa Legba opens doors for you.

Mama Hodap's words came back to him but he still didn't want to invoke the god to get through this door. He couldn't help but think she had some other door in mind. This was still just a physical door and he had rapidly come to learn that all physical doors are made to be kicked down. He sidestepped quickly to his right and wrapped his hand around the grip of the ax. He yanked hard but it was firmly planted in the woman's chest. He grunted and yanked again as the first dogman pounced on him, knocking him back onto the floor and clamping his teeth to his neck. His hand groped for the ax but found only air.

The dog certainly had the killer instinct.

And Myron should be on his way to death right now but knew he wasn't. He'd made the offering to the Baron. Even better than a regular offering, it was a blood offering, however inadvertently that had been.

So let the blood flow.

Let the bullets fly.

Let the knives plunge and the teeth gnash.

With the dogman's jaws still clamped to his neck, its head jerking back and forth to rend the wounds even wider, Myron rolled over onto the dogman. He clamped the jaws shut with his hands, squeezing with his new strength. He could feel the blood pumping out of his neck. It was blood he didn't need. Not here, anyway. Until Papa decided to swing open death's black door, Myron wasn't going.

The dogman kicked beneath him, Myron's blood filling its mouth.

He thought about the stock certificates being shoved down his throat and clamped the dogman's jaws shut even harder. It gagged and tried to spit beneath him. Blood frothed out of its nostrils.

Myron wondered why the other dogman hadn't attacked him from behind. Maybe it was afraid. Maybe it didn't care. If they were Todd and Steiner, Myron figured they had been vicious backstabbers in the real world and didn't know why they would be any less so here.

The dogman stopped twitching beneath Myron. Its eyes rolled back in its head.

When Myron stood up, he found out where the other dogman had gone. It was sniffing the crotch of the sacrificed woman. Even if it was part man, it still had the brain of a dog.

Good boy, Myron thought, as he finally managed to work the ax out of the woman's chest.

"Stay," he said, and barely managed to suppress a laugh.

The dogman continued to lick at the blood caked between the woman's legs.

Myron raised the ax back over his head. He brought it down as hard as he could. The dogman had a thick neck. The ax severed the half closest to Myron. A torrent of blood sprayed out over the woman, some clinging to her pallid skin, some dripping down the strange bone desk.

15.

It wasn't a door guarding him from Chambers' office so much as more membrane. Thick and oozing from the boned frame. Myron clutched the ax tightly and stepped through the opening. The membrane stuck to his skin. He walked slowly into the center of the breathing room. The sensation was almost like being on a boat, rocking back and forth in gentle waves.

The room glowed brightly. It was strewn with cash, gold, stock certificates, and currencies from around the world. He almost didn't see Chambers sitting on something resembling a throne made from bones roughly where his desk used to be.

Like in a dream, the thing sitting there looked nothing like

Chambers, but Myron knew it had to be. He was naked. His skin stretched tightly over his skeleton, pale white but gorged with blood, giving him an almost rosy complexion. Dark red nails grew from his hands and feet. A sickly smooth pouch replaced his genitals. His eyes were small and black.

And, it took Myron a moment to realize it, but Chambers was pulsing, his whole body expanding and contracting with the rhythm of a heartbeat.

Thud. Thud. Thud.

Myron almost wanted to touch him just to make sure he wasn't imagining it.

"What are you doing?" Chambers' voice sounded like sandpaper gargling blood, but with the same gruff cadence it had before.

Myron thought about charging him with the ax, chopping him up until there was nothing.

But he couldn't move. He was rooted in place. The membrane had thickened and become like a rope, clinging to his clothes, reaching into his clothes and adhering to his skin.

"You know what I'm doin," Myron said. He felt stupid opening his mouth around this man. He felt small. Poor. Dumb. Uneducated. But he knew none of those things made him any less than this man.

Chambers chuffed out a laugh.

"I know what you're *trying* to do but let me assure you: Many have tried and many have failed. You don't know what you're up against."

"I have a pretty good idea."

"Is that so? Let's hear it."

"A monster."

He coughed out a laugh again. "You wish it was that easy. You're a simpleton. You don't know what it's like to become."

"Become what? A monster?"

"A god."

"You're hardly a god."

"You're right. I can only aspire. But the gods will continue to give me power if I continue to serve them."

"I don't serve gods. Any gods."

"Well, then you are even simpler than I thought. You're used to the gods of civilization." Chambers picked up some coins to his right and let them plink back down into the pile. "The gods of this. That's what makes you so civilized. The gods you've known don't know the meaning of chaos and survival within that chaos. The gods of civilization were made to be housed by churches and books. They are gods of convenience, there to serve the believer when convenient. It makes it easy to deny their existence. I haven't seen any proof myself. But my gods are the old gods. The oldest gods in the cosmos. And getting some of their power is as close as any one of us will ever get to them."

"The only god you serve is greed."

"Greed? Greed for what?"

"Money."

"Money? Hardly. Although my gods did create money. In order to collapse a civilization, you have to give it the tools to build itself so that people can forget about the old ways. So people can forget what it's like to live in fear. Fear of their neighbor. Fear of the creatures in the night. Fear of starvation. You have built walls between yourselves and fear. And you let us build these altars to the gods. Our gods. And we found a way to turn currency into souls. We found out how to deaden them, eat them. And with each soul death, we move a little deeper into your world. And people like me, we are the hearts in these altars, moving the blood of our gods from hand to hand and taking it back and hoarding it when we need to. Tell me, Mr. Barnes, how's your soul doing? Bet you still wish Joanie and what's her face were around. Don't be surprised I know all this about you. I knew when you called. I knew how you pleaded with the clerks. But none of that helped. It amused me, sure. I don't know how many laughs you gave me. You lost your job. You lost your money. You lost your house. You lost your family. I can see inside of you. I can see how small you are inside. Now you're just a pawn in someone else's game and you're trying to turn it into something more than it is. I think you got back to the fear. Might have even found some gods of your own, despite what you said."

"It's so much more than that."

"Is it?"

Myron felt the membrane separate into something like tentacles, reaching up through his shirt and coiling around his neck, around the wound from the dogman. Myron felt no pain.

"Let's be honest, Mr. Barnes. You've said you don't serve gods so the only things you have left are life and death. You're alive, playing the game, being a pawn for some nigger who lives in the sewer, or you can die and hope there is some afterlife to reunite you with your family. Or . . ."

"Or what?"

"Or you can follow me through this door." Chambers motioned to the door behind him. It was the same door Myron had seen back in the real world, looking strangely anomalous amidst the bones and ooze. He'd wondered what was behind it then and he still wondered.

"What's behind the door?"

"Behind the door is the world you left behind. So you can go back to that world and I can make you a very rich man. All that worrying about money you've done over the course of your life would be over. You can start a new family. You can still remember your old family, but you'll have to start this new family just to show them how well you can provide for them. And I could give you the means to provide for them. You would have everything you need. You could give them everything they need. Your sense of worth would finally be restored."

"In return for what?"

"Nothing at all. You will, of course, be serving my gods, but you already said you do not have faith in your gods so, really, what difference does it make?"

"All the difference in the world." Myron raised the ax.

"You don't want to do that."

But he did want to do it. He could stand here and listen to Chambers talk for hours. Promise him things. That was how Chambers had gotten where he was today. Talking. Promises. Getting people to do things for him and offering what in return? Money? For what Chambers was asking for, money seemed a poor compensation.

Myron hoisted the ax above his head and threw it with everything he had before the membranous tentacles could wrap around his arms and restrain him. It sailed toward the pulsing heart of the old gods.

The ax struck Chambers in the shoulder and blood exploded outward. More blood than could possibly have been inside him. It spewed out in a slowly dying fount, covering the room, covering Myron.

The floor tilted beneath Myron. He thought about all those collapsed buildings around it and wondered if this one was collapsing too. Or maybe it was some kind of freakish earthquake.

The building lurched to the other side.

A deafening sound rumbled through the building, up behind the walls.

He reached down to begin tearing the tentacles away. Wrapping his hands around their slimy surface, he could feel the same breathing sensation he had felt since entering the place.

The breaths were further apart than previously.

He continued tearing at the tentacles, not knowing what he would do once he was free.

The building lurched again.

16.

The building was moving. Myron had to find a way out.

With each lurch, the treasure in Chambers' office jostled around. The paper currency stuck to the membrane and blood while the coins and the gold clattered together with a happy jingle. The thickening membrane moved over Chambers, pulling him against the wall, cocooning him. The ax still jutted from his shoulder. The building moved with a slow gait. Myron wished there were windows. He wanted to see the absurd spectacle of this building lumbering down Wall Street, in between the crumbling ruins, trodding on the piles of dead bodies.

He pulled the last coil of membrane from around his ankle.

He moved toward Chambers. He pulled the ax from him. He looked at the heavy door set into the bones and the ooze. He wanted to open it. He wanted to see what was behind it. Would there be some kind of answer or just more nothing?

Myron chopped Chambers free from his cocoon.

He felt the building lift. The trotting gait no longer disrupted the office. Now he had a plunging feeling in his stomach and a feeling of weightlessness.

Was the building flying?

He slung Chambers over his shoulder.

Again he looked at the door. He turned the handle but it wouldn't budge. It didn't turn at all. Myron wondered if the handle was even real. He thrust Chambers up higher on his shoulder so he could hold the ax with both hands. He drew it back and slammed it against the door even though he wasn't sure it was made of wood. Wasn't sure the ax would do any good.

It didn't.

The ax shattered—metal and wood—and it felt like Myron's hands shattered along with it. Deep vibrations rattled through his bones, reaching all the way back to his spine.

He would have to take his chances.

If this wasn't the door Papa Legba was supposed to open then maybe he was making a horrible mistake. But he didn't have any other choices.

He invoked the image of Papa Legba standing by the door. The deity looked at him as if to ask if he was sure this was what he wanted.

Myron nodded.

The door opened.

17.

What he saw beyond was swirling blackness. A dark night over New York or this other world he had fallen into. He walked to the edge of the door. The building was flying. Black water churned below him. The building had been flying but now it seemed to be descending. Chambers had said the building was an altar but could he have been wrong? Could he have been lying? Could the building have been the old god? Could Chambers have been the heart of the old god? And now the old god was trying to go home, to the depths of the ocean, back to some pre-civilization where chaos was the norm?

There were too many questions for Myron.

Perhaps he would ask Mama Hodap about them some other time.

For now, he had to get out of the building. Away from this dying god. He had to go through the door.

He clutched Chambers tightly and leapt through the door.

He felt himself falling rapidly through the rain, felt the water sting his face, saw lightning flash around him.

He closed his eyes and opened them back in Chambers' real office. The one in the Chambers building at the corner of William and Wall.

In one hand he held an ax. In the other hand, he held a black, meaty heart.

The office was still in relative disarray. Blood was everywhere. Todd and Steiner lay on the floor, sprawled out and mauled. A dog sat above each one of them. Both the dogs looked content, panting happily. They made no move to attack Myron.

Money, shit, and stock certificates were mixed in with the blood. The smell was ferociously terrible.

Chambers' desk had been uprighted. Chambers lay on the

surface, naked, the flesh of his torso ripped open to hang in flaps on either side of him.

Myron grabbed a wad of the stock certificates and wrapped them around the heart and put it in the pocket of his worn coat. He wiped his hands on some hundred-dollar bills and let them flutter back down to the floor. Myron left the office and wondered what the police would make of this when they came upon it.

The receptionist area was relatively clean.

He wondered if the sacrifice had been claimed as brutally as she had been in that other world or if she had managed to escape. Had Lora managed to escape?

These were things he would happily put behind him.

He took the service elevator down to the lobby and slinked out the service exit like the under man he was proud to be. He was going back to the bottom. Back below, and he was taking a little piece of this place with him.

Disorientation dizzied him as he stepped back out onto Wall Street.

The furor and chaos had died down.

Most of the brokers had probably gone home.

The whole area felt decompressed.

The streets and sidewalks were wet with rain and there was a chill in the air. He breathed deeply.

"Hey, buddy, ya got my money?"

The hotdog vendor was pushing his cart along the sidewalk. Packing it in for the evening.

"I said I'd pay ya back."

"Hey, buddy, I was just givin ya a hard time. One hotdog ain't gonna kill me, right?"

Myron reached into his pocket and pulled out the two hundred dollars.

"Look, mister, you ain't gotta . . ."

Myron handed him one of the bills.

"I can't take this, mister."

"I insist. You . . . performed an invaluable service. Besides, I still have another one right here, huh? Hey, between you and me—this is free money."

"You steal it?"

"I *look* like a thief?"

"Nah, you look honest."

"Take it and do somethin nice for your wife and kids."

The vendor looked down at the bill and shook his head. "It's been a weird goddamn day."

"For you and me both."

The vendor slipped the bill into his pocket and glanced around suspiciously like he was guilty for having this much money handed to him at once.

"You have a real good evening, mister." The vendor went back to pushing his cart.

Myron turned and walked in the opposite direction, flipping a dismissive wave behind him.

He hailed a cab. He slid into the back. The cabbie was listening to the radio. The market had finished down for the day. Tough economic times were coming, all the experts agreed.

Myron sighed with relief. It felt like all of his tough times were coming to an end.

18.

Later, in the sewer beneath Harlem, after leaving the cabbie with the remaining hundred-dollar bill, Myron watched Mama Hodap's face light up as he presented her with the heart. The other members of the Enclave seemed ecstatic as well. It was a small victory. One they celebrated by roasting the heart over a pitiful fire and dividing it equally before eating.

There were still people like Chambers out there.

Still people who served the old gods.

The news spoke of a collapse and Myron knew this meant the hearts of Wall Street might lie low for a year or two years or maybe even more, if they were really serious about it. But they would be back. They would make another move to stake a claim on the modern world. And Myron and Mama Hodap and the rest of the Enclave would be there to try and stop them.

CANDY HEART

IN THE MIDDLE of the woods, Diane Celine whirled around, her pulse quickening. Sudden movements snapped twigs around her. Her eyes stabbed the moonlit darkness, trying to find the source of the noise. Madness gnawed at her, the culmination of weeks of worry.

If she stopped to think about it, if she stopped to think why she was standing out here in the cold, purplish darkness, beneath the bare trees and the fat moon, she could *almost* see the lunacy of her situation. Almost, but not quite. Maybe another month or two of fruitless searching and she would be there, ready to bow to sanity and run the opposite way . . . but not yet.

Joey was gone. Her madness wouldn't bring him back. She didn't know who would take a six-year-old boy but she had seen the news enough to know it happened all the time.

Yes, those things happened all the time, only the television glass always added just enough of a layer of fiction to them so her thin wall of safety remained. That wall was gone now. All the faceless psychopaths she had heard about on the television had finally found her. Actually, they had found *Joey*. And now she was prepared to do anything necessary to bring him back.

If something in her gut told her to leave the house and come out here to this clearing in the woods then that was exactly what she was going to do. If that gut feeling had told her to wake up and drink a pint of motor oil, she would have done that too. She didn't have to explain herself to anybody and if something happened, if one of those gut instincts panned out and she found Joey, the need for explanations would be erased.

Again, there were those scurrying sounds off in the woods, heavy and so *quick*. Her head whipped to the side, breath spuming out like factory steam.

Probably just a deer, she thought.

Then a pain ripped up her spine and she dropped to the floor of the woods.

The weeks had passed in a darkening whirlwind where some things, mental things—thoughts and memories—were smashed, shattered, or devoured completely.

It began with the morning she woke up and found Joey gone. His father had run out on them a long time ago and now it was just the boy and her, living alone in a ramshackle house between a winter quiet town and hibernating woods. Amazing how she could live alone like that and never have so much as an inkling of fear. Also amazing was how fast the fear could wrap its steel-thick trapjaws around her heart, lungs, and mind.

The day was off, not quite right, from the moment she woke up on the couch in the living room. It took her a couple of minutes to put things together. She was confused, unable to recall the last time she had fallen asleep anywhere except her bed. Maybe she had dropped off while watching television.

She searched her mind for an explanation.

The pills.

It had to be the pills.

She had changed doctors last week and the new doctor (she remembered jokingly referring to him as "the incredibly hairy Dr. Bath" to Joey) had changed her pills. He told her these new ones would still help her sleep at night when the red anxiety crawled all over her skin, but they wouldn't leave her feeling so groggy the next day. She wasn't used to them. That must be why she fell asleep on the couch. But she still couldn't see how that fully explained it. She always doubled up on the old pills during this most special time of the month because they helped with her cramping and bloating as well as her anxiety. Sometimes she thought the pills were like some magical cure all. Now if they could just take care of excess weight, depression, and a tight financial situation . . .

Not only had she passed out on the couch, she had also overslept. The angle of the meager February light coming in from the windows told her she should already be at work and Joey should already be at school.

With her heart pounding and her head in a foggy spin she started to run down the hall and wake Joey before something caught her eye.

Glass double doors faced the woods, taking up half of one wall in the living room. It provided a good view. It was one of the things that made her decide to rent this place upon walking into it, despite it being a little out of her price range. There was something smeared across the doors—a clear, hardened substance—something that reminded her of snot.

She stopped before turning into the dim hallway. A thought popped into her head, reaffirming her assertions that she *needed* the pills she took. She had to get rid of whatever that was on the doors. She would not be able to think of anything else until it was gone. She would yell at Joey and be tense all day at work if she knew that single streak of yuckiness was still there.

Rushing into the bathroom, she grabbed some paper towels and Windex, opened the double doors and vigorously cleaned the snot-like substance from them. The streak was about six inches wide and, at its arc, reached her chest. It made her think of a large drooly dog. Maybe a coyote, she thought, for she had heard them howling at night.

Once the streak was gone, she immediately felt a little more clear-headed, now able to go wake up Joey and get ready for work.

She glanced into her bedroom as she passed it and noticed a light flashing from her answering machine. A digital red "2" blinked repeatedly as she approached it.

Shit, she thought. The first was probably Joey's school, calling to find out where he was. The school would have probably called her work, also. The other message was probably from work.

Way to get everyone all worried, sleepyhead. How was she going to excuse Joey? Give him a note letting the teacher know that his mom was an anxiety-ridden pill popper?

She hit the play button and listened to the messages robotically spurt from the machine while she hurried to Joey's room, not knowing why she now felt so sure he wasn't going to be in his bed. Until that point, that pinprick of panic, she had simply thought he would be in there sleeping because she had not woken him.

Please let that feeling be wrong.

She saw a lump in the covers and her hopes rose until she reached the bed and punched down on the hollow fabric, feeling nothing, her heart beginning to steadily increase its rate.

She could only hope one of the messages was from Joey or somebody who could tell her he was safe and sound. It *was* perfectly possible he had woken up on his own, gotten dressed, and gone out to wait for the bus. But he just seemed too young for that.

Her feelings were right about the messages. One of them from Joey's school, one of them from work. Both of them sounded vaguely concerned but more concerned with her complete failure to call and report either of these absences than any kind of panicked, *genuine* concern like that which now surged through her body.

The alarm she felt held court with an overwhelming sense of guilt. The last time she had seen Joey, she had sent him to bed early because he had scattered little candy hearts she had bought for him on Valentine's Day around the house. She had been incredibly mad at him. Even after yelling at him about the mess, he had tried to smuggle some of the hearts into bed with him, the palm of his sweaty little hand multi-colored pastel after she pried them from it.

She spent the next hour searching the house inside and out, not finding anything.

He was gone. How could she have let this happen? Before letting panic punch a devastating hole in her sanity, she tried to seize on the only rational explanation.

His father had somehow found a way into the house and lured the boy away. He had been threatening to do that ever since the divorce three years ago and now she figured he probably had. A secret part of her, buried beneath the hate and resentment, almost *wanted* this to be the case. At least then she knew he would be safe, or as safe as a child could be in the company of a womanizing alcoholic.

Now she figured his father could probably make an actual case for gaining custody of Joey, coming into the house to find her whacked out of her skull on sleeping pills, completely neglecting Joey's education and her means for financial support. What would it matter that he had only before come to see Joey sporadically, at best? Or that he had paid her exactly nothing in child support?

She wanted to call the bum, but she just couldn't bring herself to do that. He would just lie to her or try to make her feel smaller than she already felt.

She did the only thing she could think was left to do. She called the police. Officer Branson was very kind to her. He asked all the right questions. He kept her calm. He asked her about her ex-husband, Stanley. Surprisingly, she was able to answer most of the officer's questions in a reasonably intelligent manner, even though it felt like her brain or her heart was going to swell and pop out of her body. Branson assured her they would contact the police in Stanley's area and have them check out the situation.

That afternoon, she called Officer Branson again, wanting to know if they had any leads. Branson told her they had questioned Stanley and were not under the impression he had Joey. Stanley had let them come in and search his house without a warrant.

She had already known this. Stanley had called her as soon as the officers left, out of his head with anger and frustration. Of course he blamed her and she didn't think she had a right to disagree with him. He said he was going to search on his own before hanging up the phone.

That evening, the police came to her house, dusting for prints, looking for any evidence of a break-in. Other officers searched the woods, questioning the occupants of the houses located closest to hers.

The next day, Diane broadened her own search to the woods. As the investigation progressed, she went back there every day, mentally mapping the dead trees as landmarks so she wouldn't end up searching the same area over and over. Sometime during the second week, she found something that gave her both a sense of dread and a faint glimmer of hope.

She almost didn't notice it at first. It could have been any tiny piece of debris. It was the *color* that caught her eye. Bending to pick it up, she saw that it was a pastel green candy heart.

The inscription on the tiny heart said: MAYBE.

She knew it was stupid. She knew it meant no more than what the kings of holiday commercialization intended it to mean but, under these circumstances, it seemed to contain some kind of mystical prophecy, like a girl on a first date opening a fortune cookie that says, "You have found the love of your life."

Maybe, she thought. *Maybe he is out here.*

She continued to search the woods all through the bitter cold days. She didn't know what she was looking for and she didn't know how she would be able to deal with it if she actually came upon his dead body lying out there somewhere.

All of her searching led to nothing. Only more panic, more depression, more guilt, an increased feeling of doom.

Down on her knees in the woods, a month later, staring longingly at the pale moon, everything came back to her.

The new medicine wasn't working.

The old pills had kept this . . . this *changing* away. Images of this night the previous month flashed through her dulling mind, before what was human was completely devoured by what was animal. There was just enough human left to grasp those fleeting animal images and feelings.

She had locked herself outside because she felt strange and she hadn't felt that way since before Joey was born and she knew what feeling that way meant.

She had tried to get into the house, tried so desperately, beating her snout against the door until she finally found one flimsy enough to batter open.

Only she hadn't had to batter it open at all. It opened for her. And Joey stood on the other side, looking at her with a combination of awe and fear until he realized what was in front of him. He took off running for his room, screaming. She had dragged him out here. He had yelled for her to stop. And she had tried to communicate to him that his time had come.

Oh my God, she thought. Had she murdered her own son? But before she could answer herself, those thoughts were gone, surrendered to the animal thoughts, the ones that could only focus on hunger and scent and desire.

Jeff Branson didn't know what the hell he was seeing. He didn't know why this shit always happened to him. He guessed that was what he got for trying to be a responsible officer, a good cop.

He wasn't even on duty, but there was something about the Celine woman's case that had really gotten to him. He didn't have any children of his own but, if he did, he would want to know that, should one of them go missing, the law would do everything in its power to bring them back. Jeff had taken a very active interest in her. It probably didn't hurt that he was single and she was single and not at all bad looking. He reassured himself it was more than that. The FBI and the state police, though informed of the disappearance, didn't really seem to be doing a damned thing about it. Diane had called him and told him about the clue, the little candy heart, and that had given him renewed desire to search for the boy.

Every chance he got, he had come out here to the woods behind the house. He didn't think it would hurt anything to wander around in the woods with his shotgun. If another clue didn't turn up then he figured that, at the very least, he might be able to bag a deer. Part of him wanted to tell the woman the boy was gone, that he probably would not be seen again. That was what his gut told him. It seemed like he had been through this too many times before. Not here, of course. Things like this didn't happen in Twin Springs, Ohio. But, fresh out of the academy, he had served on the Orlando force for three years. That had been enough for him. He couldn't find any comfortable resolution with the little children like he could manage with teenagers. Teenagers had ways of taking care of themselves. Some of them just ran off. Some of them were mixed up in really weird shit. Children did not just run off. They were usually taken. And the people taking them usually did not have wholesome goals in mind.

So tonight he had put on his plain clothes, his heavy winter jacket, grabbed his shotgun from his house, and come out here to wait. Maybe he had heard too many horror stories but he had visions of some crazy, child-abducting family living out here in the woods. They were probably cannibals, to boot. He knew there were a few communes on the surrounding farms. While many people saw this as a nearly Utopian attempt at peaceful coexistence, he could only think of the Manson family and cults. And he was hoping to catch one of them passing back and forth here in the deep night hours, thinking they were operating in complete secrecy.

Branson was more than a little surprised when he saw Diane stumble into the woods. He was going to approach her until he noticed she acted differently than the woman who had presented herself in front of him before. She seemed, not so much hysterical, as *wild*. He decided to watch and see what she was going to do, where she was going to go.

Suddenly, she stopped in the clearing and fell to her knees. He would have dismissed what happened next as complete fiction if he wasn't observing it firsthand.

The woman grew large. Hair sprouted out all over her body.

A werewolf, Branson thought, wanting to dismiss the idea as ludicrous as soon as it popped into his head.

But it was hard to dismiss as ludicrous when he could stand there and watch the face reach out into a snout, the teeth elongate and yellow, the ears grow and bend back, the clothes rip and fall away, the legs and arms deform, lowering the woman. He'd seen this occur in a number of horror movies and had always wondered why the person just stood around and watched this transformation happen. It never went quickly. Why didn't they just plug them? He figured it was just one of those movie anomalies, something that had to happen and shouldn't be thought about too much. But here he was thinking about it. Hell, here he was *doing* it. And he had the answer. Because a werewolf is not just a monster. It's almost always a person the watcher knows. And maybe they know that person as a decent person. It wasn't like the movies where the good guy hunts down the serial killer and stands paralyzed while the psycho soliloquizes.

Now fully formed, Diane sniffed at the ground, looking hungrily up at the moon. Branson crouched down but it didn't matter. She had already seen him. The doglike thing turned its head in his direction and growled, baring those sharp yellow teeth.

Now that it was a matter of self-defense, Branson took aim with the rifle and fired as the wolf lunged across the clearing at him. He doubted his bullets were silver and wondered if that even mattered.

He pressed the trigger again and again. The first shotgun blast sheared off the wolf's right front paw. The second blast took off a hunk of the snout, collapsing the thing. After the second shot, the gun only clicked as Branson pulled the trigger. Empty. He stayed where he was, just slightly occluded behind the bare shrubs.

The body of the wolf slowly turned back into the Celine woman. Branson felt like this would probably spell his end as a police officer. It was frowned upon to kill the people who you were trying to help. He felt certain he would eventually have to draw someone's attention to this naked, shot-up body that happened to belong to a woman he had somewhat openly taken a "special interest" in.

Another sound from the far end of the clearing.

What now? Branson thought.

Then he saw Joey. At least, he thought it *had* to be Joey. It was a smaller wolf than the one he had just shot and even though it was completely animal there was something about it that made Branson think of all those pictures Diane had shown him prior to the search. It was like watching a cartoon where the animated character vaguely resembles the actor doing the voiceover. The wolf strolled out into the clearing, approaching the body on the ground. It licked at the woman, nuzzling its wet nose against her neck and Branson swore he heard a whimper that sounded very much like a human cry.

The wolf looked into the woods where Branson crouched and issued a growl. Then it came at him. He couldn't load his gun fast enough. The wolf threw itself on Branson, its jaws gnashing in front of his face and Branson smelled, just faintly, the sugary smell of candy hearts. He wanted to laugh with the absurdity of it all but sharp teeth tore through his jugular and he was pretty sure he would never laugh again.

THE PHOTOGRAPHER

VERNER STOOD ON the balcony of his 23rd floor penthouse suite. The city, with all of her glittering lights, still seemed cold to him. Despite the warm breeze coming in off the Pacific, the city was still cold. Was the feeling one of physical cold or was it one of isolation? That wasn't a question Verner asked a lot. Truthfully, he didn't really give a damn. It didn't really matter the city held all the grandeur and mystery of a corpse laid out on an autopsy table. What mattered to Verner was the power he held over the city. Like the woman in the other room, the city was something he would demolish.

Only, the woman in the other room wasn't really a woman at all, was she? No, Verner admitted to himself, she was probably just a girl. He doubted if she was more than fifteen or sixteen. Didn't matter now, did it? His business with her was done. How many others like her had there been? Countless, like the cold cities he moved through. Countless. Worthless.

Verner pulled his silk robe around his freshly bathed body and lit a Dunhill. He sighed, blowing out a stream of smoke. Tomorrow, he had to go into the Santo Corporation and tell the company president which people to terminate. It would be roughly half the corporation. Santo was the largest employer in the city. The move would be devastating. Tomorrow, as he had been so many days in the past, Verner would be God. As mysterious as God, too. The people who would find themselves without a job would never see him, would never know his name.

Verner went back into the expansive penthouse, figuring he'd have a scotch before retiring for the evening. He reminded himself to call a cab for the mess in the bedroom before completely retiring. Bringing the cigarette up to his mouth, he noticed a speck of dried blood under his thumbnail. Must have missed it in the shower, he thought. He sat down on the couch and took the top off a large, ornate wooden box sitting slightly crooked on the glass coffee table. That's where he kept all the random things like fingernail clippers, lighters, batteries—all the stuff there wasn't much of another place to put. Instead of the miscellany he usually saw, there rested a letter-sized envelope.

That's odd, he thought. He couldn't quite remember tossing it in there. Before eagerly tearing into the envelope, he noticed it hadn't come through the postal network. No return address. No postmark. Maybe it was something he'd carried home from one of the corporations.

He took out the few small pictures and it all came back to him.

It must have been a little more than thirty years ago now. The air raid had flushed them out. Well, the air raid had dropped the bombs that flushed them out. Verner's decimated troop was so terrified they were simply mowing down anything in their way.

Verner wasn't terrified, though. Each night, he slept soundly, awaking in the morning with a feeling of exhilaration rushing through his veins. War was quite simply a game where the strongest, the most cunning, survived. Verner had no doubt he was the strongest, both mentally and physically. There was slow-witted Tibbs from Tennessee. Wallace from someplace like North Dakota who always thought a snake was going to slither up and bite him while he shat. Bergman from New Hampshire acted like he'd rather be in Canada or Mexico, anywhere but here. There were others. Verner hated them as much as he did the people on the other side. More, probably, since he had to listen to all of their idiotic little conversations that usually involved the girl back home. Verner wanted to tell them that girl was undoubtedly getting her brains fucked out by some guy who was just waiting for them to leave—in short, someone like Verner.

Yeah, the bombs flushed them out.

And Verner and the rest surrounded the ramshackle village, waiting for them to run through the smoke jabbering their idiotic mutant chatter. That's when they opened fire, aiming for the nameless figures. Sometimes, it amazed him to see how many came running.

Off to his right, he noticed one of them running away.

"Three o'clock!" Verner shouted to Tibbs.

"Fuck! Let it go!" Tibbs shouted back. If it hadn't been for the bullets in Tibbs' gun, bullets that may eventually find their way into the enemy, Verner would have killed Tibbs, simply because of the weak look in his eyes.

Verner took off toward the figure. Of all the ones he hated, he hated the ones who almost got away the most. This one was fast, running in a jagged pattern. Verner didn't fall for it. He kept straight on, waiting for the smallest mistake. He got close enough to the figure to be able to tell that it was a woman. This spurned him on even more. The figure darted off to her left, a little wider, and Verner continued straight.

After a couple of seconds, he cut quickly to his left, holding his gun diagonally across his torso, thrusting himself into a collision. She was the one who went down, of course.

Sprawled on the ground, panic danced in her eyes.

To make sure she wouldn't be going anywhere, Verner brought the butt of the gun down on her ankle. He circled her, the sound of gunshots rolling in the distance, the pealing screams of someone cracking up or melting down. He could already feel himself stiffening.

That had been only one incident. There were a number of others. He'd probably been mythologized as some kind of monster in their language. He never killed them. No, that was too easy and, in the end, did death really make much of a point or was it just something that had to happen? No, what Verner did was much worse than death—and much more memorable.

The girl in the other room moaned. Probably just cleaning out a wound, Verner thought.

After looking at the first photograph, Verner had moved back out onto the balcony. There were several more. All of them in vivid color. The dominant color was red. Verner dragged on his cigarette. What was it he felt? Pride? Maybe, a little bit. Confusion? Probably. How the hell had the pictures got there and, more importantly, who had taken them? It was a question that couldn't be answered, of course. It was like a paradox. Who takes the pictures when there's no one around? It certainly wasn't him. That would have been too messy.

But there was another feeling Verner felt. A new feeling. It was the feeling of inconsolable dread.

Verner turned and let the pictures float down over the city, vulgar confetti.

The heavy door to his bedroom creaked loud enough for Verner to hear it out on the balcony.

The figure that came out wasn't the young girl he'd taken in there just hours before. The only thing similar was the smooth skin hanging from the seeping organic shape inside. A row of faces descended down the front of its torso. All of them similar, none of them the same. All were recognizable.

"Someone had to die!" Verner barked at the monstrosity. Claws like razors came out from what Verner guessed were the hands. They clicked against the coffee table.

It spoke in the soft voice of the girl he'd picked up that night. The one who called herself only "Li."

"Yes," it said. "Someone had to die."

Even though the hybrid was far away from Verner, everything slammed into him at once. He was helpless and he knew it. It moved toward him, standing at the balcony's threshold.

Verner thought about what he'd done to his victims. He couldn't let that happen to himself. He remembered their screams, remembered the way the skin sounded as he tore it apart, remembered the feeling of power as he stood over top of them. He remembered the look in their eyes—the complete absence of sanity. The hybrid reached out those razor fingers, grunting as Verner had when he thrust into those countless girls, all on separate occasions, all together now.

Verner lashed out at the hybrid, gouging at the eyes rapidly emerging from the filmy skin. Anger numbed him to the slashing razors. He braced himself against the railing, kicking out with his bare feet. The hybrid got hold of his feet and swung them around, sending Verner to dangle over the city, his hands clutching the top of the railing. The hybrid stood there for a moment, making sure each of its myriad eyes took in Verner's situation. Then, as slowly as it had come out to the balcony, it reached out a hand and gracefully sliced through Verner's fingers.

With a final shout, he fell away from the balcony, plummeting down into the cold bowels of the hot city.

The hybrid watched as its personal demon, *their* personal demon, bombed his way down into the darkness. Turning away from the city, the hybrid split apart, beautifying itself, becoming countless, becoming whole.

CRUEL WOMEN WITH WHIPLIKE SMILES

HUTCHENS TOOK UP space in his customary seat in the back corner of the bar for quite a while before he saw the woman come in. Sitting in that particular spot allowed him to see everyone coming and going. A few moments before her entrance, Hutchens was about ready to call it a night. The smoke in the club seemed a little too thick. The alcohol had gone to his head, making him tired rather than exuberant. The house band's rendition of "Kind of Blue" seemed to drone on endlessly and the trumpeter sounded like Miles Davis if Miles had chosen to play the trumpet with his ass.

When the woman came in the door, alone, there was one of those unique pauses in everything. Even the music seemed to stop for a few seconds. All the old cliches were resurrected, ringing with a new truth. Every man watched her because they wanted to be with her. Every woman watched her because they wanted to be her. What it came down to, he supposed, was rape and envy.

She took a seat, by herself, at the far end of the bar. What life it had rushed back into the club. Hushed conversations of girlfriends chastising their boyfriends inevitably blossomed even though the women knew perfectly well why their boyfriends were staring. But Hutchens didn't have to hear any of that tonight. He didn't have to look into angry eyes, the anger only a thin coating over the jealousy—that wounded jealousy that was somehow worse than the anger. No, none of that tonight. Tonight he was alone.

He lit a cigarette and stared at the woman. She sat sideways on the barstool, her legs crossed beneath an above-the-knee jade dress. Nothing fancy. It didn't have to be. She held her drink in her left hand and watched the band intently. He found himself admiring every touch—her jet black hair pulled back and swept off her neck, her red lips, her black choker and black fingernails and the pale white skin coming out of the dress like smoke. For once, he was glad this was one of the most well-lighted clubs in town.

The band finally finished its number and the woman put her glass down to clap quietly. As she clapped, her lips drew back into what she may have thought was a smile. But there was something about the smile, something insincere and mocking, something that demonstrated how an object of true beauty can never really appreciate what is beneath it. That's when Hutchens realized he had to approach her.

These cruel women with whiplike smiles were exactly the type of women he went for. Actually, they were the only ones he could approach. There was apparently something weak and motherless about him, for these women said yes much more than he would ever have thought likely, undoubtedly realizing their sadistic control would be appreciated. And when they said no, well, it was to be expected and he didn't feel any less about himself.

Hutchens teetered toward the woman and sat rather gracelessly on the empty stool beside her. It was enough to put him in the range of her scent, which was also flawless. It was somehow very dark and clean and exotic, if that were possible.

When he turned to look at her, he noticed that she was already looking at him and he almost lost his nerve.

He wasn't a line kind of guy and all women, even cruel women with whiplike smiles, made him nervous. He said the first thing that popped into his head:

"I'm a chronic masturbator."

She didn't laugh, only smiled that enticing half-smile.

She looked at him for a long time, the way a man looks at a woman when he thinks she doesn't see him, before speaking. "I'm not much of a conversationalist either. I think we both know why you came over. Would you like to see where I live? Maybe we can do something about your problem."

Before he could answer, she noiselessly slid off the stool and headed for the front door. He followed, bathing in the scent unfurling behind her.

He followed her out into the welcome cool of the parking lot.

"Would you like to follow me?" she said.

"Sure," he said and went to get in his own car.

As he slid into his car he saw her pull around in a small black

Mercedes. *All that and money, too,* he thought.

Staying as close behind her as possible, he followed her out into the countryside. She managed to go ten to twenty miles over the speed limit the entire time. Within the confines of his small Chevrolet, its lawnmower engine wheezing and groaning, he felt like she had to be having a lot easier time than he was. They sped around twists and turns, up and down small hills, out into the low, flat country where the huge plantation houses were scattered sparsely, set back off the road. With one of these illuminated, monolithic structures looming in the distance, the woman slowed down and turned onto a blacktopped driveway.

I should just drive on, he thought. *I have to be in way over my head.* Suddenly, he felt like a mouse in the hands of a sadistic cat.

A large, luminescent fountain bubbled in front of the house, the moonlight sparkling over the black water. The woman pulled her car around the arch in the driveway and he pulled in after her.

The woman got out of her car and, without acknowledging him in the least, went straight to her front door. He followed her through the cavernous, darkened house and into her kitchen. She grabbed two wineglasses and a bottle and continued with her strident pace. He almost wanted to call, "Hey, wait up!"

The word "agenda" came to mind and he started to wonder what hers was. Maybe she had found out her husband was having an affair and this was her way of making up for it. Other things crossed his mind. *Or maybe,* he thought. *Maybe she's just like you and this is all she wants. Just one night that neither party will remember too well years in the future.*

Maybe, he thought.

She led him through the house and out the back doors. Once outside they were in a huge garden, the like of which he had never seen before. Back there was another fountain, this one smaller, in the middle of the garden. There were also a number of statues—almost enough to be gaudy—arranged sporadically throughout the garden, a small underlight illuminating each one of them. There were men and women in various poses and they reminded him of the sculptures of Roman gods.

The woman split off the cobblestone walkway and, kicking off her shoes, sat down on a mat of depressed ornamental grass. She looked up at him before he sat down, her mouth twisting into that malicious little smirk and there was a look in her eyes that told him exactly what she wanted. Following her lead, he kicked off his shoes, peeled off his socks, and took a seat next to her.

"Do you drink wine?" she asked.

"Yeah. You know, I'm not real picky."

"If you were, you wouldn't have a problem with this at all. I could tell you that it was Rollin 1946, but you wouldn't know what that was, would you?"

"No. I definitely wouldn't. Stuff's a little out of my price range," he said, immediately feeling kind of dumb.

"Well, then let it be a mystery to you." She picked the bottle up and held it, her large eyes running up and down the length. "I need to go back in and get the corkscrew. I always forget the corkscrew." It sounded filthy, the way she said "corkscrew."

She stood up and moved back into the house. He picked up the bottle. It contained no label or anything hinting at its contents. *Well, this is it,* he thought. *She's brought me here to poison me.* But he couldn't see how that would benefit her at all. Then she would just have a dead body on her hands.

The woman came bouncing back out with her hands full. She sat back down across from him, childishly criss-crossing her legs. "Would you like to do the honors?" She handed him the corkscrew.

He went to work on opening the bottle.

"What's your name, by the way?" she asked.

"Oh, Elliot. Yours?"

"Magdalena."

"That's beautiful."

"That's trite. But thanks."

The cork came out with a small pop. He smelled the opening and was surprised at the sweetness of it. He had lied when he told her he would drink anything. He hated wine almost as much as he hated champagne. "This is a nice place you have here."

"Thanks. You state the obvious really well."

"Are you married?"

She laughed. "Of course. Why? Does it matter? Besides, why do you ask?"

He couldn't really give an answer. He didn't mind at all. As he approached middle age, he found married women to be the most abundant.

"Because you don't know any rich women? A woman can't have a nice house and drive a nice car if she's not married?"

"*No.* I only asked because you seem pretty . . ."

"Forthright?"

"Yeah, I guess. Is he coming home soon?"

"Let me give you a quick lesson about the female psyche, Elliot. Women want fucked as much as men. Maybe more, sometimes. A man could probably get off by rubbing up against a tree but it's not that easy for a woman. We ache. And the ache is way up inside and it has to be teased, coaxed, or simply beaten out. Only then do we get release. We may be a little pickier than men but the longing, believe me, is still there. The only difference is that a woman doesn't have to work to get fucked. We can . . ."

"Just go to a bar and sit down?"

"Exactly. Unless she's married. Then she gets to fuck when the husband wants to fuck." Again, her mouth formed that derisive smirk. "Here, hold this." She handed him one of the wineglasses and filled it full.

"Shall we toast?" he asked.

"To . . . to . . .?"

"To fucking," he said.

"And the night," she finished. They clicked glasses and quickly polished off the first round.

Magdalena was right. She wasn't much of a conversationalist. They sat in relative silence and drank a couple more glasses of wine. He found it quite agreeable. He sprawled out in the grass and looked up at the fat moon, listened to the night birds call out to each other from their separate cells of isolation, watched the slow flapping of the trees and the unmoving grandeur of those statues.

Startling him, Magdalena sprang to her feet and said, "Catch me if you can," and took off running through the garden.

Hutchens, battling with his alcohol-soaked body, struggled to his feet and trudged in the direction she had gone although he could no longer see her. Slowly, he stepped his pace up to a slow trot and jogged around the flowers and shrubs, undoubtedly trampling some of them. Once he got about halfway around the perimeter of the garden, he stopped, winded.

"Magdalena!" he called.

Some feeling other than drunkenness settled into his bones. Now he thought for sure the wine had to be spiked or poisoned or adulterated in some fashion or the other. The whole garden brightened somewhat, became somehow richer, like all the green seemed to stand out, painting itself over a black, foggy canvas.

"Magdalena!" he called again. *Shit,* he thought, *what the hell kind of game is she playing?*

After thinking that, he saw something like a path open up—a green, liquid path. It wound around a series of small yew trees and disappeared behind a huge magnolia. Now he started to feel a duel sensation. His skin and viscera felt light, his hair stood up all over his body, shivers down the spine, like it was all trying to crawl away from him. But from the middle of his body—his lower stomach spreading down to his sex—he felt a heavy thickening. This animal desire combined with a revelatory high gave him renewed zeal in seeking out Magdalena. He was going to give her what they both came here for. Relishing in the intensity surrounding him, he slowly started down the path floating through the garden like an ethereal river.

Visions ripped through his mind. He made no effort to try and force them out. The red raging fires of hell gave way to a group of sweaty, naked primitives, background drums beating as they coupled with wild ferocity. He saw a shimmering blue church and heard, from within the church and somewhere very far away, the slow chanting of "Ave Maria." A whip came down on a sublimely porcelain and feminine back, lighting a red gash. Lightning ripped through a dark sky. Waves pounded a black coast. He saw dripping, hairless vaginas and throbbing, ejaculating cocks. He could smell lilac, the mighty river, the sultry air of the Gulf and somewhere, even farther away, the scent of Magdalena.

He crept behind the magnolia and saw her there, standing still. She took off running through the dew-slicked grass, back toward the house. Determined not to lose her this time, those visions still raging through his head, those feelings still surging through his body, he chased after her.

She splashed through the fountain and threw herself down in the grass on the other side of the walk, her dress sliding back on her thighs. Hutchens landed on her, shoving that dress up above her waist and taking down his pants and underwear with one motion. The only thing he could think about was tearing her apart. He forced her legs open and moved up inside of her moistness.

Magdalena grunted hungrily as he thrust up into her. She ripped his shirt off and bit his chest. He moved one hand under her ass and the other behind her head, moving it around to the neckline of her dress, yanking it down and kneading her breasts. Lasting only a few short minutes, he experienced everything—heard the wet grind of their skin, the soft and rhythmic rasps in her throat, felt the pumping of her blood around him. He shivered to a climax and rolled off beside her.

They lay there for a few moments, breathing heavily.

"Would you follow me anywhere?" Magdalena asked.

"Yes," he replied.

"Will you follow me inside?"

"Yes."

But maybe dreams were just starting to mix with reality because he didn't really remember saying anything at all and after they had this exchange they both still lay there. He felt too heavy to move. It felt like he was sinking into the soft mat of grass and he couldn't imagine her house, however accommodating it looked, being more comfortable than that patch of grass under that moon with that thick night air washing over his skin.

Then he watched as Magdalena stood up and sloughed off the scrap of green dress. She reached down for him from somewhere impossibly far away and he felt his hand in hers and his body slowly rising to its feet. She kept her arm behind her, leading him along. He looked at her exposed backside, the red marks from his rough hands smudged along her back and buttocks.

She led him back to their original spread. Her hands were all over him, pressing one of his arms down to his side and crossing his other arm between his chest and his stomach. Magdalena got down on her knees before him and closed her mouth around his cock. He looked down at her and she returned his stare. Her eyes were green and vibrant. Was that the first time he had noticed her eyes were green?

She took her mouth away and said, "I love to taste myself," before going back to her suckling. He felt his sex stiffen again. He looked up at the sky and then back down. She held a cup, wine remnants sloshing around the bottom, and pulled her mouth away just before he came into the liquid.

Magdalena stood up and held the cup to his mouth. "Would you like to taste yourself?" she whispered into his ear, her hot breath running down his spine.

He wanted to object, knock the cup away or something, but he couldn't move. She put the cup to his lips and tilted it up. He felt the warm liquid slide down his throat and hit his stomach and then felt like he had to be sleeping because he couldn't move and everything was black.

Slowly, the blackness of night gave way to the gray dawn. A cacophony of birds unleashed itself upon the garden. He thought he must have gone to sleep out there and tried to roll over, half-expecting to see Magdalena still sleeping beside him, but he couldn't move. He looked around the garden, verdant and dripping with life. He looked at the statues, the well-built men and women, dark gray with the night's dew. They were full of life, too, weren't they? he asked himself. A sickening dread hardened the inside of his body when he realized his fate.

Time was not a factor. For days, weeks maybe, he drifted in and out of consciousness. Every now and then Magdalena came into the garden, sometimes to sketch, sometimes just to take her morning coffee, sometimes to take a lover and drink wine, the last thing Hutchens had tasted, mingled with the last bit of life he had. Other times, she brought patrons out to the garden, told them lies about the statues. Sometimes the patrons offered her vulgar amounts of money for them. Smirking with the knowledge that she had things people wanted, Magdalena sent them away disappointed. Sometimes she would stand in front of the statues, staring up at them. It was at these times he wanted to be free, but only so he could once again feel Magdalena's skin in his hands and lose himself in that whiplike smile and those clover eyes.

AIR CATHEDRAL

THE ROOM CHOKED on blue dawn bitterness.

"Why don't you show me?" Arthur asked the bleeding heap, the mere puddle of a human, behind him. Arthur did not look at the priest when he asked him this question. He sat in the old wooden chair, a blood-stained Styrofoam cup of cold coffee in his right hand, a burning cigarette in his left, staring out of the partially open window in front of him.

The man on the floor behind him didn't say anything. Of course he didn't say anything. Arthur figured he was probably dead. Beyond dead, even. Mutilated. Arthur fought the urge to turn around and look at him. To study him as some people study paintings, sculptures, or the beauty of a chosen sex.

He wanted to look at the priest because he thought the priest could show him something. Arthur still wasn't sure what this something was, but he knew it was there. It had to be in one of his victims or else his work had all been fruitless.

How many had there been?

It was countless.

Only, it wasn't really countless at all. Eighty-six. That was a very exact count. Eighty-six priests going back twelve years.

Arthur didn't know why he had chosen priests.

No, that wasn't true either. He chose the priests because they were eager for someone to hear their confessions. And Arthur was that person. Before using the knife or the gun or, in this case, the drill, he listened to their confessions. Everyone had confessions, he was sure, but there was something about the priests' confessions that seemed weightier. Maybe it was because they, after hearing so many confessions themselves, knew how to tell a confession. Or maybe it was because their confessions were somehow entwined with all the confessions they had heard over the years, like the confessions they'd heard were some kind of bassy backbeat to their own.

Some of the priests' confessions were quite nasty. Some of them made what Arthur was doing look like the work of a saint. Others were beautiful. These were the ones Arthur had the most faith in. These were the ones that filled him with the most hope.

Ultimately, he guessed he had initially sought out his first priest because that was who he had first shared his confession with. It wasn't just a confession. It was a dream. It was a life's journey. It was something he knew he had to find. He wasn't sure if it was a place or just a something, some disembodied structure lodged in the reaches of his subconscious, but he knew it existed and that it was out there somewhere.

Come to think of it, it was hardly a confession at all. When he had told that first priest, it was more like a statement or a declaration. The priest had scoffed at him. Told him it was all metaphor. Tried to tell him he was on the path to righteousness and he needed to follow the footsteps of Christ.

But, well, Christ had never done *this*.

Now he sat on the third floor of an old abandoned warehouse, looking out over the city, where people were just filtering out of their apartments, getting into their cars and going off to work. This was a world he was not part of. There was a certainty to this thought. A certainty that could not be denied.

This was a time of reflection for Arthur. Reflecting was something he was not a stranger to. He sat there and wondered why he had chosen this particular priest. It wasn't just accessibility. No. It was something in the old man's eyes. They were the same blue Arthur had seen in the sockets of a hundred Irish Catholic priests but there was something else to this man. There was a certain twinkle, a certain knowledge. And the complete ease with which this priest (who would not give Arthur his name) died hinted at something greater. Perhaps this man contained the peace and serenity Arthur had sought for so long.

He set his cup of coffee down on the splintered wood windowsill, tossing the burnt nub of his cigarette into its dregs. He stood up and knocked the chair over as he did so.

"You're the one," he said as he stalked over to the body of the priest. "You have to be."

The priest was a mess. Arthur's gorge threatened to kick up as he approached him, knelt down beside him.

Arthur reached into the wound running down the priest's torso, pulling it open with his hands, leaning down into the sick warmth of his body, the smell of early decay already there.

He swooned, his balance thrown off. He pitched forward and thrust his arm out, his hand hit the blood-sticky wall and he hovered above the priest, drunk off the rush of scent rolling around in his head.

He stood up and walked back over to the window.

Time had jumped forward.

This was not unusual for Arthur. Strange gaps in memory. Time racing forward. No, not racing, *jumping*, like frames cut from a film. He was here, he was still here, but everything and everyone around him was suddenly five minutes or a half an hour ahead. He had to catch up with it, time, them. He felt dragged along, a slight nausea slithering in the back of his head as he stepped into the present.

Time jumped forward. It always did.

The city bustled now. Thronging with a thick presence seemingly borne out of its hard, manufactured surface, the city bustled. Car horns. Shouting. The whole sick and violent world thrown into motion for yet another day. He looked west out the window, over the buildings, toward the heart of the city and that was when he saw it.

This was the first time he had seen it in twelve years and this time, this time, it wasn't just some image from a dream. It was something in front of him. In the distance but still vast. Vast and real, as solid as it could ever be and very much *there*.

The air cathedral.

He didn't know of any other way to describe it. It was like all the cathedrals of his boyhood only this one was more immense and promising and looked like something Dalí would have painted. It wasn't simply a bricks and mortar cathedral floating in the sky. It looked like it was actually inscribed in the air. There and not there at the same time.

A feeling came over him that he couldn't describe. Seeing the cathedral was not enough. He had to be inside of it. He had to walk its crystalline halls and look down at the strange worlds it hovered over.

Arthur walked back over to the priest.

"How do I get there? I know you know. How do I get there?"

But the priest wasn't talking.

Arthur went back over to the window. He shoved the window all the way up, never looking away from the cathedral glittering in the air miles ahead of him. He thought about jumping from the window but couldn't put that much faith in anything like that. And if he was wrong, that would mean his quest was over. He also thought about running through the street, never taking his eyes off the cathedral, just running until it was right above him. But one did not run down crowded city streets while covered in blood and reeking of death.

So he sat on the ledge, only to be closer to the cathedral, feeling the cold wind swirl up from the cold street.

It was truly beautiful, how it hung there in the sky, looking more like a castle than a place of worship.

Then things got jumbled up inside of Arthur's head. He didn't know what happened but, suddenly, he desperately wanted to be off the narrow window ledge. He wanted to be back in the room, his feet planted firmly on the ground. But he couldn't seem to move and when he finally managed to turn his head around, the priest was there behind him, smothering him in that bloody scent.

This could not be happening, Arthur's mind shouted. This could not be happening. Arthur faced the priest, noting the way the air cathedral gleamed in the reflection of each eye.

"You wanted me to show you," the priest spoke through vocal cords Arthur had ruined hours ago. "You wanted me to show you and I did."

Arthur wanted to speak. He wanted to argue with the man but a loud bleating was the only thing that came out.

"And now you want me to take you there."

The priest pulled Arthur back into the room. The room was now full of people, all dressed similarly to the priest. Arthur didn't have to count them to know how many of them he would find. There were eighty-six of them in there and something screamed inside Arthur's head. These people were not priests. They were not priests at all.

"We can take you there," the priest said. "It is not a pretty place."

Suddenly, Arthur didn't want to go. He didn't know what he had been doing all these years. It fell away. His whole journey fell away or, rather, he realized that maybe it wasn't *his* journey but *their* journey. He felt all of their cold hands on him, looked at the wounds he had inflicted, and tried his best not to scream as they took him to the air cathedral. His life sprawled out behind him like a horrific photo album and all of that was nothing compared to what he was about to see.

had inflicted, and tried his best not to scream as they took him to the air cathedral. His life sprawled out behind him like a horrific photo album and all of that was nothing compared to what he was about to see.

163

A BUTTERFLY IN ICE

1.

J OEL."

The voice came from very far away, swimming toward him.

"*Jooooel?*"

The voice was unrecognizable.

Joel Vernon struggled to open his sandy eyes. Scraping open, he had the feeling they had been closed for a very long time. He stared into blackness.

No. It wasn't blackness. It was . . .

Pupils.

"Good," the man who owned the pupils said softly, pulling his face away from Joel's. "You're awake."

Joel resisted the urge to speak. Didn't even know if he could. He resisted the urge to ask the man in front of him a million questions. Already, a frantic feeling of dislocation rolled around in his brain. He sensed rather than felt his eyes darting around the room. A room unlike any other he had ever seen and the man in front of him was unlike any other man he had ever seen.

The man's black pupils, set in irises just as dark, were the only breaks in the monotonous white of this room. Even the rest of the *man* seemed to be white. His hair was white, even though the taut skin of his face suggested he was not old enough to have a head of totally white hair. His skin was very pale and not reddish pale but powder white vampire pale. He wore a white outfit Joel immediately thought of as a uniform. A name was embroidered into the chest of

164

the uniform's shirt, right over the heart, and Joel didn't know if it was the man's name or some kind of logo. The embroidery was white. It said: SNOW. So this man in front of him was potentially "Mr. Snow," Joel thought. He couldn't think of a more appropriate name for this man to have.

Joel scanned the entire room. There wasn't really anything to take in. It was like trying to take a drink from an empty cup.

Everything was white.

White walls. White door. White floor. White ceiling. White bedside table. White chair in the corner. White blinds covering a window. After spotting those blinds, Joel wondered what would happen if he lifted them. Would everything outside be white, also?

This made him wonder how long he had been here, wherever *here* was.

"How long have I been here?" Joel asked, not really knowing why he put this before the other obvious questions like "Where am I?" and "Who are you?"

Snow looked at Joel with an expression he couldn't quite place. He didn't think there was caring in those eyes. Neither did there seem to be any malice. Sadness, maybe.

"You've been resting here for some time, Joel," Snow said, his voice low and soothing.

"Where am I?"

"Well, that's difficult to explain. You're in a hospital of sorts."

"Of sorts? Which hospital?"

"You need to rest, Joel. *Rest.*"

So maybe this man, Snow, was a doctor. Dr. Snow. Apparently, Snow noticed the wildness in Joel's eyes. He held up a small sky blue pill in front of his face.

"Here," he said. "This will help you rest." And then he placed it into Joel's mouth. His fingers, while gloveless, tasted of latex.

Something inside Joel revolted. He didn't want to swallow the pill. He didn't want to swallow anything this man was going to give him.

Snow rose from the bed to his full height. From Joel's position on the bed, Snow seemed very tall.

"I'll return shortly," Snow said, leaving the room.

Joel raised his hands up to pull the pill from his mouth and noticed he had no hands. The sleeves of his thick white shirt descended past his hands, where they were sewn tightly shut. Quickly, before the pill dissolved, he turned his head and spit it onto the floor.

Bad idea, he thought. The semi-dissolved pill made a small bright blue splash on the harsh white of the floor. Sliding out of the bed, he attempted to stand up, his rubbery legs immediately dumping him back on the floor. Panic seized him. What the hell was he going to do with the pill? He took another quick scan of the room, searching for a bathroom door. Surely there had to be a bathroom in here and if there was then he could just take the pill in there and flush it down the toilet.

For a few frustrating seconds, he tried to pick up the pill, succeeding only in making a bigger mess. The blue was all over his elongated sleeve. How could something as small as that pill make such a big mess? Finally managing to pick up the pill, he stood, contemplating where he could put it.

No. There didn't seem to be any bathroom doors in the room. None at all. This worried him on a whole other level but the only thing he could think about for the moment was getting rid of that funny blue pill. He looked toward the window. Deep down, he knew it wouldn't open but he decided he had to try. He crossed the room to the window and pulled on the white cord he thought would lift the blinds. They didn't budge. He reached under the blinds, thinking maybe he could pull them out a little but they seemed to be fastened to the wall. Now he was as thirsty for a glimpse outside as he was to find a place to stash the pill. He attempted to pry a couple of the slats apart so he could look out of the window but there weren't any spaces in between them. They were like very convincing faux blinds. Like they were just carved out of the wall or something. He doubted there was even a window behind those blinds.

Snow said he would be coming back but he did not say when he would be coming back and there was still the matter of hiding the pill and then trying to get the stain off the floor, knowing it would just end up on his sleeve.

He took a firm grip on the pill. He had an idea of what he could do with it. He slid his covered hand down the back of his pants. Before he could really think about what he was doing, he pushed the blue pill between his buttocks and into his anus just far enough for the sphincter muscles to close around it. When he pulled his hand back up there was some brown now mixed with the blue on his shirt.

More like a straitjacket, he thought. Why the hell would they need to put me in some kind of straitjacket? Why am I even here? Do they think I'm some kind of danger to myself?

With the pill safely hidden away, he crouched down on the floor and spit at the blue spot, vigorously wiping it with his sleeve and wondering how he had arrived here. And for the first time since being conscious he was gripped with a single emotion.

Fear.

True and pure, it dripped ice down his spinal column.

It rattled his bones as he climbed back into bed, grateful to give his wobbly legs a rest.

2.

Maria Pearl. That was who he thought of when he went to sleep. Maybe it was more than thinking of her. Maybe it was dreaming her because here, in his dream, he wasn't sure she had ever existed. He saw her laughing face, green eyes winking out of sunsplashed red cheeks, orange hair flaming crazily away from her head like the sun's corona.

She was a dream . . . maybe. If he had ever had her, he couldn't imagine letting her go and if he had not had her, then he realized his life still had a purpose.

She wasn't the only thing in the dream. There was a whole other place there. A summer place. Joel heard the shrieking of the insects, reveled in the sight of the swollen green trees. A stream trickled lazily in the distance.

Suddenly, Maria's smile faded. She looked at him and said, "We have to go. I think there's someone else here."

And, just like that, the dream was gone.

3.

He woke up, shivering, searching the room. How could he have let himself fall asleep? Did he even remember being awake? Was that the first time he had been awake?

Snow stood over by the window. The blinds were now open, pulled all the way to the top of the window frame, and Joel wondered how this could be since, only a little while before, he had found the blinds to be completely impenetrable. As if sensing he was awake, Snow turned toward him, approaching the bed, moving slowly and languidly, those black eyes swimming in a sea of white.

167

"You're awake," he said.

"I have questions." Joel didn't know how he was going to force those questions out, didn't know if he was going to be *able* to force those questions out when it seemed impossible to make his brain form words.

"We *all* have questions. I don't expect you to answer any of *my* questions."

Joel didn't know what to say to that but he couldn't just lie back in the bed. He couldn't just lie there and not do anything. He didn't know why he was here. He didn't know if he should even be here. He didn't know where here was. But he didn't know if this man, Snow, was to blame. Joel's first instinct was to attack him. To get past him somehow . . . but what if Snow was there to help him?

Snow rubbed his powdery hands together. "Actually," he said, "I do have one question you could answer for me . . . At least, I think you can answer it. Stand up." Snow, now bedside, reached down and helped Joel out of the bed. Joel stood up, his legs a little less shaky. Maybe, he thought, that was because he didn't take the pill. The pill *this man* had given him.

"Let's come over to the window," Snow said, cradling Joel's elbow and leading him. The only thing Joel could see from where he stood was a vast expanse of blue sky. "There's someone I would like you to identify for me."

Joel stood at the window. His eyes widened. He didn't see whoever it was Snow was talking about. The only thing he could see was that it was summer. Joel didn't know why that knowledge aroused such emotion within him but, just standing out there and looking at the foliage beyond the window, the bright flowers in bloom, the trees growing mammoth past the parklike ocean of green, blowing lazily in a sultry breeze, made him want to shatter the window to be out there in all of that sun and warmth. To be out there in that climate that was the complete antithesis of the climate currently enveloping him.

"You're looking off in the distance. Look down. Down there on that bench. Do you see that girl?"

Joel saw her and, as impossible as it seemed, his eyes widened further.

4.

The first time Joel saw Maria Pearl was in a summer sculpture class at Gethsemane College. It was a sprint class, mostly intended for people who needed a few credits in order to graduate on time. The class met three times a week at four hours a meeting. Joel had taken his customary seat on a bench in the back corner of the room. Maria was a good fifteen minutes late. There was a universal pause as she walked into the classroom, made her apologies to the professor and came to the back of the class, taking up the empty bench next to Joel.

He found himself staring at her all through the class. They were stolen stares, sure, nothing too open, but he found himself glancing at her every few seconds. Red hair. Green eyes. Pale skin flushed red. A baggy t-shirt. Baggy blue jeans, cut low enough so Joel could tell she wore black underwear. The underwear contrasted with the paleness of her skin. He felt like an ogling pervert and realized he didn't care. He was shy by nature, had never approached a girl before in his life but he determined, from first laying eyes on Maria, that he was going to attempt to get her to go out with him.

Turns out it wasn't as hard as he thought.

After the class was over, she stood up from her bench, arms dusty up to the elbows with dried clay, and looked at Joel. Maybe she sensed some desperate, urgent longing in his stare.

"I'm Maria," she said. She pulled an odd-looking sculpture from her canvas bag so she could put her sculpting tools in it.

"I'm Joel. That's cool," he said, pointing to the sculpture.

"Thanks," she said. "It's called 'A Butterfly in Ice.'"

"Cool name." Jesus, he felt like a putz. "So I haven't seen you around campus. Are you new?"

"Kind of. My parents moved here from Arizona. Dad's with the Air Force. We moved too late for me to enroll in the last semester so I have to do the summer thing."

"Welcome to Ohio," Joel said, feeling stupid. He was still marveling at the fact this mysterious girl now seemed so down to earth, with parents and everything. It seemed foreign to her.

"What do you people do for fun out here," she asked, pulling her heavy backpack off the floor and slinging it over her shoulder. It pulled her shirt tight against her breasts. She picked up her sculpture and, watching the muscles in her forearm flex, Joel noticed the sculpture *did* look like a butterfly trapped in ice, in an abstract kind of way.

"This is the Midwest, we don't have fun," Joel said.

She laughed briefly. Joel's insides melted.

"Right . . . but I thought you like watched racecars and farmed and shot guns and stuff like that."

"Well, maybe I'm not the best person to ask about recreation."

"Why not?"

"Not many friends. I don't really do much. Study. Read. Study."

"Well, you have another friend now . . . what was your name again?"

He coughed, ready to tell her his name when she put a hand on his chest, stopping him.

"I know," she said. "It's Joel. I was just kidding."

She drew her hand from his chest, kind of sliding it downward as she did and asked if he wanted to do something this weekend.

"I'd love to."

And then they went their separate ways. At the close of the next class, they made plans to go out on Friday after class.

The rest of the week was interminable. The class ended in the afternoon and they went to a bar close to the campus. They were both kind of drunk and decided the bar was too full for them. They went to a park and sat in a pair of swings, the empty park somewhat spectral in the moonlight and Maria told him she had never seen the ocean. Joel, whose family made regular trips to Florida, told her they would have to change all that. They ended up in his car, racing east on the highway. Sometime the next day they were in North Carolina at a nearly deserted expanse of beach.

"Well, here we are," Joel said, as though they had taken a quick trip around the block.

The weather couldn't have been more perfect. The sky was blotted with far away puffs of clouds. They ran along the beach all day, the water warm, splashing up around them, the sun baking them. There was a lot of laughter. Joel couldn't remember laughing like that since he had been a kid. He couldn't remember feeling that unabashedly *good* since he had been a kid. And it wasn't just his lust for Maria making him feel that way. They had not done so much as hold hands at that point.

They stayed on the beach until sunset. Once the sun was out of sight, they retreated up to his car in the deserted parking lot.

"Maybe we should rest before driving back," she said.

He couldn't argue with her, having been up well over twenty-four hours. They both crawled in the backseat of the car and there they kissed for the first time. To Joel, that was what made the whole day a dream. Those innumerable seconds with his lips pressed against hers assured him he would be able to remember the day in shimmering glimpses at best. It was this he would remember in its entirety. He fought the urge to let his hands explore her. He didn't want her to feel like she had to let him just because he had driven all this way and was her only real way back.

"Now, was that fun?" she asked.

"Yes," Joel said. "That was fun."

They fell asleep in the backseat, Maria's head resting against his shoulder, the wild fragrance of her hair there to stimulate even his sleeping mind.

They awoke just before dawn, climbing out of the car to stretch and move into the front seat. In this meager blue-gray light, the beach now seemed sullen and cold, summer faded in a night. An old man walked slowly along the beach, casting awkward glimpses at the car.

The trip back was not nearly long enough for Joel. They talked about books and music and movies, told stories from their childhoods, lived nearly a continent apart but with eerie similarity.

5.

"Familiar, huh?" Snow said, his breath icy on the back of Joel's neck.

"What the fuck is going on?" Joel said. "I want to talk to her."

"Why? She wouldn't know who you are. That's not who you think it is. That's her twin sister."

"She didn't have a twin sister."

"How well do you think you really knew her?"

"What is this? Is this some kind of game?"

"This is life, Joel. And you're making a mess of it. Not quite following orders. I can tell when you do not do as you're told. It's all over your sleeves. It's all over the floor. I want you to get back in the bed."

"And what if I don't want to get back into bed?"

"Then you will never know what happened. I have the answers. You have the questions. Who has the power?"

Joel didn't know what to think. He knew what he wanted to do. He wanted to tear through the glass in front of him. He wanted to float down on the summer breeze until he stood in front of that model of perfection sitting languidly on the parkbench. Maria didn't have any twin sisters. He would have known if she did. Even though he had never been invited back to her house (there hadn't been any time for that) he knew she would not have left out a detail such as that. Nevertheless, his mind raced. Part of him still wanted to believe what this man was telling him. That was the same part of him that wanted to believe Snow was there to help him.

"Get back in the bed, Joel . . . and I'll tell you a story."

Reluctantly, Joel pulled himself away from the window. What could he do, really? Would there be any escaping this man in his current weakened and doped-up state? He didn't think so. There wouldn't be any fighting. There could be little resistance of any kind. Even without Snow's suggestions, the only thing Joel really wanted to do was to get back into bed, curl up under the white blankets that afforded at least a modicum of warmth, and listen to the air conditioning hum continuously from the vent overhead.

Joel climbed back in the bed, his muscles hungrily reaching for the mattress, wanting nothing more than to be immobile. Snow came and sat on the side of the bed, staring off across the room. He took a deep breath, preparing to tell Joel why he was here.

6.

The first time Joel had sex with Maria was like this:

It was the weekend after their beach excursion.

He had driven them to the nature reserve at dusk. He was pretty sure they both knew what it was they wanted. They found a clearing located deep enough in the woods for them to hide and spread a quilt out on the ground. He had stuck some incense into the soft earth around the quilt and lit it. Soon the air was redolent with the sweetness of summer and the perfumes of nag champa.

It didn't take them long. They greeted each other's bodies with near ferocity and, afterwards, they lay there in silence, smoking cigarettes and looking at the stars. She lay on her stomach, her legs bent so her feet dangled above her rounded ass. He stroked the two strange, nearly-identical scars on her back and fought the urge to ask her how she got them.

"This is our spot," she said out of nowhere.

"What?" he asked.

"This is our spot. The next time we do this, it has to be right here. For now. And then we can make more spots."

"Sticky spots," he said. He wrapped an arm around her shoulders and pulled her nakedness closer to him. There they kind of drifted off.

And awoke nearly an hour later to a rustling in the woods.

"What is that?" he asked, startled.

"Some kind of animal," she said.

"Then it's a fucking huge animal," he hissed under his breath. He figured it was more likely a park ranger and, gathering their clothes and the quilt, they both sprinted along the trail until they reached his car.

7.

"I'm surprised you don't remember what happened." Snow's voice was annoyingly calm. Devoid of any compassion whatsoever. "It was so tragic. But I guess some minds can simply erase tragedy. You've been here ever since."

"What happened?"

"You really don't remember, do you?"

"You promised."

"It was a terrible car crash. You were driving. You were a little more than drunk. Shouldn't have been driving. You swerved to avoid something in the road. Your car turned over and slid down a hill. You went into a coma. This morning was the first time you came out of that coma. Maria was killed. Not instantly. No, for a while, she was here with you. She died this morning. That is her sister out there, ready to go home, ready to begin preparations for the funeral. It's a short story really."

Joel didn't know what to think. His heart thudded sickeningly in his chest as he lay there. Why did he have any reason to doubt this man? What else would explain why he was here in a hospital?

"How long have I been here?" Joel asked.

"Three months."

"Why am I wearing a straitjacket?"

"It's not a straitjacket. Your hands are covered so you won't scrape out your eyes in your sleep. We've discovered some people

173

who undergo violent trauma suffer very physical rages even while in a coma."

"Why is everything white?"

"Lack of stimulus."

"But you let me look outside."

"That was because I wanted you to feel like you were looking at Maria for one last time. Trying to trigger some memories. I shouldn't have done that. It's not in the rules."

"I'm glad you did."

"I need you to take this pill for me."

Snow placed the pill in his mouth just as he did last time. Then he stood to leave. This time, thinking he was some kind of murderer, Joel took the pill, let it slide down his throat, hoping it would quell some of the strong emotions that had risen within him.

8.

The next weekend and the next weekend and the one after that, they went to their secret place in the woods. There was always a sound to creep them out, always the thought of someone looming just outside the perimeter of the clearing, watching them, listening to them, consuming them. Maybe it was just some sick voyeur or maybe it was a park ranger or maybe it was some horrifically huge shaggy beast. Neither of them knew. Neither of them cared. They left fulfilled.

On their last night together, a stranger thing happened.

After their lovemaking, they lay in their customary position, Joel flat on his back, Maria curled up between his arm and torso. He saw something flutter just above them.

"What is that?" She had seen it too.

"I think it's a butterfly," he said. He reached up casually, not expecting to catch it. But it seemed like the butterfly wanted to be caught. At first, he had thought it was just one of those butterflies you see flapping through summer fields, the small white kind.

After bringing it down into his palm, he saw that it was different. It looked like it was covered in ice crystals.

"Oh, this is beautiful," Maria said and Joel could have sworn the butterfly turned toward her voice, acknowledging her in some way. "It's just like my sculpture."

"Touch it," he said. "It's cold."

She reached out a finger and stroked the back of the little white butterfly. "Feels like ice."

"Weird, huh?"

"Put your clothes on. Let's let it go and see where it lands."

He had realized she was able to make a game out of just about anything. He was usually willing to play along and he always enjoyed himself.

The night was strange. A clear full moon kind of night that seemed way too bright. A night full of shadows that moved.

He put his clothes on, watching Maria slide into hers. He had always found this nearly as sensual as watching her slide out of her clothes. Once clothed, they chased after the strange icy night butterfly. And it was like the butterfly wanted them to follow it, the way it hovered there at the edge of the clearing, never letting itself escape their range of sight.

Beckoning, he thought. *It's like the butterfly is beckoning us.*

9.

Again, consciousness found him. Opening his eyes in the winter room, a sudden panic seized him. He had to get out of here. He had to get out and get as far away as possible because this place was not any good. Not any good at all. This place was a prison, an icy prison, and he knew the longer he stayed, the thicker and stronger the ice would freeze until he would not be able to even entertain any thoughts about escaping.

He melted from the bed. Some form of stored heat inflated his muscles, making him feel strong again. He didn't think his legs would give out anytime soon. He half expected Snow to be there in the room with him, there to shove him back in the bed and cram another pill down his throat, to ice the sweat beading on his forehead.

Joel ran to the door and pulled at it. Locked. Of course. This only reinforced the idea that this place was a cell.

He crossed the room until he reached the blinded window. How had Snow made the blinds go up? Joel ran his fingers around the edges, not finding so much as an opening. He wanted to scream but knew that would not do him any good. Screaming would only attract attention. He went back to the bed, pulling on it, sliding it out from the wall, thoughts of dismantling swarming his brain. Memories trickled from his thawing thoughts. Memories, he knew, that were the correct memories. Even though they were not as solid and resolute as the memories Snow had supplied for him, he knew they were the correct memories because they were *his*.

10.

Maria *hadn't* wanted to follow the butterfly. She chased him chasing the butterfly through the woods. They were not on one of the main trails. This trail was narrow and unmaintained. Hardly a trail at all.

Strange feelings tugged at Joel. This was the first time he had ever felt badly when in the presence of Maria. They jogged down a slight hill and the thought, more like a warning, popped up in his brain . . . and she just kept yelling at him to stop.

Something bad was going to happen.

And looking ahead in the oddly luminous night, he noticed the woods didn't look right. He wanted to heed her warnings but he couldn't stop.

The woods ahead of them were melting.

No longer individual rigid structures, the trees and shrubs became something like richly colored water. All the daytime green, painted purple in the night, slowly ran down the canvas of the horizon. Peeking through was something that looked like ice.

The butterfly swam through the air as if desperate for this new, surreal landscape. Joel watched it disappear into the waterfall of the woods and staggered backward with a blinding light and shocking force. Like a block of ice hitting him in the chest.

11.

Try as he might, Joel was not able to dismantle the bed. It was like the whole structure was made from a single piece of metal. That meant he would have to use the bed itself as a weapon. He squeezed in behind the head of the bed and waited, readying himself, his muscles tense.

He didn't know how long he waited for Snow. He was about ready to give up. There was probably a camera set up somewhere, watching his every move. He didn't have much faith Snow was going to open the door and walk into the trap Joel had laid for him. But he wouldn't give up there. He would give it a few more minutes and if Snow had still not come back then Joel planned on going over to the window and pounding on that. He would use the bed if he had to. Rage made him strong. Rage made him burn.

Just when he was about ready to give up, Snow opened the door. Joel drove the bed forward. The foot of the bed slammed into the doctor, knocking him into the far wall.

Now, however, the bed obstructed the doorway so Joel had to waste precious moments pulling the bed back into nearly the same position it was before. By the time he did that, Snow stood in the doorway, a gun in his hand. The gun was white, small and sinister-looking.

"Stop," Snow said.

"I didn't think doctors carried guns."

"I didn't think patients tried to kill their doctors."

"You fed me lies before. Who are you?" If he was going to die at the end of this man's gun then he felt he at least had the right to know why it was he was dying.

"You've seen me before. I'm surprised you were so shocked to see me here . . . in my home."

"What do you mean I've seen you before?"

"And I've seen you. I've watched you for a long time. Actually, that's not true. I've watched Maria for a long time. And then you came along. Did you ever feel like you were never alone?"

"You were the one." Joel should have seen this before. The shivers in the bushes. The man on the beach who had only been mistaken as elderly. This man was Joel and Maria's collective unease.

"Do you know what it was like watching you take something I've wanted for so long?"

"You're sick."

"Yes, Joel. I'm glad you realize that. In fact, I don't think you know just how sick I am. Do you know how many times Maria has moved in the last ten years, ever since she turned twelve?"

"She moved around a lot."

"It's not because her dad was in the military. Everywhere she went, there was someone there, stalking her, making her feel like a victim . . . or at least a potential victim. The police were called a number of times but they could never find anything. Not as long as I had this place, all wrapped up in ice and hidden just slightly behind reality."

"But that's insane."

"Who's to say what's insane anymore? You're here, aren't you?"

"But why . . . why her?"

"Let's just say that I'm not fully human, Joel. I'm not a god. Nothing as glamorous as that. But I was close. An angel maybe. I wasn't always a bad person. I was given this home and the ability to change some things. To *influence* some things. But then I saw this girl one day. It was in Maine. I'll never forget it. She was in the lake and the undercurrent was pulling her down. I had the ability to become the undercurrent, to change it. And that was what I did. I became the undercurrent. I released her and she swam to safety. But I couldn't stop watching her. And it didn't stop there. Over the next several months, I couldn't take my eyes from her. Eventually, I was told I had to quit this voyeurism or risk losing my powers. It was an easy choice to make. But I didn't lose all of my powers. Only the ones that gave me any sense of self-worth. So I hope you understand what I am about to do. I hope you understand because I have sacrificed everything I once had to have Maria here, in the closest thing I have to a home. And you are not going to keep me from that."

Snow raised the gun and fired at Joel. Joel threw himself to the side, the bullet catching him in the left arm. A spray of red cascaded across the pristine winter room. Joel rolled toward Snow, knowing only that he wanted to be close enough to get him out of the way. Instead, he made himself an easier target. He looked up to the gun hovering only inches from his face.

And then he heard a loud sound.

Metal on bone. Bone or ice?

Joel saw the metal bar hit Snow's head. And he saw Snow's head erupt in a frosty shower like a shattered ice cube. And then Snow changed. He shrunk, becoming the butterfly that had led him to this place. Standing where he once stood was Maria.

She smiled down at him.

"Are you ready to get out of here?"

"What about him?"

"He's just a butterfly."

12.

Joel followed Maria out of the house, into the heat, into the summer. He held Maria in his arms, looking back the way they had come. On the floor of the forest was a large block of ice and, inside that block of ice, there was a frozen butterfly, its wings spread wide. He had to look hard to see it. It could have just as easily been a bubble in an ice cube. This, he realized, was Maria's sculpture.

"I'm still not sure I understand," Joel said.

"Well, that's because you never believed in angels."

"I'd never given it much thought."

"Snow was a foolish one. Self-righteous. Always thinking he was the only one being punished."

"What do you mean?"

"When an angel wants something that is human, they become human themselves, possessing only powers of destruction." Maria approached the block of ice and put her hands onto it. Joel watched as the block melted into a puddle, the butterfly wriggling in the middle of it, before the puddle burst into flame.

"Are you . . ." Joel started.

"You were eleven the first time I saw you. You were flying a kite in your backyard. I made myself an eleven-year-old girl, knowing one day we would meet. I hope that doesn't frighten you. Snow had no idea I had fallen from grace when he tried to save me. That was probably what attracted him to me . . . because I was so much like him."

Joel didn't know what to think. He was just glad to be alive. He was glad Maria was alive. Everything else would have to come after those two facts. There were so many questions.

"You're not going to freeze me in a block of ice?"

"No. I promise."

"Then I guess I'll have to be okay with that. How do you know *I'm* not an angel?"

She grabbed his hand and put it on her back. He rubbed the smooth scars between her shoulderblades.

"Because you don't have these."

RUNNING FROM THE ROSES

THE OLD WOMAN lay on the bed, arms against her sides, eyes and mouth closed. Chloe thought her grandmother must be the only person who looked severe even when sleeping. Countless times Chloe had stood beside this bed, staring down at the old woman, waiting for the cessation of the covers' rising and falling. A part of Chloe looked forward to this. When she wasn't staring at the woman, she stared at the wallpaper, crawling with green vines and red roses. She didn't want to seem cruel and even though, in her grandmother's better days, the two women had fought continuously, Chloe didn't want to think she hated the woman.

She didn't want to think she was doing any of this out of hate.

Hate was the furthest thing from her mind. What she thought about on this sad day was love. It was her intense love for a boy named Jack Kettering that rooted the decisions of which the seeds had been planted much earlier.

Jack was on his way. Together, they were going to go to California and leave Twin Springs, Ohio, behind.

Her meager suitcase sat beside the front door inside the ramshackle house.

She stood over the bed, looking down at Grandma Elly and wishing things could have turned out differently. It was late summer and Chloe wore a black skirt that cut off just below the knee. Wind came in from the windows, touching her pale legs under the skirt and above her combat boots, making her feel amazingly alive in this, the most depressing stage of her life.

But she was young. Wasn't it okay to feel alive? Shouldn't she feel like the world was hers, spread out before her?

She pulled the uncomfortable wooden chair from in front of the wall over to the bed. She sat down and crossed her legs, leaning toward her grandmother.

The wind whistled as it was cut to pieces by the screens in the western windows.

"I won't leave if you just say something. Anything at all, Grandma."

But she knew the old woman wouldn't say anything.

Chloe felt feverish. Cold sweat stood out on her skin. What *should* she be feeling? She didn't know. She was only seventeen and nobody had ever sat her down and explained to her how one feels when confronted with this type of thing. She was too young to remember her parents dying. And that was different anyway. They were not the ones who had raised her. Who had loved her through everything since she was a baby. They were not the ones who had made her life a living hell for the past two years. And the only mystery they had left her with was the mystery of who they were and what they were like. She didn't expect them to be anything *but* mystery.

But her grandma *shouldn't* have been a mystery. Chloe wasn't an idiot when it came to human nature. Her grandma should have been an open book to her but she knew there were things about her grandma she didn't know about. Dark things. Maybe even scary things.

Off in the distance, the faint rumble of thunder rolled out of the hills.

"Jack's gonna be here soon, Grandma. I'm gonna go with him. Do you want me to go with him? Because I'll stay if you need me."

And she knew the old woman needed her. Of course she needed her. Chloe was the one who fed her. The one who changed her bedpan. The one who made sure a nurse came over once a week to check on her. She was also the one who made sure her grandma wasn't put in a home because that had been her last wish before lapsing into whatever complacent vegetable state she had lapsed into. Chloe knew it wasn't just pride keeping her out of the home. It was something else. It was that secret.

The sky darkened, throwing shadows across the room.

Chloe stood up from the chair and paced around the room, the room with the busy wallpaper that reflected a simpler time, a time when painted roses could almost pass for the real thing.

"You know, this hasn't been easy for me!" she screamed, knowing she didn't have to. She had screamed countless times before. It didn't matter whether her grandmother heard her or not. She wasn't going to respond. Nothing was going to make her respond. She wasn't screaming at her grandmother anyway. Not really. She screamed because she felt like she had to. It kept the madness at bay.

The sky darkened further. The room dimmed along with it, the deep red roses of the wallpaper turning almost black. She imagined fat, malignant tumors covering the wall, held together by vines that were actually thick tendons, metastatic tendons carrying the malignancy from one tumor to the next.

"What's wrong with you, Grandma? You know I can't take it anymore, don't you? Why didn't you just let me put you in a home? Is it because they would run too many tests on you? Is it because they could take samples of your blood, samples of your skin and find out what you really are?"

She surprised herself with this last thing she said. It was the first time she had allowed that thought to be spoken aloud.

Growing up, it had never crossed her mind that her grandma was something else, something other than human. Something called, around town, a Zwinn. The Zwinns were myth, legend, scapegoats for the unexplained. Vampires, maybe. Maybe witches. Near demonic familiars that somehow took the place of their human counterparts. It made sense, now that she thought about it. It made even more sense when spoken aloud. Until then, she didn't think she believed in the Zwinns. She certainly didn't actually think her grandmother might *be* one. Chloe's idea was not unfounded. She was able to recall the genesis of that idea perfectly and, thinking back on it, was surprised it had taken her this long to give voice to her suspicions.

She had been young. Eight or nine. She woke up in her bedroom, the remnants of a terrible dream squirming through her head. She still remembered the dream vividly. She and her grandmother were running through the woods. It was dark. The moon hung full overhead only it wasn't the moon at all but the pale waxy face of a man. A terrifying man who struck some chord of familiarity within her. It was a face she would never forget and hadn't seen since but, nevertheless, she had often found herself wondering just who it was. Scared, she had wandered out of her bedroom. She heard voices coming from down the hall and figured her grandma must be out there watching television. She hadn't even thought her grandmother might have visitors because no one ever visited this sad old house unless it was one of her friend's parents coming to pick her up for a sleepover.

First checking the family room and finding it empty, she then went into the kitchen.

She squinted her eyes against the blue fluorescent glare of the light. The light seemed comforting at night when it was her and her grandma in there baking cookies or eating dinner, but now it just seemed harsh. Harsh and obtrusive. Obtrusive because there were people standing in the kitchen and the brightness of the light prevented Chloe from really focusing on them. There were three of them. Chloe moved a little closer, her eyes gradually adjusting to the light, able to make the figures out a little better. Two men and a woman. One of the men spotted her and flashed her a wan, secretive smile but didn't say anything. Didn't hint to her grandmother they were being spied on. And didn't that face look familiar? Wasn't it the face she had just seen in the moon, in her nightmare? Now it didn't seem so terrifying, just . . . familiar. Where had she seen that face before?

The woman was the most beautiful woman Chloe had ever seen. She wore a very black, almost floor-length dress. Chloe couldn't identify the fabric in this lighting. Her black hair was pulled away from her face, high cheekbones, large eyes, large red lips. She was fashion magazine beautiful, Chloe thought. Now able to focus perfectly, she noticed the woman's eyes and, even from this distance, she could see the woman's green eyes sparkling—green bordering on yellow like some undiscovered gem.

Everyone in the kitchen whispered. At least Chloe thought they were whispering. They may not have been speaking at all. Chloe imagined a telepathic communication. Chloe's grandma was the only one who sat. She sat in a kitchen chair and had her right arm raised. The beautiful woman held her hand in both of hers. Chloe thought the woman held her grandmother's arm like a bottle of precious wine. She didn't know why she thought it but she wondered if these three people hadn't just been drinking from her grandma's arm.

It was a strange picture, a strange thought, but it was one that would come back to her many times over the years and it was the last night she remembered her grandma in quite that way because, seeing the older woman there in the chair, with her hand raised, was the last time she would think her grandma was being honest with her. There was a rift. It went unspoken but it was felt and that lack of verbalization only seemed to make it grow deeper.

Once her grandma knew she was standing there, she was quickly shooed to bed and, every day since then, Chloe had known the woman was keeping something from her. Something secret. Something Chloe desperately wanted to know. And there were times when Chloe would catch her grandmother staring at her and wondered if the old lady was reading her mind. That would certainly explain why she always managed to be a step ahead during their arguments.

That was the only time she had seen the strange people come to the old sad house but she knew they had come on different occasions throughout the years. She knew this because, when they visited, her grandma's physical condition deteriorated at an alarming rate. She couldn't help but think her grandmother was being bled dry. Bled dry by this triumvirate of mysterious people she had seen gathered in the kitchen that one night. But why? That, she didn't know. Perhaps her grandmother's life was precious to these people and slowly, slowly, they were sucking away the last of it. And then, two years ago, it had happened. Her grandma had gone from a woman of sixty-five to a woman who was on her deathbed.

And on her deathbed she had stayed.

Now, as the first of the rain started to water down on the house and all the huge trees around it, she sat on the side of the bed, wrapped in that clean linen scent, placing a hand on her grandmother's sallow chest.

"I think I know what they were, Grandma. But I want to know *who* they were. I want to know you didn't have a chance before I do this. I want to know I'm not helping to end any sort of life at all."

Thunder cracked outside. A gust of air, almost cold, swept into the room. The meager sunlight caught on the rain beading the window and added it to the already busy wallpaper. Now there were a lot of little gray tumors to go with the fat black tumor roses.

"Jack's going to be here soon, Grandma. Give me something. *Please.*"

Still, the old woman said nothing.

Thunder cracked again. The blazing glow of the lightning popped into the room for a split second. It was like an x-ray and, when she looked at her grandmother, the only thing she saw beneath the skin was dust.

From outside, she heard a car horn. Jack. Beautiful Jack, come to take her away.

She reached into the waistband of her skirt and pulled out the handgun. She didn't know much about guns. She didn't know what kind of gun it was. She didn't even know the name brand. She had fired it exactly once, into an old board out behind the house, to make sure it worked. It did. Not only did it work, it looked like it left a big enough hole to properly cremate a potential suicide's brains.

She held the gun over her grandma's nightstand.

"This is for when you wake up and realize I'm not here."

The *clunk* the gun made against the wood of the nightstand was as lethal sounding as the actual report the gun had made going off out behind the house.

"I'm sorry," Chloe said, the words sounding weak as they came out of her mouth. From all around her, the roses like tumors or hungry mouths seemed to wriggle across the walls. Breathing. Whispering her name. Begging her to stay.

She turned her back on her grandmother, turned her back on the hideous hungry roses, and left the house.

The storm raged down, spitting at her, and there was some deeply rooted religious part of her hoping God was not going to strike her down for what she had just done. She opened the passenger door of Jack's ancient Volvo and threw her suitcase in the backseat.

"Is everything okay?" Jack asked her when she slid into the passenger seat.

"No," she said, tears trying to claw their way out of her eyes. "But I knew it wouldn't be."

"We don't have to go," he said.

"Yes, we do. And you can't let me come back here, Jack. *Ever.* Do you promise?"

"Sure. I promise."

With that, they pulled away from the house, Jack commenting on the uselessness of his windshield wipers, talking about how he should have been better prepared. Chloe barely heard him.

He drove the first leg of the trip. She sat in the passenger seat with her eyes closed, feigning sleep in order to avoid conversation. She was much too sad and sick and confused to really fall asleep or to open her eyes and talk, for that matter.

She pretended to wake up just before midnight and they pulled into a rest stop somewhere in eastern Illinois. Jack said he was tired. She told him she would do some of the driving. They fucked in the passenger seat, Chloe straddling him. It was quick and furious. She was barely aroused and it was nearly painful but, for some reason, she had wanted to feel the solidity of Jack inside her, hot and real, stabbing her insides while his arms wrapped around her. Ever since she had met him, it was always this gesture that made her think things just might turn out all right.

She sat in the passenger seat with his come leaking out and into her ass crack. He put his big, warm hand on her knee and said, "What's the real problem?"

"I don't know," she said. She was crying again.

"You can tell me everything, you know? That's what this is really all about. That's why we're going away together. It's kind of like a marriage. Anything that bothers you, I want it to bother me too."

"You'd think I was crazy."

"We're from Ohio, remember? Crazy is relative. Actually, it's most of our relatives that are crazy."

Without expecting it, without really wanting to, she launched into the whole story. She told him everything. He didn't seem as concerned about the crazy supernatural stuff as he was about the gun she had left at her grandmother's bedside.

"If there's a gun involved, they'll come looking for us. You know that, don't you?"

"Well . . ." She tried to justify herself. "She said she didn't want to go into a home. I figured that, in the off chance she actually woke up and was somewhat aware of herself, she could, you know . . ."

"Chloe, this is the kind of thing the news gets ahold of and . . . and then we're finished. Then we have to come back and God only knows what happens after that."

"Maybe it was stupid," she said.

"No, no, we can fix it. We're not that far away."

"No, Jack. We can't go back. We can't. Nobody's going to come looking for us. It'll look like suicide."

"The gun's gonna have your prints on it. If she wakes up and does away with herself, you're going to look bad either way. You're either going to look like you abandoned her and were too gutless to call an ambulance or you're going to look like you shot her so you could get away and live your teenage life."

"No. It wasn't like that at all. I just didn't want anyone to find out about her."

"I know that. But think of how crazy that's going to sound to anyone else."

"And when we go back and find that nothing's happened . . . what then? We can't take her to a home. Then they'll know. Then they'll all know. And we can't live there with her."

"Why not?"

"Because I just can't. What we have . . . it's beautiful. I don't want it mixed up with that. I want to make a clean beginning."

"Well, maybe we'll have to wait until she's gone before we make our beginning. I don't mind, Chloe, really I don't. I'd do anything for you."

"I know you would. That's what makes me so scared."

"Forget about all that Zwinns stuff. It's all just rumors and lies."

"Okay. We can go back. But if we go back, we're getting someone to take care of her. Are you willing to work enough to support that?"

"I'm willing to do anything you ask me to do."

"Who's driving?" she asked, turning petulantly in her seat and reaching in the floorboard for her underwear.

"I'll drive," he said.

"Let's get this over with then."

Jack drove. She watched the rain beat against the windshield and she couldn't think of anything except the wallpaper in her grandmother's room. She didn't know why she thought of it. Maybe she thought of it in order to take her mind off all the other things she could have been thinking about. Maybe it was the intricate pattern of the wallpaper that kept her mind busy, tracing it over and over. No. Not *it*. The *memory* of it. And she still thought of the roses as tumors and the raindrops as little baby tumors but, after a bit of driving, she saw the tumors clearing up. Like they were going away. Mouths closing, satiated. Memories were tricky things.

Something inside her told her that her grandmother was better now. Another part of her told her this was insanity and, even if that was the case, then maybe it was Chloe who had made her sick these last couple of years. Maybe her being gone was the best thing to happen to her grandma. Or maybe it just meant things would work out. Things would be different. If she had Jack there to help her with her grandma, maybe things wouldn't be so bad. Or if they put her grandma in a home. Really, what was stopping them from doing that? The Zwinns weren't real. Just like Jack said. They were made up. They were a scapegoat for what ailed the town. *Reality* was what really ailed the town.

In her mind, she saw the wallpaper in a sunny room. All the tumors were gone and now it was just the roses, dark red with deep green vines against an off-white background. Normal roses. Normal wallpaper. A normal life. The way it should be. It wouldn't be the ideal beginning but Chloe thought, maybe, it was the only way she could be truly happy—to have both people who mattered near her at all times.

The trip back seemed to go a lot quicker than their abbreviated trip toward their nonexistent California dreamland. Sometime before dawn, they reached the sad old house nestled at the edge of the woods, surrounded by towering trees.

"I guess we're here," Jack said.

"Yeah," Chloe said. She didn't want to go inside but knew she had to. Going inside, coming back, that was doing the right thing. She didn't know what she had been thinking. She wasn't that type of person. The type of person who leaves a dying old woman in bed with a gun to off herself if she came to and found herself alone. Jack wasn't that type of person. Of course, she had never told Jack about the gun until they were at the rest stop. She had told Jack someone would be there to look after her grandmother. Now they were back and that was that. That was doing the right thing. It felt good.

"I guess I should go in," she said.

"I'll come with you."

"No," she said. "I mean, I think I should go in alone. I don't want you to see anything you shouldn't see. This is my mess."

"Are you sure? I want to. I mean, I wouldn't mind."

"Yeah, I'm sure. You stay here. Let me make sure everything's okay. I'll come back out. I still don't know what I'm going to do."

"Just don't do anything stupid."

"You mean like use the gun myself . . . on her, just to put an end to it?"

"That's exactly what I mean."

"I couldn't do that."

"I know you couldn't . . . wouldn't . . . Okay, I'll be here. If you're gone too long, I'm coming in to check on you though."

"Kay."

Then they kissed and she didn't want to release his lips. The second she pulled away from him, she felt an overwhelming sense of emptiness. The time for hesitation was over. She had to do this. She had to go back in. This could be a beginning too, she realized, even if maybe it wasn't the beginning she had originally wanted.

The door creaked open. The house was dark and scary. She couldn't remember a time she had ever been scared in this house. The night she had seen the strangers, that didn't even make her scared. It filled her with something else. Something like wonder and awe. But what she felt now was fear and she didn't know why she felt that way.

She flipped on a light as soon as she found it, hoping it would chase some of the scariness away.

The light came on, spreading through the hallway like a beacon to her grandmother's bedroom door. Even though she had only been gone for a few hours, the house looked different. It looked and felt even sadder and she didn't know why she had come back. Coming back was perhaps the stupidest thing she had ever done, she now realized. They couldn't do this. She and Jack would not be able to live in this house with that woman down the hall. Of that, she was certain.

She walked down the hallway, wanting to get it over with, wanting to confront those crazy fears raping her mind. She wanted to get to the end of the hallway and go to her grandmother's bedroom and see that the woman was just as wooden and dormant as always and then she could call the ambulance and they would come and take her away because even if they took her in and ran tests on her they weren't going to find anything, were they? Of course they weren't. Because the Zwinns didn't exist. They were myth. They were legend. They couldn't be part of her.

Chloe flung the door open and her heart stopped for just a second.

The old woman was not on the bed.

The first thought she had was that the roses had climbed down off the walls, *grown* down off the walls and covered the bed, ate her grandma with their hungry mouths or ultra rapid cancer. Then her heart sped up. Of course those weren't roses.

They were bloodstains.

Her grandmother had woken up and found the gun. The gun lay in the middle of the bed, covered in those vulgar, drippy-looking roses.

But where was her grandmother?

Had there been time for the ambulance to come and find her? Had she called them before doing it?

Her heart doubled its pace.

She had to get out of here. She had to get out of this carnage. She didn't even care about answers anymore. She just wanted to grab Jack and then they could go off and do what they had planned. What they had wanted to do for so long now.

But the door was blocked.

Her grandmother stood in the doorway, flanked by two of the people she had seen in the kitchen the one night. Her grandmother's long gray hair was down, falling around her shoulders in bloody clumps. Her mouth was blackened. Chloe gagged, went down on her knees, staring at the atrocities in the doorway. To her grandmother's right was the beautiful woman. To her left was the man whose face Chloe had seen in the moon.

In that instant, she understood everything, knowledge as ubiquitous as the coppery blood smell around her.

"Why didn't you tell me?" she mumbled through a mouth gone cotton.

"Thank you for making me free," Chloe's grandma said, approaching her.

"Stay away!" Chloe spat.

She knew who the people with her grandmother were. Those were Chloe's parents. She was surprised she didn't notice the resemblance that night in the kitchen. And it was true, they had died in an accident but they had become something else. Something that fed off the living. Something nightmares were made of. And her grandmother had lived so that she could feed them only, eventually, the old woman had dried up. Her parents looked gaunt, wasted.

Chloe knew exactly what they wanted of her. Maybe she would just grab the gun and explode her head and give them what they wanted, give them the blood, give them the life. In her mind, she mapped where the gun lay on the bed. She needed to have it in her hand only she didn't know whom she was going to use it on.

Her grandmother stayed out of Chloe's reach but continued to talk.

"I'm glad all the secrets are out. Now we can be like a family again. There's nothing we can do to help it."

"I'm not going to be like you," Chloe said. "I'm not going to turn myself into a wasted wreck so you can continue being whatever you are."

"There's nothing you can do to stop it," her mother said.

"The fuck I can't," Chloe said.

She sprang up to her feet and grabbed the gun, putting it to her temple.

"Chloe, no!" Jack shouted from the doorway, shoving her family aside and flinging himself on her.

He grabbed her wrist and yanked the gun away from her head. But Chloe was not going to let him stop her. She pulled the trigger and the gun went off with a deafening explosion.

Chloe never felt the impact.

She reeled back on the bed and looked around her. Jack stood at the foot of the bed, the top right half of his head blown away. But he didn't drop. He didn't go down.

She wondered why it had taken her until now to recognize him for who he was. He had been in the kitchen that night also. Maybe it was the way the dawn slanted in through the window, reflecting off all the roses scattered across the bed and the floor and Chloe's arms.

The roses were hungry.

She knew that, no matter how many bullets she decided to put into Jack, in any of them for that matter, they would not die. Because they were already dead. Or, perhaps, beyond death. So, doing what she had originally planned, she put the gun to her head and pulled the trigger but the gun didn't fire. She tried again and again—nothing and nothing. Jack approached her, removed the gun from her hand. She thought about struggling but didn't know what value struggling would have. Jack had been the dream, or at least part of the dream, and now he was part of the nightmare. He pushed her back on the bed. She extended her arms out to either side and, with deathbright eyes, the Zwinns tore her open and fed from the blood coursing through her veins.

Chloe thought about a little girl she had seen downtown the other day. Perhaps she could take that girl. Take her and call her her daughter. Bring her here, tell her lies the entire time she grew up. Maybe she would even tell her about the roses on the wall. Tell her they were really like tumors . . . or hungry mouths. Tell her they would consume everything she knew and loved. Or maybe Chloe would just tell her to run. To run and run until she was so far away from this place it was just a distant memory. And, if the girl ever saw any strange visitors, Chloe could tuck her into bed and tell her it was nothing. Really, it was nothing. Just a bad dream. Just a nightmare. And everybody knows nightmares end when we open our eyes.

THE WARM HOUSE

SCHOOL LET OUT early because of the snow. Amy Bradshaw pulled her car to the curb in front of her house. There was already at least a foot of snow on the ground and her cheap car with its bald tires (a perfectly good car for a sixteen-year-old girl, according to her father) had barely made it from the high school. On the way home, she had listened to the weather reports on no fewer than three different radio stations and they all predicted the same thing—blizzard. When it got dark in a few hours, the temperature was expected to drop even further and the winds were supposed to pick up. They were advising businesses to close and motorists to stay off the road. There would be white-outs, the weather people said. They advised against the elderly and the infant leaving their homes.

Great, Amy thought, I'm going to have to be a shut-in for the next three days. Maybe she could go over to a friend's or get one of her friends to come over to her house so she wouldn't have to bear the company of her parents without some kind of a buffer. She was an only child and often hated this fact of life. The fact that she was the only one for her retired parents to focus their considerable attentions on.

My little princess, her dad often called her.

Yes, it seemed like he called her that every chance he got and she was getting sick of it. She no longer wanted to be anyone's princess. Sadly, her parents' affections were making her hate them. Maybe she was just getting older. She wanted to go off to college, someplace very far away and maybe only come back to visit during holidays and summers. She felt bad for feeling these things but, nevertheless, the feelings were there. They brewed to a thick froth with each passing day.

She thought all of this as she sat there in her shit car in front of her (her *parents'*) large house and took a deep breath before getting out. She pulled her coat tight around her neck and decided not to bother grabbing her backpack from the passenger seat. She probably wouldn't need it until Sunday. Today was only Thursday. She counted on school being canceled tomorrow.

The car door opened with an ancient squeak, wind biting into her skin.

Getting out of the car, she plunged ankle-deep in the snow and cursed it. She went around the front of the car and cautiously walked up the walk leading to her house.

Reaching her front door, she was surprised to find a package waiting below the mailbox. Hopefully, it was something for her. Maybe something she had ordered from the internet and completely forgotten about.

It was a simple rectangular box sitting with its length vertical. The side of it, in green lettering, read: "OPEN IMMEDIATELY OR-GANIC MATTER ENCLOSED."

Maybe someone sent me flowers, she thought. It *was* getting close to Valentine's Day. She quickly laughed that thought away. High school boys were not considerate enough to send packages.

A disappointing affirmation flooded her as she cleared some of the dirt from the address label. These weren't for anyone in her house. The label read "1311 Oakmount Dr." They were for the neighbor. The toad who lived next door. She could probably tell her dad they received a package in error and let him be the one to take it over but Amy thought it might buy her a few more minutes. Not to mention that she would, hopefully, be able to get a glimpse of the way the toad lived. She loved finding out things about people. The man had lived next door for nearly a year and she didn't know anything at all about him. She knew he was ugly, middle-ageish, lived alone, and rarely left the house. This chronic indoorsiness led her to believe he did not have a job. Of course, the neighborhood was relatively affluent so maybe he did something over the internet. Or maybe he collected disability. Or maybe he lived off an inheritance.

Suddenly, her interest was piqued.

Besides, it was very cold outside and if the box did contain flow-ers then she didn't think it was such a good idea to leave them sitting out there any longer than was absolutely necessary.

She picked the box up, holding it delicately with both hands, and walked back down the snow-covered walkway. The snow had picked up; big fat flakes that accumulated fast and stuck to the road. Maybe she would walk to Jennifer's later. She was the only one of her friends who lived in the neighborhood and she certainly didn't think she would be driving anyplace for the rest of the day.

Reaching the end of her walk, she turned right and walked the short distance to the neighbor's house on the obscured sidewalk.

Then she turned another right and started up the neighbor's walkway.

Curious, she thought. His house wasn't covered in snow like all the other houses in the neighborhood. The roof gleamed black as though it *had* snowed on it and now the snow had simply . . . melted off. That didn't seem quite right, she thought, but she guessed stranger things had happened. Maybe it was just the way his house sat or something. Maybe the wind had peeled off most of the snow and she was just imagining it looked wet. It was possible the meager sunlight hit his house in a more direct way than it hit the other houses.

As she reached the porch, she noticed the windows were also steamed up and while this didn't seem exactly normal, it didn't seem to be any reason for her to run screaming or anything. Maybe the guy just liked it warm. And speaking of the guy, she realized she didn't even know his name. Live next door to someone for nearly a year and you don't even know their first or last name. That didn't seem right, either. Suddenly, that seemed just as strange as the lack of snow on the man's roof.

But she had just seen his name, hadn't she? On the mailing label of the box. Why hadn't it stuck with her? She glanced back down at the box.

Brent Johnson, the man's name was. Totally inoffensive and unremarkable. No wonder it had simply bounced off her memory. Sometimes it amazed her how shallow she could be. How could she be truly interested in people and not remember a name, however forgettable, for two minutes?

Oh well. She was cold. She now wanted to be done with this business. Dump the package on the poor old ugly guy, pop in and say "hi" to Mom and Dad and then head on over to Jennifer's. Maybe Jen had managed to score some more vodka from her friend who worked at the drive-thru and they could warm up their evening that way.

Sounded good to her.

She rang the doorbell and waited.

She tapped her foot in the slush at the bottom of the door and rang the bell again.

Waited.

Jesus, it was cold. And the wind had already picked up.

She was about ready to simply set the package on the porch swing to the right of the door when she heard a voice call from inside.

"Coming," it said.

The door swung open and a tired-looking man opened the door. Her breath caught up in her throat. No, she realized, she didn't know anything about this Brent Johnson at all.

What startled her was that he wasn't as ugly as she had imagined. Only he was. She didn't know exactly. It was like he was probably really attractive at one time but, somewhere along the line, scars had happened. A lot of them. His face was covered in a series of thin, spiderweb-like scars, reaching down his neck and into the collar of his shirt. It made her think of looking into a fractured mirror.

Definitely disability, she thought.

He also wasn't as old as she had thought. Certainly not old enough to be retired. He was maybe only ten years or so older than she was. He had beautiful eyes. They were something like blue but not. Or not like any blue she had ever seen before.

She coughed, trying to break her trance. It wasn't her intention to make him feel like some kind of circus freak.

"Umm, sorry, Mr. Johnson. I think this is for you."

Confusion filled his eyes until she proffered the package toward him.

"I think it's flowers or something," she offered. "I didn't think they should be left outside."

Then his eyes lit up and maybe, just *maybe*, there was a little bit of madness there.

"Ah, yes! That's very good indeed. I can't believe they sent them to the wrong house. Come in out of the cold. Please."

"Well, I just live right next door. I'll be okay."

"No, come on in. You have to see this flower. A girl like you should appreciate beauty like this." Her cheeks blushed past their already cold-reddened state. He wiped a hand across his mouth, his eyes now greedily glued to the package. "It only takes a minute to look, right? Besides, we won't see flowers for months around here."

He took the box out of her hands quickly and turned around, heading into the house.

She hesitated for only a second before following him. There was something inviting about his house once she stepped all the way inside. It was incredibly warm, for one thing. Balmy. And it smelled good. She struggled for a second to think of what the smell reminded her of and then she had it. The ocean. Brent Johnson's house smelled like the ocean.

He set the box down in the center of the oak kitchen table and grabbed a knife from one of the drawers to the right of the sink.

"You're not going to believe this," he said. "I bet you've never seen anything like this at all."

Expertly, he sliced open the box. Rather than just cutting the tape and lifting the flower out of the box, he cut along three edges of the side that faced him. Then he slid the knife out of the box and held it up to the fluorescent light hanging over the table.

"Would you look at that," he said, his eyes sparkling with wonder, his lips turned up in a smile, deepening all of the scars covering his face.

She didn't know what to think. She didn't really pay that much attention to flowers but this one was certainly impressive. It reminded her of an orchid, the way the blooms hung at the end of a long stalk. But the blooms were huge, probably the size of her fist. They were a purple color, deep deep purple and it almost looked like they had been dusted with glitter. And they looked wet, as though something was oozing out of them.

"That's very pretty, Mr. Johnson."

"Oh, please, call me Brent. I'm so sorry. So distracted by the flower that I didn't even get your name."

"Oh, I'm Amy Bradshaw, from next door."

"You must be the daughter."

"That's right. What do you call it? The flower."

"Well, see, that's one of the good things about the flowers *I* collect. They don't have names."

"But I thought people who collected flowers were like obsessed with names."

"Some of them are. Some of us aren't. These flowers don't really come from your standard-type places. I don't know how to explain it, exactly. I think the name removes some of the mystery from them. When I look at my flowers, I see them for what they are. It is more complex and runs deeper than any word could ever describe. Would you like to see some more of my flowers?"

"Sure, I guess." She didn't think it would do any harm and she found herself feeling pretty comfortable in this house and, besides, what could possibly happen with her parents right there next door?

She followed him through the house and down into his brightly lighted basement.

What she saw down there hit her all at once. She felt like she was going to be sick but, for some reason, she didn't run.

"When you woke up this morning," Brent said. "Did you ever think you were going to die?"

This knocked her even further off guard.

She tried to back up but could barely move. She felt limp. The heat or bright lights or the things dangling from the walls stole something from her. I feel wilted, she thought, collapsing onto the bottom stair, desperate and terrified. Those weren't the only things she felt. Somewhere deep inside of her sparked the smallest grain of excitement. Or maybe it was adrenaline. She didn't know, didn't have time to analyze it. She only knew that it was something she hadn't felt in a very long time.

"You don't really want to leave," Brent said, wiping his mouth in that way that made her think he needed a drink of water.

Maybe he was right, she thought. At least, for now, maybe it was best to make him *think* he was right. It would give *her* time to think of a way out.

Tasting bile in the back of her throat, she looked around the brightly lighted basement. The gentle cerulean walls were only a background to the horrors standing out from them—a mixture of exotic plant life and human death. Or something like death. She wasn't really sure if the people hanging, pressed against the walls, were dead or not. Dismembered certainly, but maybe not dead. If they *were* dead, then they had been preserved remarkably well. Their skin still shone. Some of them appeared to breathe.

But everything breathes if you stare at it long enough.

She counted to ten.

Whatever they were or whoever they had been, they were something else now . . . That something else wasn't as disgusting as she had initially found it to be. The closer she looked at them, the more beautiful they became.

Across the basement, in front of her, hung a woman. Her left arm was gone. A thick, bright green vine grew out of the shoulder, as if replacing the arm. In place of her eyes were two deep blue blooms, undoubtedly larger than her eyes had ever been. A dark green carpet covered her legs. Was it some kind of moss? Amy wondered.

To the woman's left was another figure. She couldn't tell if it was male or female. Its head was thrown back in something like revelation or ecstasy. The body's torso was either missing or hidden, serving as fertilizer in some form of sick flowerbed. In its place, in a sloppy vertical line, grew three bright orange blossoms.

She should have turned and run. She knew this. She wanted to. Everything inside of her, everything in her being except for that wilted feeling and that spark of excitement, told her she *had* to get out of this place.

"Lovely, isn't it?" Brent asked her.

"Are they . . . are they dead?" Her voice was thick. It was an effort to push out any sound at all.

"Dead? No, they're not dead. They won't be coming back to this world anytime soon, though. They have gone some other place."

"Where did they go?"

"Well, I can't say exactly. I've only seen it in glimpses myself. I think of it as the land of the flowers. That's where all of these come from. The flowers take you to the land and they come from this land and it is all very confusing. The flowers are not very good at, uh, invoking clarity. And this land . . . it . . . *changes* with each flower."

He stopped talking and surveyed the basement, as though drinking in the ugly beauty surrounding him.

"Perhaps I'm getting ahead of myself," he said. "See, this place, I can only get there by consuming the flowers. I don't know where the flowers come from. I *think* . . . I *think* they come from over there. It wasn't until I moved here that I started getting them. Each month, these boxes would show up. The first one had instructions in it. Very explicit instructions on how to eat them. It was like something out of *Alice's Adventures in Wonderland*. I had to try it. The first time, I tried it alone. It changed me. I won't lie to you. I haven't been the same man since. But, after that first time, I knew it wasn't something I wanted to do alone. No, it was something I wanted to share. And that's why the others are down here. I know it looks like I have done something bad to them but, truthfully, I don't know if it is all that bad. And I can tell by the look on your face that *you* think I've done something bad to them. So maybe I have but . . . well, let me ask you this . . ."

He crossed the room and held his hand in front of one of the flower figures, one with a radiant and fleshy purple bush for a head.

"Does *this* sound like pain?"

He rubbed his hand down the figure's side. A moan came from somewhere on the figure, perhaps somewhere in the bush that had replaced her mouth. It certainly wasn't a moan of pain. Amy had made moans like that with her first and only boyfriend. But it went even beyond the moans she had given her boyfriend. The moans she had given her boyfriend were more for his benefit and ego. This moan escaping the woman hanging from the wall . . . *that* moan was what an orgasm would sound like, Amy thought.

"Now I have to ask you if you would like to go to this place with me. I won't lie to you. You might end up just like these people. I really don't know. Maybe it's happiness. Maybe it's misery. I wouldn't know, because I'm never allowed to stay. No matter what happens, I always come back. I don't know why it happens. I don't really even know what happens when I'm over there. I just know that I come back and I have more scars to mark my voyage and a sense of longing greater than any need I have ever had before. But *these* people . . . these people are there all the time."

Amy didn't know. She didn't feel like she had a whole lot of time to decide. In front of her sprawled a fate that was horrifying yet wild, mysterious, and potentially pleasurable while, out there, well, *out there* just seemed so boring now. How could she ever go back *out there* without having at least given this a chance?

She knew that was what every addict thought when trying their chosen vice for the first time.

A thick sweat had greased her skin since coming to the basement. She felt light-headed. She raised her head up from between her knees and said, "I'll go. Just tell me what you want me to do."

As she spoke the words, she was surprised. That was not what she wanted to say. Clearly, something had happened to her since coming down here and now a sudden panic gripped her. What if this enchantment could not be undone? What then?

Now, even while thinking about how much she wanted to quit this insanity, she spoke again, "What do you want me to do?"

"Oh, well, it's nothing too complex. You are the youngest one to go with me. That concerns me a little bit. See, when I told you before that I didn't name flowers, well, that was a little bit of a lie. The flowers all had names to begin with."

He walked over to one of the figures that had something like calla lilies growing down her left leg and patted her. She moaned as his hand touched her.

"This one," he said. "Is named Monica. That one . . ." he pointed to the one next to her. "Is named Celina." He pointed to one on the far side of the room. "And that one, unfortunately, is named Tonya."

Then he held out the flower that came for him today, elevating it under the bright fluorescent light so the light caught on the sparkles covering the petals. "And this one," he said. "I suppose this one will be called 'Amy.'"

He plucked off two of the petals, balancing them gingerly on the tips of his index and middle fingers.

"All you have to do is eat this. It doesn't really take any time at all."

Slowly, he crossed the basement toward her. Swiping the back of his right hand across his mouth, he extended his left toward her, the petals softly sitting on the tips. A cough would have sent them spiraling to the floor.

Without hesitation, she reached out her own hand, taking one of the purple petals into her slender fingers. More to fully savor the experience rather than any sort of cautionary measure, she held the petal up to her nose and inhaled a deep breath. It smelled like fruit. No fruit that she could place immediately, but it smelled fresh and wonderful, whatever it was. Brent stuck the remaining petal onto his tongue and chewed it slowly. Following his lead, she did the same, thinking of it as some kind of bizarre communion wafer.

An impossible amount of juices splashed the inside of her mouth. It didn't seem right that something so small as a flower petal could contain that much liquid and that much intense flavor. The potency of the flavor was almost biting but there was an underlying sweetness there. That sweetness, that was something she immediately wanted more of. She had the instant urge to run to the plant sitting on the floor of the basement and begin pulling the petals off and shoving them into her mouth. She forgot about Brent entirely. The only thing she wanted at that moment was to have another taste of that flower because the petal she had put into her mouth was already gone, all dissolved, and it had taken its taste with it, rudely gobbling it up like a miser, leaving nothing in its place. Nothing. And this sense of nothingness felt even greater because what it was the alternative to was so great . . .

Amy wasn't in the basement anymore.

She didn't know how that happened. The plant had taken her to this other place. Instead of the rich sweetness of its taste, the plant now offered her this dreamscape.

She stood in the street, in front of Brent's house, her own house behind her. Theirs was a dead end street and she should have been staring into a field on the other side of a rusted barb-wire fence but what she stared at instead was a vast ocean. It was a beautiful blue ocean. More beautiful than the waters she had seen in travel brochures for the Caribbean. And above the ocean sprawled a sun-filled, deep blue sky. What made this odd was that, where *she* stood, on her street, she stood in ankle-deep snow and darkness. She should have been cold but she wasn't. She was merely filled with the desire to walk toward the ocean, to feel its warm waters wrap around her.

She was aware of something else too. She didn't know where it came from exactly. It felt like something else opened up in the back of her head. It was like a window. She didn't understand it. She didn't know if she *wanted* to understand it.

In this window, this spooky ghostplace at the back of her head, she saw Brent. At first, she was afraid he could see her and then she realized he wasn't paying any attention to her whatsoever and even if he *was* there wasn't really any physically possible way he could be living inside her head. At least, she didn't *think* there was. But her thoughts still didn't seem entirely her own.

He looked at himself in a mirror and smiled, as though he were posing for a picture. When he smiled, all of the scars on his face bunched up, making him nearly repulsive. He was naked to the waist and the same scars etched their way across his pale torso. He held a large knife in his hand. He placed the blade to the right corner of his mouth and pulled the knife toward his ear so the skin opened up into a gaping red wound. Then he did the same to the other side, blood running down his neck and onto his chest. Now he would be smiling whether he liked it or not . . . permanently.

The result was monstrous.

What was the point of all this? Amy wondered. But she only wondered what the point of Brent's actions were. They seemed so tragic and awful compared to what lay in front of her. What lay in front of her didn't make her feel bad at all. It made her feel ecstatic. She ran along her road, the wind whipping around her body, oblivious to its cold sting. Running like that, *thinking* about the one simple act of left leg-right leg, took her mind's eye away from the glowering image of Brent.

Her road ended in a cliff tumbling straight down into the ocean's depths. What lay just beyond that cliff was what really captured her attention. What she saw was something that looked like an island paradise. Only the island was very small. Perhaps the size of her backyard. And it was as high up as the cliff, tottering there, the top of it fatter than the bottom. Amy didn't think it would take much to knock it over. But she planned to go there.

The window in the back of her head opened up again so she could see what Brent was doing. He was in his basement.

Blood covered him. In one hand he held the same butcher knife he had used to slice his face and in the other hand he held a huge pair of gardening shears.

It took her a second to realize what he was doing.

He was *pruning* the women in the basement. The pruning shears went *snip-snip* with great dexterity, taking a leaf here and a finger there, flesh and vegetation treated as though they were the same. Then he leaned over them, the blood spilling from his wounds, "watering" them.

How long would it take him to realize she wasn't there? How long would it take him to realize he didn't have the latest flower he needed? The latest flower he *desired?*

For a second, she contemplated running back to her parents, charging through the front door and telling them about everything that was going on. But she didn't do that. She didn't think it would help. Didn't even know if it would be possible. Besides, she didn't think she was in any condition to know what was going on herself. She imagined herself jabbering on, half-incoherent, spouting nonsense about thoughts not being her own.

What she wanted was the island beyond the cliff in front of her.

In her mind, she watched as Brent sliced an earlobe from one of the women. The woman cried out in some kind of ecstatic agony and something resembling a poppy took the place of the earlobe.

Above Amy, the sky was dark and purple, clouds ominously swirling. In front of her, the blue sunfilled sky. She wanted that.

She stood at the edge of the cliff and opened up her arms to the sky, opened her arms to the wind, letting it take her, letting it gather itself around her clothes, bearing her up and toward that island.

She closed her eyes, smelling the sea as she crossed overtop of it, hearing the waves crash down on the rocks below.

Then she felt ground beneath her feet, smelling the fragrant jungle around her.

She opened her eyes and gagged.

The view around her was similar to the view in Brent's basement only a thousand times worse.

Amy knew these people were not living. That was impossible. Maybe their bodies experienced some kind of unknown sensual pleasure but none of it was of their own choosing any longer and she didn't think that could be considered life.

She didn't want to be on the island anymore.

But she didn't know if she had a choice or not.

She turned to go back the way she had come but Brent blocked her path.

How did he get there? she wondered.

It wasn't important, she figured.

He moved up close to her, grabbing her around the waist. She smelled his blood. It opened up her nose and poured through her body in a way none of the flowers could.

"Let me go," she said, still choking.

"Where do you want to go?" Brent said, his ghastly smile directly in front of her face.

And suddenly, much like the window in her mind that allowed her to see what Brent was doing, something else opened up and she thought she knew what he was thinking. He wanted her to stay here with him. He wanted her to be his queen in this sick, warped world of half-life and half-death. He wanted her to let him slide that giant knife down her skin, open up a vein and let her blood spill out so he could drink it. So he could absorb a little more of the things growing around him.

"I just want to go home," she muttered.

"I think you'll like my home much better."

"No," she muttered. She tasted doom on the back of her throat. He seemed so much stronger than her. She struggled against him but it didn't seem to do any good. He could drag her down into the soft dirt and do whatever he wanted to do with her.

But then his grip lessened somewhat and a hurt look blossomed in his eyes.

Amy took this chance to stumble back from him and his blood-spattered knife.

Behind him stood, if one could call it that, something that was half-man and half-bush. His arms were missing. In their place were two vines with lavender flowers dangling from them. And beneath the lavender flowers were thorns no fewer than six inches long. This man wrapped one of his arms around Brent's neck.

Amy wondered if Brent was the one who had created these awful things or if he was just fulfilling someone else's destiny. She turned away from the scene, away from the island, running toward its edge. She stopped at the lip of the island, teetering over the drop and the ocean below.

The ocean wasn't there, she told herself. The ocean had never been there because all of her thoughts were her own and the person who was thinking all those other thoughts for her was left to deal with his own nightmarish fate now. Holding out her arms, she let herself fly into the blue day, sinking slowly down to the warm waves that were not there.

She woke up on the floor of Brent Johnson's basement. No sign of the plant people were down there, just the strangely cerulean walls that now seemed comforting. Maybe she had just come down here and passed out somehow. Maybe the whole thing had been a dream.

She stood up, the aches and pains in her body telling her it wasn't just a dream. Her throat felt scorched. She felt cold.

She walked up the stairs and through the house. The house was bare, like no one had ever lived there, like there had never been a person named Brent Johnson.

Out of the house, she continued to walk, into the snow, the cold scalding her tender skin. She didn't bother with the sidewalk, she walked straight through the yard and up to her porch.

A box sat beneath the mailbox to the right of the door. She recognized the printed message on it. She cleared off the address label, half-expecting to see next door's address on there. Instead, what she saw was her name and her address.

Strangely, she found herself tempted to open it. She wanted, so desperately, to know what was inside the box. But she already knew what was inside the box. She wanted to taste it. She wanted to feel it run through her. But she didn't want to go where it wanted to take her.

Picking up the box, she marched around to the back of the house and put it into the trashcan with the address label facing down so it was just a box and nothing her parents would be too suspicious of.

Then she took a deep breath of the cold, let it fill her lungs, pulled a forbidden cigarette from the pocket of her coat and lit it, looking around at her mundane little neighborhood, all covered in snow and the first thin strands of dusk.

THE NOWHERE ROOM

ANNA SEIFERT SAT in front of her computer, trying to work on a literary paper about the writings of Ambrose Bierce. So far, she hadn't made it any further than the title page. The cursor blinked in and out of the grayish-white background, after the terminal "t" of her last name.

It was a beautiful early summer day. She stared out the window. Her study felt like a prison. The window afforded a perfect view of the children across the street. Three kids who looked to be around the age of five ran around the neighborhood yard in an insane pattern, no doubt driven by a perfectly understandable kid-logic. The next minute, she was yanked from their sunny imaginings and thrown to the floor.

It had been a while since she'd had one of these attacks but she immediately recognized it for what it was.

Once again, her memory was trying to kill her.

On the floor, struggling to crawl across the carpet and pull herself up on something, her vision turned a screaming red.

Her head throbbed.

Her muscles knotted up.

Her gorge rose and she exploded a pool of stinking vomit, some unseen hand forcing her down into it.

And then she heard the voice, calling her name like metallic fire and brimstone scraping at the inside of her skull, the backs of her eyes.

"Anna!"

She tried to answer it, but her gorge came up again, turning her vocal cords acid and watery.

"Anna! Anna! Anna! Anna! Anna!"

The voice always liked to wait until she was alone. Sure, it removed embarrassment but it also removed any sense of comfort she might gain from those around her.

The angry swarm in her mind and viscera, like a vicious hybrid of psychic bees, screamed on for a few more minutes before leaving her stunned, squirming in her own vomit, piss, and shit. Her pride was gone someplace else but the past, the past was right there in front of her.

Anna saw a small abandoned house in a stand of trees behind an empty field.

She saw a small fire burning in a thickly rusted grill without legs.

She saw a sixteen-year-old girl named Carmen.

She saw visions and colors, some of them beautiful, some of them horrible. She felt a glittering, revelatory magic in her veins and felt it turn ugly.

She rose from her expulsion, went into the lonely bathroom and washed the stink from herself. It had taken years but she now knew what she had to do.

Once she started for Gibraltar, there was no turning back. Something pulled and pushed her along, forced the whining engine of her car to give as much as it could. Intense tunnelvision melted Anna's eyes to the road, keeping her mind free from distraction. Almost eagerly, she cruised along the boondocks, those rural islands of Ohio, sandwiched in between the industrial sprawls.

Soon, with the gray coming of dusk, she reached the tiny town of Gibraltar. It was roughly the same size as Red Oak, the college town where she taught, but completely different. It was precisely the beaten down, worker-drone mentality of Gibraltar that had pushed Anna through the ranks of the university. When she finally received her Ph.D. from a small school in Pennsylvania, she hung the certificate by her desk and it was only then she felt separated from Gibraltar. Wherever she moved afterwards, the doctorate came with her, hung someplace where she could see it nearly any time she wanted to—hung up as a reminder. She couldn't explain it, exactly. She just always had this fear that, without as much education as she could possibly get, she was forever in danger of sliding down some dark rabbit hole and becoming one of Them.

And now, as she entered the town, the same force that had been speeding her along slowed her down as if to say, "Look." She cruised down Main Street, her eyes scouring the shabby buildings, the run-down storefronts, the three bars with spraypainted, particle-board windows. A man stepped out from one of the bars, his skin as gray as his hair, thin shoulders protruding from his ancient flannel shirt. He stared at the sidewalk as he ambled along, his whole body leaning toward the ground, toward some premature death. Anna thought they should change the town's name to Sorrow. The depressing sadness that had ridden with her the first eighteen years of her life was back.

Luckily, the town proper wasn't that large and she was soon out on the state route, cutting through fields of low corn.

Memories trickled through her head and, for the first time in a long time, she thought of the Infinity Room.

Anna had discovered it the summer she was twelve and had immediately told Carmen about it. Carmen had dubbed it the Infinity Room without any real reason, they just decided they liked the name. Furthermore, it was a name they could agree on. The small, one room house in the middle of the woods became like a slice of adulthood for them. They went there and talked about whatever they wanted to as loudly as they wanted to. Sometimes Carmen stole cigarettes from her mother and, together, they smoked them in the Infinity Room. They got drunk their first time in the Infinity Room. Anna lost her virginity there when she was fourteen. It was with one of Carmen's cousins who had come down for the week. He was seventeen and told her he had already initiated Carmen. It lasted only a couple of minutes and ended with the boy awkwardly masturbating in her face. She didn't learn until later that was how they did it in pornos.

She cared nothing for the boy and nothing for the experience although, over the next couple of years, she took a few more boys to the Infinity Room. When she was sixteen, she realized she only liked boys as friends. Carmen was who Anna was attracted to. Other women would come later but, at the time, she thought only of Carmen. That summer, the Infinity Room blossomed into something very much like a house with Carmen and Anna playing the parts of newlyweds. Slowly, as the summer drew on and rotted into fall, a taint came over the Infinity Room. For the first time, there were arguments. The girls said things to each other they didn't really mean.

Things were done that shouldn't be done. The winter and early spring were unbearable, a screaming black Rorschach blot of heart-broken teenage depression. It was here Anna's memory broke up and turned to static.

"Carmen," Anna said, barely audible. It felt good. It was a name that started all the way at the back of the throat, brought the lips together and exited the mouth with a soft air, the tongue left to caress the roof of the mouth.

"Carmen."

Her car left by the dirt access road, Anna approached the small house in the early moonlight, her heart leaping around in her chest. Choked with memories, she pulled open the door and stepped into the familiar smell of old rotting wood and all the familiarity of the past.

With an electric rush, it came over her. Veins pounding, skin crawling, she remembered what had happened on that April day just after turning seventeen.

It had been a rough morning. Anna had fought with Carmen the previous night and it looked like they might finally go their separate ways. Wanting to get away from her mother's questioning (*Are you using* drugs, *Anna? No boy's worth all this, Anna.*), she went to the Infinity Room.

She remembered everything now with a distilled clarity.

The way she had stalked up to the old house, wanting only to sit and sulk in one of its cool corners. Sit and sulk and be alone and think about how she would have to get used to that word: "alone." She remembered the way she had yanked the rickety old door back on its tenuously moored hinges. The way she had felt when she saw the boy on top of Carmen, working away. The look in Carmen's eyes that said, with glistening surprise, things could never be the same again.

Anna felt hackles rise all over her body. A previously unfelt electricity started in her stomach when she saw Carmen's hips, pale and perfect, below her upraised cotton dress, rising to meet the boy's thrusts. Unbridled, Anna felt the electricity, the energy, explode from her skin.

She screamed. Powerful and focused, she directed that energy to the sick revenge taking place on the floor of the Infinity Room. Then it was their turn to scream.

The poor boy didn't even know what hit him.

He had come down somewhere on the state route. The trucker who rolled over him said he never even saw him. It was like he came out of nowhere. The papers, of course, never said he fell from the sky. It was speculated that he had simply wandered out onto the road at the wrong time. There was alcohol in his system, never mind that it wasn't enough to write his accident off as a drunken mishap. The papers never mentioned Carmen and Anna. The girls were the only ones who knew about that, about Anna's awful power.

Carmen, poor Carmen, would never be the same again.

And Anna turned her back on it all. Left to throw herself into her studies, to busy herself with the creation of a purely intellectual world she could shape and control with all the tools of her trade.

Now Anna stood in the Infinity Room, so much cooler than outside. Outside where there was life—the rattle of cicadas, the chirp of crickets, the ever growing and twisting of the trees and vines. In here there were only memories.

Anna circled the small iron top of the thickly rusted legless grill, something she and Carmen had dragged here to build fires in. Fires that melted away their inhibitions and their childhood.

Looking down into it, she saw red-hot coals flicker and ignite into a small flame.

Anna wasn't very shocked. She expected things like this to happen when she came back to the Infinity Room.

Looking around, she noticed not much had changed. There were new things spraypainted and chalked on the walls: OZZY RULES, THE BREW CREW, SENIORS 91, FUCK ME MARYLOU, PO-OPTOOTH LIVES. All of the scribblings stood out as epithets toward her memories.

Then she saw Carmen, faintly at first and then drawn into sharp focus. The insubstantial figure walked toward the fire, toward Anna, coming out of nowhere.

"Carmen," Anna said.

"Anna," Carmen said back.

"It's good to see you."

"You knew I would be here. I've always been here."

"Well, I knew you would be here in spirit."

"No, you saw to it a long time ago that I would always be here. Why did we call it the Infinity Room? Do you remember?"

Anna shook her head.

"We should have called it the Nowhere Room," Carmen said. "Because that's what it is. You know, I've been right here ever since that day, waiting for you to come back. I knew you would."

"You haven't been here since that day. I watched you walk away . . ."

"But I was never the same, Anna."

Anna used to like to hear Carmen say her name, but now it contained all the beauty of a racial slur. It was something spit or thrown out of the mouth.

Carmen continued, "You stole something vital from me that day. Just like how you managed to throw Peter nearly a mile away. You stole something from him, too. And you, you were too self-involved to even realize what had happened. What would your students . . . what would your precious *colleagues* think if they knew you could wipe them out with a single thought?"

"Carmen . . . I didn't mean . . . I was just so mad. I had no control over it. I never . . . It's never happened since. I've learned." Anna's body was trembling.

"The Nowhere Room, Anna. This is where you left my insides when you scraped them out. But you wouldn't know. You've never come back to visit."

Warm tears coursed down Anna's cool cheeks. "I'm sorry, Carmen . . . If I had known, I would have . . ."

"Would have what? Come back so you could piss on my soul. Take it out of nowhere and put it someplace worse. You say you had no control over it, but what about after that incident? What about when you saw me walking down the halls at school, a hollow shell? What about after I got sick and laid in bed for months? I had *strangers* coming to visit me, Anna. People I didn't even know. And where were you? Where were you at my funeral? Another room filled with strangers."

"My parents wouldn't let me go."

"You were nowhere."

Sobs and sadness rippled the muscles in Anna's face. She drew in a snotty breath and said, "Carmen, I only wanted to be with you . . . Since then, you're the only one I've thought about."

"Is that what it was all about? Because you couldn't have me. Because I liked boys better than you?"

"No," Anna sobbed.

"Well, you had me and then you let me go. I think you could have brought me back from nowhere and I still think you will. I've learned some tricks of my own over the years."

"To say the least." Anna thought about the unseen forces that had attacked her over the years, things she had always thought were part of her own mind until earlier today.

"You've noticed," Carmen said.

Now Anna's black memories turned to an even blacker tumor of fear. From inside her head, she felt a sickening twisting metal feel, the one that had driven her to the floor earlier. But this time it pulled her toward the fire. The nausea blossomed like a mushroom cloud and she bent to throw up and found herself unable to fall to her knees, her puke hanging from her chin and sizzling onto the fire, fueling it rather than dampening it. And then she stepped into the small grill, felt the flames at her feet, licking at her jeans and crawling slowly upward until they licked at the backs of her arms, up her stomach, her breasts, her neck, her spine, her hair, her chin, her lips, her cheeks, her eyes.

And she heard Carmen's voice saying, "I'm going to get out of nowhere and you're going to take me. I am the fire around you. I am the Nowhere Room. I am the trees and the snakes and the wolves and the dirt and the air and the stars and the moon. I consume you, Anna. *I consume you.*"

Anna felt the fire burning the moisture out of her skin, shrinking it. She felt her skin crack and pop open and heard her vital fluids hissing onto the flames.

Slowly, skinless, Anna stepped out of the fire. With a new vision, she looked around the Nowhere Room and saw it for what it was: Nowhere. On tender feet, she crossed the warped wooden floor and exited through the door.

Outside, the balmy night breeze rustled the trees and moved over her moist, raw body. Everything was bright and purple and she felt magic snake through her exposed muscles and veins. Relishing the night, she walked deeper into the woods until she reached a small clearing. Here she smelled the earth's dark loam and almost thought she could smell each mineral in the soil, hear them slowly dissolve into the trapped rainwater. She felt the dark decay of the dead leaves and felt the slow growth, so full of life, of the trees around her.

Then she heard the banshee-like yattering of wolves, all of them responding to one another, their collective howls and yelps rising to an ear shattering crescendo.

They surrounded her.

"I am all that surrounds you," she heard Carmen whisper in her head.

Slowly, they closed their circle on her. These were not the beautiful, powerful wolves she recognized from nature photos. No. These were the Gibraltar version. What wolves looked like in Nowhere. They were thin and mangy, yellow-eyed and decrepit. Wild dogs. They looked so underfed they would eat anything and, eagerly, they sniffed at the meal at hand.

Anna was not afraid.

Fear was not an option.

She felt their wet muzzles on her glistening body. She felt their tongues lapping at her blood, sucking it from between muscle and tendon. Sensing the competition amongst them, they all tore in at once and Anna felt their broken teeth rip into her meat and drag her down into their pack. She felt and smelled their greasy fur rubbing up against her and longed for their filthiness. She felt one of them between her legs, nuzzling at her burnt sex before digging in with its teeth. She felt her meat come off her bones and stared up at that faceless purple sky, glittering with the icily indifferent stars. She felt herself go out into that sky, something inside of her rising above the wolves. She felt herself circling the earth, pulled toward the sun and burning up in the atmosphere, fires exploding behind her eyes and through her viscera and she exploding with them.

When she came to she was curled up beside a long dead fire in the thickly rusted legless grill of the Nowhere Room. The oily, burnt charcoal smell cloyed at her. Dawn trickled in through the windows.

She took deep breaths. She ran her hands down her body.

She was alive.

She was whole.

Thank God.

Slowly, like somebody coming upon a new world, she walked out of the woods and down the dirt access road walled in by those fields of corn.

She remembered leaving the keys in her car, ready to make a quick escape, and hoped no one had stolen it.

Heavily, she trudged along in the dirt until she reached her car, the door handle feeling cool, clean, and good.

Anna sat down and turned the ignition.

She reached for the power button on the radio, wanting some loud music to wipe away the darkness of the previous night. She still wasn't sure what had happened. Wasn't sure she really *wanted* to know.

With her fingers on the tuner, another voice, a foreign one, came into her head, "What are we going to listen to, Anna?"

"Carmen," she whispered.

Without controlling them, her fingers pressed the tuner until it landed on a jangly rock song.

"There, that's good," Carmen said.

Anna pulled away from the gravel roadside feeling both extremely sad and happy. She realized she no longer controlled her body, it was Carmen. From within her own head, she could feel out Carmen's thoughts and they were not her own. Carmen wanted to see her new house. Carmen wanted to meet her new coworkers, people who had only been faces across a metaphysical void. Carmen wanted to feel a man between her legs, his cock battering her insides. Nausea racked Anna but she had no way of being sick, her body no longer hers. Anna sensed the new duality of her existence, heard the yammering voice of another person's thoughts, and felt the first powerless fingers of madness.

"Welcome to the Nowhere Room." Carmen laughed with Anna's mouth, checked her soul behind Anna's eyes in the rearview mirror, and sped down the state route.

DURNING

THE HIGHWAY THRUMMED beneath them.

"It's nice of you to give up your break just to come with me," Christina Johnson said from the passenger seat, her delicately pale hand reaching out, stroking his knee.

Adam Strafe squinted into the sunlight beading through the dirty windshield and said, "I'm not really giving up much."

"I'm sure you miss your family, though."

"Maybe. I don't know. My parents are pretty preoccupied with the younger ones and . . . well, Maine isn't really pleasant this time of year. Not very springlike."

"I can't wait until you meet Mom and Dad. They're gonna love you."

"I'm looking forward to it."

That wasn't really true. Adam didn't really care about meeting her parents. He had a couple of motives for spending his break with her but meeting her parents definitely wasn't at the top of the list. First and foremost, he was hoping to finally be able to sleep with her. He had the whole scenario worked out in his head. Mom and Dad Johnson would make him a bed on the downstairs couch and he would sneak up to her room after lights out. This, he reminded himself, would be her teenage high school room. There would probably be posters of rock stars on the walls and stuffed animals tucked away in the corners of the closet. And there, maybe, he would have her.

"I might just have to show you off to the whole town," she said, smiling that perfect smile, all those straight white teeth beneath the freckled cheeks and coffee brown eyes.

"Durning, Ohio," he said. "I can't wait to see if it's everything you've made it out to be."

"Oh, it is. It's the perfect town. Almost magical."

Looking at her, he almost believed such a town could exist. He had met her in an undergraduate philosophy class at Shartles University in Pennsylvania. He sat to her right. He could almost smell the apple pie clinging to her hair. He was reminded of the part in *Annie Hall* when Woody Allen's character first meets Annie Hall and thinks of her as, "Annie from Wisconsin." That was how Adam thought of Christina. Christina from Ohio. Durning, Ohio, more specifically. The perfect town. Where the mail always ran on time and the neighbors not only knew but *loved* one another. That was his other reason for coming with her. He couldn't imagine such a town. Where he came from—Salt Port, Maine—the winters were long and mean and the people were almost as harsh. Growing up, he remembered the sky as a desolate slate of gray.

"So what's the weather like in Durning?" he asked, making small talk, car talk, something to while away the time.

"It's usually pretty nice. Especially this time of year. Not too hot, not too cold."

"Probably raining though, huh?"

"It doesn't rain that much in Durning. It must have something to do with the way the land lays or something. You know, like in the Pacific Northwest?"

He was clueless. He shook his head.

"There's Seattle, right? And everybody knows how much it rains there. But just to the east of Seattle, it's practically a desert. That's because of the Cascade Mountains. At least, I think it's the Cascades. They hold back the clouds and that's why it rains so much to the west of them but hardly at all to the east."

Ah, Christina from Durning, Ohio. Adam didn't know if anyone else could be truly enthralled by such trivialities. He loved it. It was almost enough to make him love her but he didn't know if he was ready for that yet. He didn't know if *she* was ready for that yet. It didn't seem like she had enough of the world on her. Let her season, let her experience some things, ferment, and then he would see what kind of person she would become.

Continuing on I-70 West through the mountains and the Amish country of western Pennsylvania, they crossed into Ohio and Adam asked if they were close yet.

"About another hour or so," she said, staring wide-eyed out the window.

They continued to make small talk. Christina talked nearly non-stop about Durning. He had heard about some of the people before. But she had different stories for them.

And pictures. She said she had taken a roll of film and went through town snapping pictures so she could remember them all. Adam glanced from the pictures back to the road, Christina narrating each picture. There was her dad, Thomas, smiling into the camera. He was a milkman. Adam said he didn't know towns still had milkmen. There was her mother, Angelica. She was, of course, a stay-at-home mom. There was Town Hall. There was Memorial Park, in the center of town, landscaped perfectly, a wide expanse of lawn covered by picnickers and boys playing catch and girls playing with hula hoops. There was the soda shop/drugstore. Another throwback. And Mr. Daniels, the proprietor, wore one of those paper soda jerk hats on his head. Adam wondered if he was the pharmacist, also. He didn't know if he would want drugs from a man wearing a paper hat. The photos revealed women who were matronly but not unattractive. The men were lean and hard-jawed but their eyes twinkled with kindness. Unreal. Adam wanted to be cynical about the whole thing but it all sounded pretty good. After he finished doing all the things he felt like a young man had to do, he could see himself settling down in a place like Durning.

"Low on gas," he said, noticing the gauge bobbing in and out of the cautionary orange block.

"You should probably stop at the next gas station. That'll probably be it until Durning."

A few minutes later, he pulled into a gas station. They both got out, arching their backs in the pleasant air. It was early April and there was just a hint of summer balm in the air. Adam went around to the tank, twisted off the cap, inserted the pump and started filling.

"I'm gonna go in and get some coffee. Want some?" she asked.

"Sure. Thanks."

He put the pump on automatic and watched her as she walked in.

She was perfect. He didn't really want to admit that. He thought maybe he was too young to say he had really discovered perfection but there she was, strolling through the parking lot with her confident head held high. The pump stopped itself and he started for the store to pay. Spying him through the window, she motioned him away. She was paying this time too even though it was her car and she had paid before they left. He was okay with that. He would pay on the way back.

He got back in the car and watched her come toward him. Toward *him*. He couldn't really believe how she had even taken an interest in him. Maybe over the summer, he could take her back to his home town and show her the backwoods shacks, the abandoned houses downtown, the junked cars littering the yards of the shoddy suburbs. He grimaced at the thought.

"Thanks," he said as she slid into the car, handing him his jumbo Styrofoam cup of coffee. He took a sip. Gas station coffee always tasted like it was made with pencil shavings but it had caffeine and the caffeine was what he needed to get him through this last jaunt.

The last half hour or so they sipped their coffee and talked about other things, mostly common professors or projects they were supposed to be working on over the break.

She directed him off the interstate and onto a state route and then through some winding backroads. Ohio had yet to become flat and some of the turns were pretty wicked. Then they turned onto a gravel road and rose up a steep hill that wanted to be a mountain. When they reached the top she told him to stop the car.

"Here?" he asked.

"Yeah, you can see the whole town from up here."

"Oh, cool," he said. He always liked those sorts of bird's-eye-views of towns.

He eased the car over to the side of the road and downed the last of his coffee. He looked at her and she smiled and made him feel things he had never felt before.

The road dropped away on her side of the car and he crossed over to her.

"Isn't it beautiful?" she asked.

He looked out over the valley and saw nothing. Was he supposed to see something? The only thing he saw was the gravel of the road give way to the grassy hillside and descend into a grassy meadow. A small knot of fear began in his gut.

"What are we looking at?" he asked, putting his arm around her.

"Durning," she said.

He had never thought she was insane before that instant and it was so fleeting he almost wanted to laugh it off.

He did laugh. A low chuckle that got caught up in the back of his throat. He coughed and felt his head swim. His vision blurring, the whole green meadow swooned in front of him. His stomach kicked up. Damn the coffee, he thought. Cheap ass gas station coffee always made his stomach burn. And when was the last time he'd eaten?

"I'm not feeling so well," he said.

"Maybe you need to lie down," she said, beaming, moving in, kissing him on the cheek, running a hand softer than cornsilk down his forearm.

"Yeah," he choked out.

He didn't even remember making it back to the car.

"You've finally come to," Adam heard Christina's voice through a thick haze.

Yes. He had finally come to. He wondered what had happened to him. He opened his eyes, expecting to feel her cool and comforting hand on his forehead.

But he had trouble opening his eyes. He couldn't focus. Once he finally got them opened, it still didn't feel right. His vision was limited. He couldn't see anything to his left. He felt that eyelid opening and closing but there wasn't anything there.

What the hell? he thought.

He tried to raise his hand to touch his eye because he didn't know why he couldn't see anything out of it and he wondered what that ache was. That ache, so hollow, throbbing at the border of his brain.

And why couldn't he move his arms?

Something was wrong. He was now sure of that. He was either more than just sick or . . . or Christina had done something horrible to him.

With his one eye, he looked down at his lap.

He was seated in a wheelchair.

A wheelchair? he thought. Maybe he had been out a lot longer than he thought he had. Maybe he had gone into some sort of coma.

No. No, that couldn't be. Looking ahead of him, he saw the meadow he and Christina had looked down upon only the sunlight had disappeared and a little wind had picked up and it felt a lot colder now.

His hands were strapped to the armrests of the wheelchair. His heart skipped and thudded in his chest when he saw that his right hand didn't look right. Three fingers were missing. It wasn't until noting their absence that he felt the pain there too. A different kind of pain than the one in his eye but a very real pain nonetheless.

Where was Christina?

He turned to view the panorama before him. He spotted her to his right. She was bent down about four feet from his wheelchair, her back to him.

"If you're wondering about your eye, I took it out."

He wanted to laugh. It had to be a sick joke but he knew she wasn't joking. He could see that some of his fingers were missing, why should he think his eye was anything but gone?

"*What?*" he coughed out.

"You heard me. If you're wondering about your eye, I took it. We needed a theater."

She patted the ground with her small hands and stood up, dusting them off on her jeans.

"Did you *plant* my eye?" he asked.

"Of course. How else would I grow a theater?"

She came over behind the wheelchair, leaned down close to his ear and said, "This is going to be the best town yet. I'm sorry you never got to see Durning. Kenneth Durning was this absolutely beautiful boy I met in Idaho. He was beautiful but so naïve. You wouldn't believe the things I wanted to do to him. I told him all about those things but he wasn't interested. You could practically smell the fucking apple pie on him. So I planted him somewhere in Missouri. That's where Durning really is. It's a beautiful place. Real fucking pure. Just like him.

"I wonder what kind of place Strafe will be. I give the theater two months before they start showing porn."

Christina pushed the wheelchair along. Adam jostled himself about, trying to topple the thing.

"Just let me go, Christina. Let me go!"

"You know I can't do that."

"Why? Just let me go. I need a hospital. I need a doctor."

"The town needs a concert hall. Where do you think we should put it?"

Hot pain. Slicing down close to his scalp. Screaming behind his ear.

Christ! She just removed his ear.

"Christina! Christina!" he shouted.

She walked in front of the wheelchair, in front of him, now to the other side of him, and planted his ear in the grassy ground.

Adam could feel himself sliding into shock. He realized he was alternately screaming and sobbing but he couldn't do anything to stop that. He couldn't help it. His chest rose and fell rapidly. He was very aware of the blood covering his body.

"Christina, just let me go and I swear, I swear to God I'll do anything you want me to just please please please don't do this."

"You talk too much."

She grabbed some other instrument from behind his head. It was a long knife. She drew it back on each cheek, severing all of the muscles controlling his jaw.

She doesn't want me to bite her, Adam thought. Oh my God, she doesn't want me to bite her. And that meant she was going to do something even worse.

She reached into his mouth and grabbed his tongue. Adam tried his hardest to jerk it away but she clamped with her thumb and fingertips and it hurt. Amazing, he thought, with all the other pains in his body, the way his tongue was able to take center stage and hurt the most.

Sticking the knife back to his throat, she drew the blade along the back of his tongue and the only sound Adam could make was with his now ravaged vocal cords. She held the tongue up in front of him.

"I wonder what we'll do with this. A tongue can become many things. A church that spits lies. A coffeehouse of bad poetry. A townhall of bickering dissent. The rundown house of the finest whore in town."

Adam sat in the chair, his body rigid, his one eye bulging toward Christina as she held the tongue up appraisingly. She turned to plant it in the ground. Now he couldn't smell any trace of apple pie on her. The only thing he could smell with his last trembling breaths was the stink of death and he didn't know from which of them it came.

GLOWERS POINT

KAREN BRUCKNER HAD just finished knotting the condom when the phone rang. She looked apologetically at Keith and took the cordless from its charger. Instinctively, she knew who the caller was and didn't really know why she resented him so much for calling. Trying to sound like she hadn't just had an orgasm, she said, "Hello?"

"Hey babe, it's me." It was Dan, his cell phone making him sound like he'd had a stroke.

"Where are you? The signal's terrible."

"That's a good question. I seem to be in the middle of Fucking Nowhere. Do you know where that's at?"

"I've been there before."

Keith ran a hand up her inner thigh and she gasped slightly.

"So what're you up to?"

"Not much, really."

"Are you alone?"

"For now. Allison and Kim are coming over in a bit. I think we're going to dinner or something."

"Okay. I was just calling to let you know I'd be home tomorrow. Oh, here's a sign. I've just entered Glowers Point, Ohio."

The Point, Karen thought, her heart leaping around in her chest, stealing the words from her mouth. Although the place name had no significance to Dan, merely hearing the name spoken aloud ripped open a dam of memories for Karen. Immediately, a sense of doom enclosed itself around her bones, robbing her of that post-coital wave of relaxation she'd been feeling.

Something bad was going to happen.

The signal got choppier. Smacks of static punctuated Dan's words.

Karen swallowed, a dry click from her throat echoing back to her.

"Be careful, dear," she said. "I'm gonna let you go. I can barely hear you." She hardly even heard her own words. She was someplace else. Closer to Dan than he realized. Someplace that had an insane logic of its own. Someplace that she never wanted to hear of again. Someplace that she certainly never wanted to visit again.

The Point, as the locals had called it.

"Okay. I love you . . ." There was another sound, louder than the static. Different. What came next didn't really surprise Karen. It was like something inevitable finally being fulfilled.

Dan screamed, "Oh dear fucking God!" The signal ended with a chaotic sonic jumble, followed by silence.

"Dan?" Karen said. The bad doom feeling intensified, turning into something close to physical pain. "Dan!" She knew he wasn't there.

"What's wrong, baby?" Keith asked, moving his hand up to her breasts.

Men are so fucking clueless, Karen thought, scraping his sweaty hand off.

"It's Dan. Something's wrong with Dan."

Immediately, Karen was out of bed and pulling on her clothes. She felt Keith's eyes rolling over her body.

"Aw, fuck Dan. Come back to bed."

"Shut the hell up."

Less than five minutes after Dan had called, Karen was in the car and headed for I-71 southbound, thoughts caroming violently around in her head. She was impulsive, sure, but she had no idea why she was doing exactly what she was doing and yet it seemed like the only thing she could do. Maybe it meant she really cared for Dan although, at this point, she saw it more as a responsibility. Her feelings for Dan were certainly something she hadn't been so sure of lately. She definitely didn't think about Dan when Keith was all over her, except maybe about his fumbling ineptitude. With Dan, it was clothes off, him on top for a few minutes before pulling out and coming on her stomach. If he felt really imaginative, he would aim for her breasts or, sometimes, her face. Whenever he did that, she always wanted to ask him where the camera was.

Keith wasn't like that. Today, he'd fucked her in her car in the parking garage at work and fucked her again when they got back to her apartment. But, with Keith, it was just that—fucking. Even though it had been going on for quite some time, there was no love there. No connection. And his virility had a tendency to turn brutal. She never really had to worry about sore jaws or a raw ass with Dan. Keith treated them as standard fare. With Keith, the words, "That hurts," were said in a wasted breath.

But now she wondered if there even was a Dan. She knew it sounded severe, but Glowers Point, the Point, despite all its rolling hills and full-bloomed splendor, was a very severe place.

Her thoughts ate up the road and turned the dusk to dark.

Around Columbus, the traffic thickened and she pulled off an exit. She decided she had to find a phone. Unlike Dan, she wouldn't have anything to do with a cell phone, although she wished she had one now so she could make the calls without burning time. She pulled into a BP and used her credit card to call information.

"City and state," the bland feminine voice asked.

"Glowers Point, Ohio," Karen spat. Not a religious person in the least, she had the urge to cross herself after speaking those words. She became aware of how impatient and out of breath she was.

"That's another number. Let me get that for you."

Karen wondered if operators were aware of how monstrously slow they were. The recording gave her the number and, having no pen or paper, she chose the extra toll to be connected automatically.

"City and state?" Another bland feminine voice. This one maybe a bit more Appalachian.

"Glowers Point, Ohio."

"Go ahead."

"I need the number for the Glowers Point Police Department."

Again she chose to be connected automatically. The phone must have rang fifteen times.

"Glowers Point mergency." A uniquely twangy female voice this time.

Karen paused. What was she supposed to say? The words tangled in her mind and got stuck in her throat. The whole purpose of the call hinged upon the fact that Glowers Point wasn't the same town it used to be. That is, a town with a secret. A secret that all the towns-people knew and never talked about. She would be able to tell by the dispatcher's voice if it had changed or not. There was also the possibility that maybe Dan had had an actual emergency. Maybe he ran off the road or hit a deer or, Christ, she didn't know, suffered a fucking coronary there in his car.

"Hello?" the voice said.

"Uh, yeah, sorry. Is this the Glowers Point Police?"

"Police, Fire, and Ambellance."

Of course, Karen thought and then said, "Um, okay. I need to find out if there's been an accident."

"Ain't been none all day. Usually there is, but we ain't got no calls bout no accidents today."

No. The town hadn't changed a bit. The woman's voice made Karen think of walking into a room with your skirt tucked into the back of your hose and trying to carry on a normal conversation while the person you were talking to tried not to laugh. But there was something inside Karen that wouldn't let her drop it at that. It was futile, she knew, to try and penetrate their shell, but she pressed on anyway.

"Can't you radio someone? To make sure."

"Naw. There ain't no need fer that. If there'd been an accident, I'da hadta pers'nally call in the county."

"Okay," Karen said, trying to think of a million other questions to ask this woman. Trying to create a conspirator for her madness but, she knew, both she and the other woman were already part of the madness.

Before Karen could think of anything else, the woman said, "Okay? Bye now, honey."

Karen hung up the phone, feeling lost. The call should have made her feel relieved but it served an opposite purpose. At least, she thought, Dan's probably not dead yet.

There are some things worse than death.

No. She didn't want to think about anything like that, the creepy cult stuff. Besides, Dan was a grown man, he could take care of himself.

Karen laughed. She knew there was no taking care of yourself in the Point. Being there was half the problem.

As Karen wandered across the greasy parking lot to the store, only vaguely aware of what she was doing, the image of Jordan flashed through her memory, ripping in and gouging blood.

There are some things worse than death. There are some things worse than death. There are some things worse than death.

It was like she had to keep those words going like a chant so she didn't have to actually think about what those things were.

She sat in the car and unfolded the Ohio road map. Karen could never forget the way to Glowers Point. She had always remembered it. Although, she had always thought she was remembering it only so she could avoid it in the future. She bought the map because she thought there might be some new way to get there. Perhaps a state route had been extended or a new highway created. Hell, maybe there was even a second Glowers Point in Ohio. The last few minutes were completely gone, eclipsed by the first sixteen years of her life. She didn't remember going into the store. Didn't remember buying the map. Didn't. Remember.

What she remembered was this:

She and Allison and Jordan, Glowers Point High's most innocent threesome, had all gone down to the creek for a night of camping and drinking. After a couple hours, Jordan left the campfire to go squat in the woods. Time passed, but it was drunk time, moving way too fast. It was probably an hour before Karen or Allison wondered where Jordan was. She wasn't anywhere in the area immediately surrounding the fire. They made torches and searched a wider perimeter. Together, they scoured the trails, calling Jordan's name.

Nothing. Throats full of dread. That was it. Had the rumors finally come true for one of them?

By four a.m, Allison and Karen had given up hope. "Maybe she just went home for some reason," they thought. They went back to Allison's and called the local police department and were immediately told that, no, no there wasn't anyone fitting that description— no one picked up for public drunkenness, no one murdered, no volunteer emergency calls. They called the hospital over in Dayton, too, just to make sure. The only people left were Jordan's small circle of friends.

Karen called the first one, the phone ringing. On about the fourth ring, from behind her, she heard Allison say, "Oh my God," and put her hand over her mouth. "Put down the phone, K. She found *us*."

The voice on the other end picked up. Karen heard Jennifer Gentry's mom sleepily say, "Hello," while Karen was in the act of placing the phone back in its cradle.

Karen followed Allison down the stairs and out the front door.

Through the early dawn ground fog, they saw Jordan. Only she didn't *look* anything like Jordan. Once she saw Allison and Karen, she collapsed onto the front yard. Allison and Karen went over to her, inspecting the damage without touching her.

"Call the police," Karen said.

"No!" Jordan shouted, a spray of blood coming from her mouth, ropes of it dangling from her bottom lip. Her eyes darted around in her head.

Allison, disregarding Jordan's demand, rushed into the house to make the call. Anything to take her sight off the grisly heap in the front yard.

The only thing Jordan wore was a bra, relatively mangled at this point. Blood covered her from head to toe. It was heavier in parts, like where clumps of her hair had been ripped out. As Jordan struggled to sit up, Karen noticed the series of deep red gashes down her back.

Jordan reached out to Karen and said, "He said he was going to make me like him. Something about tormenting. I think he was one of *them*."

"It's okay," Karen said, placing her hands on Jordan's shoulder. *There are some things worse than death.*

Karen knew what Jordan meant by one of *them*. They were the Tormented. Karen had always figured they were as much myth as reality. Something for parents to scare little children with so they wouldn't wander off into the woods. But as Karen got older, into her teenage years, she began to see maybe a little bit of truth behind the mythic exaggerations. It didn't take her long to realize something was wrong when there seemed to be a student a week missing from the high school.

Historically, the Tormented were as old as the town itself. Call them the first rebellious teens in that area. The Tormented were a group of adolescents, between the ages of thirteen and nineteen, who broke off from the adult, church-centered society to found their own little cult. From everything Karen had heard, they'd been a peaceful lot. Their premise seemed to be that, rather than acting as slavehands on their parents' farms and being expected to follow their rules, why not work for themselves and make their own rules. Karen suspected that sex was somewhere at the center of it.

The adults claimed they were decimating the innocence of their children. They ordered the youths to stop practicing but it didn't work. Eventually, the members of the congregation decided the Tormented needed to be scared back into their senses. The adult church corralled the townspeople and stormed Black Hill, where the Tormented called home. The adults went about setting several fires, hoping the Tormented would come down from the hill and repent. Like any stubborn, rebellious teenagers, they stayed put, headed for martyrdom. The fires raged to the top of the hill but the Tormented didn't go away. Over the years, they continued to grow. And more teenagers turned up missing. After seeing Jordan that night and hearing the things she said, Karen believed every word of it.

Of course, that was only one of the legends . . .

It wasn't even that night in particular as much as the things that happened after.

Maybe what happened to Jordan hadn't been worse than death, but it seemed that way to Karen. As Jordan's wounds mended, her hair growing back, something inside of her seemed to be dying. Her eyes grew listless and vacant. Her skin became not just pale but nearly gray—ashen. And then, one day, she was gone. No one knew where she went but, Karen knew, *everyone* knew where she went. She was a Tormented now, no longer alive, no longer really human.

That was when Karen got really scared. She felt hunted. One of her friends was now missing from the circle. Would she be next? Whatever the Tormented were, however many good intentions they'd had, they were something different now, something akin to vampires. Vampires that, more than blood, wanted innocence and sacrifice. Karen had seen the type of kids that disappeared from the high school. It wasn't the oversexed football players and cheerleaders. It wasn't the boisterous class clown or the hoody girl who was rumored to sleep with the teachers. No. It was the shy ones. The wallflowers. The ones who went unnoticed and probably turned up at church on Sunday for lack of anything better to do. In short, it was people like Karen.

There were times she went to bed at night and swore she heard someone else's breath in the room with her. Out the window, she saw flashes of white, someone's face. She answered telephone calls with no one on the other line. Three or four of them a day.

On the night she left the Point, she woke up with one of them in her bed. She remembered him as the boy with the scar over his left eye and, amidst his pallid skin, those dancing orange eyes. She woke up because she was choking. The boy's hand crushed her windpipe and she had the panicked feeling that this was it. Images of Jordan skipped across her head, giving her an angry strength. Somehow she managed to pry the boy's hand from her neck. She had a large butcher knife in the nightstand she had started keeping there for safety. If she could just get to that. Her hand reached out. She made eye contact with the boy. His eyes were deep, the orange rimmed with black, but she didn't think they looked soulless.

"I know what you are!" she spat at him. "You took Jordan. You took Jordan! You took *Jordan*!"

Her hand clasped around the handle of the knife.

"We need you," the boy said.

Karen quickly brought the knife through the air and rammed it into the boy's side, ripping downward. He moaned and rolled off the bed. Karen kept the knife in front of her until the boy was out the window.

Karen took the keys to her parents' car and drove it until it ran out of gas. She never called back home. Tried not to think of it ever again. There were nights when she missed her family. Anger usually dismissed that feeling—how could they possibly keep her there if they knew what was going on? Sixteen and alone, she stripped in clubs until she turned eighteen. The especially seedy places didn't care how fake the ID was. Once she was eighteen, life got a little bit easier. She was able to get her GED and start college with no questions asked. Now she was almost thirty and headed back to every childhood fear she'd ever had.

She turned the radio on and up, driving the programmed route until fatigue overwhelmed her. She pulled off into a rest stop and convinced herself Dan was in no immediate danger. She convinced herself the whole situation was, maybe, just a coincidence. Crazily, exhausted, she convinced herself Dan had somehow found out about her secret childhood home, found out she wasn't from Idleville, a small town outside Richmond, Indiana, and had concocted this whole thing to show her she couldn't keep secrets from him. She convinced herself to sleep.

She woke up at dawn and stepped out of the car. After a good stretch, she went in search of the coffee machines, pushing the 'Extra Strong' button and waiting eagerly for the small paper cup to fill up.

She got back into the car, a sheen of sweat already covering her. The sweat would be with her all day, slowly oozing out. Karen cursed the car's aging air conditioner. Resting the coffee on the dash, she pulled the map onto her lap and dug in the console for a pack of

Camel Lights that had been there for about six months. It was half empty. A little more than one cigarette a month wasn't too bad, she figured. She lit it with the car lighter and breathed in the stale smoke. Her muscles relaxed a little bit. Thank God for tobacco, she thought.

Studying the map, she thought maybe, in the previous night's fatigue, she had missed some other way. No. Nothing new. Nothing quicker. Frustrated, she crumpled up the map and tossed it in the passenger-side floorboard.

And what if she just turned around? She almost had herself convinced she would simply run into Dan when she got back to the apartment. By that time she would be too embarrassed to tell him about her excursion. He would interrogate her. He loved to interrogate her. Sometimes she thought maybe that was the reason she was fucking Keith on the side, to see if she could still pass Dan's interrogations. If she let him beat her down mentally, then the last shreds of what they had, whatever it was, were gone. If she did find him down here and something had happened to him, she would tell him what she'd been doing and put the decision in his hands.

If *you both come back.*

There are some things worse than death.

But she didn't want to think about that.

There was something inside of her telling her maybe this didn't even really have anything to do with Dan. Like maybe she wasn't going down there out of any concern for him as much as the fulfillment of some sense of duty. It may have seemed self-involved but, ever since Jordan's disappearance, Karen felt like she had been chosen for something. She shuddered at the thought of what that thing might be.

Tossing her cigarette out the window, she lit up another one and forced the thoughts out of her head. The trees stormed by the window. The road thrummed beneath the car. Karen stared blankly ahead.

In a couple of hours the coffee was long empty and the highway was way behind her. She turned onto a state route and stayed with that for a while, winding and twisting for miles, the summer foliage threatening to take over the road, the bugs hitting the windshield like soupy rain. The turnoff was around here somewhere. She almost thought she'd missed it until she saw a green sign, the gray-white reflective letters reading: GLOWERS POINT 5. Almost there. Just stay on this road.

Where are you, Dan? she thought. And then, *Let's get this the hell over with.* Whatever it is.

She couldn't help but speed, the feeling in her veins a collision of excitement and dread. She reached for the pack of cigarettes and lit another one, not even remembering tossing the last one out the window. The car had reached 80 by the time she saw the yellow and black sign indicating a sharp right turn. Shit, she thought, and nearly slammed on the brakes. She managed to take the turn more gracefully than she would have thought, the finesse of her youth, the ability to take these back country woods turns half-drunk with nothing but a learner's permit in her pocket, coming back to her.

Karen pictured Dan's car going off the road. Only he said he'd passed a sign saying he was *in* Glowers Point. So it had to be after that. Immediately after that. Not that it mattered, she would be able to cover just about every road in the Point in a few hours. And then she saw the sign, hanging upside down from the two iron poles. She pulled the car over to the right.

The road she was on was the one veering up and to the right, into the hills. This was the road that could take her into town. To the left, the road forked. This road was gravel, weeds sprouting up here and there. This was the road that would take her down into the Point proper. If she followed that road, it wouldn't be long until she ran into the small trailer park by the river where she had lived out her first sixteen years. She walked over to the other side of the road, tossing her cigarette away, and stood where the asphalt became stone. She tried to figure out how many seconds it had been from the time Dan said he saw the sign for Glowers Point and the moment the signal ended. She looked for some sense of trauma amidst the shrubs and undergrowth by the side of the road. Something roughly the size of a car.

She took a deep breath. Out here, she couldn't smell anything but the woods.

Karen had come all this way and only had an inkling as to what the hell she expected to find. The car idled behind her. That was how hopeless it all felt, she hadn't even bothered shutting off the engine. She sighed deeply and put her hands on her hips. Did she even *want* to find him?

But he's *not what this is about.*

This was about her. She realized that. If something happened to Dan, then so be it. He was a grown man. If he was dead, then she would have to deal with that. If something else happened to him (*something worse than death*) then he would have to rely on some other source of help. The best thing she could do would be to get back in her car, drive back up north, and let Keith fuck her until Glowers Point was just a fading memory. She wasn't responsible for Dan. He didn't even know of her association with this place. He came in without me, she thought, let him get out without me.

Taking a final cursory survey, she turned to go back to the car. *Wait.*

She saw something. Didn't she? Sure. That little blotch of white way off to her right—in the midst of all that green. Instead of heading back to the car, she took a couple steps to her right, one foot on the road, one foot on the wild grass descending down to the creek bed, getting wilder as it went.

She turned and put both feet on the grass, the woods in front of her. The wind picked up, blowing up under her shirt like a cold hand, coaxing her deeper into the woods, down into that nearly dry creek bed.

What the fuck are you doing? an inner voice screamed at her. *You're Karen Bruckner. You're twenty-eight years old. You're from Idleville, Indiana. You're not sixteen. It was all behind you. Leave it there.*

They took Jordan. They sent me screaming from my home. They took Jordan. They took Jordan and dragged her into something that was worse than death.

She found herself scrambling down the slope and stupidly thinking, *Dan wears a lot of white.*

Thunder rumbled and Karen looked up to see dense black clouds rolling over the top of the hill. The white thing moved. Did it move? Wasn't it over there just a second ago?

The thunder hollered through the hills, blowing through Karen's skull. She had forgotten the intensity of it. The rain started heavy, soaking her hair and clothes.

"Dan!" she shouted. "Dan! Are you down there?"

Not about Dan.

She couldn't see the white thing at all anymore and it was getting very dark, like going from noon to dusk in under a minute. Karen stood in the creek bed, water up to her ankles, smelling the clean ozone.

There are some things worse than death.

She saw the white thing (*worse than death*) and it looked like it was running. Without hesitation, she took off running after it, the rain and the water at her feet making her feel like she was running through a dream.

"Dan!" she called, trying to cover up what she was doing with some type of semi-rational pretense. She couldn't really admit to herself she had come back to the Point to stalk down all the nightmares of her childhood, but that was exactly what she was doing. Karen had been strong. The fear had broken her down. It had broken down all of her friends. After Jordan's disappearance, the fear became real. There was nothing horror movie about real fear. The talk of finishing up high school and running off to the same Ivy League college vanished. They were broken. They were afraid.

That feeling came back to Karen. That feeling of lying in bed every night, a butcher knife in the nightstand beside her. And most nights she would wake up, one of an eventual many, and feel that blade at her throat. Always, always the feeling of someone just outside her window, or just outside her door, or just beside the bed. Sometimes she woke up because she felt a cold hand, sometimes at her throat, sometimes on her cheek, sometimes running slowly up her inner thigh. Was that what they wanted? Her fucking *virginity*? Sorry guys, she thought, I gave that away to the first fat fuck to give me a job. And that was when she had felt the fear the most. When she had left the Point and was all alone, doing things she never would have done otherwise. Things she did solely in extremis, to stay alive another day, another week. That's when she hated that place the most. That's when she blamed the Tormented the most. When she was doing things she never would have done otherwise.

Karen struggled to the further bank of the creek, regaining her footing, and continued after the thing in white. Rain and darkness separated them. Karen's breaths became wet and ragged. A scream of thunder. A flash of lightning and everything lit up for only a second. But a second was long enough to recognize the face of the figure as it turned to look behind it.

It was Jordan.

That's impossible.

But hadn't everything else seemed impossible, too? Why, at this point, should she question anything? How *could* she question anything?

Another belt of thunder. Another flashbulb of lightning and Jordan was gone. The thing in white had vanished.

Karen kept running.

A few more yards and she came upon the place where she had lost track of Jordan. She stopped, standing there in a sort of bemused stupor. She ran a hand through her hair, holding it out from her scalp and feeling it smack wetly down on the back of her neck. To her right, from the creek, she heard a sucking sound.

Here, the creek widened in a circular pool nearly twice its usual width. Instinctively, she knew what she had to do.

That's great. Come all the way out here to drown yourself in a fucking creek.

Jordan had vanished. Karen realized part of her problem when she was sixteen was she had never really questioned where Jordan had gone to that first time. Now, here she was, faced with that dilemma again. Only, this time, she wouldn't pacify herself with answers and legends and fear. Sometimes you had to do stuff you were afraid of. She realized that now.

She looked up at the sky and wondered, for just a moment, if there was a God up there. She laughed crazily. If there was, he has to be the sickest son of a bitch in the universe, she thought. She looked at the spiraling whirlpool and, without another second's hesitation, dived in.

She half expected the water to be freezing, but it wasn't. It wasn't even the texture of water. It was somehow lighter than water, silkier. Being surrounded by it, she thought of amniotic fluid, like she was in the womb. Ridiculous, of course. Time got messed up while she was in there. It felt like it came and went within seconds but when she emerged at the end of it, on the other side, she had the feeling weeks, possibly years had passed, or reversed. Yes, that was it. She was sixteen again, or felt like it, walking slowly toward the black maw of her fear.

She opened her eyes and looked at her new surroundings. It was nighttime but Karen didn't think it seemed like real nighttime. It was like what she imagined a movie set would look like if the director called for darkness. She realized it was a full moon. The sky overhead was totally clear and starless, void of anything except the moon's alien surface, reflecting back a cold light.

The trees here were squat and without leaves and yet the air on her skin didn't feel like winter air. It was chilly, but there was an underlying balm she found comforting. Was she still in Glowers Point? Was she still even alive? There was something of an afterlife in this new landscape. Some ethereal quality. A certain level of unreality.

She captured a scent of earth, good clean dirt, rising up from the ground. There was another scent there. The smell of a smoldering fire, after the fire and smoke and coals are gone and the only thing left, like a memory, is its odor.

She should have been afraid. She had been terrified just a few moments ago, her feet on familiar ground. Now she was surrounded by something she was totally unfamiliar with and the fear had vanished. In front of her, close and looming, was what looked like a church.

The Church of the Earth, of course, she thought. The Tormented's place of worship. How was it still standing? She thought for sure she remembered hearing about how it had been burnt to the ground. Nevertheless, there it was, right in front of her, majestic in its lopsided decay.

The windows were gone. The wooden slats of the exterior were shiny burnt black and brittle-looking. The steeple truncated two-thirds of the way up. She wondered what type of symbol had adorned the top of it. Maybe it had been a cross. From everything she'd heard it didn't sound like the Tormented had developed a religion in any way similar to Christianity. The doorway was one of those enormous, arching, double-door affairs. The doors were gone, some of the heavy stones used to make the arch had fallen away as well. The whole structure seemed to somehow *lean* toward her, like the front of it was sinking into the earth. This gave the entranceway the appearance of being like the opening to a grave, leading down into the earth. She would be going in there. There was no other choice.

Slowly, she walked toward the church.

As she drew closer, she noticed the dim blue light glowing inside. There would be someone there to welcome her then. Her sense of fear was admonished by need for closure. Whatever waited for her inside, she had no doubt it was going to be some kind of ending, either the end of her or the end of Glowers Point and its ongoing pull.

Closer now, she noticed other details about the church. On either side of the doorway, hanging like porchlights, were her parents. Their hands and feet were bound. Their faces looked skyward, mouths bent and twisted. Their bodies were blackened, most of their clothes burnt away. This should have stopped her in her tracks, but it didn't. For her, her parents had died a long time ago. It had been easier to get through the day if she told herself they were dead.

She stepped into the Church of the Earth.

Is this my something worse than death? she thought, looking around her.

The hanging, charred corpses lined the inside of the church, suspended precisely at the same level like Bible pictures. On either side of her, worn stone pews rose up out of the ground. People sat, here and there, on the uncomfortable looking things. They turned their sullen faces toward her as she approached the altar. Above the altar was the pulpit. Behind the pulpit were the choir risers. These were virtually filled, the same sullen faces as out in the pews, piously turned up from their stained white robes, except these were more plentiful and mostly female. All of them looked very young to Karen.

Softly, from the risers, a voice sang out. She looked up to meet the voice and saw that it was Jordan.

"Jordan!" she called.

More voices joined in the soft chant.

To her right, she heard footsteps. She looked to see a man, a boy, emerge from a small, wasted door. It was the boy with the scar over his eye, those crazy blazing eyes honing in on her and closing the distance.

"Karen," he whispered.

"Who are you?" she asked.

"Does that really matter? This is my church. You came here. I should ask, 'Who are you?' But I know who you are."

"What do you want with me? What *did* you want with me?"

The boy laughed. "So much older and still so innocent."

"Is that what you wanted? My innocence? My virginity? You're way too late if that's what you wanted."

"Oh, I know that. The bar in Newport, where you got your first job? Remember that fat greasy man who didn't bother taking the cigar out of his mouth when he fucked you in the ass?"

Karen looked at the boy, her fear slowly returning. Staring into his face, his expression somewhat bland, she saw it shift from his own handsome face into that other face she would never forget, although the name she had long since put out of her head, and then dissolve back into the boy's original face.

The boy laughed and his face changed again, kaleidoscoping into a multitude of other faces. Some of them were men who had been nice to Karen, men she wanted. Others, a good many others, some of them forgotten, were men she had slept with just for a place to stay, maybe something to eat. Finally, it shifted into Dan's and then Keith's.

Holding out a hand, the boy braced himself on the pulpit. "My God," he said. "I think I almost made you depraved."

Karen felt as though something essential had been stolen. The fear had slowly welled throughout the boy's demonstration and now pounded along like a train at full speed.

"So if you had me all those times, why now, why here?"

The boy moved closer to her, cradled her chin in his hand. "There's more to it than just sex. You make everything too simple. In a way, this doesn't even have anything to do with you."

"I don't understand."

"I wouldn't expect you to. Here's what you need to understand: when I wanted you to come, you didn't. You had your chance to get it over with and you chose to draw it out. But the conclusion is inevitable. Can't you smell the death?"

She wanted to turn and run but the boy's grip had dropped to her neck and tightened.

"Fuck you," she said.

"When you pass through Glowers Point, you enter an agreement whether you want to or not. If you are young, then you belong to us. If you are older, then you mean nothing to us. You stand in direct opposition to us. Look around you."

Karen looked at the people hanging from the walls. Some of them were people she recognized: teachers, shopkeepers who worked in town, random faces. None of them were teenagers.

"Why does it keep happening?"

"A long time ago, there were atrocities played out here. The town had to die. The young people had to be turned away from their parents' way of life. They had to become something different. Somehow, you got away. You didn't give us time to react. But I have you here now and you're too old for the turning."

Summoning all her strength, she attempted to bolt. The boy's grip tightened, shutting off her wind, and he drove her to the floor of the church. Within seconds, two members of the congregation had risen and moved toward her and the boy. Each of them grabbed a hand. The boy moved in front of her and pulled a whiplike thing from the sleeve of his shirt. It had the diameter of a quarter and ran the length of his arm. At the end, it had a curved piece of metal, like a talon.

She tried kicking but the boy held her legs down and put a foot on each ankle. He bent to raise up her shirt, exposing her tender back. With a quick gasp, he brought the whip down across her back. She shrieked out in pain, her fingernails biting into her palms. Unlike a clean cut from glass or a knife, a cut that somehow caused numbness, this cut burned with savage life. She could feel the wound hanging open, as though the very atmosphere irritated it.

The boy brought the whip down again and again. She couldn't help but scream. The fear consumed her. And it wasn't just the fear of death, it was the fear of living. In only a few minutes, the boy had told her the life she thought she had led wasn't really her life at all. She was merely a pawn. Insignificant.

The other two members of the congregation moved away. Karen realized, somewhere, in the course of this, the choir's chanting had risen in volume and intensity. The boy knelt down beside her, placed a hand just inside one of the gashes in her back. The pain disappeared.

"There are some things worse than death," the boy said, stroking the lip of the wound. "Join us," he whispered. "Join us in death."

She felt his hand probe deeper into the wound. And then another hand. She felt more and more hands on her and the chanting rolled through her head, dragging some inner part of her to some other place.

From behind her, she heard the sounds of celebration, the soft crackle of a fire. Karen realized her something worse than death was finally happening.

THE CALMING WOOD

A MAN NAMED Figg wandered across several states searching for a certain geography. That was the only way he could really think of it. He was not a spiritual man. He'd led a rough life. Always, he found himself in a town or even just a piece of wilderness or countryside, and eventually he had to move on. But his back had begun twisting up on him and he trembled even when he tried to stand still. The grinding sound in his head had become unbearably loud. If he found his special place, he didn't think he'd be moving on.

There were some thick woods in these parts but, already, farmers had begun clearing away the trees to make room for fields to plant crops. Farming was becoming a big business. Living off the land by killing it. That was no way to earn a living. The man didn't think *working* was any way to make a living. He'd made do without a job most of his adult life. His memories of childhood were cloudy things. His father had made him work despite Figg being a sickly child. If there was ever a day Figg wasn't able to, his father had him make up for it the next day.

One morning Figg stumbled onto a narrow dirt road. It was relatively flat and he could see farther then he'd been able to see for days. It looked like it was going to be a perfect spring day. It was about time. Here it was the middle of May almost and he'd bet it hadn't reached seventy until a couple days ago. The sky was a sweet, brilliant blue, puffy white clouds hanging still like the exhalations from a kind god that didn't exist in Figg's world.

And under that perfect sky, the landscape rose slightly and the already narrow dirt road seemed to disappear in shadow. The man knew that was the place. Somewhere cool and dark and quiet, like a grave above ground. The man didn't like the sun and the light the way he used to. Hell, even then he'd only seen it as something like a cleanser for his late nights. The things he'd seen and done in the shadows were best left there and while he managed to thrive in that environment, there'd always been a part of him that looked forward to waking up in a sun-filled room. He guessed most people were supposed to like the light and warmth more as they got older. Common belief held that a warmer climate would make his back feel better but it just made him feel like more of an ailing, monstrous old man. It was like lighting a lamp in a filthy room, the grinding in his head there to match the frantic scurry of cockroaches.

He moved so slowly it took him all day to reach that shadowy place on the horizon. He traveled south on the road, the sun stinging his right side. But even that began to diminish as he moved closer to the woods. At first he thought maybe it was already sunset and the sun had tucked itself beneath the earth for the night, but there it was hanging in the sky. It should have been intense but, somehow, it wasn't. It was like, not even in the woods yet, the shade was already keeping the sun from him. This was a good sign.

A small furl of smoke climbed out of the woods and dissipated in the sky.

Now he even had an exact destination.

He reached into his pocket and pulled out his knife and sharpening stone.

Someone living all alone in the woods like that . . . Well, Figg thought that person was probably a lot like him. Meaning he probably wouldn't be missed and maybe even had a reason to be living so far from people.

Figg just hoped it wasn't a family. It wasn't that he would feel any guilt. Figg had heard that word—guilt—but had never experienced the feeling. When there were more than one or two people, he tended to like it too much. He really lost himself in it and usually paid for it the next day. It had been a while since he'd had to do it but the memory of last time was still quick to bubble up.

When he finally stepped into the woods, it was like all the crazy nattering in his head went silent. He'd once taken an apartment next to a glass blower's shop. Every morning, Figg would be woken up by the sound of the man sweeping glass shards out of his shop. Until then he'd never really had a close comparison to the sound that was almost always in his head. It lessened a little around nightfall on any given day and quieted almost completely if he was staying in one of his good places. The only time it stopped was when he did what he felt like he was born to do. And, well, probably when he was sleeping but he was unconscious and couldn't enjoy the silence then. A tree falling in a forest with no one around and all that.

He paused to take it in. If it wasn't so welcome, he may have thought of it as eerie. He didn't hear any birds or insects or animals, although he could see them.

He was locked into his path, gliding through the dim woods, sharpening his knife on the stone and not hearing the gritty sound of the blade becoming more lethal.

He spotted the dim glow from the cabin just as the light seemed to die completely from the air around him. There was a yellowish window, probably lit by a candle or a lantern. There wasn't much of a clearing. Like whoever had built this shoddy, ramshackle cabin had cleaned out only enough trees to fit it. Figg liked that idea. He never could understand the concept of a yard. Wide open spaces only made you more vulnerable.

There was a single crooked step before the door.

Figg knocked on the door and waited. He heard footsteps and slid the sharpening stone into his pocket, tightening his grip around the haft of the knife.

The man who opened the door was black and this momentarily surprised Figg, but not enough to derail him.

The man looked just as surprised to see *him* but Figg was sure to make eye contact and say what needed to be said:

"I've come to take up residence here."

He heard his own voice from a distance and it didn't feel like it came from him.

The man looked slightly confused but before he could even back away, Figg had already slashed the knife across his throat. Figg had done this enough to be sure he'd done it correctly but it was hard to see the blood against the man's skin so he didn't feel completely confident until he saw the front of the man's grayish shirt turn dark. Once he saw that, all the sounds of the natural world came back to him. The brain sound stayed away.

Figg could have continued stabbing but didn't know exactly how long he was going to be here and didn't want to damage more of the body than was necessary. The man dropped to the floor and clutched his throat. As long as he didn't have a gun on him or within arm's reach, Figg didn't figure he had much to worry about. Mostly he just stood where he was and tried not to get too much blood on him.

Figg surveyed the tiny shack in the dim glow. He was wrong about the candle or lantern. The fire was the only source of light in the room. Maybe the man had been asleep already. He wondered why he'd just opened the door like that. It seemed like he should have been a little more cautious. Maybe he'd been expecting someone. That didn't make Figg as nervous as it probably should have. Maybe this man just wasn't running from or hiding from something like most of the black men Figg had encountered. The fireplace looked like a good one. There was already a metal rack for cooking in it. Most of them didn't have that. A relatively comfortable, though narrow, bed was pushed into a corner. The man probably lived alone. There was a wobbly table against the wall below the solitary window. Figg was grateful to look up and see a sturdy beam running through the center of the room. Various pots, pans, and burlap sacks hung from it. Figg poked a couple of the sacks until he came to one that, hopefully, contained what he wanted. He lifted it from the nail and glanced into the opening. Salt. A lot of it. Good. He suspended the sack back on the nail. He didn't want it to get soaked with blood.

Figg unspooled the rope wrapped six times around his waist. He must have lost some weight on this latest journey. His pants almost slipped off his hips. He waited for the man to stop flopping.

When he was pretty sure the man was finished, Figg bound his ankles with one end of the rope and took the other end over the beam. He hoisted the man so he hung upside down. A steady trickle of blood continued to pour from his throat. Figg secured the rope around the beam and made a slash along each of the man's wrists. He'd wait till the man had bled out before splashing the floor with a pail of water. The house wasn't constructed particularly well and he was pleased to see most of the blood already finding its way to the earth from in between the floorboards. It wasn't overly hot so he didn't think he'd have much to worry about. He was tired. That bed was starting to look pretty inviting. He'd earned a good night's rest. Tomorrow he'd get up and begin the carving. Hopefully he'd have everything ready to start drying and curing the meat for the day after that. He wasn't sure how much it would yield. It would probably be more than enough. And if he ever got sick of eating it, he could probably find a town to sell some in and maybe make enough for some steak and eggs. He usually told folks it was ostrich jerky so they didn't have anything to compare it to.

Figg fell asleep to the soft thick drip of the man's blood.

When he woke up early the next morning, the man was gone.

That had never happened before.

Figg inspected the rope coiled on the floor. It didn't look ripped or shredded at either end. Supposing the man could have lived through the bloodletting—a feat Figg was pretty sure was not possible—maybe he could have chewed or gouged the rope loose. But given the shape of the rope, that definitely was not the case. Something like that would had to have woken him up, anyway.

The front door was open. Figg walked outside and looked around. If the man had managed to free himself in some fit of post-death strength, he couldn't have gotten far.

The trees greatly diminished visibility, but Figg didn't see the man lying on the ground or any sign of movement.

Given the unsecured nature of the rope, the open door, and the fact there wasn't a trace of the man, Figg could only think of one solution: someone had taken the man—a member of his family or something. Hell, maybe even someone like Figg. Someone happy to discover most of the work was done.

Just thinking about his loss made Figg's stomach rumble.

He went back into the tiny shack and found two potatoes on the brink of going bad in a wooden bin near the fireplace. He cut them up, fried them in a pan, and ate them outside while sitting on that crooked step and surveying the dark shadows of the wood. The potatoes didn't satisfy his growing hunger but they'd have to do for now.

In the distance he heard a dog bark and a little girl scream. He guessed if worse came to worst, he knew where to go.

Last night he'd had his plans for today all worked out but now he found himself with nothing to do. He decided to explore the woods even though he knew his body would make him pay for it the next day. He never worried about getting lost. His sense of direction was perfect. Once he'd locked the location of this shack into his head, he could walk a thousand miles away from it and still know where to return to should he decide to turn around. There were a number of tall dark pine trees mixed in amongst the elm and oak and maples, which was odd for this part of the country. Not that Figg minded.

He liked the gloom they produced. A damp chill hung in the air and he imagined there was a river or creek somewhere in the area. A ready source of fresh water was always a good thing. The shadows and the perfumed air put him in something of a spell as he spent the majority of the day wandering through the woods. He didn't stumble upon any more houses and when he thought about returning to the shack it took him longer to find it than he thought it would. He cautiously approached it. What if the man or a member of his family had returned to find it empty? What if they had decided to take it back? Figg had his knife ready as he slowly opened the door. He surveyed the small space and found it empty and exactly as he had left it. When he took a jug of water out to the step and sat down, he saw the black man wandering through the woods. He had the carcass of a dog slung over his shoulders and clutched the hair of a bloody and mangled girl's corpse, dragging her through the dirt and dead leaves. Figg again removed his knife from his pocket and clutched it hard in his hand, feeling the closest thing he'd felt to fear since his father had beat it out of him.

The man didn't seem to notice him. Figg watched him shamble through the woods with no attempt at stealth, burdened by his dead cargo. Figg knew there was no way this man could be alive. What Figg had done to him last night was something he'd done countless times before. Many times he didn't even bother making the incisions on the wrists. He'd only done that because of the man's size and possible virility. So how was it this man had managed to free himself? How was it he now managed to walk amongst the living with enough vigor to take the lives of others? Figg had heard about certain black magic practices and rituals. He'd lived throughout the Deep South and in some of the poor areas of this country's larger cities where those sorts of beliefs were common. But even good old Christianity had its belief in a number of strange, dark fantasies. Figg had avoided all of it. Now the mere thought of it sent tendrils of unease uncoiling through his body. This man, this creature, was shattering the calm wood he'd found. Already, Figg could hear the grinding glass sound. It was faint right now, but he knew how it would go. It would start at the top of his spine and slowly infect his whole head until he moved on to some place else.

Unless he kept on top of things.

Unless he could trap the man and destroy him.

He wished he'd paid more attention to what those believers had said.

Figg went back into the shack to search for a gun. Someone living all alone out here in the woods was almost certain to have one. But if this guy had kept one, Figg couldn't find it. Maybe he hadn't needed one. Aside from hunting and killing, Figg reasoned the gun's existence was due to the fear of death. A man kept a gun, ultimately, because he was afraid of dying. So, he reckoned, a man who couldn't die would have no need of a gun.

But how did he hunt?

The imagined answer to that question made Figg nervous.

He could see that man, that thing, wrapping his large hands around the dog's throat, taking a deep and savage bite from its jugular, snapping the girl's neck when she came to the aid of her pooch.

Some men sure were sick, ferocious bastards.

Figg had trapped both men and animals before. Okay, so usually he'd trapped women and those he kept around for more non-dietary purposes, but he felt confident he could do the same with this . . . creature. The only way to get rid of the thing once and for all would be to completely destroy the body. First he would sever the head and burn that. Then he would sever the rest of the limbs and feed them into a roaring fire. He would find the creek running through the woods and dispose of any remaining bones. And if the grinding glass sound didn't go away, he would move on. He might have to move on anyway, if he couldn't manage to find a lasting source of food. He would have to remember to start decapitating his supply. And also maybe destroying the head just to be on the safe side. He didn't really enjoy the brains and eyes much anyway and the neck muscles were always tough and stringy.

The man had now shambled out of sight.

Figg supposed he could have gone after him but his walk had left him feeling tired and listless.

The day was practically done anyway. He withdrew inside. He nailed a board across the door, removed the legs from the table, and nailed that over the single window. He didn't really know if he'd be able to fall asleep or not but, if he did, he didn't want to wake up to that thing's teeth at his throat. Figg found a small pipe and a pouch of tobacco in a tin on the mantle. A quick inspection of the leaves revealed that it wasn't tobacco but maybe an herb or a weed. Figg decided to smoke it anyway, thinking it might diminish the grinding sound. The only things he knew to stay away from were the mushrooms some of the Indians liked and the consumption of alcohol. Both of those made his thoughts too weird. They made him lose the tight self-control that had kept him alive all these years. The mushrooms had made him think he was a god and the alcohol just made him tell everything to whoever would listen. He was lucky that the one time that had happened, the person he had told all his secrets to was trussed up and in the process of bleeding out. No lasting harm there.

After smoking, he lay in bed and stared at the shadows on the ceiling. He'd neglected to start a fire and was happy it wasn't very cold. He went over his plan again and again. Maybe he should just get out. What was stopping him from doing that? Nothing, really. That would certainly be the easiest thing to do. He could try to get a decent night's rest and head out that door first thing in the morning and hope like hell he didn't run across that thing creeping through the woods. But he knew he wasn't going to do that. This man's resurrection had been something of a defeat to Figg. He didn't like to lose. It was one of the reasons he'd never joined the ranks of decent society. He wasn't on their playing field and would have lost repeatedly because he didn't have the proper skill set. He wouldn't have even been able to take the small daily failures. He would have probably ended up in jail. Just to prove he'd beaten his father once and for all, Figg had carried the man's severed penis in his pocket until he'd lost it during a month-long bout of youthful indiscretion.

He woke up the next morning unaware he'd even fallen asleep. He drank some water and pissed into the fireplace. The pain in his back was excruciating and the clamor in his head was back with a vengeance. The door and window seemed to be unmolested. He pried the board off the door. The dead man had left something for him.

In front of the step was the carcass of the dog with the little girl's head in place of its own. The hair was dirty with leaves entwined in it and her milked over eyes stared right at Figg. Beyond this creation was another one. A stake impaled the girl's body between the legs. The dog's head sat atop her body. Both creations were crawling with flies that Figg couldn't hear over the deafening roar in his head. He went back into the shack and shut the door.

The things outside bothered him in a profound way. In a number of ways, really. Figg had, over the years, made it a habit to kill people so he could eat them. It seemed like a rational, pragmatic, although perhaps ghoulish, thing to do. There had been some women he had had to kill to keep them from talking. He had usually ended up eating them, too. He would never describe anything he did as senseless or mindless. Not that the constructions outside were completely mindless. He thought there was definite intent there. Which brought him to another thing that worried him. Killing a black man who lived alone in the woods was one thing. Now he had the corpse of a little girl and her dog outside the place he'd overtaken. Not just their corpses, but their mutilated and molested corpses. Even Figg thought it was sick and he had a pretty bizarre code of ethics. Whatever was happening with the man he'd killed was not normal. Maybe he should invent a clause allowing him to leave without feeling as though he'd lost some battle. As far as he knew, he'd never had to deal with the supernatural before.

But he knew he wasn't going to leave.

He still had some rope.

He could build some kind of trap with that. Snag the monster around the ankles and dismantle him before moving on. Maybe he could even salvage the meat from the girl and the dog and plant himself here for a while. After all, he'd need sustenance and if he planned on staying, he'd need to get rid of the evidence. People *would* come looking for them. He guessed he'd go out and get started on the trap right away. If he stayed cooped up in this shack all day waiting for that thing to come back, he'd go insane.

He smoked some more of the herbs and took the rope out into the woods.

He'd need a sturdy branch.

This time, passing the jumbled corpses and walking into the woods was like submerging himself in the ocean. Maybe the clamor was still there but it was pushed down to a level just above audible. He heard nothing else and seemed to be only aware of his surroundings by about a three-foot radius. He reached up and tested some branches, searching for the right amount of spring and sturdiness. He'd been here less than twenty-four hours and nothing that had happened had seemed right. He'd seen many strange things but nothing as strange as this. The rope trailed in the dirt and brown pine needles. He thought he saw the monster man at one point and froze up. Figg couldn't go after him. What would he do if he caught him? There was something off about this place. He knew he'd sought it out, wandered until he found somewhere that felt good to him.

Someplace that felt *right*. This had always worked for him. He'd always had success. Like a farmer finding the right plot of land, he'd always had a good yield and managed to pull out before he got caught. He'd never attributed anything otherworldly to this ability, just experience and instinct. It was like a transient's education. But he was starting to think there was something about this place that had seduced him, even lied to him. He knew he should get out. He should definitely get out. He shouldn't even bother returning to the shack. There wasn't anything of his in there anyway. Nothing he really needed. He should keep going. Follow the sun west. Go all the way to the ocean. Maybe even sign on with some kind of vessel and go someplace far away like China. No place would be far enough away from here. Maybe not even the heavens. But even as he thought this, he was wrapping the rope around a branch and testing its sturdiness, creating a sort of slipknot with the other end.

He saw a man walking toward him. It wasn't the monster. This was a white man. He held a rifle. His mouth was moving but Figg couldn't hear anything coming out. He dropped the rope and reached for his knife but something had him around the tops of his arms and he didn't even realize it was another man until yet a third man reached into his pockets and emptied them of their contents and when he did this Figg's pants almost came down and he was pretty sure his cheeks colored with shame and, like that, all the pain and all the sounds came back and it was like exploding to the surface of the green ocean.

"Stay still!" the man in front of him shouted.

Figg noticed the badge.

The man behind him bound his wrists behind his back.

"What is all this? I didn't do nothin!"

Figg refused to walk so they dragged him over to the dirt trail that would eventually lead into town.

The road was lined with unspeakable atrocities.

The monster had been very busy.

It was tough for Figg to hear the men over the noise in his head.

The school had gone on a field trip to the woods.

No one had returned.

Worried parents.

What kind of sick man does this?

Blood and limbs and flies everywhere, lining the trail like a road of horrors.

The trial was short. Many of the parents cried for hanging. The sheriff agreed with them. Mr. Elias Figg should certainly be hanged. He should probably be drawn and quartered. Possibly even castrated. But the judge had a better idea. Twin Springs was new. It was going to be a growing village, maybe even a town or a city one day. There was work that needed doing. There certainly wasn't a lack of volunteers to oversee Mr. Figg in his labors. And if ever he should escape there was certainly no lack of volunteers to go looking for him and bring him back.

There was always someone there to watch him. Even when he was alone in his cell, there was someone watching him to make sure he did not take his own life.

Figg lived a lot longer than he ever imagined he would.

He managed to escape a number of times but never got very far. The repercussions were always very severe.

Now a very old man, every part of his body screaming with pain, he managed to escape and make it all the way back to the shack in the woods. No one had reclaimed it. It was a haunted place and, while it had been somewhat battered and abused over the years, it had never been lived in or destroyed. Still free, Figg struggled up into the shack—the step had long since rotted away. He lay down in the middle of the floor and stared at the shadows moving across the ceiling. He didn't think about everything he'd done and not done. He closed his eyes and did the one thing he'd come here to do in the first place.

DEATHTRIPPING IN NEW ORLEANS

FOR TWO YEARS, Tod Hoskins had followed a voice.

The voice was an insubstantial, shadowy thing. He was never really sure if it was inside his head or coming from somewhere externally, brushing past his ear like a moist whisper. Sometimes, he didn't think it was a voice at all.

No, it *was* a voice and it *did* have an owner.

Unfortunately, Tod was only able to find this owner during moments when he doubted his mental faculties the most: just before sleep or immediately upon awakening, deep in the throes of drunkenness or simply in a darkened room where space was nonexistent and time yawned like an empty chasm.

Sometimes he thought he wanted the voice to go away. Sometimes he thought he could chase it away so the only voice left in his head would be his own. But he knew that wasn't true.

If he lost the voice, then he lost *her.*

Her.

The voice was the last thing he had to remember Althea Jones.

It was *her* voice that called to him, nearly inaudible, intangibly soft, teasingly close, impossibly distant.

The voices had started after the car crash, two years ago, when they were both seventeen.

Tod was the passenger. He lived, emerging from the accident without a scratch, merely suffering from shock. Althea had died instantly, the steering column pulverizing her chest, crushing her heart.

Now, only memories and her voice. He did what he thought the voice wanted him to do, going wherever it told him to go.

Now it was September and Tod found himself standing at the far end of Jackson Square in New Orleans at the edge of a hurricane and he couldn't think of any reason he was there, save for the voice.

He wasn't a stranger to the city. His family had lived there until he was twelve, before moving to Ohio. He had always liked New Orleans. It seemed to have more than just a physical presence. There was another layer, another dimension to it. Maybe it was the strange history of the city itself. Maybe it was the city's fascination with things like voodoo and the dead. All those rumors of vampires and zombies. Maybe it was the heat and the humidity. Undoubtedly, it was all of these things, forming a ghastly mélange that crouched in the brain and wrapped the skin.

He liked being there. Not only was he following the voice, he also took an adult view of at least one part of his childhood. Something that made him think about full circles and how beginnings are so often endings. Tonight, however, would be his last night.

He would leave feeling somehow empty and unfulfilled. He had become accustomed to disappointment. Many times, he had gone where Althea's voice told him to go only to find nothing there. And so far, there didn't seem to be anything here either. Just emptiness.

According to the weather reports, a hurricane was only a few hours away. People had begun fleeing the city this morning. Tonight, it was practically empty. Businesses, not all of them, but most, had closed up, the owners shuttering their windows and going someplace safe to pray that the winds didn't tear their buildings down.

He had always thought of any tourist city as being very similar to a whore. Visitors come to leave their money, have fun, and maybe look at the beauty, however decadent, she has to offer, but then they leave with only a foggy memory. And tomorrow, by plane or by bus, he would do the same.

For now, there was the gentle beauty of the nearly empty city, the damp darkness softlit by gas lights, and the winds that were hard, constant and vaguely refreshing coming, as they were, at the end of a massive heatwave. He continued walking through Jackson Square thinking he had never seen it without any pedestrians or musicians or tarot card readers. There was something spectral about the empty benches.

But Tod was wrong. The Square wasn't completely empty. Maybe it had just been the murkiness of the night, but he had failed to notice the man sitting at the far end of the walkway. The man sat on a red milk crate, a brown man in a brown suit strumming a battered brown acoustic guitar. Tod came up behind him, veering off to the man's left so he didn't startle him. Tod waited until he was parallel with the man and began circling back toward him. The musician noticed Tod and nodded an acknowledgement.

Tod couldn't tell if the man was playing a song or not. The man strummed the guitar and hummed a tune that was maddeningly familiar but still unnamed. A small white bucket sat in front of the musician and he nodded toward it. Tod always hated it when the street performers more or less asked for money. But something inside of Tod felt sorry for this poor guy, sitting on the edge of a hurricane and playing to an empty street. Tod reached into the pocket of his jeans, pulling out a dollar and approaching the musician.

Tod leaned down to put the dollar in the bucket before the musician's leathery hand reached out to block him.

"You hang onto your money," the man rasped.

"No, you deserve it," Tod said.

"I'm not asking for money." Tod looked at the man's watery green eyes. The man looked down, voicelessly telling Tod to look in the bucket.

When Tod looked into the bucket, he saw that it was filled with black and white flyers.

"Take one," the old man said. "That's your free admission to a bit of fun on this most lonesome of nights."

Tod picked one of the flyers up, read it, and said, "Thanks."

The man nodded. Didn't say anything.

Tod glanced down at the flyer in his hand.

"But there's no address," he said.

"You'll know it when you get there. It'll be the only place with its lights on."

The voice, Althea's voice, whispered across Tod's ear, sending a shiver down his spine. He knew he would go.

"Well, thanks again," he said to the musician before turning and walking away.

"Have fun," the man said and went back to strumming his guitar.

Tod looked down at the flyer in his hand. It was an index cardsize piece of white paper and, in big black blocky letters, it said:

FREE

SHOW

Simple enough, he thought. Now I just need to find it.

He nodded to the guitar player and turned around. A brief moment of hesitation filled him and he considered turning back to the guitar player and asking, "No, really, where is it?" but decided not to. A man who followed voices of dead girls to strange cities across the United States could not really spend too much time questioning himself about where he should go. Instead, he held the flyer out in front of him, almost like a flashlight. He glanced up at the green and white-striped awning of Café du Monde, noting the umbrellas on the tables had been removed, and turned to his left. The guitar player was right. Except for the street lamps, there wasn't a single light glowing. No one was home. The city's emptiness grew ever more palpable.

Aimlessly, he wandered up a couple of blocks and turned left.

Aside from the darkness, the city was ominously quiet. The only thing he heard was the wind in his ears. With a sudden exhilaration, he wondered when the hurricane was going to break over the city.

Damage.

That was what all the news reports had predicted.

Severe damage.

And he decided he didn't care. If he was going to be caught out in the storm, he welcomed it. He wanted it to rage over him. He wanted the cold air to strip back his skin, lay his soul bare and run its icy fingers through him.

If it killed him, it didn't matter. Two years of misery had him convinced that any sort of happiness, any lifting of his black cloud, was not going to come. Maybe that was why he heard the voice. Maybe that voice was death. Maybe that was what he secretly hoped for every time he boarded an airplane or got in his car and raced down the highway. Maybe he wanted some fiery death to claim him, twist his body up with metal.

And he knew Althea would hate him for thinking that.

Althea—the beautiful young girl with the old-sounding name. And just thinking her name sent a tight shiver down the center of his body. That feeling bothered him. There was almost as much fear as love in that feeling.

Lost in his thoughts, he stopped when he came to an opening in between buildings. An alley. Looking down the alley, he convinced himself he saw a light gleaming somewhere back there. On the building to his right was a black sign with white lettering advertising the opening as Ohio Alley. He had never heard of it. Normally, if the city wasn't deserted, he would not have wandered down a dark, narrow alley but surely the pickpockets and thieves wouldn't see a profit in stalking a dead city.

With the paper still held out in front of him, he started down the alley.

And that's when he first got the feeling that, somehow, things just were not right. The darkness, the emptiness, the quietness—all of that was explained away by the hurricane. That was not part of the strangeness he now felt.

Now, being in the alley, it felt wrong. The buildings were higher than he remembered them. And they weren't just darkened, they were black. The broken cobblestones beneath his feet didn't feel entirely stable. They felt spongy, threatening to open up and suck him down. This was a prospect he would have completely welcomed. He wanted the earth to take him. It was what happened in the end, eventually, inevitably, anyway. Why not let it consume him now?

The air whistled through the cramped alleyway. For a moment, he felt like the alley was breathing around him, the mushy ground vibrating with a steadiness reminiscent of a beating heart. At the end of the alley, he could see faint yellow light pouring out of a door or a window. That had to be the place.

He walked the remainder of the way on legs that did not feel entirely his own.

The soft light at the end of the alley flickered in and out. *Were the winds that heavy?* he wondered. Could the power already be threatening to go out? It was possible, he guessed. Maybe the storm had already landed somewhere and would be on top of the city in no time at all. If that was the case, he should have been glad he was moving indoors only . . . he wasn't. He could have stayed out in it. He could have let it take him and that wouldn't have bothered him at all.

He reached the light. Something about it invited him toward it. It was meager lighting, not even bright enough to strain his night-focused eyes. The light invited him inside. Suddenly the light seemed the answer to his loneliness and his darkened mood. Inside, maybe there were people. And, inside, there was definitely that damp old wood smell he would forever associate with the city. It was a smell he found comforting. It reminded him of his grandma's house.

He stood in the doorway and, at that moment, couldn't remember a time when he had stood anywhere else. Suddenly, he didn't remember where he had come from and had absolutely no idea of the black death he had been chasing for the past two years. He had no idea where he was going. He had no idea that was where he wanted to go because he was standing there in front of some kind of shelter. That was what the light and the scents told him. That this place was there to protect him.

There *were* people inside. Six of them. Three couples.

Tod went in to join them, still clutching the flyer in his hand like he would need it for admission. When he saw the others seated in old wooden chairs he knew he no longer needed his flyer and there was a sudden sinking inside of him. There wasn't anything to do here. It was just someone's idea of a cruel prank. Some malicious soul probably paid the street performer off to sit there and hand these false promises out to the last of the storm's stragglers.

But, because he hadn't felt quite right all night, Tod decided to sit down and give his legs a rest.

The others were seated in an evenly spaced out fashion, as though afraid of anyone else overhearing their hushed conversations. There were sixteen chairs. Four rows of four, separated by a narrow aisle. Tod counted them because he had nothing else to do. One of the couples stared intently toward the front of the dingy yellow room. Another couple sat in the back row and snickered over their own private jokes. The other couple stood up. They had been sitting in the first row and passed Tod as they left.

"This is some kind of fucking joke," the guy said.

"Yeah, like what the *hell?*" the girl said.

When they got to the door, the guy announced, "You all might as well go home. Nobody's coming. They do this all the time."

There was an uncomfortable tension before the guy finally escorted his girl out into the night. Tod understood the tension. He felt sure the others now felt exactly like the guy who had just left but to stand up and leave now would be too much like following orders and people do not often want to look like sheep. At least not overtly.

So that left the five of them waiting in the room with the flickering lights and the warm smell. The couple in the front row continued to stare intently forward, unmoving and not talking. The couple in the very back row continued their conversation. They were like himself and Althea, Tod thought. They could have gone anywhere. They were just happy to be in each other's company. Even if they were in a room staring at nothing. That didn't matter because they *were* each other's entertainment.

And now Althea was dead and Tod didn't think he could ever feel that again. He would never again feel what that giggling couple in the back row felt. That warmth. That belonging. That sense of togetherness. Of being a part of someone else's life.

After thinking that last thought, the power went out.

The girl in the front row screamed and then things got really weird.

The room went black. Much blacker than it should have. Tod stood up from his rickety wooden chair and, upon standing up, lost his balance and collapsed to the floor. Whoever had been in the room with him before was now gone. He waited for a crack of thunder, a flash of lightning, anything. But all he got was the constant howling growl of the wind.

He didn't know what was happening.

The room swirled around him. He no longer knew where the door was or where it had been. He didn't know which way was the front of the room.

And he didn't care. He was ready to lie down on the floor and let the entire structure rain down on him. That was what he had wanted since the beginning anyway, wasn't it?

But that didn't happen. The room shook violently, still in that disorienting black. He felt the wind rage over his skin and it didn't feel like anything he would run or seek shelter from. He liked the way it felt. It was cold in the stifling New Orleans humidity. Even more than that, it filled him with something he hadn't felt in a long time.

He didn't think he wanted to die anymore.

Now all he wanted to do was lie there and feel the wind rage across his body. That would have been enough for him. And as quickly as he thought that thought, the wind stopped.

He realized he had closed his eyes, half-expecting some kind of grim final climax to it all. But that wasn't what happened. Instead there was a quiet calm.

He opened his eyes.

He was no longer in the room.

He was outside of a cemetery and he wasn't lying down anymore. He was standing up, right in front of the twisted wrought iron cemetery gates hanging slightly ajar. To the right of the gates, someone had written the phrase "THERE ARE GHOSTS IN THIS CITY" in black spraypaint. For a moment, he didn't know if the graffiti was talking about the city of New Orleans itself or this city of the dead in front of him.

He could still smell the storm in the air but it was no longer on him, if it had ever even come. Maybe it had passed. Tod didn't have any idea. Looking around him, he wasn't even sure he was still in New Orleans. It was like the cemetery occupied a sphere of existence all its own.

In his ear, Tod heard the whisper—Althea. Beautiful Althea breathing across the side of his head, beckoning for him to follow her.

Tod walked into the cemetery, the mausoleums towering around him, some of them fresh and clean and gleaming white beneath the moon, others in a state of complete disrepair, as though whatever had once been contained within could come crawling out at any moment. From the corner of his eye, he saw a movement and from somewhere within the back of his brain, he found a memory.

It was a violent memory.

It surged up behind his eyes, the flashing whiteness of his car cutting into the electrical utility pole.

But it wasn't his car, he told himself. It was Althea's car. She had been driving and she had died.

He shook the memory from his head. That wasn't the Althea he wanted to remember.

The Althea he wanted to remember was in front of him, sliding past a crumbling gray tomb.

"Althea," he said.

"Tod," she said back. "We need to talk."

"I know."

"It's not what you think it is."

Tod drew closer to the ghost (was it a ghost?) in front of him.

"I know what you're going to say. I need to get on with my life. I need to stop following you. I need to stop trying to die."

"That's not it at all."

"What then?"

"I want you to join me."

Another memory, cascading through his brain, caused him to take a step back from Althea even though she was pale and beautiful and standing right there in front of him, everything he remembered about her made crystalline and drawn into sharp focus.

Why was he stepping back?

"We could do it, Tod. Me and you could be together. Just like we used to be. All you have to do is not go back. If you never leave this cemetery, you can be with me forever."

"I loved you, Althea." But even as he spoke the words, he doubted the weight of them. Doubted the truth of them. Another memory stabbed at him and he dropped to one knee. This one was harsh and fuller than the rest. More than just a fragment.

In the memory, Tod was driving the car. He fought with the steering wheel to keep the car on the road but it was a battle he lost. And there was something else in the car with him but not some*one*. There was something else in the car with him, in his head, and there was a reason he had aimed his car at the lone pole to begin with.

"You know you want this, Tod."

"No," he said. He stood up, shaking the memories out of his head, swelling with the new memories flooding into it. The memories he had had before the car crash. The *real* memories.

"I don't want it."

"Why not?" she asked, her lips gone pouty.

"Because you never were."

"But here I am, Tod. How can you say that I never was?"

"You were the figment of a lonely boy's imagination and when I wanted you to go you wouldn't and so I had to destroy what created you . . ."

"Yourself. Oh, you've grown so clever in your manhood. But dreams don't go away that easily, Tod. I will be with you until you die."

"No, you won't."

After saying that, the storm broke over the city of the dead. He crawled into an open mausoleum, one not yet used, to escape the winds, and Althea crawled in with him.

The chill of the winds was replaced with all the warmth of a fever. The sweating thing that never was lay beside him in this cramped quarter, trying to coax Tod in any way plausible. Trying to get him to acknowledge her in some way because the more he acknowledged her, the more he addressed her, even if it was to tell her she was just something he had dreamed up, the stronger she became. So he lay there, huddled up into himself, his eyes drawn tightly closed as her hands roamed over his body and her breath swept his ear and his scalp. Hands and breath, nothing more. Nothing more physical than that. Nothing more physical than what could have passed as wind.

Nothing there, Tod had to continue telling himself, listening to the cold winds around him and feeling so very hot inside. Like he was going to erupt in fire. But that was exactly what he couldn't do. When he had dreamed her up, Althea could do anything. She could take him to whatever pleasure limit his mind wanted to go. She could do all of that, Tod now realized, because she *was* his mind. He quivered, feeling the cool stone push against his fevered back, as he felt Althea's hands move lower and lower, reaching between his legs, preparing to administer the final test. Tod knew what she wanted. He knew she wanted to find rigid stiffness there. Hardness to enclose her breath around and then, eventually, her sex. She wanted to drag him back up within her.

But what she found was nothing. Tod started to laugh. A crazy man in a tomb during a hurricane trying not to let himself be raped by his own mind. He laughed away the past, fits of coughing turning into a bout of vomiting but, sometime during the course of this fit, he felt something whoosh out of him. His head, if it was possible, felt *emptier*. After that, he relaxed, sprawling back, his puke warm against his back.

He didn't know how long he stayed like that, but eventually he found blackness. A blackness more comforting than he ever thought.

It felt like years before he opened his eyes again. In reality, it was probably little more than a day. But, in another way, he realized, it was years. He felt like he had regained the lost years after the crash. He felt like he had regained a certain amount of sanity. A sense of purpose and a sense of light filled the space he had emptied. He slid out of the mausoleum and into the wet dawn.

He walked out of the cemetery and thought about trying to board a plane or a bus back to Ohio but he suddenly found he was terrified to step foot on an airplane. Maybe, he figured, this was the place to begin his new life. With his wet clothes sticking to his skin, he turned to his left, wondering how he had made it so far out here, and began walking toward the dark and sinking city before him.

THE FUNERALGOER

THRIP HAD A lot of problems.

He found it impossible to explain most of his actions.

He did not have a job. He did not have any friends. Other than obtaining the bare essentials of life—food, coffee, and cigarettes—he rarely ventured outdoors. Besides those bare essentials, a funeral was the only other thing that could draw him from his cramped, cavelike apartment. Over the past sixteen years, ever since turning sixteen, he had been to two-hundred and eighteen funerals. He had seen *Harold and Maude* and knew what he was doing was not wholly original but, like most other things, he could not explain it.

However infrequently he did so, it seemed impossible for him to leave the apartment without incident. Part of the reason for this was his appearance. He stood well over six feet tall and was rail thin. Normally, he clothed himself in layers of old clothes, allowing them to grow pungently filthy before washing them. Greasy black hair fell in a tangled mass down to his shoulders. He rarely shaved but his facial hair was thin, looking more like a layer of grit on his bone pale face. His so-brown-they-were-almost-black eyes were normally bloodshot because he did not sleep very well. His fingernails, which he rarely cut, were thick and jagged.

Thrip could not help the incidents. When he went out in public, he grew anxious. And when he grew anxious, he did things that were clearly not right.

Like this morning . . .

On the way to the Thornburg funeral, he had stopped at a gas station for some cigarettes. Upon leaving, he saw a small girl sitting in a car while her mother went in to pay for the gas. Thrip, noticing the girl staring at him, bounded over to the car and, pressing his face nearly to the girl's window, ran his fingernails down the glass, shooting a wild-eyed stare at the girl. She screamed, her face turning red, forcefully cradling the doll in her arms. The girl's mother had seen this and come running from the gas station, shouting at Thrip to get away. The woman waved her arms in the air and shouted, "Get away from her! Get *away* from her, you horrible man!"

Thrip bowed his head and slinked away. He knew nothing would come of the incident. He was as much a part of the town as the corner drunk or the star quarterback. There were stories about him and he knew the town would not be able to live without those stories. Not only that, he had the police in his pocket.

Whenever there was a murder in the town, of which, admittedly, there were very few, the police came to Thrip. And he, unfailingly, could give them an accurate description of the murderer. Consequently, a murder had not occurred in Olden in six years and, while it was a peaceful town, this was some kind of record. Thrip wondered if all of those cutesy housewives who vilified him knew he was the very same man who had put an end to murder in Olden.

He had an interesting knack for feeling what the dying felt, of looking through their eyes. If anyone had cared to ask, he could tell them what the old man dying from a heart attack felt too. He could tell them there was a Heaven for some, a Hell for others. He could also tell them about Purgatory and the endless Void. But no one asked about *that*. No one truly wanted to believe there could possibly be nothing at all after death.

Lately, however, the funerals had disturbed Thrip. The murders had stopped but another mystery had risen in Olden.

His suspicions had culminated at the Thornburg funeral. Actually, the thought had popped into his head when he had crossed Alma Bentley's grave. She had been buried yesterday afternoon but, now walking over the grave, Thrip had the distinct feeling it was empty. Under a cool gray sky, he stood in the back of the group gathered around the Thornburg grave but he couldn't stop thinking of the emptiness just a few yards behind him. Before the service was over he had pointed at Mrs. Bentley's grave and shouted, "That grave is empty! She isn't there! There's no one in that grave!"

The pastor looked up from his thick Bible and went back to reading from it, paying no attention to Thrip. Two large men in the

Thornburg party advanced on Thrip, helping him out of the cemetery.

"Get the fuck away," one of them said. "You're ruining my dad's
funeral."

"You don't understand," Thrip said, practically pleading with
him. "Mrs. Bentley's grave . . . it's empty. You don't want that to
happen to your father, do you?"

The man drew back a meaty hand and rammed it into Thrip's
nose. "You're sick," he said. "You're a very sick man."

Thrip, on his knees, stayed there for a while, holding his bloodied
nose and staring up at the incline of the cemetery, wondering what
had just happened. Eventually, he rose, headed back to his small
apartment in town.

That incident, that feeling, continued to plague him. He wondered why he went to funerals at all. They were all basically the same
and he wondered why this was. Hadn't all of these people led wildly
different lives, wildly *individual* lives? Why were all of their services
conducted in the same manner, as though it could be anyone going
into the cold earth? Had he just shouted those things to try and
breathe some life into the funeral, to give the funeralgoers something
memorable?

He wanted to think that. He really did. Because the alternatives
seemed to be so much worse.

That night he tried to sleep, waking up to a shattering pain. Somewhere, someone had just taken a nasty and fatal fall down a flight of
stairs, pushed by the blind hand of fate. Thrip was up the rest of the
night, shaking, knowing there would be another funeral in a couple
of days. But he didn't want to wait that long before going back to
the cemetery.

Thrip slept fully clothed. He pulled himself up to the head of his
small bed and waited, knees pulled into his chest, arms wrapped
around knees, staring frightfully around the room until the cold gray
dawn came up over the town. Still shaking, the meager light bleeding
through the curtains, he left the bed and pulled on a couple more
layers of shirts and a ratty black overcoat.

The morning traffic had not yet begun and he made his way to
the cemetery, some unseen force hurrying his footsteps through the
cool mist that monochromed everything.

Once in the cemetery, he approached Alma Bentley's grave.
There was still a bit of a swell, a bit of a mound, to the freshly turned

earth and the sod had not yet taken. Thrip stared at the headstone, not yet made colorful with years of lichen and mildew. He did not really want to do what he was about to do. But he did it anyway.

Knowing the force of what he was about to feel would send him reeling, he dropped to all fours and sort of *crawled* onto the grave, staring down at the grass almost as though he was able to see through it. Of course, he couldn't actually see through it. He knew that. He could only feel what was supposed to be below there. And he could only feel what was supposed to be below there if it was death. Death had a way of calling to him. Death, the cessation of all feeling, had a way of sparking *his* feelings until they came alive and sent a scary kind of electricity rushing through his veins.

Thrip felt nothing.

And that was how he knew the grave was empty.

Cautiously, unable to take his eyes from the grave, Thrip stood up, backing away from it.

Would anyone listen to him? he wondered. Would anyone pay the least bit of attention if he ran up to them and told them about how some of the graves in the cemetery were completely empty when there were supposed to be people in them?

No. He knew they wouldn't listen. And maybe he didn't want them to listen. Thrip felt something interesting pass through his brain. A flicker of a thought. A wash of excitement.

What if this was what he had been waiting for?

He had attended all of these funerals, drenching himself in death, wanting to gain some sense of finality to its mysteries, wanting to find some proof of something more than just these bland family re-unions there to placate the attendees with foggy candy- coated memories.

Maybe this was that something else. Maybe there *was* something else after death. Some form of life after death. Maybe it wasn't all so final and bleak. Maybe there were other options besides Heaven and Hell and Purgatory and the Void. He straightened his clothes, planning to go over to Travis Thornburg's grave and see if he could still feel the death below or if it would just be more of the empty nothing that infested Alma Bentley's.

Movement caught Thrip's eye. He turned his head to see a small man standing at the crest of the hillside. Briefly, Thrip thought he was going to get kicked out of the cemetery again. He was well out-side of visiting hours and although he wasn't doing anybody any harm, he knew the caretaker to be a restless and trigger happy hill-billy who had never really liked him from the second he had seen him.

This wasn't the caretaker.

The man raised an arm over his head and beckoned Thrip to come over to him.

Thrip made his way over the soggy cemetery grass until he stood out of the man's reach but close enough for conversation and ob-servation. The man was considerably shorter than Thrip. He wore a conservative gray tweed suit with an out-of-place bright pink derby on his head. He looked vaguely familiar to Thrip but he couldn't put a specific time or place to him. The man smiled jovially and raised the hat off his head.

"Ah, Mr. Thrip, just the man I wanted to see."

"You . . . you wanted to see me?" Thrip asked, finding this en-counter odd on a number of levels.

"Oh, I most certainly did."

"Why?"

"Because, out of everyone in this town, I think you are the only one who would be interested in us."

"And who are you?"

"Yes, yes, I'm getting ahead of myself. I'm sorry." The man's small brown eyes blazed with a cross between good humor and cra-ziness. "My name is Gregory Nascent."

The man stuck out his hand. Thrip moved closer and took the man's hand in his own. "It's very nice to meet you," Thrip said out of politeness more than any genuine affection.

"I would like to invite you to a funeral. You're always up for a good funeral, aren't you?"

"I go to every one I see listed in the paper."

The man looked down at the ground, his smile fading for just a second, before looking back up at Thrip. "I'm sorry to say this fu-neral will not be in the paper."

"No?"

"Most certainly not. Truthfully, I don't really suspect many would attend."

"Why not?"

"It's kind of a unique funeral. Would you like to join us?"

"Who is 'us'?"

"You'll just have to come down and see. It begins at midnight. I trust you will be there."

Nascent had turned and left before Thrip could give him an answer.

Something about the man left Thrip feeling slightly off, like the man had taken a piece of his soul. He couldn't describe it any better than that.

On the trip back home, he kept his head down, staring at the ground, having traveled this route so many times he didn't really need to look up and see where he was going. Once inside his apartment, he lay down on his bed, staring up at the water stains on the ceiling and thinking about who that strange man could have been and how he had never seen him before and why the man would have approached him this morning of all mornings. Surprisingly, he fell asleep.

The night was cool, dark and gloomy. The fog milked the sky gray. Not a single star was visible. The moonlight was murky but ample enough for Thrip to make his way to the cemetery. After bypassing the gates, a shiver wiggled its way through his body. Excitement and fear mingled within him as he climbed the gentle slope to the dark figures gathered around Mr. Thornburg's grave.

Upon spotting him, Mr. Nascent approached Thrip and held out his hand, "Ah, I'm so glad you could make it."

Thrip did not know what to say. He shook the man's cold hand. The others gathered around the grave seemed to be in high spirits as well. Looking at Thrip, they spoke excitedly, albeit in hushed whispers. There were maybe fifteen people in all. Something Nascent described to Thrip as a "pitiful showing."

"So what happens here?" Thrip asked Nascent.

"Well, that is why I invited you. So you could see for yourself."

"Very well."

"I invite you to put your hand on the grave. Tell me what is beneath it."

Thrip looked at Nascent, somewhat distrustfully, approaching the grave but not taking his eyes off the small man. He put his hand on the dew-slicked earth and said, "Death. Mr. Thornburg is in there. He's dead." Thrip took his hand away before the sensation of nausea could completely wrap him and rock him to the ground.

"So we are agreed upon that?"

"Yes. I guess." Thrip found himself more and more confused.

"Now, what you are about to see is a funeral like you've never seen before, Mr. Thrip. It is sort of a . . . *reverse* funeral."

"You're going to raise him from the dead?"

"That is exactly what I am going to do."

"But why?"

"Because sometimes the dead can't forget. Sometimes the pull of life is too great and they are not ready to relinquish control of that."

"But this is an abomination."

"Be careful of what you say in mixed company, Mr. Thrip. You never know who you might be insulting."

"You're dead."

"No. I *once* was dead. Now I am very much alive." Nascent grabbed Thrip's hand and placed it on his heart. Thrip felt the organ beating slowly but strongly against his palm.

"Let us begin the funeral," Mr. Nascent said.

He pulled a heavy black book from his overcoat and stood at the foot of the grave. The others at the ceremony gathered around him as he read in a language Thrip did not recognize. Not only was the language unknown to him, the intonations were strange and garbled, like nothing he had ever heard before.

Thrip watched as the ground trembled slightly, the grass and dirt being pushed away before Mr. Thornburg pulled himself up, dragging himself from the earth. The process was slow, Nascent's chanting oration hallucinatory. With Thornburg halfway out of the grave, a burly man in a tattered tuxedo who Thrip identified as Dr. Kittinger came to aid him in his further struggle. Now all the way out, Thornburg looked around at his surroundings, confusion naked in his eyes.

"It is not unlike birth," Nascent said. "But imagine being born with all of the faculties you had at your death."

Thrip turned his head away. He didn't want to make eye contact with the risen man.

"Kittinger? Could you lead him away? Let him know what is happening to him."

Kittinger led the man into the fog on the far side of the cemetery.

"I've seen enough," Thrip said. He didn't think he could bear it anymore. If there was one thing he had gained through his funeral attendance, it was an immense respect for the dead. Since he was unable to rationalize death in any other way, he could only truly see it as a final, eternal rest.

He turned to leave but Nascent grabbed his arm.

"Now, Mr. Thrip, wouldn't you like to know why we invited you here this evening? It seems we are not the only ones with abominable skills."

"I would turn it off if I could," Thrip said. "Please let go of my arm."

Nascent gripped stronger. Others from the funeral gathered around him.

"One of the interesting things about death, Mr. Thrip, is that the deceased never really remember what death feels like. We don't even remember exactly how it was that we died. Can you imagine having those gaps in your life . . . in your life after death?"

"I don't know what you're getting at."

"I think you do know what we're getting at. I want you to come with us. I want you to tell us the stories of our deaths."

"I can't do that."

"You don't have a choice. And . . . Yes. There's something else."

"Just let me leave."

"I can't let you leave. If I let you leave, then I don't get to hear the story of my death. Nor do I get to fulfill my life's work."

"What is your life's work?"

Nascent gripped Thrip's other arm, pulling him closer to his gaunt, dead face.

"Look closely. Think back about six years."

Thrip studied the man's face, recognition flooding him. Thrip remembered being in the body of a twenty-year-old woman, staring at the face in front of him as the life left her. At the time, the face was a little thinner, a little hairier . . .

"Oh God," Thrip said.

"That's right. She was not the first. She was merely the apex. I had developed quite a taste for murder and you stopped that. Well, you stopped *me* . . . The taste is still very much there."

More and more of the incident flooded back to Thrip. The girl's murder had not been quick and painless. It was the most drawn out, excruciating death he had ever experienced, keeping him awake for two days while some hidden part of his psyche felt it all. The man had kept the woman blindfolded the entire time but, at the end, during the last few seconds of her life, he had removed the blindfold. Thrip felt stupid for not realizing who Mr. Nascent was from the beginning. But, aside from the surface physical differences, the context was completely different. Like seeing one of your grade school teachers in the grocery store. Besides, he had spent years trying to forget that face, trying to forget that entire episode, just like he did after every death. Most of the time, he could even manage to forget the name of the deceased. But not this time. Melinda Kendrick. The name stuck with him, always somewhere in the back of his mind.

"You're a monster," Thrip said.

"Oh, that was just the beginning."

Thrip struggled to get away but Nascent's grip proved to be almost supernaturally strong and Thrip was not exactly powerful to begin with. There were others surrounding him, grabbing him, others every bit as strong as Nascent. The more he struggled, the harder they gripped.

"The best part of this whole death business," Nascent said. "Is that, the more people we kill, the stronger we grow, the greater our numbers."

As a whole, the funeral party dragged Thrip into the woods behind the cemetery. And there, they made him repeat the stories of their deaths. Most nights, Thrip was only able to get through one story. The stories left him bereft of nearly everything except sorrow. He ritualistically collapsed onto the ground, weeping and shaking, wanting desperately to be away from these people, wanting to get beyond the cemetery gates so he could breathe a single breath of life. And each night, the strange tribe claimed another victim, bringing them from all over the country but always making sure they died within the borders of the town, within the perimeter of Thrip's knowledge. The Olden Memorial Cemetery had long since been used up. Now there were only the new arrivals and the ones they murdered themselves. Their reach was staggering.

The dead had no concern for him, using him only for the individual stories of their deaths. And the stories were always told on an individual basis, the deceased and Thrip, away from the ear shot of all the others because, in the end, death was a very personal thing. The deceased were given a gun to shoot Thrip with if he tried to get away. They were instructed not to shoot with intentions of killing.

Afterwards, the gun passed like a morbid baton, they gathered around one another, some exchanging their new found information and wondering if death would find them a second time. They speculated on how they would take the next victim, inventing new ways so the story would always be entertaining. In a way, Thrip thought, they told the stories themselves.

Soon, Thrip begged them to kill him. He refused to eat so they beat him until he did so. Nascent told him they could not let him die. Once they killed him, Nascent said, all of the stories would go with him, along with the memories of his own death.

And, of course, Thrip thought of other ways to die besides starvation. Like escaping just long enough to take his own life. Or removing his tongue and then his hands so he couldn't write the stories down. But they guarded against this. He was watched at all times. And there he stayed, in their keep, waiting for insanity or a natural death to claim him so that he could, for once, be done with death. Then he thought about what Nascent had said about all the dead retaining the faculties they had gained in life. And Thrip knew they would continue to keep him around. His "gift" would not leave him. He would have to escape.

Months later, a man named Alex Kendrick died from complications due to liver cancer. One night thereafter, the man came to Thrip to learn of his death. Thrip sat on an old tombstone by a small fire, still shivering. He was always cold these days.

Kendrick was a thin man, ravaged by his disease and, perhaps, Thrip thought, he was haunted long before that. He sat down across the fire from Thrip.

"So, I'm sure it was the cancer . . ." Kendrick began. "I just want to know if my wife was there. Was she holding my hand? Did she say anything?"

Surreptitiously, Thrip surveyed the surroundings. "You know," he said. "This doesn't have to be the end. This doesn't have to be your afterlife."

"What other option do I have? Lying in a hole in the ground until the worms come?"

"The afterlife is whatever you thought it would be before these . . . ghouls came and dug you up."

"It's too late for philosophy, I'm afraid," Kendrick said.

"Did you have a daughter named 'Melinda'?"

Kendrick's eyes grew wide.

"Yeah. How did you . . ."

"She was murdered, wasn't she?"

"Yeah, she most definitely was. It was a tragedy. So young. So beautiful." Thrip knew the man would have cried if the dead were capable of tears.

"I can tell you who did it."

"I already know who did it. His name was Gregory Nascent. He killed a number of people in this area and . . . Hey, are you the one who tipped off the cops?"

"I am," Thrip said, wishing he could feel good about it. "And I guess you haven't exchanged names with all of your . . . cronies, yet?"

"There seem to be an awful lot of us. Soon we'll outnumber the living."

It was true. There must have been nearly a thousand of them now. They had moved from the surface of the woods to an elaborate underground city beneath the cemetery. Odd that they would choose a place so similar to where they would still be if they had never risen.

"The man who killed your daughter is there. I'm sure you'll meet him eventually. I can describe him to you if you let me go."

"I can't let you go. They've told me what happens if I let you go."

"What? They kill you?"

"Something like that."

"But maybe that's not such a bad thing."

"I don't know. I know that now, I'm able to walk around, I'm able to experience life."

"Have they told you about the murders yet? About how they go out hunting at night? Why do you think there are so many of them? They get you hooked on this perverse life after death and they bleed everything else from you. They wouldn't let you strike out and do what you want. So kill their leader and become their new leader. Tell them what they have to do."

Kendrick looked at the ground, ran a hand across the stubble on his gray cheek.

"How many people get the chance to avenge a loved one's murderer with no repercussions? You're beyond the law now. All you have to do is let me walk through those gates."

Kendrick took a deep breath.

"And I suppose I'll never know what happened before I died?"

"Do you really want to know? It's never as good as you want it to be."

Freedom was so close. Thrip could feel it in his cold, thin fingers.

"If I saw him, I would recognize him," Kendrick said. "And then I would take him apart. I don't really need you. If I let you go, it'll be like bringing a house of cards down on myself."

"So you really think you'll recognize him?"

"How could I forget? You know, I was there, when they put the needle into his arm. He looked happy. That face is in my brain for good. Definitely. I couldn't forget him."

"Mr. Kendrick!" a voice called out from behind Thrip. Nascent.

"Others are waiting, good sir!" Nascent said.

"Recognize *him*?"

"Of course, that's the man who resurrected me."

By this time Nascent was standing next to Thrip.

"He's out of context. Look closely," Thrip said.

"Closely at what?" Nascent asked but, as though he knew what they had been talking about, his hand clamped around Thrip's thin arm. Thrip would have pulled away if he had the strength.

"Nothing," Kendrick said.

"One does not ask a person to look closely at nothing, Mr. Kendrick."

"You know all of the stories, don't you?" Kendrick asked. "Even the private ones?"

"Of course not."

"But you listen in. Like you were just now."

"Only because you're a special case."

"Why?"

Thrip felt like a third wheel. Kendrick hadn't believed him. Thought for sure he would recognize his daughter's killer. He was trying to get Nascent to confess himself.

"Oh, I think you and I both know, don't we, Mr. Kendrick?"

"By the way," Kendrick said. "I don't think we've been properly introduced yet. You know my name, probably read it right off the headstone, but I didn't get yours."

"Would you like to guess?" Nascent said.

"Rumpelstiltskin?" Kendrick said. Thrip almost laughed.

"Close," Nascent said.

And the night exploded in gunfire and pain.

A bullet tore into Thrip's upper arm where Nascent had held him. But Nascent's hand had been torn to gore, along with part of Thrip's arm.

Everything in slow motion, Thrip turned to see Nascent staring at Kendrick. Nascent held the stump of his left wrist out before him.

Thrip was already moving away, out of this chamber and toward the surface. He hoped no one tried stopping him. The gun fired continuously behind him.

By the time he reached the cemetery gates, Thrip felt, for the first time, what it was like to feel someone die a second time. Once safely outside the gates, he collapsed onto the ground, reeling with the vast torment of Nascent's afterlife. If the man had escaped death once, Thrip didn't see how he was going to escape it a second time. Not with his body as torn apart as his soul.

Thrip watched the dawn gray the dark purple of the sky. His first dawn in months. He picked himself up from the ground, damp with dew, and went in search of a convenience store. He desperately needed a cigarette.

SAD CLOWN, KENTUCKY

1.

MOMENTS OF CLARITY. A fleeting moment when every-thing makes sense. An instant when a decision is made. A life-altering decision. Charles Zasper had a moment like that. It wasn't the moment he found his mother dead. No, his moment of clarity, his epiphany, came later. But it couldn't have happened if his mother had not died. In fact, he would realize later, perhaps to relieve him-self of any guilt he felt, that everything had to happen exactly the way it did for him to get where it was he was going.

2.

Charles Zasper was not an extraordinary man and the circumstances that brought him to live with his mother were not extraordinary cir-cumstances. In the life of Charles Zasper, things just happened. And, up to a point, they happened in an ordinary fashion.

Charlie graduated from Oretown High School in southwestern Ohio with average grades. He selected an average community college to attend, planning on majoring in computer science when he fin-ished his requirements. When he was twenty, he met an average woman, although it took him a while to realize she was average. It was also when he was twenty that he dropped out of school and went to work in one of Oretown's many factories. It wasn't a spec-tacularly high-paying factory, for those did exist in Oretown. It was an average factory, a paper mill that made boxes for White Castle

274

restaurants that paid average wages and had average benefits.

Charlie and his wife, Nora, bought a house in one of Oretown's many average suburbs. There they ate, slept, fucked, argued, and talked about having kids. But Charlie had a low sperm count. Even *they* give a lackluster performance, he sometimes thought. When he was twenty-five, Charlie and Nora went through an average divorce. They had simply grown tired of one another. The good days were no longer good enough to cancel out the bad ones. Charlie quit his job at the paper mill and moved in with his mother. Between his half of the divorce settlement that came from selling the house and splitting the money in half and his mother's social security, Charlie didn't figure he'd have to work again for a long time, if he lived modestly.

Which was good, because Mother was getting on in years and Charlie didn't really have any intention of ever working again. He didn't see the point in it. It felt like he was working for somebody else. Besides, Mother needed somebody to look after her. Ever since Charlie's dad died when he was twelve, Mother had been fiercely independent. But now it was nice to have someone go to the store for her, or make out the bills, or help with some of the more laborious upkeep of the house. Charlie was that person. It was something he didn't mind doing. He loved his mother and it was nice to spend time with her before she died. It was clear she was going to die soon. At least, it was clear to her.

"The beautiful place is calling my name, Charlie," she would say. He didn't really want to hear it. He didn't want to think about her dying but he knew it was inevitable.

Charlie spent most of his time at Mother's house stoned during the day and drunk in the evening, watching television and reading books. Well, he had started out splicing his TV watching with reading but then he realized most of the books he had thought he enjoyed contained stuff he didn't really want to think about. The television was different, though. It didn't really matter what was on, Charlie watched it. Day after day, he sat frozen in front of the TV. Sometimes he laughed only to wonder, a couple of minutes later, what it was he was laughing at. Sometimes, whole days would pass and, when he went to bed at night, Charlie had no recollection of what happened that day. Well, he'd watched TV all day, of course. But what had he watched? He couldn't remember. The talking heads simply ate away his memory. So from the time he moved back in with Mother until she died was really one long continuous daze.

3.

Mother died on March 23rd. Charlie knew she was dead when he went into the kitchen and saw that the coffee hadn't been made. Mother always made the coffee at 6:30 in the morning, just like she had when Charlie's dad was alive and Charlie was rushing off to elementary school. Without fail Charlie was greeted, every morning, with the aroma of Mother's strong coffee. It was a welcome scent and the absence of it that morning stopped him cold.

Hurriedly, he went about making the coffee himself, as though it could revive the dead. He knew it was hopeless, but it was like the whole house was lopsided and insane without that scent. Once the coffee was on, maybe he could think a little bit. Maybe it would get some of those cobwebs out of his head.

While the coffee brewed, he crossed the house to Mother's bedroom. The door was slightly ajar. It was always slightly ajar when she was in it. It came from pushing the door against the frame but not hard enough to make it click shut. The slight unevenness of the old house caused the door to creep back into her room.

Mother was slightly cold to the touch. He watched her chest for any rising and falling. He checked her pulse. He held the back of his hand against her nose and mouth. Nothing. She was right, Charlie thought. She knew she was going to die. It was just a couple of nights ago she had warned Charlie about her black dreams—black cars, black curtains, black horses, and black seas. Shadow children calling from outside her window, wanting her to come out and play. And now the blackness had settled over her. It had drowned her and it wasn't going to cough her back up.

Charlie went to call the hospital and then decided not to. Maybe he should have some coffee first. Smoke some pot to calm his nerves. Pick up the house a little bit. Mother would hate anyone being in the house when it looked the way it did.

Later that evening, Charlie went to the phone again. This time he figured he'd better call the police but, picking up the phone, he couldn't do it. He was too drunk and high to handle the house being filled with cops and paramedics.

He went back into his mother's room. It felt colder than the rest of the house. Outside, the March winds rampaged, slinging icy rain against the window. Charlie pulled the quilt, something his mother had made herself, up to her chin. He sat down on the edge of the bed, put his face in his hands, and cried. For some reason, he couldn't see her as completely dead until she was in the ground. He imagined her spirit stuck in some kind of middle-ground, trying to reach her beautiful place. He hoped she could find it. He didn't want to leave her side. Not that night anyway. He went to her nightstand and rummaged until he found the only two books she ever read. One was the Bible and the other was a beat up historical romance paperback. Alternating, he read her passages from both of them. There were times when it felt awkward, reading the romance passages to his mother, but it was better than trying to think of something to say.

Some time just before dawn, Charlie got tired. He put the books on the nightstand, kissed his mother on the forehead and, pulling her door tightly shut, he went out into the living room to fall asleep in front of the television. He wouldn't open her door again for nearly a month.

4.

He woke up the next afternoon and contemplated calling someone about Mother again. Before he even got up to go to the phone, Charlie realized that an interesting sort of paranoid paralysis now crawled through his veins. If he called someone, wouldn't they know how long his mother had been dead? And wouldn't they find it peculiar he hadn't called them yesterday, as soon as he found her? Wouldn't it be considered gross abuse of a corpse or something? Christ, he didn't want to go to jail.

Eventually, Charlie settled down into a fogged routine. Every day, he tried to forget he was ignoring the fact that something had to be done about Mother. He woke up, made the coffee and took a daily trip to Hapsburg's Corner Store to buy wine and cigarettes. At first, he just bought one bottle of wine but then he found himself going for three and then four. He smoked five packs of cigarettes a day.

All day, he sat on the couch in front of the television, ripped on wine and laughing like a madman, a cigarette always burning between his fingers. The morning after he woke up with headaches and a persistent cough, wondering why he felt that way and proceeding to do the same things over. He didn't turn on any lights save the flickering glow of the TV. He didn't open any blinds. He couldn't recall eating anything. For nearly a month, and it really felt much longer, it felt like the only life he knew, Charlie lived like this.

5.

It wasn't until a day in late April that Charlie had his epiphany. Actually, it was like several small epiphanies leading up to one huge revelation.

The day began like any other day. He woke up. He made his coffee, took the pot into the living room with him and sat in front of the television. Shortly after noon, he went to Hapsburg's. This time he just needed wine. There was still a half a carton of Lucky Strikes back at the house so he wouldn't need any more for at least a day. He jingled the door open at Hapsburg's and went along his predestined route, staring down at the tiles peeling back on the yellow water-stained floor. Charlie always wondered how it was the health department never managed to close Hapsburg's down. Charlie liked it because it was convenient, but he didn't think he would ever buy any food from there. But it was all right for wine and Charlie loaded up his arms, carrying the bottles to the front counter.

As always, old Hapsburg was there. Charlie had never figured out his first name. Charlie also realized he never made eye contact with old Hapsburg. Usually, the transaction took place with Charlie staring at his chest until the old man held out his gnarled hand to give him change. Today, however, Charlie looked up at old Hapsburg. What he saw made him stumble back a couple of steps, only far enough to where he could loop his arms out and seize the wine bottles.

It looked like Hapsburg had aged to the point of death. His once ruddy complexion was now a chalky gray. His wrinkles had become trench-like furrows cutting through that pallor. And his eyes, when Charlie met them, were a milky white. "Thank you," Hapsburg said before his eyes turned black, some type of fetid pus rolling out and onto his cheeks, diverted by the wrinkles around his mouth.

Charlie was speechless. Not bothering to reach out for the change, he pulled the bottles in close and charged out the door, his heart beating harder than it had in a long time. He didn't slow down until he was at the corner and across the street. *What the hell?* he thought.

Once across the street, he slowed down. On one hand, Charlie was terrified. On the other hand, he felt more alive than he had in years. Adrenaline sparkled through him. His skin felt hot against his clothes. His heart leaped around in his chest.

All around him it was a nice day. The electricity of spring held on. Overhead, a bruised mass of clouds floated rapidly across the sky but, here and there, he could catch the blue behind the clouds and it was magnificent.

Charlie paused at the next corner, looking around at the blooming trees and the early stages of the neighborhood's gardens. He breathed in the air, a rare fresh and clean scent for Oretown. It was only clean, he figured, because it came from some other place. He imagined the flat farmlands of Indiana. Off to his right, he saw a woman ambling from a few yards away. She pushed a baby carriage and it looked like she had on a short skirt. Charlie found himself vaguely aroused. He had forgotten how good it felt to be in that state, even if it just meant going home and jerking off over the sink.

The woman drew closer. She seemed, in fact, to be coming at a somewhat alarming rate. As she closed the distance between them, the terror Charlie felt back at Hapsburg's came back. The woman was almost right on him now and he saw that she wasn't attractive at all. She was emaciated and deathly, tight brown mummified skin wrapped around her bones. Her hair hung in dirty strands and clumps. She smelled like decay. She stopped the carriage just in front of Charlie and turned to look at him. Her eyes were black sockets. Yellow pus oozed from her blunted, truncated nose. She put up a hand to one withered breast and lasciviously rolled her green tongue out to Charlie.

Forgetting himself, he bent over the baby carriage to vomit. Inside was a stillborn, its purple body drawn up, an umbilical cord ascending to who knew where. Charlie let go with the puke, wanting only to be away, and felt the baby's sinister soft stroking of his cheek.

Charlie uprighted himself and took off running. He was only a couple of blocks from home. Ducking off into an alleyway between two shops, he pulled to a panting stop. Christ, he felt like he was dying.

Looking up at the sky, he saw the sun desperately trying to break free from those heavy clouds, lining their contours with a glaring white gold.

"What the hell are you trying to do to me!" he shouted. He didn't know if he was yelling at God or Mother or his whole sad life. "What the *fuck* am I supposed to do?!" The amazing thing was that he felt capable of doing something, anything.

He pulled a wine bottle out from his jacket. Rearing back his arm he threw it as high up in the air as he could, aiming it right at the clouds. He heard it pop on one of the roofs. Charlie imagined his blood spewing from the shattered dark green glass.

"Why don't you let the sun go, you little shits!"

He threw the second bottle. "She could burn you up if she wanted to!" Charlie threw the third and then the fourth before he took off running back toward the house, chasing down the cloud shadows racing along the asphalt.

6.

Once back at the house, Charlie realized he didn't want to go in. He thought it would be too much like walking willfully back into a coma. The inside of that house was a dense fog of twisted, half-remembered memories.

Bracing himself, he opened the door, went in, and turned on all the lights.

The place looked like a warzone. He was amazed he was able to wreak so much havoc in so short a time. Indescribable stains covered the floor, creating a sticky sheen. More stains were splashed upon the wall. A dank, heavy odor took his breath. Pizza boxes and junk food wrappers surrounded the coffee table and couch, some of them containing a decomposing mass of the original contents. The coffee table was covered in ash and cigarette stubs. A pile of empty wine bottles mounted itself against the back of the couch.

"Christ," Charlie muttered.

It was at that point he knew what he had to do. He had to get out of Oretown. To stay there was a slow death. But there were other things he had to do first. Things that would free up his mind. First, he had to stop and think—where was he going to go?

He went around behind the easy chair in the living room and grabbed his dad's old Rand McNally road atlas. It was still there. It was amazing how little certain things changed over the years. Trying not to look around him, he took the atlas out onto the cement front porch and sat down on the top step.

Age had turned the pages of the atlas yellow and crinkly. It carried a musty scent the fresh, damp air seemed to exorcise. Charlie didn't know where to look first.

He lit a cigarette and started at the beginning, reading the names of towns and cities in each state. Some of them he spoke half-aloud, rolling them around in his mouth to see how he liked the sound.

He sat there for over an hour, hardly moving, letting those names and the abstracted topography of America silence the voices screaming up from his viscera. By the time he reached the end, he had it narrowed down to two places. Going by the names alone, he figured it had to be either Nothing, Arizona, or Sad Clown, Kentucky. Practicality dictated that it would be Sad Clown, Kentucky. Charlie didn't think the car would make it all the way to Arizona and it was just his luck that it would break down in some place called Centerville or Middletown. Some generic, pre-fabricated place too much like Oretown.

Another Oretown, regardless of how far away, would still be Oretown in the end. No, Charlie had lived his entire life in Oretown, experienced life and marriage and death in Oretown. Charlie was finished with this Oretown and all the other Oretowns in the world.

His mind made up, he tossed the atlas off to one side of the porch and walked around the house to the garage. He pulled the door open and let the smell of the garage hit him—a smell he'd always found unpleasant. It was like gas and rubber and antiseptic cement with a layer of unidentifiable grime. No matter how clean it was, it always smelled that way. Charlie sidled past the car, not knowing why they even bothered putting it in a garage, and made his way to his mother's gardening tools.

Beside the table covered in flowerpots and old dried bulbs, Charlie found the items he was looking for. There was a small, motorized tiller and a shovel. He grabbed them up and went back to the house.

Before going inside, he looked around to make sure no one saw him carrying these instruments into the house. Later, when the authorities found the house abandoned, Charlie didn't want one of the neighbors to say, "Well, come to think of it, last time I seen him he was going into the house with a shovel and a tiller." That could breed suspicion and Charlie didn't figure it would take people too long to start thinking maybe he had killed his mother. That wouldn't be fair to either one of them. Charlie didn't want an exhumation to disturb his mother's resting place.

7.

Trekking through the wreck of the house, Charlie eventually reached the basement door and skillfully maneuvered both instruments down the stairs. The floor down there was a hard-packed dirt, greasy with age and a virtual lack of sunlight or organic activity. There were the narrow, rectangular windows on three sides of the house, but they were so grimed over that any sun coming through was pale and sickly.

Charlie knew he would have to use the tiller to break the initial layer and figured he could probably get down three, maybe even four feet before hitting bedrock.

It proved to be a lot more difficult than Charlie had at first suspected. Digging it took him up until nearly dawn. The old dirt had covered his sweaty skin and he felt like he wore a coat of mud. His palms were blistered and bleeding. The bottom of his right foot throbbed from coming down again and again on the metal lip of the shovel. Once he stopped, he didn't think he'd be able to raise his arms above his chest without wincing. But he wasn't tired. Not once during the whole night had he felt like going to sleep.

He stood back and surveyed his work, wondering, "Is it a grave if there's nobody in it, or is it just a hole?"

Sticking the shovel in the pile of loose dirt he'd dug up, Charlie went upstairs and out onto the porch to take a breather. He pulled a cigarette from his breast pocket and lit it, resisting the temptation to sit down on the steps. If he did that, he knew he'd stiffen up and be unable to go back to work. Because, of course, only half of his work was done. But he didn't really think of it in those terms. This next part was ritual, ceremony, something he should enjoy doing.

It was going to be another mild day. At this hour, the sun merely burned the horizon gold. Low, thick gray clouds rolled slowly overhead. Last night had been a full moon, or close to it, and Charlie felt as much surrounded by twilight as dawn. Off in the distance, a factory billowed its white steam. Muffled by the morning moisture, a train horn sounded, dragging its sad cargo along the cold rails. The world had not woke up yet and Charlie stood there, still, feeling like the possessor of some secret knowledge.

Flicking his cigarette out into the yard, he went back into the house. Still trying not to look around him, he went to his mother's room and turned the knob of her door. Bracing himself against the fetid smell, he swung it inward and then his breath got caught up in the back of his throat. His throat closed up and his heart hammered against his breastbone—

His mother, crouching in the corner, stood up, moving too rapidly, brushed the wrinkles out of her dress and came toward him. She made a hideous kissing gesture with her mouth and said, through windpipes riddled with decay, "I'm not there yet, Charlie. I ain't made it to the byootiful place." And he smelled her rose perfume covering up that fecal urine reek and closed his eyes, waiting to feel her cold cold hands on his cheeks only—

He didn't feel them at all. Pressing himself against the doorframe and trembling, Charlie opened his eyes.

There, on the bed, just as he'd left her save for looking a little more dead, lay his mother.

"Jesus," Charlie said aloud, putting a shaky hand to his chest and waiting for his heart to stop trying to explode. He thought about going into the kitchen to get some wine until he remembered he didn't have any.

Charlie crossed over to the bed and thought, "Well, I guess I have to do this." This was the part he dreaded most and he found himself questioning the reality of it. The whole thing just didn't seem like something he ever saw himself doing. It felt like he had become someone else, living some other life.

The smell of death hung around his mother. There was some familiarity in the stink. Charlie had smelled it when they went to visit his great-grandmother in the rest home. He had smelled it in hospitals. It was like the body gone bad, turning like milk or meat or fruit. There wasn't any other way to think about it.

Charlie went around the bed, undoing the four corners and tossing them toward the middle. Gathering quilt and sheet around Mother, Charlie bent down and heaved her up, slinging her over his shoulder. There was a sickening crack as his Mother met his shoulder with some stiffness before her torso went limp and draped over his back. If it weren't for having to focus on some level of physicality, that sound and that feel would have made Charlie nauseous.

Cautiously, he crept through the living room and down the stairs as they creaked beneath the added weight. Once in the basement, Charlie hurried to the hole and, as tenderly as he possibly could, turned the hole into a grave. He climbed down in the grave with her. The mounds of dirt were well over his head and he felt instantly claustrophobic. As though he was going to be buried in there with her. He figured he had managed to go a good three and a half to four feet deep with the grave.

Charlie bent down and made sure the sheet or quilt covered all areas of her body. It would seem too disrespectful to just throw the dirt right on her. He scrambled out of the hole before panic attacked him.

He stood there, looking down at her and feeling like something was missing. Mother was not the most religious of persons but Charlie felt like some type of prayer was in order only he didn't know any prayers. Suddenly, he ran upstairs and grabbed the two books out of her room. He dropped the romance in there with her and said, "In case the Beautiful Place has a restroom." Then he flipped around the Bible until he found "Psalm 23." Nervously, he read it aloud over her grave, not fully understanding it and not entirely sure he wanted to.

With that, he closed the Bible up and delicately lowered it into the grave until it rested against Mother's still heart.

"God bless you, Mom. You deserve so much better than this."

And just before he threw the first shovelful of dirt on top of her, a streak of sunlight came through one of the basement windows, impossibly bright, and shone across the dirt floor and across his mother's brightly colored quilt. Not pausing, he went about hurriedly shoveling the dirt onto her, trying to capture as much of the sunlight as possible in the dirt before the sun went away.

By noon, Charlie finished placing the last of the dirt and packing it down. The sun had long since fled the window. Charlie thought about marking Mother's grave somehow. He thought about putting her name or something like, "Here lies the sun," or, "She rests in the Beautiful Place," but it seemed too risky. He didn't want any potential owners to know someone was buried down here. He settled on a cross, two very thin lines made with the tip of the shovel, and figured that would have to do. If anybody actually happened to notice that, they'd just think it was one of those spooky religious coincidences.

Charlie breathed a long sigh of exhausted relief. He picked up his instruments and headed back out toward the garage, careful to shut the basement door behind him.

Braving the kitchen, he crossed over to the sink and, from the cabinets below it, found the jar where he had put all the money from

Mother's social security checks. He cradled that in his left arm, added the half-carton of cigarettes from the top of the refrigerator, snatched the car keys from the small brass hook in the wall and started out for the car, bending on the porch to pick up the atlas.

THE SUMMER OF FLIES

I N MAY, MARCUS thought of it as the hottest summer he could remember. By August, he thought of it as the summer of flies. But it wasn't just the flies that were bad that summer. All of the other insects seemed to be out in abundance, as well. Every day, waking up in his fly-infested apartment, he would find another mosquito bite, looking more like a welt. The flies were the gross kind, slow and green, the kind Marcus always imagined liking shit. Another disgusting thing Marcus realized about the flies—where there were flies, there were maggots. He imagined them under the damp kitchen tile in his apartment, squirming together in trashcans throughout the town, preying with militant glee in the graveyard.

The maggots were there. The flies were there. But the flies, as they swarmed and irritated everyone, were not the only things making the summer memorable. There were also the disappearances.

The early afternoon temperature was in the mid-90s. It would hover around 98 before the sun went down in the evening. Marcus had finished sweeping up those fat flies littering the floor, the victims of daily pesticide spraying, when he decided to go sit on his second-story apartment balcony and lazily flip through the classifieds.

Not finding any jobs, he put the paper down, lit up a cigarette, and leaned back.

Fuck it, he thought. I'll look tomorrow.

It was eleven o'clock and he already wanted a beer.

Marcus contemplated going to the refrigerator to get one when something caught the corner of his left eye. It was a girl, a teenager by the looks of her, wandering aimlessly down the sidewalk. Her bright orange tank top was what caught his eye. The thought of what was underneath held his gaze.

She also wore a pair of cut-offs and Marcus watched her legs as she sat down on the retaining wall in front of the library.

Probably waiting on someone, he thought.

He stood up, arched his back, and went into the house for that beer. In the kitchen, he took his time. He'd drunk ten of the twelve-pack last night, contemplated waiting until later and then convinced himself he would just drink the last two, since he'd have to leave to get more anyway. A big black roach, the size of his thumb, scurried under the refrigerator. Marcus watched it with bland indifference.

He went over to the turntable, flicked a couple dead flies off the dusty plastic lid, and put on a Ramones record, turning the speakers so he would be able to hear it from out on the porch. He didn't think the neighbors would mind. He hadn't seen them for days. Grabbing a fresh pack of cigarettes from the carton on top of the refrigerator, he went back out onto the balcony, ready to do some heavy duty lazing. He became nearly giddy with the prospect. This is what every American wishes he could do, Marcus thought.

The girl was still there, looking this way and that. Like she was waiting for someone. Marcus drank her in, wondering if she even noticed him up there. He got up to change the record three times. He'd smoked through half the fresh pack of cigarettes, finished up the second beer, and had to dip into the Johnnie Walker Black.

The girl never moved.

Christ, he thought, she has to be baking.

But that wasn't all he thought. What he really thought about was the complete oddness of the situation. Ever since May, there had been two to three disappearances a week which, in a town like Green Grove, significantly diminished the population. He knew many families, especially those with kids, had fled the Grove. The police force, small to begin with, was depleted. But fear became the new law, exercising its control. As he sat there staring at the girl on the wall, it dawned on him that she was the first person he'd seen outside in nearly a week. He hadn't seen any children or teenagers in probably a month.

After another shot of scotch and a joint, smoked with abandon on the small stoop, he decided it would simply be the neighborly thing to do to offer her a ride. Maybe she was in shock or suffering heat exhaustion or something. He pulled on a t-shirt and went downstairs, crossing the street in the midst of the lengthening shadows. Unlike a lot of girls in the Grove, this one got more attractive the closer he came to her. Her body filled out the top and shorts and Marcus put her age at sixteen or seventeen. And, at that point, his interests weren't solely prurient. She looked lonely. If, as he drew closer to her, he noticed a lazy eye and a harelip, he would have still offered her a ride.

"Get the fuck away," she spat at him just as he was ready to open his mouth.

"Look, I was just going to offer you a ride."

"I don't need one. Fuck off."

He thought about arguing but, as he opened his mouth, he realized he was way too hot, high, and drunk to go forward with it. Instead, he retreated slowly and cautiously back to his apartment where he shut himself up in the bedroom and turned the ancient window air conditioner up to its most frigid level. He made himself comfortable under the sheets and drifted off into some winter dreamland.

When he woke up, he put a Miles Davis record on and went over to the balcony to take in the evening air and smoke. He opened the door and nearly tripped over the girl sitting on the balcony. Surprise ran through her eyes as she adroitly leapt to her feet.

"Oh. I'm sorry. I didn't know it was *you*," she said.

"It's okay," he said. "I don't know what your problem with me is."

"It was shady up here. It looked cool, all right."

"That's fine. You could have come in if you knocked. I have an air conditioner."

"And I'll tell you what my problem is . . ." She wiped a sweaty strand of brown hair off her forehead. "My problem is these disappearances."

"I've heard about those."

"I'm sure you have. Anyway, I really need to find out who's doing this and I thought to myself: I'll just go stand someplace and mind my own business and the first person who comes along and offers to give me a ride or any shit like that, that has to be the murderer . . ."

"I don't quite understand your logic. So you think murderers are basically friendly people? And besides, how do you know they were murdered? They could have just run away. Or been kidnapped or something. Or gotten sick and been part of some government cover-up. I've thought about these things too, you know."

"No, they were murdered." She looked at a spot somewhere off behind Marcus, phasing out, before snapping into the present and saying, "Hey, give me a cigarette."

"How old are you?"

"Look, burn out, I'm not a cop."

"Okay. You want some pot?"

"I'm not a burn out, either. Sorry."

Marcus flipped a cigarette through the torn opening and held the pack out to her, taking one for himself. He was afraid she was getting ready to go and realized he kind of wanted her to stay. It was somewhat intoxicating just to be standing close to her, smelling her scent. How long had it been since he'd talked to anyone except the old man at the carry-out?

"So," he said. "What makes you think these are murders?"

"I know where the bodies are."

Marcus coughed out a sputtering spume of smoke. "You what?"

"I've seen the bodies. I've counted them. The paper said there's only been ten disappearances, but there's been a lot more than that."

"Like how many?"

"Uncountable."

"You wanna come inside?"

"Bet you'd like that."

"I would. A lot, actually. You wanna come in and sit down?"

"You wanna go for a ride?" she said in a voice mockingly similar to his.

"Look," he said. "That's weird shit." But even as he stood there, rambling, thinking she was probably the crazy one, he knew he was going to say yes. He had to say yes because she was standing there in the damp night air, the nearly full moon illuminated just over top and to the left of her head, casting an exotic purplish glow over her face. And there was this look in her eyes. Something that made her seem either incapable of lying or so hypnotic that a small lie, even a huge one, didn't really matter.

"I'll be waiting down on the sidewalk," she said.

He looked at the back of her neck. She had her hair pulled up and he noticed she had a small mole to the left of her spine and just under her hairline. Marcus went inside and grabbed the keys.

When he got down to the street, she was standing beside his truck.

"It's unlocked," he said.

"I'll drive."

"Do you have your license?"

"No. Does it matter?"

He tried not to look at her. It was when he looked at her that his will power seemed to break. She brushed a fly off her chest. Marcus tossed her the keys.

"Are you even sixteen?"

"You seem to have this hangup about age."

"I have a hangup about being arrested."

"Just relax. I've been wandering around all week and haven't seen a single copper."

"Where are these bodies?"

"Do you know where Womack is?"

"Womack's a long road. Which part of Womack?"

"Out near County Line."

"Okay."

She seemed way too small for the big truck. He enjoyed looking over at her seat, watching her leg muscles as she worked the accelerator and clutch. She'd obviously driven before. They slid along all the back country roads, in between the deep, high fields of corn, never passing another vehicle. Reaching Womack, they turned left.

Womack was an amazingly straight road. That was the thing Marcus had always found interesting about this part of Ohio. One minute, you might find yourself on a road with so many twists and turns, ups and downs that it felt like Tennessee. The next minute it would be flat and straight as Kansas.

"So, you've seen these bodies, huh?" Marcus asked.

"Yes," she said.

"By the way, what's your name?"

"Does it matter?"

"Yeah. Kind of. Unless you want to be remembered as 'That Girl.'"

"Maybe I don't want to be remembered at all."

"God, you're difficult."

"My name's Ellen, okay. Relax."

She had the truck up to eighty, the old tires flapping away under the rusted body.

"So do you really think going back to look is going to solve anything?"

"Maybe."

"What are you hoping to find?"

"The killer, for one thing."

"So, you're hoping he comes back?"

"So far, he's come back again and again. At first I find two dead bodies. Then there are four. Then eight. And now . . ."

"Think maybe you should have told the police?"

"I told them after the first two."

"And they're still there?"

"Go figure."

"I think you're fucking with me."

"I don't see much point in that."

"Maybe you're just taking me out here so you can kill me. Do you have a gun?"

He reached over and put his hand on the back of her shorts, knowing there wasn't a gun there. If there had been one, the shorts were way too small to hide it. She swerved the truck savagely to her right, dredging up the dirt shoulder and rolling him back to his side.

"Get the fuck off me!" she shouted. "How do I know that you didn't come along just so you could get me out here and rape me."

"More and more, it's starting to cross my mind."

"That's not even funny."

"Fuck you."

"Don't you even care that people are dying?"

"Of course I care, but you have to understand how abstract this all sounds to me. You just seem crazy."

"Shut up."

"I mean, come on, you sit outside all day when it's like a hundred fucking degrees. I try to give you a ride and you tell me to get the hell away. Then I find you curled up on my porch and begging for a ride. After accusing me, in so many words, of being a murderer."

"I told you . . . it looked shady up there. And I don't beg for anything."

"Let's just go see the bodies. My name's Marcus, by the way."

"Oh."

"Oh?"

"I don't care much for the name Marcus, is that okay?"

"Whatever."

Ellen slowed the truck way down and came to a stop by the side of the road. She creaked the door open and hopped out. Marcus got out his side and walked around the front of the truck.

"I don't see any bodies," he said.

"The bodies are way back there." She pointed to a narrow dirt path, perhaps big enough for a tractor. If he had driven down the road with the corn this high, he wouldn't have even noticed it. "You have to walk back this little path quite a ways. Just before the corn becomes the woods, there's like this clearing . . . that's where they are."

"Couldn't we have done this during the day? Why does he just leave them out in the open?"

"It's not exactly out in the open back there, is it? Besides, most of those serial killer types want to get caught."

"You bring a flashlight?"

"Did you find a flashlight when you felt me up back there? It's a full moon. What more do you want? Look, it's bright enough to see your shadow."

It *was* amazingly bright. Ellen headed for the path and Marcus went behind her, watching the moon light up her body and trying to figure out how many months it had been since his last sexual encounter. He realized that, by focusing on the prospect of sex, he relieved a little bit of the uneasy tension twisting his neck muscles up in knots.

"Why didn't we just drive back here?" he asked her.

"I didn't want to surprise anyone."

"How long is it?"

"Probably almost a mile."

"How did you find this place, anyway?"

She didn't answer immediately. He almost asked her again, thinking maybe the crispy rustle of the corn and the crickets had drowned him out, but then she said: "Me and my boyfriend used to come back here."

"Oh, all that personality and she puts out too."

"It was more than that. We were gonna get married when we turned eighteen. This place was kind of like what we thought marriage would be like. You know, kind of a place away from the parents."

"A secret place."

"Yeah. Or so we thought."

"What happened to your boyfriend?"

"He was the first to go. The first to disappear."

"I'm sorry."

"We should be quiet now."

They continued down the moonlit path, in silence, for a few minutes. The clearing was now in eyesight. It was like driving toward the ocean and finally coming upon that strip of blue beneath the horizon.

"Follow me," Ellen said, cutting to her left and into the corn. At the perimeter, she turned and barked, "Quickly."

Marcus was suddenly and overwhelmingly filled with terror. Maybe it was just the fog of his various addictions, but he hadn't really taken any of this seriously until now. All the childish fears, those moments when certain feelings washed over him and lit that burning pit of dread in his stomach, all came scouring over him, rooting him to that narrow dirt path. He looked over to where Ellen entered the corn and the absence of her by his side forced him to move.

The corn was sharp and itchy on his arms. A hand reached out and took his.

"Come on," Ellen pulled him after her.

Blindly, they made their way through the corn, still headed toward the clearing but comforted with a blanket of seclusion.

"Why don't we just run for the truck?" Marcus thought about his sunny, music-filled apartment and realized he desperately wanted to be back in it.

Ellen turned around, getting closer to him than she had been all evening. Her eyes were wild, dancing around in her head, an indiscernible color. "I'm not turning around now. I have a lot more in this than you. If you're scared then just stand here. That'll be safer than running back to your truck. But I'm going some place where I can see that bastard throw out another victim. I'm gonna get close enough to see his face."

Marcus lowered his head. He didn't have a macho streak in his body but she had somehow made him feel low. He began to understand the significance this had for Ellen.

"I'll come," he mumbled.

"Then let's go," she said.

There was enough of a breeze so their movements weren't too noticeably loud. Nevertheless, the closer they felt they were getting, the more they slowed down and tried to squeeze between the stalks. Once they could see the clearing, they stayed back in the corn, using it like a security blanket.

In the distance, Marcus saw the bodies.

There was something infinitely sad about the way they were piled up there in the clearing.

Knowing the answer, he turned to Ellen and whispered, "Is that . . . them?"

Gravely, she nodded her head and said, "Let's move in a little closer."

"What about the killer?"

"I don't see him."

Well, that's obvious, Marcus thought.

Stepping out of the corn was like losing your clothing. They were naked now. If there was a killer on the loose, running around stark raving mad, they had little chance of hiding now. Running, maybe, but hiding was definitely out.

Marcus followed Ellen.

The grass in the clearing was worn down, as though it had been trampled quite a bit. Marcus thought it was probably from someone driving a truck out here. As they drew closer to the body pile, the stink intensified to a truly nauseating level. Marcus grabbed Ellen's arm. She turned to look at him, her stare pinning him where he was. Since coming out here, something had changed about her. She came off as a little flaky before but now she just looked insane.

"I don't think I can get any closer." Marcus pulled his shirt up over the lower half of his face.

"Have some fucking respect, Marco," Ellen said, shaking his grip from her arm.

Through the noisy, insectoid country night, Marcus heard a singular sound resonate—the humming of flies. *My God, there must be millions of them on those bodies.* He even thought he could hear the wet squirm of the maggots twisting through decomposing flesh. His gorge rose and sat stinging at the back of his throat.

"I'm gonna go wait in the truck," he said.

Ellen turned to him once again. The craziness was gone. She had put on her seductive face. Pouty and girlish, it was the look she had used to get him to give up his keys. "Come on, Marcus. It's just a few more steps. You'll get used to the smell."

"Why don't you tell me what we're really doing here and I'll think about staying."

"But you're already thinking about staying, aren't you? Don't you know what we're doing here? We're trying to find the killer, remember?"

"If that was the case then why aren't we still hiding out in the corn?"

"You can't catch anything by hiding."

"Nobody said anything about *catching* anything. I'm not a cop."

Marcus looked into the heap, arranged in a semi-circle. It had to be most of Green Grove in there. Exposed to the elements, they had decomposed rapidly, their skin gray, pieces of skin peeled back, probably the result of wild animals. All of them were rendered unrecognizable.

Ellen wandered right up next to the bodies and dropped down onto her knees.

"What the hell are you doing? Can we just go?"

"I'm saying a prayer. Can't I do that?"

"Just hurry the hell up."

Marcus turned around and looked up at the moon. What a night this was turning out to be. He turned back around and Ellen was back on her feet.

"Come here," she said.

"I'd really rather not."

"I'll make it worth your while."

"Jesus," he muttered, thinking, I'm here anyway, aren't I?

He slowly walked over to her and she turned, grabbing him around the waist, pressing herself against him. Her eyes gleamed with a wild urgency. He bent down to kiss her and leaned into the smell of a hundred rotting corpses. She fastened her mouth around his, trying to bring him down to the ground. His stomach fought to come up and he put his hands on her hips, nearly encircling her bare midriff, to try and push her away.

He felt the twitching of her skin like something was fighting to get out. Just when he couldn't hold the vomit anymore, he let go, but it was forced back into his throat. He coughed and backed away, stumbling to his knees. Before he could stand up, his stomach convulsed again and he heaved, expecting the wet acid of his puke. Instead he felt the flies crawling over his tongue and all around the inside of his mouth. He looked back at Ellen and the crumbling wall behind her. The corpses were animated, Ellen standing at their center, flies crawling through her hair, covering her eyes and body.

Marcus bolted toward the corn, but the dead were there also.

They had shifted, surrounding him. Flies crawled from their skin and hollow eye sockets, forming a cloud that blotted out the moon's glow.

The circle tightened and Marcus waited to feel their hands on his body. From behind him, Marcus heard Ellen whisper, "You're the last one, Marcus." And he felt her hands, hands that he would have welcomed a half an hour ago, slide down his stomach and crush his sex in an unforgiving grip.

"What happens now?" he begged.

"You taste death," she whispered. "The killer is here, somewhere. Only he didn't kill just my boyfriend. He killed me too."

"What does this have to do with me?"

"A soul is not free until his work is done. He made that clear. You're the last one." With that, Ellen snapped his neck and let him fall to the ground.

It was a strange night that Marcus spent, lying on the ground, his body getting colder, his heart inactive in his chest. By morning, he had joined the pile, become food for the flies as he remained still throughout the rotting day. The next night, the dead rose again, dragging with them their veil of flies, and moved in to the next town, each of them intent on doing what had been done to them, hungry for some shred of justice.

LAUNDRYMEN

"HAVE YOU SEEN my shirt?" Barry asked.

"Which one?" Michelle returned.

"The brown one. You know, my favorite shirt. The button-down one?"

"Good Lord. It probably curled up and died." She walked over to the blinds in the western-facing window of the apartment, closing them against the last fragments of that day's sun. "Are you sure you washed it? I mean, that thing like never leaves your back. Speaking of which, I think I left my black bra over here the last time. Have you seen *that?*"

"Yeah. Here you go." Barry tossed her the black bra.

The rest of the laundry was organized and sorted on the kitchen table in front of him. He rubbed his forehead.

"No," he said. "I know I washed it. I specifically remember grabbing it from that chair in the bedroom. I'm missing those pants too."

"Which pants?" Michelle collapsed onto the couch, grabbing the remote and turning on the TV.

"The gray corduroys. Have you done something to them?"

"You figured it out, Barry. Yes. I have your clothes. I love them so much that I stole them and, on days that I'm not over here, I'm wearing them all over the place. A big brown shirt and gray corduroys. I'm trying to start a new trend. I hear the frumpy look is coming back in style."

"You don't have to be *so* sarcastic."

"I wasn't being sarcastic. I was being completely serious," she said absently, flipping through the channels. "You probably just left them at the laundromat. Why don't you call?"

"No. I guess I'll just go back over there. That's almost where they have to be. I know I took them. I know I washed them. Probably just left them in the dryer."

Barry grabbed up his keys and headed for the front door.

"You coming?" he asked Michelle.

"Think I'll pass on this one. The Great Clothes Hunt. Nah. Not today. Maybe if it were those jeans I like so much . . ."

Barry ran back over to the couch and gave Michelle a quick peck on the mouth. "Be right back."

"I hope your clothes aren't some part of an international conspiracy."

"Never underestimate the power of Mr. Brown."

Michelle chuckled. "Oh my God, you've *named* it."

"I'm very close to it. I'm sure he's been very lonely, trapped in that dryer all by himself."

"But your pants are there to keep him company."

"Still, they shouldn't be left unsupervised."

"You better hurry."

"To the Batmobile."

Then Barry rushed out the door, regretting the fact he had to leave Michelle alone in his little apartment and hoping she would be there when he returned.

Barry rolled the car windows down and enjoyed the early summer breeze as he drove to the laundromat. Children ran throughout the town, happy to be out of school. There weren't any parking spaces directly in front of the laundromat so Barry circled the block and ended up parking a few doors down.

He got out of the car and took in the smell of the clean night air. He looked up at the sky, deepening into purple, casting a twilight glow all around him. Taking his time, he strolled down the sidewalk to the laundromat.

Once there, he stood outside, staring into the laundromat's harsh fluorescent lighting. He didn't know why he didn't just walk right in. Was he hoping to spot his clothes lying around somewhere? Did he think they would have them hanging in the window like some flyer from someone who had found a stray dog?

Barry reached for the door to go inside when he saw the man.

The man, standing back at the line of dryers embedded in the far wall, was wearing Barry's clothes.

That's ridiculous, Barry thought. It's entirely possible someone else has the exact same clothes. Besides, he figured, he wasn't even really close enough to be sure those *were* his clothes adorning the man.

Barry opened the door and stepped into the humidity of the laundromat. Instead of walking directly toward the man, Barry wandered off to his right, around the islands of washers.

Christ, he thought, I'm sneaking up on this man.

And that's exactly what he was doing. The closer he got to the man, the more Barry realized he *had* to be wearing his clothes.

The man was perfectly normal looking, close-cropped black hair, tan skin. Somewhat thinner and shorter than Barry, the clothes were baggy on him.

Barry moved up next to him, prepared to begin his spiel by saying, "Excuse me . . ."

Just as Barry opened his mouth, the man turned and saw him. Then, lightning quick, he reached out a hand and shoved it into the middle of Barry's chest, taking him by surprise and knocking him to the floor before running through the laundromat's side door. Barry fought to stand up as quickly as he could and follow the man out the door. Now, everyone in the laundromat looked in his direction.

Barry burst through the door and out into the twilight. He saw the man running off to his right and ran in that direction himself.

Barry had not run in a number of years and the man lost him by cutting into the first alley he came to, disappearing into fresh shadows.

"The clothes!" Barry screamed. "They'll never fit you!" As if that statement would cause the thief to have some sort of understanding, some complete change of heart and come running back.

Then Barry had another idea. If the man was at the laundromat, surely he must have some of his own clothes there. When Barry had first approached him, the man was bent over one of the tables. Maybe he was folding his own clothes. He had to have been wearing *something* when he entered the laundromat.

Barry went back into the laundromat, his head hung low, trying to avoid eye contact with all the people who had seen him get shoved down. He crept over to where he had seen the man. He looked for something on the table, the same table Barry had used an hour ago, but didn't see anything. He looked at the row of dryers and saw one with a few meager items lying lifeless at the bottom of the stopped dryer.

Those must be them, Barry thought.

He stepped toward the dryer but just as he got ready to reach out and open the door, a burly woman beat him to it, shooting a dirty glare at him. Barry watched her pull out a giant thong with hearts on it and a blue halter-top. A shiver ran over Barry's skin.

"You can use it now," she barked at Barry. "If that's what you was wantin."

"Thank you," Barry said, but he felt numb. Absently, he turned and wandered out of the Laundromat, back to his car.

By the time he sped back to his apartment and raced up the stairs, Barry was sweaty and out of breath.

"Good God, what's the matter with you?" Michelle asked.

Barry slammed the door behind him, went over to the couch and collapsed onto it. "You're not gonna believe it," he said.

"You should try me."

Michelle was standing, her coat on and her purse slung over her shoulder.

"You look like you're going someplace," Barry said.

"Yeah, Brandon called. He's over at Derek's. Wants me to pick him up. He's been pretty clingy lately. I don't think he wants me and you getting too close, you know. I'll be back tomorrow though. He has school."

"Okay, I'll make it quick."

Barry told her about what had happened at the laundromat, his voice as full of bewilderment as it was of anger.

"Oh well," Michelle said. "Stranger things have happened, I guess. It could have been your wallet or something."

"I know," Barry said, resigned. "It's just, I don't know, it was so fucking odd. I mean, why would he want my *clothes*? Wasn't he wearing any clothes when he came in? Wouldn't somebody have noticed? Who goes to the laundromat to steal people's clothes? Why not dig through dumpsters or something. Did he put them on *over* his regular clothes?"

"Everything doesn't have a rational explanation. You're old enough to know that by now."

"Oh, I'm well aware of that but it's just . . . *frustrating*."

"Well, as much as I'd rather stick around and hear you mope

about your lost clothes, I'd better go. See you tomorrow." She came over to the couch and kissed him deeply. He ran a hand up the inside of her smooth thigh, beneath her loose skirt.

"Sure you can't stay for a few more minutes?"

"I really have to go. Sorry."

"That's okay." Barry watched her walk out the door, enjoying the view and saddened by her encroaching absence.

With Michelle gone, Barry didn't really have anything to do. He sat on the couch with the television on, unwatched. He couldn't stop thinking about what had happened in the laundromat. The more he thought about it, the more it unnerved him.

He thought about making himself something to eat and then decided he wasn't hungry.

He couldn't even really figure out why it bothered him so much. It wasn't like the clothes were expensive or anything. It wasn't even that they were *his* clothes, or were at one time. He had donated countless items of clothing to the Salvation Army and Goodwill. Hell, there was probably a whole town somewhere adorned in clothes that had once been his.

What bothered him about this incident was that it was almost like this man had gone to great lengths to . . . *abduct* these clothes. Barry felt like he had been singled out. That's what really bothered him about it—the fact that he was alone in this situation. Never had he heard of anyone else suffering this same problem.

Suffering?

Okay, maybe that was a bit too much. Sure he was a victim, but of what?

Feeling helpless, he switched off the TV, stripped down, and crawled into bed, longing for the nights that Michelle would be there beside him, his nose pressed against her strawberry-scented hair . . .

Barry awoke to a brightly lighted apartment. A quick look around told him it was his, however scarcely recognizable. The couch and coffee table were kicked over. The TV was turned up to full volume, buzzing test patterns of a station that had gone off-air. All of his drawers were open, clothes strewn everywhere. His closet was gutted. All the cabinets in the kitchen were open, the water faucet in the kitchen sink running full blast.

Three men stood in the middle of the room, staring at him.

One of them was the man he had seen at the laundromat, still wearing Barry's brown shirt and gray corduroys. The other two were also wearing Barry's clothes.

Barry fought the temptation to pull the sheet up around his shoulders and cower back into the bed. Instead, he slung the sheet off, walking up to the three men in all of his nakedness.

He drew very close to the man in the middle, the one from the laundromat and, sounding as authoritative as he could, said, "What the fuck are you doing here?"

"What are *you* doing here?" the man shot back.

"I *live* here."

"It's a shame. The place is a shambles."

"Take off my clothes," Barry demanded.

"These are not your clothes."

"Yes, they are. You stole them from the laundromat. And you two, you must have taken those right out of my closet."

"Actually, they were laying on the kitchen table. And they're not your clothes."

"What do you mean they're not my clothes?"

"We think they fit us better. These should be our clothes. Therefore, they are our clothes."

"You need to leave. Right now."

"No."

"Okay. You know what, fuck it, I'm calling the police. Stealing my clothes is one thing but breaking into my house is another. So I'm calling the police and then I'm going to get out my baseball bat and beat you fuckers until they get here."

"Oh, I wouldn't do that."

Barry went into the kitchen where the phone was. The phone was off the hook and he had to place it on the hook before picking it up again.

Before dialing the "9," Barry asked, "Why wouldn't you do this?"

"Because you're in a lot more trouble than we are."

"I think you're fucking nuts. And I think you're breaking and entering. And I think you've vandalized my entire apartment. I think you're in plenty of trouble."

"But you invited us."

"Like hell I did."

"I don't think you're aware of all the things you've done."

"I don't know what the hell you're talking about. How did you find this place anyway?"

"When a man is running, when he is desperate, he leaves behind a scent, an essence. That's what led me to the laundromat. That's how I found your clothes. And of course, your scent was all over your clothes, embedded in the fabric, smudged against the collar."

"I'm not running from anything."

"Where were you at 3:28 this morning?"

"I was . . ." Barry looked at the clock on the stove. It read: 3:28. "I was standing in my apartment calling the police on three intruders."

"But we were never here."

And then the apartment was plunged into darkness and quiet.

Barry was back in his bed.

The apartment was more than dark. Barry had the sensation of being somewhere very deep under the sea.

He heard a popping sound. And then another popping sound and felt himself rising through the sea, toward his apartment, toward his bed that felt like it was at the surface of the water.

Suddenly, he broke through the surface of the sea. Into his apartment. Into his bed.

Barry stood in the middle of the bed, aware that he was holding something heavy. When he looked down, he saw that it was an ax. And what he saw beneath that, pressed down wetly into the bed, caused him to scream.

Michelle was down there only it wasn't the whole Michelle. It was pieces of Michelle, her blood spattered all over Barry's gray pants, wetting the arms of his brown shirt and sticking the fabric to his skin.

She was red and the bed was red and Barry couldn't stop screaming.

THE SCREAMING ORCHARD

Y OU KNOW, WE could just walk," Nie said. Her real name was Stephanie, but she hated that name and all of its usual derivatives.

Chris, lying on top of the ancient baby blue Escort said, "I'm way too high to walk. Probably fall down."

"That was your idea."

"Maybe somebody'll come along and pick us up."

"Look around you, Chris. This road probably sees like two cars a day and we're one of them. Besides, you have blood all over you."

"And that, sweetie, was *your* idea."

"I thought it would be fun to get out of the house. There *are* other things to do besides messing around in your parents' basement, you know."

"Maybe for you. You're all *I* need. Besides, I promised them I'd stay and pass out candy."

"You left the bowl out, didn't you?"

"Yeah. But you know how that is. One of those punks'll come along and take all the candy, probably the bowl with it, and then some other punks will egg the house or something because they think we're *those people* who are too cheap to give out candy."

"Christ, you think too much."

"I *think* we should have stayed there."

Nie looked around them, the endless fields of golden brown corn divided only by the narrow strip of the gray road. *At least it's warm,* she told herself. A perfect day to go trick-or-treating, if she were like four years younger. She had been looking forward to going to

Donna's party and Chris's indifference was really starting to irritate her.

"What the fuck are you supposed to *be*, anyway?" she asked him.

"I'm a butcher," he said, staring up at the clear blue sky.

"And that's scary how?"

"I don't know. I just thought it looked grisly." He sat up, brought his feet around the side of the car and scooted off.

"You look like a murdering soda jerk."

"Do they still have those?"

"I don't know."

"Butchers wear hats, don't they?"

"I don't know *what* butchers wear."

"And what are you supposed to be?"

"I'm a ghoul."

"I think this is just your excuse to look goth."

"Well, I don't know what a ghoul looks like."

"That's okay. You look hot. I mean it."

"Didn't you get enough last night?" She pulled her black shawl over the cleavage showing above the black corset.

"Enough of you? Never."

"But you're too high to walk?"

"Completely different muscles."

"Pervert. Besides, I couldn't possibly fuck anyone who has their hands in animal parts all day."

"Jeez, vegetarians."

"And my boyfriend's vegetarian. He wouldn't like that."

Chris walked up to her and put his hands on her hips. "Have I told you how much I like role playing?"

He leaned down to kiss her black lips and she pulled away.

"Car," she said.

Chris turned and squinted down the road.

"Van," he said. "A white, unmarked van. We should hide rather than trying to bum a ride from them."

Nie watched the van come toward them from the darkening eastern horizon.

"But," she said. "If we can get them to take us back to your house then I can call a tow truck and we can take your car to the party. I'll make it worth your while."

She reached down and cupped his stiff penis with her palm and whispered into his ear, "Don't you want to know what it feels like to fuck the dead?"

Chris smiled and said, "Okay, okay. You win."

Men are such suckers, Nie thought.

They both edged up to the side of the road and waved their hands.

The van, all white with tinted windows wrapping around the side and back, pulled to a stop just past them.

Chris ran up to the driver's side door. The tinted window rolled down and Chris struggled not to laugh at the man in front of him. The man had curly brown hair that looked like it was either a bad perm or a wig, cut in half by a white headband with a red stripe running along the middle. His face was full and round, outdated aviator sunglasses covering his eyes. A brown mustache occluded his top lip. The same exact-looking man sat in the passenger seat.

"Anything we can do for you?" the driver asked.

Chris stammered and then said, "Yeah, my girlfriend's car broke down and we were wondering if you could possibly give us a lift back into town."

"Well, we was kinda headed the other way."

"We could pay you for gas and time. Just tell me what you need." Chris thought about Nie's promise and realized how desperately he wanted to get home.

"No, that ain't necessary. We can probably just go through town and get where we was goin just the same." Then he turned to his partner. "You think?"

His partner bobbed his white man's afro in agreement.

"Great." Chris smiled broadly. "Thanks a lot, you guys."

"Yeah, no problem. Y'all can just climb in back there."

Chris walked around behind the van and jerked his head at Nie. He let her get up close to him and said, "These guys are kind of strange," before yanking back the van's sliding door.

"Hey there," the guy in the driver's seat said when he saw Nie.

"Hi. Thanks guys," she said, pulling the van door shut.

"Looks like you guys are ready for Halloween."

"Yeah," Nie said. "What are you guys supposed to be?" She asked that because she was convinced they were both wearing wigs and, once inside the van, she noticed they were also dressed the same. They wore matching, outdated track uniforms, white tanktops stretched over their doughy skin and old red running shorts that were way too short. Without seeing them, Nie could imagine the knee-high tube socks, red stripes at the top.

"Whaddya mean?" the driver asked.

"For Halloween?" Nie said.

"Oh," the driver chuckled. "We ain't dressed for Halloween. We're twins. Name's Vincent. Both of us. Our parents' way of a sick joke, I guess."

"I'm Chris," Chris volunteered, since Nie was still choking on her foot. "This is my girlfriend, Nie."

"*Knee?*"

"Yeah, spelled different, but said just like those things in the middle of your legs."

The van slowly pulled away from the curb. The driver shook his head and said, "Fraid you're not right about that. We was born without knees. Turn around n show em there, Vince."

The passenger swiveled around in his seat and straightened out his legs to show them how the expansive lower thigh joined almost evenly with the calf. He rapped his knuckles on the flesh and it made a doughy patter sound.

"That bone there," he said. "For those that's got em anyway, is called the patella. That's what we was born without—the patella. I guess we still got the muscles and everything."

Chris and Nie gaped in awe.

After riding silently for a few minutes, Nie noticed they weren't going in the direction of town. She didn't think anything was strange at first because she thought maybe the twins were planning on taking one of the side roads farther up.

She looked at Chris and mouthed, "Where the hell are we going?"

To allay her suspicions, Chris asked, "So, you guys from around here?"

"Huh-uh," the driver said. "We're from over in Preston."

"Never heard of it," Chris said. "You know how to get back to town from here?"

"Now, we're not going there just yet. We got some stuff to do. Might could use your help."

"We kind of needed to get back in a hurry," Nie said, icy fingers of fear spreading through her.

"Well, now your boyfriend here, he was willin to pay us, said anything you want . . . I reckon we need us some help."

Nie leaned forward in her seat and said, "That's not part of the deal. If you want cash, that's fine, whatever you want, but we've got places to be and . . . parents that are expecting us."

"Just ease up, honey. We ain't a couple of sickies. We just need your help, that's all."

Nie clenched her jaws, ready to lash out at them. Chris reached over and put his hand on her knee and spoke in her place.

"What, exactly, will we be helping you with?"

"Just a little, uh . . ." the driver looked at the passenger and they both chuckled, "Horticulture."

"I don't understand," Chris said.

"You ever hear tale of the June tree?"

"No," Chris said.

"Don't rightly know why they call it the June tree, since it blooms in October."

"I've never *heard* of a tree blooming in October," Nie sneered.

"Well, this'n does. At least it's rumored to. I guess the tree must've been named June or something before."

"Before what?" Chris asked.

"The way the story goes, a number of years back, prob'ly before any of us was even born, there's this girl named June who got raped and killed out by some woods. But that ain't the really strange part. I mean, that shit happens every day. But now they say that, if you was to be standin and lookin at this old dead tree that happens to be bout round where they say the girl was murdered, and it was a full moon on Halloween, you'd see the tree become that girl. You'd see it bloom."

"That's ridiculous," Nie said.

The passenger turned around and looked at her and, for the first time, she saw that he had a red number two on his tank top. It made her think of Thing One and Thing Two, from *The Cat in the Hat*. "It's nothin to be afraid of. It's not like the tree's gonna jump out and *getcha*."

And then he shot his arms out and squeezed the inside of Nie's thighs, a little too close to her crotch for Chris's liking. But Nie took care of herself. After jumping nearly to the roof of the van, she roped out her right arm and punched the guy in the face.

The man retreated back into his seat holding his mouth and Nie was pretty sure he was sobbing. She was surprised when the van didn't stop and they weren't asked to leave.

Then she heard the passenger say, "She hit me, Vin."

The driver reached out and patted his brother's quivering

shoulder. "That's all right, buddy. She didn't mean it. Did you, sweetie?"

"Yeah, I did, shitface." She wasn't looking at the driver. She was turned in her seat, scanning the back of the van, looking for some means of escape. On the floor in front of the backseat, she spotted a shovel, a bag of dirt, and a large plastic pot. She looked at Chris and motioned toward the shovel.

He reached back for it as the driver said, "You know, you kids got a funny way of showing gratitude."

Chris quickly grabbed the shovel and, with his hands somewhere around the middle, wielded it in front of him.

"Okay, guys," he said. "Stop the van. We wanna get out."

Chris met the driver's shaded eyes in the rearview mirror as the man said, "I think you might wanna put the shovel down," and then nodded to Thing Two in the passenger seat.

Thing Two held a gun on Chris.

The driver said, "We're gonna go find the June tree. We know right where it's at and we need you to help us dig it up. There's a fella back in Preston that's gonna pay us big bucks for this and you guys are comin along to tell em it's real. That is, if it's even there. If it *is* real."

Nie sensed Chris's powerlessness as he lowered the shovel.

The sun had all but left the sky and the van seemed way too dark, charging toward the gold powder harvest moon.

"We ain't got long to go," the driver said. "You two better just sit back n relax."

Nie shot Chris a look that said, "We're in deep shit."

Chris nodded, reached over and put his hand on her knee. The touch didn't comfort Nie nearly as much as she would have liked.

The van slowed down to turn right and Nie pulled the handle of the sliding door. It was locked even though the lock switch itself said it wasn't.

Damn child safety, Nie thought.

The van turned into a heavily wooded area, making it seem even darker than it actually was. Thing One pulled the van into a gravel turn-off and cut the ignition.

"You all wanna grab that shovel and pot and shit from back there?"

Nie grabbed the shovel and the empty black plastic pot. Chris grabbed the bag of soil. It was heavy and warm. Thing One and

Thing Two got out of the van, came around and unlocked the door.

If the twins didn't have the gun, Nie was sure they would be able to outrun them. They were so short and plump, Thing Two looking pitiful with the trickle of blood oozing down from his mustache.

"Now, we're gonna take this here trail. You guys don't wanna try nothin, ya hear?" Thing One said.

He turned and stepped into the woods, Nie behind him, Chris behind her, Thing Two bringing up the rear.

Nie couldn't believe any of this was happening. She tried to think of something, but the red streaks of panic blazing through her head made it difficult.

She and Chris had darkness, the cover of the woods, a shovel and speed.

But the twins had the gun. Damn the gun. Could they even shoot the gun? They seemed to have some inept quality about them. She doubted their marksmanship.

They traveled in their single-file line down into a gully, crossed a moss-covered wooden bridge and started up the other side.

She decided the best thing to do would be to create chaos.

Quickly, she grabbed the shovel with both hands and let the pot drop. She raised the shovel. It was much heavier than she expected and rather than bringing it down on Thing One's head, she bashed him in the shoulder.

Her plan was to turn and run, charge through Thing Two before he could figure out what was happening and just hope Chris had enough sense to follow her as fast as possible.

The blast from the gun shot her plan to hell.

The body in the trail prevented her from running back the way they had come.

It was Chris, face down, the back of his head a glistening mass.

She froze. Stood there screaming.

"Shut her the fuck up, Vinny!" Thing One shouted from the ground.

Thing Two shifted the gun to his left hand and drove his right into her mouth, dropping her onto Chris, her hand coming down in his wound, sick and warm and wet.

Thing One was over by her side now, his hand wrapping up in her hair.

"You really fucked up, bitch," he said. "And now your boyfriend's dead."

Too afraid to scream, Nie blathered softly toward the moldy smelling earth.

"I'm sorry. I'm sorry," she said.

"You should be," Thing One said. "We do you a favor and you try n clobber me with my own damn shovel. Now if you don't give us any more hassle, we might think about letting you go after we visit Mr. Martin."

"Please. Please don't hurt me."

Thing One smacked her cheek and said, "Get up. We got work to do."

She stood up, her nervous body shaking violently.

Thing Two moved closer to her, poked the gun into her ass and said, "You scream any more and we might take it upon ourselves to satisfy certain urges. Understand?"

"Yes."

"Pick up the pot and the shovel."

She bent and picked them up.

"We need to hurry," Thing One said. "Grab the boy. We can leave the soil here until we come back," Thing One said.

"But there's blood all over it."

"Fuck that shit. Don't matter. It's Halloween. You think anybody's gonna think anything of comin up on a bag with a little blood on it?"

"Guess you're right."

"Besides, it'll be gone before anybody sees it. Gimme the gun."

Thing Two passed the gun to Thing One and grabbed Chris around the ankles.

Thing One pointed the gun at Nie and said, "You go first. Just follow this here trail up the hill. You run, I shoot. And then we'll take turns fuckin your corpse."

Nie turned and started back along the trail, traveling up the hill and into the moonlight. She cringed at the sound of Chris being dragged along the sandy trail.

The trail opened up into a large meadow. Dead autumn smells surrounded Nie, dried wild grasses and deep brown thistle crunching under their feet as they walked to the far side of the field. Darkness had brought fog and a chill with it. The fog, still settling, swirled gray and clean-looking over the ground.

"It should be just over here," Thing One said to Thing Two. Eagerly, he quickened his pace.

Maybe I'll get out of this, Nie thought. Immediately, she doubted herself. She hadn't thought things could get as bad as they had. She certainly hadn't thought the twins were murderers when she and Chris had first entered the van.

They came upon the other side of the field. More woods loomed in front of them. A storm last week had knocked most of the leaves from the trees but these woods contained a lot of eastern juniper cedars, making them seem darker, thicker. Nie didn't want to go into any more woods. Even though they were still in the middle of nowhere, unseen, she found a modicum of security in the clearing.

"Ah, here she is, buddy," Thing One said.

He had stopped just at the edge of the woods. Nie stood on his right side and Thing Two moved up parallel on the other side of her so they stood in a semi-circle looking down at . . . what? What was she supposed to see that she didn't?

"The June tree," Thing Two said.

"That's gotta be it," Thing One said.

The tree stood about chest high to Nie. She didn't really see anything incredibly strange about it. She supposed that, maybe, it vaguely resembled a human form. Its trunk was abnormally thick for its height. The trunk was as thick as Nie's chest. It was cruciform so it could be perceived to have a head and arms held out like a martyr.

"Why ain't it bloomed?" Thing Two asked.

"Shit, I don't know," Thing One said. "It is a full moon, ain't it? I mean, we're not like a day away from a full moon or somethin, are we?"

"No, it's full. I checked the paper, the *Old Farmer's Almanac*. I even checked online."

"Maybe it's like that old riddle. You know, 'If a tree falls and no one's around, does it still make a sound?' Maybe the June tree don't bloom unless there's somebody here to look at it."

"And maybe everyone's just full of shit. Maybe it's just a rumor."

"You think Mr. Martin would lie to us?"

"I don't know."

"You seen his pictures."

"I guess."

"Should we dig it up anyway?"

"I don't see why it would matter."

A shrill scream pierced the crisp night.

"Shit," Thing One said.

"Fuck," Thing Two said.

Nie didn't say anything.

She could only gape in amazement as the June tree bloomed.

The overall color of it seemed to lighten until it reached the color of pale skin.

"Jesus, we've gotta stop that sound," Thing One said.

The top of the tree softened, became a waterfall of dark hair spilling over the intersection of the horizontal branches.

"Take the boy's shirt off," Thing One said.

Thing Two began stripping Chris's shirt off.

Nie watched the tree as it slowly became a human female, emerging from the dirt at mid-thigh. Frantic eyes stared at Nie, shooting around in their sockets. The screaming knothole became a screaming mouth. Farther down, two rough places of bark became nipples. The tree brought her limbs down, covering her breasts and her sex, only the limbs were now arms.

Thing Two approached the tree and jammed Chris's shirt into her mouth, tying the arms of the shirt behind her head.

"All right, now take off his pants and put them over her head. Makes me nervous to look at her," Thing One said. Then he pointed the gun at Nie. "All right. You better get to diggin."

Nie put the pot down and pulled the shovel out. Again she thought about taking it across Thing One's head and remembered what they had said earlier. She had no doubt that killing her wouldn't be the only thing they did. Fucking creeps.

She put the point of the shovel in the dirt about a foot out from the base of the tree and drove it in with the bottom of her foot, suddenly glad she had opted for the Doc Martens rather than the six-inch heels.

As the shovel bit down in the soil, the tree doubled over, thrashing in pain, the pants sliding from her head. A geyser of blood shot up, spraying Nie's face.

She dropped the shovel and turned away from the tree, falling to her knees and vomiting.

"Shit," Thing One said. "We need to hurry."

Nie curled up on the ground, shivering in the cold fog.

"Fucking useless cunt," she heard Thing One say.

She couldn't bear to look at what was happening. She heard the shovel punch into the fleshy earth.

"Now we're gonna put him in her place, right?" Thing Two said.

"Yep. Take his legs off at the knee and put the stumps in the pot. She's losing a lot of blood."

Nie heard the thwakking of what had to be the shovel coming down on Chris's legs.

"Jesus, man, use your fucking knife," Thing One said.

Nie lay there and tried to concentrate on the sound the wind made as it rustled through the woods because if she didn't concentrate on that then the only thing she could hear were the muffled cries of the June tree and the squelching sound Chris's body made as they put him into the earth.

This was a far cry from Donna's Halloween party. She shouldn't have listened to Chris. She should have just walked back to town by herself. But Chris was gone now. She couldn't blame Chris.

One of the twins dusted off his hands like someone who'd just planted a garden of petunias and said, "Well, that's it. Get yer tits up here, missy. We're ready."

Nie brought herself to her feet with a faint glimmer of hope.

Maybe, now that they've got what they came for, they'll let me go.

Or maybe they're saving you for something else.

If it came to that, she would force them to use the gun.

Thing One held the pot containing the June tree, slanted haphazardly from within. When Nie looked at it, the first thing she thought of was that the tree had wilted. Her arms hung down by her sides. Her breasts appeared more pendulous. Her hair hung lank around her face.

Where the June tree had once stood, Chris was now buried to just beneath his shrunken penis. He was bent over from the waist, his face in the dirt. Nie figured he was wilted, too.

"She don't look too good," Thing One said while studying the June tree. "We need to hurry up and get that soil."

He started back along the fog-covered meadow, covered in purplish moonlight.

Thing Two held the gun in his right hand and the shovel in his left. With the gun, he gestured for Nie to follow Thing One.

Nie tried to block out the fear and any thought of escaping. She fought to clear her mind completely, free herself from the cat claws of madness scraping at the backs of her eyes.

It seemed like an eternity before they reached the blood-spattered bag of soil.

Thing Two gave her the shovel to hold and he lifted the bag easily with one hand. The same bag Chris had struggled so hard to carry.

The rest of the walk seemed like an eternity.

When they reached the van, Thing One set the pot at the rear and opened up the doors. He took the bag of soil from Thing Two and unrolled the top of it. The smell that wafted out made Nie gag. She tried her best not to vomit again, but when she saw him dump the "soil" into the pot, she lost it. At this point, it was little more than a dry heave, but it sucked her energy even further.

What came out of the bag looked like entrails and blood, all squishy and glistening. Thing One centered the June tree, positioning it upright. Thing Two handed him the shovel and he packed the offal down around the tree. Then he lifted up the pot and put it in the van, folding the bag back down on the soil and placing that next to the tree. He handed the shovel back to Thing Two and said, "Better keep that up front with you."

"Should we dose her before we get back on the road?" Thing Two said.

"I'll let you take care of that."

Thing Two grabbed her around the arm and pulled her up to the passenger door of the van. He stepped back and continued to hold the gun on Nie.

"Why don't you reach in there and open up the glove box," he said.

She opened the door, leaned over the seat and turned the faux chrome knob of the glove compartment, conscious of Thing Two's eyes burning into her ass.

"Now reach in there and grab that bag."

She felt around and pulled out a Ziploc bag, its bottom lined with blue pills.

"Pull out two of them things and pop em in yer mouth. We can't have you goin apeshit on us."

"I won't," she said quietly. "I promise."

"Why should I believe you?"

She moved closer to Thing Two and said, "If you promise you'll let me go, I'll let you fuck me."

She looked at the bulge in his red running shorts.

"I'll let your brother fuck me, too."

A sound blasted behind Nie and she saw the explosion of the gun followed by another blast.

It took her a second to figure out what had happened. The first sound was the van's horn. The fright had caused Thing Two to pull the trigger but he must have jerked too much because the bullet had missed her.

"I think you better take the pills."

She reached into the bag and plucked out two of them.

"What are these going to do to me?"

"They're gonna make you sleep. When you wake up, we'll be at Mr. Martin's and you can tell him this here tree's real."

"And then you'll let me go?"

"Just take the pills."

She put them in her mouth and dry swallowed. One of them went down and one of them stuck on the back of her tongue. She gagged.

Thing Two pressed the gun to her lips.

"Open up," he said.

She opened her mouth, the pill tickling the back of her throat. Thing Two slid the gun into her mouth, pushing the pill down into her throat. She gagged again as the pill went down and Thing Two pulled the gun out of her mouth.

"Get in the van," he said.

She climbed into the stink of the June tree's soil and Thing Two shut the door behind her before hopping into the front seat and shutting his door. Once his door was shut, she heard the automatic locks seal the doors.

That was it, Nie thought. *That was my one chance to get away.*

The van started and pulled out onto the road.

Nie sat in her seat, watching the two brothers.

Maybe I could bust out a window. Maybe if I went for their eyes. Jesus, I just want to be home. I want to be somewhere where none of this has happened. I want to wake up from this bad bad bad dream.

But even as she thought that, she felt her eyelids get heavier, her head fill up with something and she thought she could feel herself slide ever so slowly and gently out of her seat as the pill wrapped its narcotic fingers around her consciousness.

Nie didn't know how long it was before she came to.

The van was still moving, she could hear the wheels thumping on the road. She was on her stomach. Thing Two was beside her. She could smell his meaty breath. His hands were between her legs. He had slid her thong aside. His fingers played with her sex, his thumb massaging her anus.

"Man, this bitch's dry as a bone," he said.

"I told you, after we see Mr. Martin, we'll take that money down to Cincy and get us a couple whores."

"Yeah, but she's young and fresh. Her pussy's real tight."

Nie fought off the nausea and opened her eyes to slits.

The gun sat abandoned on the console between the two front seats.

The rest happened very fast.

Nie sprang.

She wrapped her hand around the gun, slipped her finger around the trigger, held the gun toward Thing One and pulled the trigger.

There was an explosion.

A spray of red.

The screech of tires.

Then she was flying.

Hitting the pavement and skidding across.

Maybe the pills were still in her body because she didn't feel any of it.

Knew she had to get away.

Thing Two was probably still alive and . . . and he was the one that wanted to . . . to . . . *do stuff* to her.

She brought herself to her feet. Jesus, she felt wet all over. Was that blood? Her ears rang and she was having trouble hearing anything else. She walked but her body didn't want to. She didn't hurt. She was numb. Numb all over.

The street was lined with houses but most of them were darkened, glowing Jack-o-lanterns sitting on porches for one final night of rot.

In front of her there was a brightly lighted house. Slowly, slowly, the house came toward her.

A woman who looked like Elvira opened the door.

"Goodness, honey, what's wrong with you?"

"Need to call police," Nie stammered. Christ, she wasn't going to be able to stand up much longer.

Then there was a man standing beside the woman. His hair glittered gold and he wore a pair of gold horns and, they must have been contact lenses because Nie could have sworn his eyes were orange.

"What's wrong?" the man asked the woman but Nie could barely hear him because it sounded like . . . *screams* were coming from the house.

"This girl . . ."

Such awful screams.

"She says . . ."

It's Halloween. It's Halloween, remember. Those are Halloween sounds you're hearing.

"That we should call the police . . ."

No. This isn't right. Those screams are real. There's too many of them. Too loud.

"Mr. Martin. What are we going to do, Mr. Martin?"

Nie stared at the man with the flaming orange eyes as he laughed. She wanted to run around and run back to the road but the road was too far away and her body couldn't run backward anyway so she fell forward, caught herself and tried to run in that direction.

There must be a phone.

Has to be a phone.

And those screams, high and ripe and she really knew that was where she was going because it was Halloween and she wanted to be surrounded by screams, surrounded by people.

She was through the house and out the back door, the night air, the sky spinning around her and beneath the sky, surrounding her, the screaming orchard.

She stopped, turned in circles, staring at the people trees around her, the mouths contorted as they screamed at the moon, some of them waist high, some of them towering against the sky, grown to gigantic proportions.

And beside her she felt the hot breath, heard the faint crackle of eyes burning somewhere under all the screaming.

A feverish hand stroked her cheek and, after a giddy bout of laughter, she heard the voice say, "Skin like an American beech. Don't you think?"

She willed herself to die. She wanted blood-loss or broken bones or ruptured lungs to take her away from these awful people and then she thought of Chris and wondered if it would matter.

Nie heard the woman laugh and say, "Oh, definitely, Mr. Martin."

Nie screamed. A Halloween scream. It was all she could do. From somewhere outside herself, she heard her sapling scream rise up and join the chorus of the other trees in the orchard.

MUSIC FROM THE SLAUGHTERHOUSE

THE MIDDAY SUN continued to burn the already brown grass in the meadow. It was the hottest, driest summer Jakob could remember. Marcie, his younger sister by two years, sat next to him under a shady crabapple tree. Together, they stared across the field at the slaughterhouse. It was owned by their neighbor, Sully Bussard. Any breeze blown from the direction of the slaughterhouse was tainted. Especially in this heat. It smelled like meat gone bad and made Jakob think about what happened in there. Maybe it was a blessing that, today, the breeze was nonexistent.

"I don't like that place much," Marcie said.

"Me neither," Jakob said.

Marcie had brought her sketchpad out. She had completed her first year of high school where she had taken an art class and been absolutely consumed with her drawings and painting ever since. She sketched quickly with her left hand, holding the big sketchpad in her smaller right hand. Jakob didn't think anything of that hand's size deficiency until she actively used it. It looked strange. He tried to think of the word . . . *Anomaly.* That was the word he was thinking of. The hand looked totally out of place. It was the hand of a six-year-old girl.

"That's a good drawing," he said.

"Thanks."

He had almost forgotten why he had come out here. Then he remembered. Marcie's friend, Geneva Kaufman. He wanted to try and get Marcie to see if she liked him. He was seventeen and desperate and didn't see anything wrong with using his sister as a pimp.

He started to ask her about Geneva when a round of bleating

came from the low white cinderblock slaughterhouse.

"Grotesque," Marcie mumbled under her breath.

"At least we don't get the smell today."

"Do you remember what dad used to tell us about the slaughter-house, when we were too little to know it was a slaughterhouse?"

"Yeah. He said they made music in there and the sound of the cows dying was just some new music that wasn't played on the radios or anything yet. He said it sounded like it came from a whole other land."

"Yeah. It kind of made me want to go, like, look around in it or something. Only, when I got a little bit older and I knew what slaugh-terhouse meant I imagined they still played music in there only they used the ribs for a washboard, the eyeballs for castanets, and a bloated stomach as the drum."

"Jesus. That's sick, Marcie."

"Well, I wouldn't have thought all that stuff if Dad didn't fill our heads with that music nonsense."

"So it's his fault you're morbid?"

"Isn't it always the father's fault? Or the mother's? Maybe both."

She set the notebook down in her lap and wiped some sweat away from her forehead with the small hand. Jakob was going to ask her about Geneva again but he remembered something he and his friend, Jeff, had seen the other night.

"Do you know if old Bussard's taken up with Darla Minnow?"

"Who?"

"Darla Minnow. The really fat librarian. You know . . . the one who's like so fat she has to use canes to walk?"

"No. Why?"

"I was just wondering. The other night when me and Jeff were out here we saw her wandering into the slaughterhouse. Well, I wouldn't really call it wandering. It was more like trundling."

"That's mean."

"I know. But why would she be there? Why would she be going into the slaughterhouse?"

"So how much had you and Jeff smoked while you were out here?"

Jakob stood up. "That's none of your business," he said. "Be-sides, you know we don't do that."

"Well, all I'm saying is you would have to be high not to notice the sort of obvious facts you've overlooked."

"Oh, well, I'm sure you'll fill me in."

"Okay. First, it's a slaughterhouse. They slaughter cows and other assorted animals so they can sell them for food. Sometimes, people provide the animal. They don't all come from Bussard's backyard. And if someone supplies an animal to be slaughtered then it only stands to reason they would have to come back to collect said animal. And, since our lady Minnow is of an expansive proportion, it would only stand to reason that she likes to eat. Maybe she lives on a farm. Maybe she had one of her animals slaughtered so she can rest easy knowing she has like a year's worth of hamburgers."

"Yeah. I guess. It just seemed kind of late."

"It's probably not like either of them had anything else to do."

"It's hot. I'm going inside. Oh, by the way, you know your friend Geneva . . .?"

"I knew there was a reason you were out here."

A few days later, Jakob lay in his bed in a post-masturbatory near-slumber when someone knocked on his bedroom door. He hurriedly zipped himself up and threw the soiled paper towel under the bed before saying, "Enter."

He propped himself up against the headboard. Marcie came in and sat on the far side of the bed.

"Why are you all sweaty?" she asked.

"Because it's hot."

"Oh, okay."

He didn't know why she had come in but she had a look of excitement in her eyes. Maybe she had finally asked Geneva about him. But she just sat there. She liked to do things like that. Like make him practically beg to get anything out of her.

"So why are you here?" he asked.

"Well . . . remember what you said about Darla Minnow the other day?"

"Yeah. And I also remember how you debunked my small town-really-creepy-love-affair theory."

"Maybe I was a bit hasty. You're not going to believe this."

Then she did it again. Just sat there on the edge of the bed with her lopsided hands clasped together, staring at him, waiting for him to ask her what it was he wasn't going to believe.

"*And?*" he said.

"Okay, so I just came back from the library. They have this really great Hieronymus Bosch book I was going to try and steal and Darla Minnow was there behind the counter only at first I didn't know it was her."

She stopped again.

"Okay," Jakob said. "If you keep making me pull the story out of you then I'm going to be too tired to pay attention by the time you're actually finished."

"I *could* just stop."

"No. Don't stop. Okay, *why* didn't you know it was her?"

"When she went into the slaughterhouse the other day, was she fat?"

"Of course she was fat. I don't know that I would have known it was her but for the girth and the canes."

"You are *so* mean. Anyway, the Darla Minnow I saw at the library was not fat. In fact, she was very thin. Like model-thin. I had a stroke of conscientiousness brought on by my curiosity and decided to check the book out instead of stealing it outright so I took it up to the counter and she got up from behind her desk to come and help me . . ."

"Did she have the canes?"

"No. No canes at all. She looked more like someone you would see dressed up as like the 'dirty librarian' in a *Playboy* spread or something."

"How's that possible?"

"That's what I've been wondering. You want to know what I think?"

"You're the brain."

"I think something happened to her at the slaughterhouse."

"That's not possible." But Jakob was already turning the possibilities over in his head.

"We should watch it tonight. See if anybody goes in. And see what they look like when they come out."

"I don't know. It just sounds crazy. I'll call Jeff and see what he thinks."

"Well, I'm going to keep an eye on it and you can listen to your stupid friends if you want to. By the way, Geneva said you don't really have a chance. And she has a jealous boyfriend who may try and emasculate you if he sees you in public. I'm sure it's all talk but . . . well, he *is* pretty big."

"Talking to you makes my head hurt," Jakob said and reached for a music magazine on his bedside table, officially ending their conversation.

When she left, he picked up the cordless phone and called Jeff, hoping Jeff would be able to refute everything Marcie had told him. Instead, Jeff only agreed with her.

Jeff worked a part-time job at Bang's supermarket. He said the manager of Bang's was an older man with a limp. Until yesterday. Yesterday, he had come in looking twenty years younger without any trace of a limp. Jeff kept waiting for someone to ask about this sudden appearance change but the only thing anyone said was, "You're looking good today, Mr. Castle." Today, Jeff said, Mr. Castle had given Cynthia Raymond a "ride home," but Jeff suspected something much more prurient was at play.

"So," Jakob said, "you want to come and scout this place with me and my sister tonight?"

Jeff agreed, called Jakob a "gentleman and a scholar," and hung up.

Disappointment washed the night. By two o'clock, Jakob was tired of being bitten by mosquitoes and he was ready for bed. The two boys' sophomoric banter had frustrated Marcie about an hour ago and she had since retreated to the house.

"So, we done for the night?" Jeff asked.

"Yeah. I think so. This was stupid."

"Not if you saw Mr. Castle."

"That's supposing he came here. We don't know that he did."

"Still, people don't just transform overnight. Even if they have some kind of surgery, they have to have some healing time."

"I guess. Maybe we could just go to the library and ask Minnow about it tomorrow."

Jeff laughed. "Why? You just want to check her out?"

"Hardly."

"I hear she's pretty hot."

They walked through the meadow, swatting at mosquitoes and gnats, the sound of peepers and cicadas providing a churning whir in the background.

"You know," Jeff said, "Marcie'd be pretty hot if it wasn't for her hand."

"That's my *sister*. Besides, the hand's not so bad. I can imagine a pedophile taking a keen interest in her."

"God, you're sick."

When they got up to the house Jakob asked Jeff if he was staying tonight.

"No. I can't. I have to get up early and go to Bang's. Maybe I'll try and buddy up to Mr. Castle. See if I can get some kind of confession from him."

"Meet back here tomorrow?"

"Sure."

Jakob went back into the house and went to bed. Lying there, he thought about the slaughterhouse. The place had always unnerved him but he found himself now terrified of it. He didn't know why exactly. If it was making people "beautiful" that should be a lot less terrifying than thinking of the slaughters it was normally used for. But he didn't like the idea. In his German class, they had discussed Faust, and it seemed like there had to be something Faustian about this. One does not get something for nothing. Then he had another horrifying thought. The thought actually came to him in Jeff's voice. It was what he had said when they were walking back from the field, "Marcie'd be pretty hot if it wasn't for her hand."

No, Jakob thought. Marcie wouldn't even think about that. He knew she wasn't a shallow person and he thought she had actually grown quite comfortable with the idea of her hand over time. If she had asked he could have told her the hands were like the *last* things guys looked at.

He couldn't get the idea out of his head.

Maybe it wouldn't hurt to get up and check on her. Act big brotherly for a change. He was the one who had brought the whole thing up to begin with. If something happened to her, he would be partially to blame. He didn't want the guilt.

The wooden floor in his room squeaked as he walked across it. He opened his door and looked down the hall. Her room was at the end of the hall and he saw that her light was still on. Maybe she fell asleep with it on. She was never up this late and she had seemed pretty tired at the stakeout. He walked down the hall and gently knocked on the door. He didn't hear any answer and just assumed she was asleep but decided to open the door and check on her anyway.

When he opened the door she wasn't in her bed.

He looked at the walls of her room, all of her drawings and paintings hung up with masking tape as though she were still deciding which ones to keep there. Dominating the wall above her bed was a painting that did not alleviate his paranoid thoughts at all. It was on an open-hardback size canvas. There was something childlike about it. It looked like she had dipped her hands in paint—the left one in primary green and the right one, the small one, in primary red—and pressed them to the canvas. Scrawled all around the colorful hands in black ink were the words: MY SCHIZOPHRENIC HANDS. Over and over.

Jakob ran out of his house and out to the meadow. Maybe he could still catch her before it was too late.

The night was a buzzing swarm, matching some internal rant raging within Jakob. He reached the rusted fence separating his property from Old Man Bussard's and clumsily made his way over the top. A dim light glowed from inside the slaughterhouse. Jakob didn't want to go in. He had never been this close to it. He didn't like it. It made his skin crawl. He slapped at a gnat that had kamikazed into his forehead.

And now he was going to go inside the slaughterhouse.

His stomach did a great turn. The smell increased as he drew closer. Standing at the rusted iron door between him and the mystery waiting inside, he wanted to be able to tell himself this was crazy so he could go back home and curl up in his bed, surrounded by air conditioning and a lack of insects. But Marcie might be in there.

No, he told himself. Marcie *had* to be in there. Where else would she be? He couldn't believe he hadn't seen the signs earlier. She had never been interested in creepy things like the slaughterhouse before. Then, after being presented with the alluring prospect of self-transformation, she had suddenly wanted to find an answer to all the mysteries.

Jakob grabbed the handle of the door and yanked it to his left. It slid into place with a clanking boom. The smell hit him, threatening to drop him to his knees. It was the worst thing he had ever smelled. Occasionally, a raccoon would get smashed on the road in front of the house and rot there for a few days until the park ranger removed it. That was enough of a deathsmell for Jakob. This was a hundred times worse. This smelled like what he imagined burying his nose in the roadkill raccoon might be like.

His stomach tried to bolt up his spine but he managed to hold it down.

He looked frantically for Marcie but didn't see her.

He didn't see anything.

Of course not. He had himself all worked up over nothing. This was, after all, just a slaughterhouse. Crazy old Bussard had probably just left the light on accidentally. Whatever he had seen previously was probably not what he thought he had seen. Maybe Ms. Minnow *had* lost a bunch of weight and maybe the person he had seen entering the slaughterhouse the one night wasn't Ms. Minnow. He doubted everything now. Maybe Jeff had made up the whole Mr. Castle scenario. Jeff had been known to tell wild stories until everyone believed him before telling his audience it was a lie.

"Marcie?" he called out, just to be sure.

No one answered him.

Okay, he had served his big brotherly duty. Now he just wanted to get out. He turned around and saw Bussard standing in the doorway.

"Lookin for somethin?" Mr. Bussard said.

"No. I was just leaving. I'm sorry. I thought my sister was in here." Surely the old man would understand that. He looked perfectly reasonable, just like he had always looked—a short man with bandy legs and a big gray mustache.

"You two playin games or somethin?"

"Yeah. Something like that. It was stupid of me to look for her in here. I'm gonna go now. Sorry if I bothered you."

Bussard stepped aside to allow Jakob passage to the outside.

"You kids get stranger every day," Bussard said. "Hidin out in a slaughterhouse." He laughed a gentle laugh. "I'll let it pass this time but you can see how it concerns me. You bein out here. Some people might wanna steal my cattle and I can't have that." Bussard stepped farther into the slaughterhouse and motioned Jakob out the door, a look something like interested disappointment on his face.

"I understand. Good night." Jakob stepped through the threshold and lost his footing. Falling forward he caught himself with his elbows. Clumsy idiot, he thought. I can't even walk away gracefully. He tried to stand up and fear seized his heart. His feet were drawn together. Bussard was dragging him into the slaughterhouse.

"You noticed all the beautiful people in town?" Bussard said.

"Let me go," Jakob said, his mouth dry, panic taking over. He struggled to scoot away but it was useless. The chain bit into his ankles and Bussard looped one of the links onto a hook.

It was some kind of pulley system. He turned a little lever about ten feet from Jakob and Jakob felt himself rising up from the ground, suspended by his feet. Jakob screamed. He screamed for Marcie. He screamed for his mom and dad.

"You can scream all you want," Bussard said. "The only thing anybody ever hears is music. Or a cow. They make what they want to out of it, I guess."

"There's nothing wrong with me!" Jakob spat. "I don't want you to change anything."

"But everybody wants something to change. Sure, you don't have any major flaws but if you looked *even better* you probably wouldn't have any problems at all."

"Let me go!" Jakob shouted, flailing his arms wildly, trying to swing on the chain and get close enough to Bussard to do some harm.

"Besides," he said, grabbing a sledgehammer leaning against the dark stained wall. "It's not so much about changin anything. It's more about dyin. And bein reborn. And me ownin a little piece of you that was all yours once upon a time."

Jakob took a deep breath, ready to scream again, before the hammer smashed into his face and everything he had ever known about life was sent spiraling into some black space.

Marcie came up from the basement. That was where the big TV was and, when she had returned to the house after the stakeout, she realized she wasn't as tired as she thought. She walked past Jakob's room and noticed his door was open. She had to admire his and Jeff's tenacity. They were really taking this seriously. Marcie was now so tired she could hardly hold her eyes open. She didn't know how Jakob was still awake. She shut the door to her bedroom, turned off the light, and crawled into bed. As she lay there in silence, she thought she heard the music from the slaughterhouse and laughed it off. She really had become obsessed over the past couple of days. It was stupid, really, she figured. Just before she submitted entirely to sleep she had a strange notion. She wished she hadn't told Jakob Geneva had said those things about him. Genny hadn't even really said that. She had actually said she thought he was pretty cute but Marcie had wanted to have fun with him. What if Jakob had gone into the slaughterhouse, seeking the same thing that Mr. Castle and Ms. Minnow had sought? All so Geneva would find him more attractive. She drifted off to sleep, convincing herself the noise she heard was just a conglomeration of the country night sounds and her speculations about Jakob were just the product of her somewhat warped creative mind.

THE EXISTENTIAL DREAD OF COMPLACENCY

1.

IT WAS PROBABLY the first time in his adult life Thurston Tremont would readily admit to being happy with nearly everything. His teenage son was doing well, both physically and in school, and seemed to be less depressed than he had been a couple of years ago. Thurston only usually saw Matthew on the weekends and it didn't really feel like enough but, in reality, they probably spent more time together than many fathers and sons. After two failed marriages, Thurston was finally with a woman who had similar interests and complemented him. She felt as much like a friend as a lover and that was something he'd never really experienced before. He didn't like to think every relationship was supposed to make you miserable at least half the time. He didn't really know where that idea came from but figured it was probably some latent misogynist notion. The woman gave the man sex and therefore he must pay for that with his misery. It relegated all romantic relationships to prostitution, essentially. But this one didn't feel like that. Oh, and the sex was great. She was a writer, too, and they spent much of their time together sitting beside one another and working on their own projects in their individual heads. They came together to share. It worked. And the books were selling reasonably well. The past year or so had seen some newfound interest in the work of Holger Blackwell and the manuscript Thurston completed for his goonish editor, *The One Who Creeps*, earned him enough in royalties to pay his rent. And the rent wasn't as cheap as it had been this time last year. He and Kara had finally bitten the bullet and moved out of their scary, tiny, ancient, but cheap apartment in downtown Dayton to a house in the town of Twin Springs. She was from up north but had fallen in love with the town when he'd taken her there one weekend shortly after they'd first met. And he'd liked it ever since going there with his friends in high school. He and his friends had mainly gone there because of the head shop and bookstore and you could buy incense and anything else you needed to turn yourself into a goofy hippie overnight. But there was more to it than that. They went to high school in the middle of a cornfield in a conservative small town. It wasn't the small town he had a problem with. He loved small towns. He did not enjoy gun toting, racist, conservative small mindedness. Twin Springs was home to Shrine College. While it had fallen on hard times lately, there was a legacy of equality and progressive politics that was still palpable. Living somewhere where they were surrounded by dreadlocked, barefoot, patchouli-wearing hippies was highly preferable to watching people get shot in the parking lot of the clubs across the street. Plus Holger Blackwell had lived there. Plus there were good restaurants to eat in and a brewery down the street that brewed awesome beer. And there were trees. A lot of trees. So they were somewhat shocked to find that the SWAT team had had to shoot the previous tenant out of the house for randomly firing his considerable arsenal out the window. They hadn't heard about the incident when it had happened. Living in Dayton, they never followed the news. It was too depressing. Or horrifying. It seemed like things like that had happened every week. But they had Googled the address and it had come up. He and Kara liked things with a history so it definitely didn't want to make them back out of it. They'd almost *bought* a house in an area where they didn't really want to live just because it had a cemetery behind it and a tombstone in the backyard.

So he was perfectly willing to admit to himself that he was happy but the most he would ever be willing to admit to someone who asked was that he was doing "okay." Because every time he'd found himself complacent in his place in the world, it had ended up crumbling around him and then he was likely to spend the next two years picking up the pieces. It was entirely possible it was that history that would keep him from being a hundred percent content. Not that he thought anyone was ever really perfectly content. But he knew he could never rest. He always had to remain somewhat vigilant. Which was maybe why he liked to spend at least an hour every night staring into the darkness and thinking thoughts he would never write down or speak aloud. This, he thought, was how adults terrified them-selves.

Or maybe he just liked the night and the quiet and the contem-plative nature of that environment allowed his mind to open up and his mental guard to relax a little while he thought about all the bad things that could happen.

It made him want to drink and smoke more. By the third or fourth beer, the night air smelled great—full of honeysuckle and something almost spicy he couldn't identify—and Kara and he would be together forever, and they were in the perfect place and he couldn't ask for anything more from his writing career and, hey, even the day job wasn't that horrible.

He took a sip of beer and a deep breath before lighting another cigarette. Sometimes thinking was the worst thing a person could do. The only things easy to think about were appointments, how shitty your life was, or how you were going to go about conquering the world. Everything else was just so many shades of gray. The im-portant thing was to find moments like this and squeeze every ounce of enjoyment from them and hope they would be abundant.

After all, when all was said and done, things were not that bad. And they could *always* be worse.

His and Kara's mutual friend, Dustin, was coming by the next day with his wife, Jessica. Thurston and Dustin shared the same deadbeat publisher. They'd wander around the town, eat good food, drink much beer, smoke many cigarettes, and trade gossip about their fellow degenerate writers.

It would be fun.

2.

Thurston got a text from Dustin saying they were almost there.

"Thank god. I'm starving." Kara put her hands over her tiny stomach like something inside of her was dying.

"I'm sure they'll be ready to get something to eat."

Thurston and Kara went out to the driveway just as the battered maroon minivan pulled in. They went around to the passenger side to greet Jessica as she got out of their van. It was both their opinion that the wives and girlfriends of their writer friends—mostly male—were woefully neglected if not completely ignored. Unless the wife was the publisher of the writer friend. This was the case with at least three of them. Thurston couldn't help noticing it looked like the back of the van was filled with trash. He wasn't really a judgmental person. It was just an observation.

Dustin had already crawled out of the driver's seat and come around to join them just as Jessica got out of the passenger side. Hellos made their rounds and they joined in a group hug. Jessica and Dustin smelled really bad. Thurston was pretty sure Jessica was pregnant. Something that had never come up.

"So you guys ready to go get some food?" he asked.

"Sounds great," Dustin said. "I hate to ask you this but is it okay if we take a quick shower first? I feel really ripe."

Of course people had asked to use the shower before, but this was the first time Thurston could recall anyone asking to use it upon arrival.

"Sure, man." Dustin and Jessica grabbed a couple of bags from the back of the van. Thurston led them into the house and Kara stayed behind to pick up the excess trash that had rolled from the van.

Dustin and Jessica dumped their bags inside the door off the carport and Thurston led them down the hallway to the bathroom. He grabbed a couple of towels and washcloths from the linen closet and held them out to Dustin.

"Here you go."

"Nah, man. We don't like the way any of that stuff feels on our skin."

Thurston stood somewhat frozen, continuing to hold out the towels and washcloths.

"So I should just . . . put them back?"

"Do whatever, man. We just need the water to get clean and the air to dry us off."

"Okay."

Thurston went to find Kara. Dustin and Jessica disappeared into the bathroom. Well, they didn't really *disappear* because neither one of them bothered shutting the door.

Kara sat at the small table on the bizarre back patio, smoking. A bag of Bugles sat on the table.

"I had to eat something," she said. "I was starving."

"Me too." Thurston sat down with a heavy groan.

He realized he probably didn't know Dustin and Jessica as well as he thought he did. Their publisher put together a convention in

Seattle every year and the authors were encouraged to attend, even though the trip out there cost roughly three times what the publisher ever paid them in royalties. Kara and Thurston had found themselves hanging around the other couple quite a bit. But that wasn't really a normal environment and they weren't really in close quarters or anything. And, he guessed when he added it up over the course of a weekend "quite a bit" was probably closer to three hours. They'd also met Dustin at a reading in Chicago and spent a few hours drinking with him afterward. But that was just Dustin by himself, not with Jessica.

Thurston sighed. "It's going to be an interesting evening."

He told her about the towels.

"And who just shows up and asks to use the shower anyway?" Kara crushed out her cigarette and immediately lit another one. "I'm starting to wish we were already drunk when they got here."

Thurston pulled a cigarette from the pack and lit it. "Maybe it'll even out."

"I hope so. What time are they leaving tomorrow?"

"I don't know. I think they were headed on to Florida or someplace so I imagine they'd want to get on the road."

"Is Jessica pregnant?"

"I don't know. That's what I thought, too. Dustin hasn't mentioned it."

They smoked, stared into the thick woods, and listened to their stomachs grumble for nearly an hour.

"Not just any shower," Kara said. "The world's fucking longest shower."

"How bout all that weight they've lost though, huh?"

"I know, right? I was going to say they'd lost a lot of weight when they got out of the van but that's like saying, 'Hey, you were really fat!' I guess that's pretty much why we can't ask them if she's pregnant."

Thurston didn't really know if the weight loss was a good thing. The last time they'd seen the couple, they'd been probably a hundred pounds heavier. Some people lost weight through diet and exercise and they seemed to maintain some kind of healthful glow. Dustin and Jessica looked like they'd been starving themselves. They looked sick. He wondered if they'd lost their house or something. Maybe they had been living out of their van. Maybe that was the reason the inside of it looked the way it did. Maybe that's why they'd lost so much weight and smelled the way they did. He considered asking them about it. Maybe he would if he got Dustin alone later. But he almost didn't want to know the answer. If he knew the answer, he might feel compelled to help. He and Kara did okay financially, but he still had his son to support and the modest surplus they were left with was really only enough to eat out a couple of times a month— a luxury they'd come to enjoy and look forward to. That left offering them a place to stay. His son still used the one bedroom when he came over but there was the library. He supposed they could throw a futon or air mattress in there. But he was getting ahead of himself. He decided if they were too irritating, he just wouldn't ask.

The screen door opened and Dustin and Jessica came out. They were both completely naked and dripping wet. They were covered in bruises and welts and Thurston couldn't help noticing that neither one of them did any bush work whatsoever.

Dustin pulled one of the wrought iron chairs out from the table and sat down heavily.

He wiped a hand across his wet brow and said, "Thanks, man. That felt great."

It was actually really hard to not like Dustin.

"No problem."

Thurston noticed Dustin and Jessica didn't really smell much better than when they had gone in. They probably hadn't used any soap, either.

"Just let us dry off for a little bit and we'll be ready to go. So what have you guys been up to?"

Jessica drifted off the patio and into the yard. She stared at the birds and tall trees and looked super stoned. Kids lived on the street and their yard was often used as a shortcut for people going into the woods so he considered calling her back but decided not to worry about it. She was an adult. She could get herself out of any situation she put herself into.

Kara and Thurston gave Dustin the rundown of the last few months. Kara provided the actual facts. Thurston provided the opinionated color.

Jessica wandered to the edge of the woods and stared into them. She may have been touching herself.

"So what's up with you guys?" Thurston asked.

Dustin was a talker, a great storyteller. It was one of the reasons he was so entertaining to have around. He just shrugged and said,

"Not much."

Jessica came charging back to the patio and said, "I saw a rabbit!" before launching into a coughing fit.

The next few minutes of conversation were stilted and awkward.

Finally Thurston gave Dustin the once over and said, "You guys dry enough to put on some clothes and get something to eat?"

3.

Dustin and Jessica each wore some kind of dashiki-looking thing, only it looked like they were made out of some plain muslin-like material.

"You guys look like cult members or something," Kara said.

"Nah." Dustin chuckled, showing a shade of who he used to be.

Their attire would have really embarrassed Thurston if they had been anywhere but Twin Springs. The place seemed to have a tolerance for that sort of thing whereas the rest of the Dayton area seemed to be almost aggressively normal.

They went to the all-organic, locally sourced Peruvian restaurant in town and had a great meal. Thurston and Kara rarely let their guests pay for anything and this was no exception. Besides, Thurston didn't see where Dustin or Jessica could possibly keep any means to pay. Their gown things were virtually transparent and didn't have any pockets. The conversation over dinner had been a little livelier although Dustin and Jessica seemed to be talking about things that had happened a really long time ago, like in their college days. There was still no clue about what they'd been up to in the last few months.

"Thanks for getting that," Dustin said as they left the restaurant. "We don't carry cash or credit cards anymore."

Kara and Jessica walked ahead of them, engaged in their own conversation.

"Are you serious?" Thurston thought maybe Dustin had been joking.

"Too confining."

"Then how do you pay for things?"

"We don't. Nobody should have to pay for anything."

"So . . . what? I should have just walked out on the check back there?"

"That would have been one option. Or we could just not have gone."

"So, okay, you don't buy food? I guess that explains how you guys have lost so much weight."

"Yeah. I feel great."

"But you have to eat."

"We do. Once we lost all that weight, we realized we don't really need that much to keep going."

"So you grow your own food or something?"

"A little. But that's a lot of work. We do take a few things off the shelf at the store but that's stuff they just throw out when it goes bad anyway."

"So you forage for the rest?"

"Yeah. Mostly. People throw away a lot of good shit."

"Oh, man. So you're dumpster diving?"

"Sure. Why not? It beats having to work to feed ourselves, you know?"

"But, dude, you're eating trash. Couldn't you work for a couple hours a day so you and your wife could eat something good every now and then?"

"We eat fine. Nobody used to really think about food. This obsession with food is just one indicator of the crumbling empire. Before the Roman Empire fell, people were eating until they vomited so they could eat more, adults introduced children into the world of sex, and a lot of other fucked up shit. Now we have the Food Network, reality television, and Facebook. Oh, and rich white men going on sex tours through Asian and Eastern European countries so they can fuck kids. Think about it."

The conversation had taken a grim turn. Thurston wanted to get back to the house so they could start drinking soon. Hopefully, Dustin and Jessica still drank. Hopefully it wasn't too emblematic of the crumbling empire. Wait, he thought. They still didn't know if Jessica was pregnant or not. She probably wouldn't drink if she was pregnant. He'd asked Dustin about the weight loss and regretted it. If anyone was going to ask Jessica about being pregnant, it would have to be Kara. He and Kara had had four growlers filled at the brewery earlier so either Dustin and Jessica were going to help drink it or Thurston and Kara were going to go into a coma. And if Jessica happened to be out, well, that just meant more for the rest of them. The way things were going, he was pretty sure he was going to need it.

"Besides," Dustin continued, "it's not just about working a

couple hours a day so you can eat. It's about conforming to a whole system. You can't just take bits and pieces of capitalism. You have to eat the whole thing. And then you're locked into the game because if you don't compete you feel like a loser. It teaches you to want more and more things, better and better things, but it keeps the ultimate goal forever out of reach. Sure, people will work increasingly difficult jobs or increasingly long hours to try and get that shit but the only people who ever do get it are the people who were pretty much born into it in the first place. And they don't even appreciate it! They have to spend money on ways to fill their copious amount of free time, which is probably the only thing someone like you wants more of."

Thurston had phased out a bit. "Huh?"

"Free time. That's what you would say you work hard for, right? You guys barely own anything."

"Sure. I guess."

"Well, see, I have plenty of that and I don't work at all. All I'm saying is: would you rather work eight hours and eat something you bought from someplace that, let's face it, still isn't that great, or would you rather have eight hours of free time and choke down an old burger you found in a McDonald's trashcan?"

"It's a little more than that. I don't want the thought of where my next meal is coming from to occupy my entire brain. Plus I have insurance and child support payments to make."

"Yeah, but what if your day job goes under and people stop buying your books?"

"I try not to think about any of that."

"I'm just saying we're probably ten years away from being a third world country. We've let the rich siphon off all the excess that was supposed to be distributed amongst the people and it's thrown things out of balance. There's no way this country can sustain itself."

They were approaching the house.

"Man, I could really use a drink. You guys still drink, don't you?" Maybe now he would find out if Jessica was pregnant or not.

"Fuck yeah," Dustin said. "As long as we don't have to pay for it."

Thurston wasn't sure if he was joking or not.

4.

It took about midway through the second growler before Dustin knocked off the adolescent political rhetoric and started to relax a little. Thurston actually agreed with most of what he said but found it overly idealistic and a horribly boring topic for party conversation. He'd always felt more than three people constituted a party and while Jessica was technically a fourth person the beer had taken what little contribution she had made out of her. She seemed almost zombified. Thurston relaxed a little. If she drank, she probably wasn't pregnant. Maybe the rounded belly had something to do with malnourishment, like those starving African kids they showed on TV.

The conversation shifted to writing and publishing, as it usually did with them. Jessica lost the last shred of interest she had in the conversation, shed her clothes, and wandered out in the yard to dance. It was dark and the light didn't reach that far and Thurston was glad because it would have made him nervous to look at her. When they began talking about some of their writer friends and the people they knew in publishing, Thurston was alarmed by the vitriolic hatred that came from Dustin. He used to be the type of person to find people's quirks funny. There were plenty of negative things to be said—it wasn't a perfect world—but everyone was pretty much there by choice and doing something they presumably enjoyed doing so Dustin's complete eviscerations of people seemed a bit much. Kara, already pretty drunk, laughed at much of what Dustin said but Thurston thought, with the way he was saying it, it wasn't really a laughing matter.

A dog howled in the distance. A June bug dive bombed the candle in the middle of the patio table and jerked convulsively in the wax, giving everyone a start. Jessica was nowhere to be seen, although Thurston was pretty sure he could hear her moving and panting.

Kara scrolled through her phone and read some Facebook posts from people they knew. Most of them were idiotic. Thurston was pretty sure the act of saying you did something cool on Facebook completely sucked the cool from it.

When they exhausted that, Thurston asked Dustin what he was working on.

"Nothing, man."

"Nothing?"

"What's the point?"

"I thought you liked doing it."

"Nah. It was stupid and childish. I said everything I had to say. I guess I'll write another one if I feel like I have something else to say."

Thurston liked Dustin's writing a lot, but he'd never thought of it as being particularly philosophical.

"The publishing business is just modern day slavery, anyway. You have a hundred slaves working for pennies so the publishers can get rich by, what? Uploading a couple of files?"

Thurston thought comparing a group of what was mostly middle age, middle-to-upper-middle class white guys to slavery was nearly offensive but, that aside, Thurston couldn't really disagree with him. It was one of the reasons he and Kara self-published most of their stuff these days. He was still pretty sure no one in the small press world was getting rich.

Kara tapped out sometime during the third growler. Jessica still had not joined them. The woods were alive with insect sounds. Heat lightning strobed the sky.

Kara told Dustin where the extra blankets and pillows were.

"Thanks but we'll probably just sleep out here."

Her hospitality thwarted, Kara disappeared into the house without saying anything else.

"You don't have to sleep outside."

"No. I know, man. Thanks for the offer. We just like it better outside. Indoors is too confining. Jessica's really sensitive to mold and mildew. She says she can smell it every time she's inside."

"There's probably more mold and mildew outside than in."

"I know, but it belongs there."

This seemed somewhat irrational to Thurston but he let it drop.

He was finally drunk enough to let his curiosity force him to ask what had happened.

"So what the hell happened, man? What have you guys been doing since we saw you the last time?"

"What do you mean?"

"Come on. I'm not the only one who's asked you about this, am I? Didn't you move out here to be closer to your parents? What do they think?" Thurston almost hoped this was where Dustin would come clean and tell him they'd moved back in with his parents. That would have made some things make a little more sense.

"We don't speak to my parents anymore."

"I thought you were close."

"They're government workers. I wouldn't feel comfortable talking to them until they quit their jobs."

"But they're both teachers. Most people see teachers as saints."

"Well we see them as tools in the government brainwashing conspiracy."

"Are you fucking serious?"

"Of course I'm serious."

Thurston wanted to ask him to go back to being the old Dustin, a fun person to be around. Crazy, perhaps, but crazy in a good way.

"So that's what you've been doing? Working on some kind of . . . manifesto that will gradually eliminate everyone you know from your life?"

"It's not really like that. Once you reaffirm your personal beliefs it just makes hypocrisy impossible."

"So would continuing to talk to your parents be hypocrisy?"

"Are you kidding? I know what it is they stand for. I know where their money comes from. And I know they're unwilling to change."

"So just spending time with them because they're your parents and forgetting about all the other stuff is hypocritical?"

"Yes."

"I guess I just don't understand the rigidity of your thinking."

"That's because you want a comfortable life so you keep your morals and personal philosophy liquid and amorphous."

"Is that a bad thing?"

"It's not for me."

"So how can you talk to me knowing that I pay taxes, thus supporting the system you hate so much?"

"Because you have to do that. You have a job."

Thurston lit a cigarette and took a big gulp of beer. "We need to stop talking about this shit. Did Jessica ever come back?"

"I'm right here." She stood less than a foot behind Thurston and he jumped when she spoke.

"Jesus fucking Christ," he said, immediately standing up. "And with that, I think I'm going to call it a night. Help yourself to what's left of the beer. I'll leave the door unlocked. There's a bed inside if you decide you don't want to sleep in the yard."

5.

Thurston lay in bed and stared at the ceiling. If he were as drunk as he'd hoped to be, he would have passed right out. But the last few minutes of talking with Dustin had made him almost inexplicably angry and Jessica finally sneaking up on him had scared him completely sober. Now he was just mostly tired and wanted to go to sleep.

That was hard because Jessica and Dustin were still on the patio and that wasn't very far from his open bedroom window. It sounded like they were arguing. He wondered what Jessica could have been doing in her time away from them. There was no way she'd been dancing around in the yard for something close to three hours. And all that shit Dustin was talking about? He almost hoped it was some kind of elaborate put on.

He heard them move around to the front of the house, their voices escalating into near hysterical violence.

Kara was still dead to the world.

Thurston decided to get up and see what was wrong before someone down the street called the cops.

A dim light glowed from the van.

The screaming and yelling continued from the inside. Thurston wasn't exactly sure how you approached people living in a van. He knocked on the window of the sliding door, realizing again how old the van was.

The door slid back and Dustin said excitedly, "She's crowning!"

"Huh?"

Thurston felt dazed. He thought, somewhere deep inside his memory, he should know what that meant.

"Jessica's having the baby."

"Shouldn't . . . we call someone?"

Dustin hopped out of the van and wrapped his hands around Thurston's arms.

"You don't understand. This is the sacrifice we've been waiting for. Once the child is born we must take it to the place in the woods where Jessica's water broke and bathe in its blood. I have the ceremonial knife right here." Dustin held it up as proof. "If we do this, no one in attendance will ever have to do anything they don't want. Do what thou wilt!"

"I don't think I can let you do that." Thurston was already sliding his phone out of his pocket. It was dead. He wasn't completely surprised. It seemed like there were a hundred apps he couldn't figure out how to keep from running.

Kara stumbled out of the house just as the first volley of the baby's cries came from the van.

"I need the knife to cut this fucking cord!" Jessica shouted.

A dog howled in the distance. Insects hummed around him. A shadow or possibly the clouds moved across the moon.

"What the fuck is going on?" Kara still looked half-asleep.

"Do you have your phone on you?"

"No. It's in the house. Why?"

How to tell her . . . Thurston wondered if he should bother explaining or just start shouting for help.

"Thurse, what the fuck is going on?"

"We need to call the cops or an ambulance or something. Jessica just delivered her baby. They want to take it into the woods and sacrifice it."

"Okay."

"*Okay?*"

"It's not our place to stop them."

This journalistic approach was expected with most things, but he didn't see how this didn't get more of a reaction from her.

"I can't let them go through with this. Kill a baby?"

She shrugged. "Are we allowed to watch?"

Jessica must have drugged and brainwashed Kara. That was the only excuse Thurston could think of. Maybe Jessica had sneaked into her room after she'd gone to bed. Maybe she'd slipped her something at dinner and had been working on her subliminally ever since.

Dustin and Jessica came around from the back of the van, Dustin holding the baby swaddled in Jessica's robe. Dustin beamed. Jessica looked weak, her thighs splashed with blood.

What if there is *no baby?* Thurston wondered.

Since he was the only one not going along with this, he thought maybe they were all playing a trick on him. Deep down, he knew that couldn't be the case. He found himself following them around to the back of the house. Jessica had definitely given birth. He'd seen her naked earlier and there was no way she hadn't been pregnant. And now she was definitely not pregnant. When he'd seen her come around from the back of the van the firm baby bump had been replaced with what looked like two feet of stretch-marked, saggy skin. And this was the first time they'd all been together in nearly a year. Why would the three of them want to spend all night acting just for some kind of ridiculous payoff?

Thurston thought he would almost rather believe anything than what was actually happening around him.

"Dustin, man, I can't let you do this." He felt like he had to say something, but felt powerless to stop it.

Dustin was suddenly in front of him, brandishing the knife with the hand that wasn't holding the sacrificial infant in a bloody robe.

"We're going through with this!" There was a look in his eyes Thurston had never seen before. "You can get the fuck away, but you're not stopping us. If you try to stop us, I'll cut your fucking throat."

Thurston thought about how this would look on a police report, maybe even in front of a jury, and wondered if it would let him off the hook as an accomplice. He put up his hands in a gesture of defeat.

Kara placed a hand on Thurston's arm. "Just calm down."

"Yeah," Jessica smiled. "That's *my* pussy fruit."

The moon was nearly, if not completely, full and the backyard was fairly well lit. Maybe someone would see them and do something. But who would see? The strange man Kara sometimes swore she saw lurking around the house? He really felt like he should turn and run for help. There were probably only a few minutes left.

As they stepped into the dark wood, he felt the last vestiges of protest leave his body. He felt like he was on acid or some other, more euphoric drug. The woods were dark but seemed to almost glow and pulse. He imagined an umbilical cord running from the woods to the house and briefly wondered which way the nutrients were going. Which was feeding which. Jessica and Dustin and Kara all seemed to be panting as they headed deeper into the woods and Thurston heard the dog howl again. This time it was almost deafeningly close and he saw that the dog, a huge black thing, was right in front of them. It lowered its head from the unobservable moon and began lapping at the ground. Thurston thought that must be where Jessica's water broke. And now Jessica stood in front of the dog and the dog began licking the afterbirth from her thighs and in between her legs. She lay on her back and spread her legs. The beast's member was huge and pink and dripping as it moved on top of her and began thrusting. Dustin slashed at the swaddle he held in his left arm. His eyes were huge and he smiled crazily. He held the baby aloft above the dog fucking his wife, the blood raining down and coating all of them.

"Do what thou wilt shall be the whole of the law!" he shouted over and over, dancing around the scene of bestiality being played out on the floor of the woods.

Thurston felt assaulted by the night and the woods. He felt the moon and the leaves and the dirt and every droplet of water on his skin. He smelled blood and sex and dog and something spicy and exotic and not entirely unpleasant. Everything spun and throbbed around him and the last thing he remembered was collapsing onto his hands and knees and vomiting onto the ground, Kara's cool hand on the back of his neck.

6.

He woke up very late the next afternoon.

His body felt stiff and abused but, thankfully, there was no trace of the nausea he'd felt last night.

Kara had already made coffee. Recently, it smelled like. She probably hadn't gotten out of bed long before him.

Last night came back to him in vivid, nightmarish detail.

He poured a cup of coffee and looked out at the driveway. There was no sign of Dustin and Jessica's hideous van.

He took his coffee out to the back patio and sat down next to Kara. He reached for the cigarettes and lit one.

He wondered if they would talk about it.

He didn't really want to.

Talking about it seemed like it would make it real.

But it was real.

He denied that thought. He felt like it was something that needed the shape of words to make it more complete.

"Sleep well?" Kara looked toward the dark woods.

"Like a baby," he said.

THE SPOT

1.

"THAT WAS NICE," Mary said.

Joe kissed the top of her head and reached over onto the nightstand for his cigarettes. Mary lay pressed against him, on her side, her left arm slung over his chest. Fortunately, Joe was able to fit a king-size bed into his apartment and they were able to gravitate toward one half of it in order to avoid the dreaded spot splashed across the other half. Tomorrow he would change the sheets. It would be the first time in a while he had had to do that.

Joe lit his cigarette and offered one to Mary. "No, thank you," she said.

"Would you like me to turn on the TV?"

"I'm fine. I'm actually quite tired. I think I'll go."

"No, stay. You don't need to be out this late."

"Are you sure?"

"Certain."

Joe smoked his cigarette and wished the TV was on but Mary seemed to be asleep now, looking so peaceful with her eyes closed, that he didn't want to disturb her. He imagined he would be joining her when he finished his smoke.

Mary was a blind date, set up by his friend Abe, from the office. He had never seen her before tonight. He wondered if he would ever see her again. She didn't really seem like his type any way other than physically and he was pretty sure the feeling was mutual, as evidenced by her current heavy slumber. Joe crushed out his cigarette and, turning out the light, thought, *Christ, I hope she doesn't snore.*

Sleep claimed him in a matter of minutes.

Later, something yanked him from that sleep.

She's just tossing and turning, he thought. He reached over to calm her and, instead, felt something cool and slimy on his fingertips. *Oh, the spot,* he reminded himself. But the spot was moving. Panic gripped Joe and he opened his eyes, groping for the bedside lamp and knocking it off before he could turn it on.

The lamps from the street let in enough pale light for him to see adequately.

Mary lay on her back on the other side of the bed. Her legs were open, her knees forming two mountains beneath the sheet. *Maybe she's ready to go again,* Joe thought. Getting up on his knees, he yanked the sheet back. The panic came back, flushing his cheeks and speeding his heart. The spot had gathered itself up and was halfway inside Mary.

"No," Joe whispered between clenched teeth. A sickening sweat covered his body. Frantically, he reached for the spot, but his fingers went right through it, coming away damp but unable to stop its journey. Feeling like a gynecologist, he got down on his stomach between Mary's legs, watching as the last of the spot slithered up into her.

He collapsed back onto his side of the bed, insane thoughts racing around in his head. By the time he could form a logical thought he had himself convinced it was all a dream. That was impossible, wasn't it? Come couldn't do that, could it? It was shot out of the body and, if it didn't find an egg to fertilize, it died, right?

Joe became aware of Mary's back against his side. See there, it had to be a dream. She wasn't lying like that a few minutes ago. But the thoughts continued to swim around in his head. Reaching over Mary, he rubbed his hand around on the sheet, seeing if he could feel the spot. Feeling nothing, he got out of bed and turned on the light.

Slowly, he walked around to the other side of the bed. *I'll see if that damn thing's still there.* He pulled back the sheet. Bending down close to the mattress, he looked for any sign of it. It was possible that it had dried, he supposed. Midway down the bed he saw something that looked like it could be an outline. The more he looked at it, the more he had himself convinced this had to be the dried stain of the spot. It *was* warm in the room and he *did* have the ceiling fan on its highest setting. It was entirely possible the spot had dried in the hours since it had been expelled from his body. *It was only*, he reasoned, *like a teaspoon of fluid anyway.*

He went back over to his side of the bed, nearly giddy with relief, and turned off the light.

"Is something the matter?" Mary asked.

"No . . . go back to sleep. I just, I don't know, must have had a dream or something."

"You'll have to tell me about it tomorrow."

"Yeah," he said. "I hope we can laugh about it."

He smoked another cigarette in the dark before closing his eyes and begging sleep to reclaim him.

He woke up later than usual the next morning, feeling well rested. Rolling over, he threw his arm across the empty bed. In Mary's place was a note.

Thanks for everything.

We'll have to do it again sometime.

And her name was signed at the bottom. Joe felt relieved. Even though his dream of last night was little more than a distant memory, he didn't care if he ever saw Mary again.

2.

When he ran into Abe's wife, Shirley, nearly a year later, Joe didn't think he would have even been able to recognize Mary if he saw her. Abe had transferred out of the office and, with that, went any connection to Mary whatsoever. Walking out of a deli with a loaf of bread cradled in his arm, on his way home from the office, he felt a tug at his elbow. He stopped and turned, half-expecting to see a bum wanting a little change.

"Joe Hauser!" Shirley's beaming face met him.

"Shirley," he said. "I haven't seen Abe in forever. How are you guys?"

They stood there in the light drizzle, exchanging small talk about their lives. It amazed Joe how little could happen in a year. Just when Joe was ready to bring the conversation to an end and head home to start his dinner, Shirley turned serious and asked, "Did you hear about Mary Tanner?"

"No. I haven't seen her since that date Abe hooked us up on. How is she?"

"I guess you *haven't* heard. Mary's dead."

"Oh my God. How did that happen?"

"I just heard about it this morning. I don't know if anybody *really* knows what happened. They think she was murdered. Her neighbors in the apartment called the police about sounds of a struggle. The police searched her apartment and, well, there was blood everywhere, but Mary wasn't there."

"Jeez, that's a shame." Joe hated that kind of thing. It had the ability to throw a pall over his entire day. He was beginning to resent Shirley for even bringing it up.

"I'll say it's a shame. I tell you, if they ever catch whoever did that I think he should be tried for double homicide."

"Why's that?"

"Oh, I guess you really hadn't heard about Mary in a while, had you? She was pregnant."

Memories of that night came thudding back to Joe, a flash here, a flash there. *The spot.* He suddenly felt sick.

"That certainly is a tragedy." Joe tried to keep his voice steady. "Listen, if you hear anything more about it, I'd like to know."

"I imagine it'll be all over the papers soon enough."

"I guess so." Joe leaned in and hugged Shirley. "Give my best to Abe. It was nice seeing you."

Shirley returned to her former beaming self. "You need to stop being a stranger, Joe. Come up to the house sometime."

"I'd like that," Joe said, turning to walk home to his apartment.

3.

Joe went home and found himself anxious. He funneled his attentions into an elaborate dinner. It wasn't until it was almost finished that he realized he didn't want to eat alone. He went to the phone and called Melissa, who said she would be right over. Joe had not planned on calling Melissa. They had gone out for a few months and she still refused to do more than kiss him goodnight. After leaving her apartment on their last date, Joe found a hooker and sought relief from her. He decided the relationship between him and Melissa was not necessarily a healthy one. But tonight he needed company.

It didn't take her long to get there. They ate dinner in virtual silence and slowly sipped some wine afterward.

"Thank you. That was delicious," Melissa said.

Afraid she was preparing to leave, Joe quickly spat out, "You want to watch a movie?"

"I guess I could stick around. What did you have in mind?"

"You pick."

Together, they went into the living room and Melissa browsed through his collection while he paced around the buffed oak floor.

"You seem agitated. Is something the matter?" she asked, tilted sideways to stare at the movies on his bookshelf.

"No. Well, kind of, I guess. Somebody I know, really more of an acquaintance, died last night."

"That's terrible. You want to talk about it?"

"No. Not really. I really need something to take my mind off of it."

"I'll make sure to pick a comedy."

She brought the DVD over and they sat on the couch, Melissa leaning into him. Joe watched the movie a lot more intently than he probably should have, running his hands through Melissa's dark hair, forcing himself to laugh at parts he thought were supposed to be funny. It wasn't long before she was asleep. Maybe the wine went to her head, Joe thought. He dozed off not too long after thinking that, leaning awkwardly against the arm of his couch.

They both woke up to someone beating on the door.

"Uh, someone's knocking on your door," Melissa said groggily.

"Sounds a little more brutal than knocking," Joe said.

"See who it is. I was getting ready to go, anyway."

Joe didn't want to go to the door. He didn't know why. It was probably just the crazy lady with all the cats from the floor below who wanted to yell at him for having his music up too loud last Tuesday. Surely, he didn't have anything to worry about. Maybe his run-in with Shirley had sparked an impromptu visit from Abe.

The pounding continued as Melissa went into the kitchen to get her coat and purse. When she came back into the living room, Joe was still standing there, staring at the door as it visibly vibrated.

"Come on, open it," Melissa said. "I need to go."

And then the door exploded inward, breaking in half, showering Melissa and Joe in splinters.

"Oh my God!" Melissa screamed.

Joe couldn't even muster a scream. He had expected something, true. He couldn't say what but whatever it was was completely overshadowed by the thing standing in the doorway.

It was the spot, grown to hideous proportions, glistening a

whitish-gray. But it wasn't just the spot. Around its waist, as though it had torn straight out of the womb, was Mary. Her middle swelled around the monstrous fetus-like thing's waist, her torso and head hanging down, back to the floor, her eyes milked over, her death-mouth a twisted rictus.

"What is it, Joe?" Melissa asked, grabbing his arms, expecting him to defend her.

The thing continued to move in toward them. Joe grabbed Melissa and pushed her toward the kitchen, not really feeling like they would be much safer in there but at least there were sharp implements, something to defend themselves with. Once in the kitchen, Melissa scrambled toward the phone. Before she could even press the first number, the thing screamed into the kitchen and launched itself at her. Melissa let go a blood-curdling scream that quickly came to a stop. With shaking hands, Joe finished selecting a knife and turned to see the phone sticking out of Melissa's eye socket, a pinkish-gray glop hanging from the antenna that protruded out the back of her skull.

He sprinted out of the kitchen, trying to make it into the hallway. The spot was too fast for him. It pounced on him at the doorway, crushing him under its weight, the back of Mary's head bashing the front of Joe's face hard enough to draw blood. He tried to stab at the thing, but his arms were pinned. Crazily, he thought of that Monty Python movie where Michael Palin sings about every sperm being sacred while his army of children dance and sing around him. He wanted to say something to it. Something that might stop it from ending his life but he couldn't think of anything.

What Joe felt next wasn't death. He felt something snaking up his penis and moving around in his lower stomach. He felt a sickening movement down there, like things were being rearranged. All the while, around the head of Mary, Joe watched as the faceless thing stared at him with dim concentration or what Joe thought passed as concentration on that slick, gelatinous caul. Joe felt the thing withdraw from inside him. The spot picked him up and threw him across his apartment, where he crashed into his bookcase and slid into unconsciousness.

4.

Months later, Joe sat on the edge of a bathtub with a razor in his hand. He knew that, in order to do it right, you had to draw it verti-cally along the veins, really lay them open. His suicide thoughts were based on crazy logic, but nothing else had made sense since that night. There were the police asking about Melissa. There was this hospital where they lobotomized people with drugs. And then there were other things—the morning sickness, the cramping. This morn-ing, Joe was pretty sure he'd felt something move somewhere just below his stomach and when he looked down, he could see the small rounded dome his belly had become. He thought about removing it and realized he couldn't knowingly unleash something like that upon the world. He imagined it slithering up out of the trashcan, ready to destroy anything in its path. He had raided the nurse's station this morning and taken what he felt was an ample amount of pills. Now, with the drugs already dulling his senses he watched as if from some-place else as he drew the blade along his arm from wrist to crook, watching the wound blossom like a long pair of bloody lips.

As he lost consciousness, he felt the thing within him struggle. And, he would never really be sure, but he thought he felt it tearing at the inside of his skin . . . maybe even breaking free.

KING CREEP

1.

HE **FOUND IT** best if he thought of himself as his stage persona—Slade Kontrol. Only there wasn't really a stage. Just a couch in the middle of his mostly bare living room, a girl who was barely of legal age (he had a photocopy of her driver's license and social security card) sitting in the middle of the couch, one huge black guy to her left massaging himself through his tight jeans, a large white guy to her right massaging himself through his basketball shorts, and himself, standing behind a camera on a tripod. Currently the only thing in the frame of the camera was the girl—Sierra Leone. He wondered if she knew where Sierra Leone was. He wondered if she even knew it was a country. Young, natural, pretty, wearing a pair of black yoga pants and a sleeveless t-shirt. She didn't look like a porn star. Really, at his level, there were no porn stars. This amounted to, essentially, filmed prostitution. Some girls he'd filmed had taken the leap out to California and made something of a name for themselves, but most of them were lazy and poor or they wouldn't need the money in the first place and most of them had a laundry list of things they wouldn't do, although that often relaxed depending on how high or drunk they were. This one had specifically said no anal, no choking, and they could come anywhere but inside of her. In Slade's experience, this usually meant they had a boyfriend who would want to fuck them later and didn't know how they made their money. It was an interesting moral code. The girl had no problems with him and his two actors fucking her senseless for an hour

352

or so but the thought of her boyfriend fucking through another man's come would just be too humiliating for him.

"What's your name?" he started the only thing close to a script. He had it dedicated to memory, pretty much.

"Sierra Leone." She smiled but still looked nervous.

"How old are you, Sierra?"

"I just turned eighteen."

"Great. Now you can buy cigarettes, pornography, and join the army. How many guys have you had sex with?"

She held up two fingers.

"How old were you when you had sex for the first time?"

"Thirteen."

"How old was your boyfriend?"

"Well, he wasn't my boyfriend. Just some guy. He was probably sixteen or seventeen."

"Do you have a boyfriend now?"

She nodded slowly.

"Does he know you're doing this?"

She shook her head.

"Do you think you'll fuck him later?"

"I'm going to tell him I don't feel like it, but he'll probably want to anyway."

"So why are you here?"

She'd been told not to say anything about money or drugs. Some of them did, but he just edited that out.

"It seemed like fun."

"Have you ever had more than one guy at a time before?"

She shook her head. "I've always wanted to but doing it with guys I knew seemed strange, you know? Like I'm pretty sure it would change things or they'd talk about me or something, you know?"

"Some people might see this."

She shrugged.

He told most of the girls he didn't advertise in their home state and a surprising amount of them believed him. Like he could even really control that. He felt like they probably knew what the internet was and were just in some kind of denial. In actuality, phase one of the advertising campaign (besides uploading a two minute clip to every free service on the web) was to send emails to accounts registered in the closest proximities to this zip code with: OMG! DO YOU KNOW THIS GIRL! in the subject line and a very clear picture of the actress' face in the body with a link to the two minute clip.

Slade continued to walk through the script. He didn't feel bad about what he did. It was legal, these girls were adults, and he never forced them to make this decision. He placed an ad as a modeling agency, they responded via email with some usually very deceptive photos attached. He wasn't that into fat girls so he just never responded to those emails. If he responded it was to make an appointment for them to come to the house. He didn't live here. He lived in a much nicer house in town. If they showed up and they were too fat or ugly to film, he asked them a few questions about their modeling experience and told them they weren't what he was looking for or, if they seemed especially delicate, that they just didn't have enough experience. If they were someone he wanted to film, he explained to them what they would be doing and, if possible, began filming within the next few minutes. A lot of girls said they needed time to think about it and left even after he offered to pay them a lot more and tried his best coercion tactics. A few of those girls got back with him but most did not. If they were up to it, they had either come in expecting what they were "auditioning" for or were up for just about anything all the time. Usually because they needed money. Probably because they had a drug habit. They were the party girls. He wasn't really sure about Sierra. Probably just bored.

"Okay, Sierra, stand up and let's get a good look at you."

She stood up. The camera ran up and down her body.

"Turn around."

She turned around. The camera focused on her ass.

"Okay. Now do you mind getting down on your knees and sucking my cock?"

She stared into the camera before looking away.

Someone was knocking on the door. It was typically Slade's policy not to answer it. He was always afraid of opening the door to find some murderously jealous redneck boyfriend standing there with a shotgun.

This girl paid more attention to it than most. Maybe *she* was afraid it was her boyfriend.

Slade rarely shut the camera off. There had been a couple of girls who'd freaked out during filming. One had complained that the guy was too big and had started, literally, crying "Rape!" Slade turned off the camera, calmed her down, let her smoke some heroin, and finished the scene with about a half a tube of lube. Thank god that shit was a write off. The other girl he'd suspected was crazy and kept yelling lies about how he'd gotten her here. But, with the rise of YouTube and some non-pornographic clips going viral in a mainstream sort of way and gaining sponsorship, Slade always thought it best to keep the camera running. As long as there wasn't anything legally damning to him.

"Do you know who that might be?"

She shook her head.

"Are you sure you didn't tell your boyfriend you were here?"

"No. Why would I do that? Everyone knows what you do in this house."

This was, actually, somewhat of a shock to Slade. He supposed it was inevitable that people in a small town would talk, but he assumed the nature of what he did would be too embarrassing for anyone to substantiate with firsthand knowledge.

"Do you want to answer the door, Sierra?"

"Were you just going to let them keep knocking?"

"Well . . . yeah."

"I can get it, I guess."

"Dude, I gotta split in, like, an hour," Black Brian said.

That was actually his two actors' "thing." Most of the time they were billed as "The Brothers Brian." They clearly were not brothers. They were, respectively, Black Brian and White Brian. They even had matching tattoos—the yin and yang symbol except, yes, with a black penis and a white penis. The adult film industry was not known for political correctness.

"I'm sure it's nothing," Slade said.

Sierra was already headed for the door off the carport. It was not, technically, the front door but since it was the one that usually had the outside light on beside it, it was the one people usually came to.

"You care if we step out and smoke?" White Brian asked.

"Just a cigarette?" Slade said.

"Yeah, man."

"Whatever."

Slade found that when some guys smoked pot it made them soft and he usually had to edit out fifteen minutes of them viciously jerking off before launching the money shot. The Brothers Brian were both so huge it looked like they rarely achieved full erections anyway. Slade didn't want to play with fire.

The Brians went out to the wonky back patio through the door in the living room.

The door to the carport was mostly glass so there wasn't any need for a peephole.

Before Sierra could open the door, Slade said, "Wait a minute."

This guy looked weird. He was bald but a lot of guys were. Maybe the harsh fluorescent from the porch light made him look paler than he actually was. But it wasn't just the washed out, almost bleached pallor of his skin. He had no eyebrows. And Slade thought that if he were to be standing closer to him, he probably wouldn't find any eyelashes either.

He stood there, dressed like a middle-age dad or a guy on vacation, staring blankly at the door. He methodically raised his right hand and knocked.

"Can I help you?" Slade called through the door.

The man quit knocking and stared intently at the door. Slade wasn't sure how well he could see inside. Slade checked the camera and made sure everything was still focused and in frame.

"I need . . . help. There's been an accident."

"Have you called someone?" Slade asked. He was getting some kind of weird, bad vibe coming off this guy.

The man continued to stand in that odd way and stare at the door. Slade looked through the camera and zoomed it forward a little to see if he could maybe get a better look at this guy without actually opening the door. The man stared straight into the camera.

"Please. I need . . . help. There's been an accident."

"Go ahead and open the door," he told Sierra.

It took him only a couple of seconds to process the reasons for doing this. First, there was always a need to catch something interesting on camera. Now that he had the chance to do that, he wasn't going to send the guy away because he didn't want to deal with him. And the man didn't look dangerous. He wasn't holding a gun or any other type of weapon. He was fairly slight of build and seemed genuinely dazed. Also, this guy was only one man while Slade was surrounded by three people, two of which were about the size of small cars.

The man stumbled past them, into the kitchen, on his way to the living room, almost like he knew where he was going.

"I just . . . I really need to sit down."

The man headed for the couch.

"Call 911," Slade said to Sierra.

She walked over to the couch, Slade focusing the camera on her ass as she reached down and fished her phone from her purse. He noticed she wore black underwear. He was already lamenting the fact that he might not get to see her out of those underwear.

There was a bright flash from outside. Like *really* bright.

It didn't help that the wall facing the backyard was almost all glass. There was a second where everything in the room was almost like an x-ray. He put the camera down and tried to blink away the black spots.

"What the fuck was that?" Sierra said.

"I don't know."

The man on the couch stared forward and blinked.

"You guys see that?" Slade called to the Brians through the screen door.

"Fuck yeah, man!" Black Brian called.

"You hear anything?" Slade asked.

"Nah, dude. Just that light."

Sierra scowled down at her phone.

"The battery's dead," she said.

Slade was momentarily excited. He thought maybe they had just witnessed something special and wondered if he'd managed to capture it on his camera. But his hopes sank before he could even focus on the viewfinder. The camera was dead.

"Fuck," he mumbled.

He set the camera on the TV stand behind him and pulled out his phone.

It was dead too.

"Hey!" he called through the screen door. "Either of your phones work!"

"Nah, man!" Black Brian said.

"Fuck!" White Brian called. Slade assumed that meant his wasn't working either.

"Shit," he said.

Sierra stood there looking nervous.

"I don't think I wanna do this anymore," she said.

"We need to get help, I think," Slade said. "Can you go knock on a neighbor's door or drive to the police station or something?"

"I think I just want to go home."

She bent to grab her bag and began walking to the front door.

Slade didn't really want her to leave but he didn't really know what to say and he was too distracted by the guy on the couch to think of anything. He guessed he could tell her not to bother contacting him the next time she needed money but, for what he was paying her and for what she would be doing, that didn't really make a lot of sense. He found himself staring at her very nice ass as she walked into the dining room, saying nothing. She left in that silent way and it seemed to plunge the house into a vacuum.

The Brothers Brian were still outside.

How long had it been since they'd opened the door for this man?

Probably only a couple of minutes but it felt much longer.

"I . . . I really need help," the man said.

He wasn't bleeding and it didn't look like there was anything outwardly wrong with him. Slade wondered if he'd been sent here strictly to fuck up his night.

"Hold on," he said. "We'll get you some help."

Just when he thought about running to the neighbor's house—a fairly good jaunt—it occurred to him that he could try plugging his phone in. He didn't know what would suck the life from every battery in the house, but it might have affected the neighbors too. He went into the bedroom and grabbed the charging cable for his phone. If this didn't work, it would probably be easier to get in the car and drive to the police station. That would only take around five minutes. Whatever was wrong with this guy, he didn't want him dying in the house.

2.

Alopecia universalis was the diagnosis Dr. Benway had given Alexander Lords' mother. Complete loss of body hair. It had happened overnight. He was twelve at the time. Now while most boys were talking wonderingly about their burgeoning pubic hair, Alexander was left to inspect himself from head to toe, hoping it would come back. It felt like some kind of outward stigma to what had happened that night, not that he felt it was anything to be ashamed of. So maybe stigma wasn't the right word. Maybe it was more of a trade off.

He wouldn't have kept it a secret if his mother hadn't told him to.

He'd finished watching *Blossom* and gone to bed. To him, and especially in retrospect, it seemed like one of the strangest shows on television. Something that had to be some kind of vehicle for a particularly nepotistic Hollywood family. He appreciated the character of Blossom. She was ugly by Hollywood standards, he guessed, but it was never really mentioned. Anything else and she would have been cast specifically as the ugly friend. Her friend on the show, Six, Alexander found oddly alluring. When he thought about her in later years, he remembered her as almost a midget and wasn't really sure why. Despite his curiosity, he could never bring himself to go back and watch it. It was probably her forehead, which had become enormous in his memory. There was Blossom's brother, Joey Lawrence. Alexander couldn't recall what his name had been on the show. He thought it was Joey but that didn't seem right. He wore a lot of clothes and was really cool. He had a lot of floppy, feathered hair that Alexander aspired to. This would later leave him feeling much animosity. Enough to where he'd apparently blocked out almost every scene Joey Lawrence was in. The most intriguing character for Alexander was the father of the family, played by Ted Wass. The supposed premise of the show was a bedraggled middle-aged dad was forced to raise his tough guy loose cannon son and ugly daughter by himself, while his daughter's big-headed midget friend came to hang out. Alexander couldn't remember if the mother had run off or died. He was pretty sure she had died. The intriguing thing to Alexander was that Ted Wass seemed supremely miscast as a TV dad. He looked sinister, evil. Like he should be playing a crime boss in a daytime soap opera. Or even a thug in a horror or crime movie. Almost anything except a single dad. But maybe it was the Cosby effect. The theory that you could soften anyone by throwing a sweater on him. This inevitably led Alexander to think that Ted Wass was *not* a good father and the real story, *Blossom*'s real narrative, was what happened when the camera wasn't running. This was what Alexander thought about as he lay in bed the night he was abducted by aliens and lost all his hair.

It was exactly as dramatic as the few abduction stories he'd heard up to that point and all the ones he would hear afterward. This was at least a couple of years before *The X Files*, but he would later watch that show with the intensity most adolescent boys reserved for sports and pornography.

He lay in bed thinking of Ted Wass as an abusive father and suddenly his room was filled with a white-bluish light. His mother rented the house from an old college friend and loved the town. The only thing Alexander really liked was the bookstore. He was more of an indoor kid.

He felt the odd sensation of leaving his body. He'd had a spinal tap once and there had been a queasy type of pressure that had felt almost like it came from *inside* his body. This was a lot like that, except it was all over rather than concentrated in one area of his lower back. He tried to scream but it felt muffled or . . . or like he lacked the physical ability to scream. Like that ability was left with his physical body that he was sucked out of and raced increasingly far from. He was a relatively anxious, panicky kid, but found that as he drew farther from his body a great sense of peace and calm began to envelop him. Where he went was mostly indescribable. He was aware of shapes around him and, maybe, they were roughly what the general descriptions of aliens were. But there was no real concrete sense of place. He couldn't remember any rooms or buildings or trees or landmarks or structures of any kind. It was like visiting a feeling. There were some colors he could recall—pinks and blues and glowing soft whites—but they were all fuzzy and throbbing, gaining and lessening in intensity almost like those cheap fiber optic things that had once been all the rage. It was like being surrounded by calm and peacefulness and tranquility with a deep eroticism humming just below the surface. This was the first time Alexander had felt this particular sensation. Of course he was as aware of his penis as most adolescent boys but he had not yet masturbated and was not aware of the feelings his sexual organs could produce. So this was all new. His penis was so hard it was nearly painful. It was like every surface of his skin was being touched sensuously at the same time. He was even aware of something moving into his anus, which he knew he wasn't supposed to like but kind of did. Of course all of this was an abstraction. He knew his eyes were open because he could see the shapes and colors but when he tried to train them on his body he was only aware that there was something that lacked specificity in its place. This was what he would later think of as his spirit body. After being there for what couldn't have been more than a few minutes, he didn't want to be anywhere else. And it continued for what felt like a very long time. That feeling in his groin would reach some pinnacle of pleasure—what he later learned was called an orgasm— and remain at that heightened level the entire time.

There wasn't an abrupt departure. He gradually became aware of leaving that place. It was like his spirit body, his alien body, had been almost large enough to encompass the whole earth and gradually shrunk into the little boy lying in his bed in Twin Springs.

He stared at his ceiling.

It felt like the life had been sucked out of the room.

He expected his mother to come rushing in or for there to be a whole fleet of emergency vehicles waiting for him. How long had he been away? It felt like he'd aged years or like he'd gained years of experience.

He looked at his clock. It was a wind-up alarm clock that read 10:04.

Later it would occur to him that, were it digital, it would have probably just flashed 12:00 at him and if it had run off a battery it probably would have been completely dead.

When he woke up the next morning, all of his body hair was gone. His mother was the first to discover this and began screaming hysterically. Alexander told her about the aliens and the only time she almost believed him was as she marveled over the absence of shed hairs in his bed.

The loss of hair bothered Alexander but, even at that young age, he understood a sacrifice had to be made.

He didn't go to school that day.

His mother had made an appointment with Dr. Benway, who'd asked him a lot of questions and provided not a lot of answers. His mother was with him the entire time. He told Dr. Benway about the aliens. His mother asked the doctor if he thought Alexander had been molested. Benway said he could examine Alexander for that too, and made Alexander spread his butt cheeks so he could peer at his anus. Alexander said nobody had touched him in that way because he'd already told them about the aliens. He hadn't told them the way it made his penis feel because he thought that was private. Benway told Alexander that if he kept talking about aliens, he could make an appointment with a child psychiatrist. The only person Alexander knew who saw a child psychiatrist was Chad Hanger and he chewed on girls' hair and occasionally shit himself in class. Alexander decided to stop talking about aliens, but that didn't stop him from reading and watching everything about them he could get his hands on. His mother probably saw this as further proof he'd made the whole thing up, even though he had not been remotely interested in aliens before the abduction.

The aliens did not contact him again until he was twenty-four, a fairly recent graduate of Ohio State University, and working as a data entry specialist at a major health insurance company in Dayton.

He had to find a child and take it to the woods behind that old house his mom had rented for probably only a year back in the nineties. Of course Alexander knew exactly where the house was. That was where *it* had happened in the first place. Ever since getting his driver's license, he'd driven by it several times. He knew it was the aliens telling him to do this because it was an *alien* thought. One he'd never had before. He knew he was attracted to young boys sexually, although this was something he'd never acted on. He had simply resolved not to put himself around them. Oh, there was a time when he'd considered entering the priesthood to gain unlimited access but, in the end, he knew it was wrong, could see it being a potential problem, and resolved to stay away. He even had every intention of becoming a middle school science teacher when he started college. He had convinced himself he just wanted to teach kids about the stars but, before so much as even shadowing a teacher in a local middle school, he had become aware of the real reason and promptly switched his major to a degree in general science. That was something he was genuinely interested in. He found himself working where he did because he needed a job and they were looking for someone with a degree, any degree, it didn't matter.

The alien thoughts did not announce themselves as perfectly formed things. He did not hear a loud voice in his head saying: ALEXANDER, YOU NEED TO ABDUCT A CHILD. No. It was a revelation he usually stumbled upon after some kind of intuition. Once he did stumble upon it—and this had, thus far, been the most potentially life-altering one—they were impossible to shake. The communications became immediate obsessions. When he received this particular one, he remembered exactly what he was doing. He sat at his desk in the huge open office on the second floor, gazing toward Angela Bent's desk. It was a Friday afternoon, not long before they'd be walking out for the weekend. Three of their coworkers were gathered around her desk. Alexander got it. Angela was what these guys found attractive. Therefore, he should have probably found her attractive, as well. But he didn't. He'd never met a man or a woman he had been attracted to. Well, not since he'd been about twelve. That he was still attracted to people that age—particularly boys but a few tomboyish girls as well—didn't strike him as particularly mysterious. Psychologically, he'd never really gone through the full rite of puberty. He'd never graduated to the next level, so to speak.

He went back to entering data from the sheets before him when that intuition became crystal clear.

Really? I need to find a child and take it to the woods behind 523 Glowers Pike?

Yes. That was what he needed to do. He would have to figure out the specifics. He would have to figure out if this was even in his moral universe. There was no real timeline. No rush. The aliens' sense of time was not like his.

Nevertheless, he found himself eager to get started.

He left work and sat around his tiny apartment that weekend mostly figuring out ways to abduct his first child. He couldn't write anything down. He realized there would be *very serious* consequences if he was ever caught and the worst thing in the world would be to create any sort of paper or data trail. This was much the same reason he'd never so much as viewed what was popularly called child pornography. The closest he'd come were some art books he'd found in a bookstore two cities away. There was no way he would buy them or even steal them. He had taken them into the restroom, even though a posted sign had expressly forbid it. In a stall he had perused the books and, yes, shamefully, he'd ended up masturbating. It did not take long. It never did. Even when the only thing he had was mental porn conjured from his memories of the couple times he'd had to shower with the boys at gym class and the one summer he'd gone to camp.

The first and most obvious question was where he was going to get this child. The farther away, the better. But it couldn't be so far away that he couldn't return home to his apartment. He wouldn't want his neighbors to notice his absence.

He would probably need to cull them from lower middle class or lower class neighborhoods. This wouldn't be a problem. Those types of people tended to breed more than the others and their parents were often more inattentive and the areas underpoliced. He would want to be as far away from the scene of the abduction as possible before anyone even noticed the child's absence.

His was pretty much a blank slate. His body type was average in every way. As long as he properly disguised himself he didn't think being seen was a big problem.

He decided he would have to try to fit in at work more, so he didn't fit the spot-on profile of a serial killer or child abductor. Maybe he would go to the mixer. Occasionally, the girls in the office had invited him along on their nights out, probably because they felt sorry for him or thought he was gay. He resolved to go the next time he was asked. Maybe he should tell them he *was* gay. Maybe that would go a little toward explaining some obvious gaps he'd have when talking about his personal life.

There were some questions for the aliens and he asked them, waiting for them to emit a response. While he was eager to get started, he didn't want to be too hasty. He had to know what he was doing. He had to know what he could expect to get out of this.

The questions were asked and the answers were given in the coming weeks.

How often would he be expected to do this?

It was hard to say. It would depend on need and transportation. Alexander's earth was not always open to these beings. He would be given advance notice and the beings would appropriately coordinate their arrival.

Would the children have to be alive?

That was not really an issue. As long as there wasn't significant deterioration of the tissue, the beings would be able to use them.

Why did they want children?

Research.

Male or female?

It didn't matter. Preferably both so they could study reproduction and the differences in the sexes.

Would Alexander ever see them again?

Possibly. If he did what the beings asked, and did a good job, there may be a special place reserved for him.

Would there be any bodies? Any evidence to cover up?

They would take care of that.

What if he got caught?

That was outside their capabilities of control. He should take every precaution.

On June 1st of that year, Alexander abducted a boy named Max Hamlisch from a small rural town just north of Columbus. The boy was walking his dog along a road just before sundown. Alexander bashed the dog's head in with a tire iron, snapped the boy's neck, and tossed him in the trunk of his car. In the woods behind the house in Twin Springs, he stripped the boy naked, violated his corpse, put the boy's clothes back on, and left the body there. Alexander didn't hear anything about it.

The next month he took a boy from a Pittsburgh suburb.

Over the next six years, there would be 43 more children. If he should ever want to abuse their bodies for too long, there was always the voice of the beings reminding him what a valuable asset he was to them. There was also the fear of recrimination and punishment. Although the more he got away with it, the more invincible Alexander felt. Most of them were boys. A few of them were girls. They were all between the ages of ten and twelve.

With the exception of one boy getting away, everything had gone off without a hitch until that night, exactly seven years later, when he left a dead boy in the woods, swerved to avoid a deer standing in the middle of the road, and lost control of his car.

He emerged from the car without really thinking. He could walk fine. He gave himself a pat down and didn't seem to be bleeding from anywhere. He felt more like he was in a daze, almost like he was outside of himself. He staggered to the house he remembered from his childhood. It was the place he'd been in least of all, and yet it was the one most seared into his memory. There had been the house where he'd lived with his mother and father. Then his father had run off and he and his mother had moved to this house in Twin Springs where they lived for no more than a year. Then, probably because of the troubles his mother was having with him, they'd gone to live with his grandparents in Glowers Hook.

Alexander approached the door to the house and everything went kind of blank for a while.

He was pretty sure he needed help.

He hoped these people could help him.

Shortly after entering the house there was a bright flash of light that seemed to simultaneously suck everything out of the air while also infusing it with some form of wild energy. That would be the aliens, he thought, coming to claim their human child.

3.

The man continued to sit on the couch, his hands resting on his knees, staring straight ahead at the dead television. His lips were moving but nothing was coming out of his mouth. Thinking he was trying to talk, Slade asked, "Huh?" the first couple of times. The Brothers Brian had quieted down on the patio.

Slade crouched by the wall outlet. Sometimes when the battery ran out completely, it took the phone a couple of minutes to come to life again even when connected to the wall. Since the lights to the house were still on (maybe there had been a brief flicker) he didn't see any reason why this shouldn't work. Unless everything was fried. That would suck hugely. He wondered if he could get renter's insurance to cover something like that. If it worked, that would be great. That meant he could get his camera running and at least record a few minutes of this weird guy. He thought it could be the beginning of one of those documentaries that said as much about the director as it did the subject. Start with this weird, pale, hairless guy sitting on his couch mumbling and work backward from there. Why was he here? Where had he been going? Why was he hairless? The reasons were probably mundane, but it was this beauty in mundaneness or in the quiet captured moments of great extraordinariness that seemed to resonate with indie audiences.

Slade glanced down at his phone. Still no sign of life.

He had not set out to make fuck videos. He wanted to make a living in the arts and this seemed to be the easiest way. He had grown up in the rural town of Glowers Hook, Ohio, and later enrolled in the film program at Wright State. He'd done well and his senior project was much lauded. His professor encouraged him to enroll it in some film festivals. On top of his already sizeable student loans he knew he was going to have to pay back some day, he had taken a bank loan to pay the entrance fees to all the festivals he was to enter it in. He did this for about a year, living with his parents and working on a feature-length script. The film was accepted into most of the festivals it was entered in. It was rejected from South by Southwest and Sundance, the two he was *really* hoping it would be accepted into. Being accepted into either of those would have probably gained him more exposure than winning a grand prize at all the other ones combined. It did take the grand prize at a small festival in Tukwila, Washington, and a "silver" prize at a festival in East Lansing, Michigan. He hadn't attended either of them and was surprised at the film's success. Both of them awarded modest prize money that amounted to only about three times the entrance fee. He was still in touch with his university professor and asked him for advice. Well, his professor said, if he was really serious about filmmaking, he'd need to move out to LA. So Slade took what was left of the loan and his prize money and moved to LA, where he shared an apartment with three other forgettable film school graduates. He shopped his script around to agents and tried to get a distribution deal for his student film. He was met with rejection for the following year. Finally he said fuck it and uploaded his film to YouTube while continuing to shop his wares. It sat there for a year where he obsessively checked its view count. It never got above 400. One night, he drunkenly made a POV film of himself fucking his girlfriend at the time and uploaded it to a porn site. By the end of the week it had over 400,000 views on that site alone. He was pretty sure it had spread itself around to other sites too. His face wasn't in it. His girlfriend wasn't as upset as he thought she would be. She left him and accepted the many, many offers that came her way. He shifted focus. Hired people to design and manage a website. Ultimately he left LA because he realized he could do the same thing back home for a fraction of the price. The women in LA wanted too much money and a lot of them thought it was a stepping stone to some fabulous career. He couldn't afford to pay them and he couldn't afford to keep paying his lawyers to fend off their lawyers. Back in Ohio, there was still enough shame attached to it that he hadn't been sued once in the three years he'd been doing this. And girls worked for about a fourth the price plus drugs. Drugs had been somewhat of a given in LA too. But even their drugs were more expensive. In Twin Springs, he could get a girl high on pot, film an hour long video where he fucked the girl in the ass and finished in her mouth, send her away with a couple hundred bucks and they felt like they'd won the lottery and were now definitely the hippest one amongst all their friends and might even get famous to boot. That video, through advertiser revenue, would earn him around 20,000 dollars, of which he would retain around sixty percent. Not bad. You just had to watch out for their boyfriends. That never happened in LA. The guys just didn't care and, if they wanted to, the girls probably wouldn't let them.

Of course, he wouldn't have to worry about any of that if all of his fucking equipment was fried.

His phone still had not blinked to life and the man on the couch was now not just moving his lips but whispering.

Slade couldn't make out any of the words.

It almost sounded like he was chanting but there was a nearly electronic sound coming from his mouth.

Still nothing from his phone.

Slade was not an overly superstitious person, but he thought maybe if he just walked away from it, it would happen. Plus he needed to get away from that sound.

He walked to the carport door and glanced out.

Sierra's car was still out there.

Of course it was. The battery was probably dead.

He considered going out to check on her and then thought, *Fuck it.*

He stood in the doorway and watched the man on the couch. He considered telling him to keep it down, the chanting had grown so loud. What had gone from being an inconvenience to a major pain in the ass was now quickly escalating into a situation that was starting to creep him out.

Obviously there was something off about the guy. Something that went beyond shock. Besides that, though . . . there was something *familiar* about this guy. At first he'd thought it was perhaps the most notable thing—the complete absence of hair. But Slade knew he'd never met anyone with that . . . was it a condition or a preference? He didn't know. Then he thought maybe it was the blank expression in the eyes. And it *was* a familiar expression, but had nothing to do with the bearer. He'd filmed enough scenes with girls who'd had one, maybe two partners in her life before suddenly getting her ass fucked by the biggest cock she would ever see in person while simultaneously having another huge cock shoved down her throat. Yeah, some of them looked a little dazed and blank afterward. Especially when this went on past the point of pain or pleasure and into numb, grinding muscle movement.

He moved closer to the man. Maybe if he placed a gentle hand on him and calmly asked him to quiet down, the guy would stop.

Slade glanced at his phone on the floor as he crossed the room. Still nothing.

He would have to ask one of the Brians to go to the police station or sit here with the guy while he did. He was feeling so freaked out right now he almost wished they *would* refuse to go.

He crouched down in front of the stranger and put his hand on his knee.

"Sir?"

Those sounds continued to come from his mouth. Slade had almost grown used to them. It was almost like they *didn't* actually come from his mouth but were made somewhere in his head and poured from his nostrils.

From this lower angle, Slade noticed his nostrils for the first time. One was round. One was tear-shaped.

Just as it all came back to him, he heard White Brian say, "What the fuck!"

Slade turned to look out the window to the backyard and saw them.

4.

That morning, it was like an alarm had gone off in William Tanner's head. William was twelve. He sometimes had weird thoughts but never with as much clarity as he had this one. It was like, for whatever question he had for the voice, the answer immediately waited for him.

What about Mom?
She will understand.
How will I find this place?
You'll just know.
How long will it take?
You will make it in time, if you leave now.

He pushed his chair back from the table and said to his mother, standing at the sink washing the waffle iron, "I have to go."

She turned, looking vaguely startled. "Where do you have to go? Nothing's open."

"I have to go," he repeated. Only this time it sounded like other sounds came out as well. It sounded a lot like the sounds that sometimes went with his weird thoughts.

His mother's expression changed. From that wide-eyed, startled look to something like resigned horror.

He got his bike out of the garage, hopped on, and rode it to Twin Springs, Ohio.

Chris Hizer didn't bother telling his mom he was leaving. This was a couple days before William left. Chris lived in Colorado and the only mode of transportation he had was a skateboard. It was going to take a while.

When darkness came to the Hizer household, it was his stepfather who finally said he was getting worried.

"I'm sure he'll be okay," his mother said.

His stepdad protested before finally acquiescing. He never really liked Chris anyway. He was creepy. One of the creepiest eleven-year-olds he'd ever met.

Penny Mugwump didn't need to tell her mother she was leaving. She no longer had one. Penny was going to tell her. She went into her mother's bedroom to tell her but she couldn't get her to wake up. Penny thought about calling 911 but the voice in her head told her she didn't really have time to do that, plus she'd have to answer a lot of questions. Not that Penny had anything to do with her mother's death. Nor did she know what heroin was. Her mother called it her medicine and said she needed it to relax. Most of the time her mother's medicine used to involve taking a pill or smoking out of a little pipe. This seemed to involve a lot more stuff.

Not that it really mattered now anyway.

Penny had a pretty strong feeling she wouldn't be coming back to her tiny house in Evanston, Illinois, anyway. She hopped on her tricycle—sadly, the only thing she had—and headed to Twin Springs, Ohio, a pretty good jaunt for a twelve-year-old girl with asthma.

5.

Slade had been eleven the last time he'd seen the man on the couch. He hadn't called himself Slade then. He was just Tyler Grimm, a small town kid with no hopes or ambitions. One ambition he knew he *didn't* have was to be kidnapped and raped by a pervert.

He'd been at the park playing baseball with his friends. This was in Glowers Hook, so the park was pretty much surrounded by woods. It would have been an ideal place for drug deals to go down, along with all kinds of other unsavory acts. But that was practically every park in this area and somehow the reputation had escaped this one. Pickle Park was what they called the one by the river where every alleged homosexual in the tri-state region met to do whatever faggots did. It would take Tyler a long time to stop thinking about them that way but that was pretty much the accepted terminology for that area of Ohio at that time.

They'd finished packing up their equipment and his friends had left him behind. Ben was already late and Layne always gave Tyler a hard time for being so slow. He would shout "Lollygagger!" and dart out of the house, often while Tyler was still tying his shoes.

He didn't think they would have left him if they'd seen the gray Honda parked in the small parking lot.

"Hey, kid!" a man called as he got out of the car.

Tyler hoisted his aluminum bat onto his shoulder, his glove looped over the knob at the end of the handle, and began walking toward the entrance of the park. He thought it was best if he pretended not to hear him.

"Kid, wait up!" the man called.

Tyler kept walking. But . . . there was something in his head telling him not to. It told him he should stop. It told him he should stop and do whatever this man wanted him to do.

But he knew this voice wasn't right.

What would Natalie think if something happened to him? She was his thirteen-year-old neighbor but she had finally let him do what he'd been begging to do for the past three months. It was every bit as good as he thought it would be, although he wasn't sure if she thought so or not. It hadn't taken very long and she had cried afterward. Nevertheless, she had a kind of power over him now.

Tyler walked faster.

He could hear the guy behind him.

"Hey, kid, wait up! I just want you to help me figure out where I'm at!"

The guy was now practically right behind him.

Maybe he wasn't a creep, Tyler thought, but wondered why he would try to get directions from a kid on a playground rather than in town or at a gas station.

Tyler stopped and turned around. Maybe the guy was legit. If he wanted to grab him, he was close enough to do so anyway. He would answer the guy's question but if he reached for him he was going to clobber him with the bat, which he now gripped very tightly.

The man stopped short.

"Thanks, little guy," he said. Tyler wasn't really that little.

Now, facing the man, he thought the guy looked weird. He had these different shaped nostrils but that wasn't the least of it. The man wore what had to be a wig under a hat that had a graphic of a police badge and the letters F.O.P. on it. And his eyebrows were clearly drawn on. And not well. It looked like whatever he'd used was already running down the man's face with his sweat.

So it's easy to wash off, Tyler thought just as the man reached out. He didn't know where that thought had come from.

Tyler didn't take the time to pull the bat back and administer a proper swing. He just rammed it forward into the guy's crotch and took off running in the opposite direction, yelling "Help!" the entire time.

It was a pretty rural area and when Tyler hit the road he was the only one on it. He heard the car crunch on the gravel of the park's lot, which meant the man was pulling out, and Tyler threw himself into the woods on his right. Under camouflage, he watched the road. He saw the front of the car pull out of the parking lot and head in the opposite direction.

Tyler sat down in the dirt, his heart hammering. He still felt uneasy but he also felt a sense of relief.

When he got home he told his mom about the encounter. She called the police and an officer came out to ask him questions and file a report. He felt nearly famous for a week or two. He also felt like the luckiest boy in the world.

Even though his mother had never mentioned his biological father, Tyler asked her, "Do you think that could have been my real dad, come back for me?"

She had rubbed his head and said she didn't think he'd ever see that guy again. He wasn't sure if she meant the creep or his dad who, he guessed, was also a creep. They probably weren't the same person. The truth, which she would never tell him but he somehow knew just by glancing into her eyes, was that she had no idea how she'd gotten pregnant. Someone would have had to have broken into her house, drugged her and raped her, all without her knowledge. She wasn't a slut. She didn't go to parties. She wasn't a virgin but it had been months since she'd had sex. She maybe remembered having morning sickness but didn't go to the doctor until her belly became distended and hard. She was afraid she had a tumor or some kind of intestinal disorder. The doctor informed her that she was probably seven months pregnant.

She told Tyler he would never see that guy again.

Now Tyler, who called himself Slade, thought his mother was wrong.

6.

"I'm not helping you," Slade said to the man.

The man's volume had increased. His eyes stared straight forward and looked filled with fear.

Slade still did not think of this man as his father. He thought of the creep who'd tried to do something to him when he was just a kid.

The light from outside was flashing, closer, making it hard to think. Shapes moved amidst the light. Maybe Sierra *had* gone to the police.

But why would they be coming through the woods?

Slade stood slowly, wanting away from the man. Now he *had* to go to the police. Who knew how many times the man in front of him had tried to do what he did to him. How many times had he been successful?

He went toward the patio door. He needed to tell the Brothers Brian to keep an eye out on this guy and to not let him leave under any circumstances.

He also needed to find out what that light was.

It was so intense it felt like it was burning a hole somewhere in his brain.

He opened the back door.

The Brothers Brian were in the chairs on the patio only . . . they had changed. Slade smelled burning. Their bodies were molten lumps, blood and unidentifiable ooze dripping from the straps of the chairs.

But Slade was having trouble making out anything.

That light. Flashing. And each flash seemed to be accompanied with some kind of heaviness that made him feel like collapsing.

But he had a sense of purpose.

He could not see into the light but, when he closed his eyes, he saw a lingering afterimage of shapes.

What the fuck was going on?

The light was so bright it illuminated the inside of the house so Slade was able to look in and see the strange man. He now stood in the middle of the living room, his arms raised to the ceiling and, even from outside, Slade could hear that alien chanting coming from him.

Slade didn't want to go back inside.

Fuck his phone. Fuck his camera. He didn't even care about

going to the police at this point. He ran around the west side of the house and stopped under the cover of the carport.

There were kids.

A lot of them.

Coming down the road in front of his house. There were at least 25 to 30 of them. They all looked young. Some of them were on bikes. Some of them were on skateboards. One had ridden a moped. Another a go-kart. One girl was on a tricycle that seemed way too small for her. Some of them were on foot. If they had one, they discarded their particular mode of transportation at the guardrail that ended Spring Street. They walked purposefully toward the house. Their eyes all shone with the blinding light that Slade now thought came from the sky. He staggered out of the carport and into the side yard. He didn't know if he was looking for an umbrella from all that glaring light or if he just wanted to be away from the house. What if whatever had happened to the Brothers Brian happened to him?

He heard sounds coming from the backyard, from the woods. It was the last earthly sound he heard.

More kids were coming from the woods. These had been the shapes he had seen. Now, as they moved closer to him, he could see their bodies glowing with the same light coming from the other kids' eyes.

Now he heard a sound like a low flying military carrier only a thousand times more intense.

The light was so bright everything looked flattened and bleached.

The children were joining hands around the house.

The house's windows shattered. Not hearing it, only seeing it, made Slade feel oddly disconnected.

Two children came toward him. One had the glowing eyes. The other had the glowing body. They held out their hands. Slade felt terrified but also strangely elated.

He let the children help him up. Their touch sent a strange current of calm through him. It was something he wasn't sure he'd ever felt before.

He joined the circle around the house.

The house was being flattened. It reminded Slade of a tornado but the pressure seemed super concentrated. Flattened and shredded, the house spiraled in the middle of their circle before being sucked up into the sky like some kind of demolished house soup.

The odd man stood in the middle of the circle, still shouting, his hands raised.

Slade felt like they were somehow helping this man and wanted to be away from the circle until—

7.

They were finally coming for him, Alexander thought.

The house was lifted away from him and he saw it disappear into the bright light. He saw all of his accomplishments, both past and future, surrounding him. All of his children, harvested from him that one night.

He felt those things reach into his head. He'd always remained open to them.

He knew he had been a sick man.

Sometimes he'd tried to convince himself they were the reason for this sickness.

What people saw as his sickness was really his earthly reward for doing their deeds. He wanted to shout at them he had taken what he deserved.

Before everything went black, he tried to recall what it had been like the last time. He'd never felt anything like it since, although he'd certainly tried. He closed his eyes and wished to go back.

8.

—the man's clothes were ripped from his body. His flesh was ripped away from the bone just as easily until he was only a skeleton and the skeleton became so much dust, invisible in all that bright light.

Slade couldn't think about anything over that deafening vacuum roar. It felt like the ground was lifting beneath his feet. Maybe he was going somewhere. He didn't want to go anywhere. He wanted to stay here. He wanted to suck everything he possibly could from life. But he couldn't move.

The circle rose toward that white light.

Suddenly everything was calm and peaceful.

Slade wondered if he would ever get used to it. He wondered if he could go back. There were colors and feelings but it all seemed too subtle and ethereal. He thought about flesh sliding against flesh. The sharp sting of pain. The explosions of pleasure. The lingering feeling in the soul of what it means to be in pain and what it means to hurt someone else.

That was what he wanted his life to be. A human life. In the midst of all that black sorrow there were pink explosions of joy and happiness. That was what he lived for.

He didn't know what this was.

He felt the alien sensation of something entering his head. It was like that voice he'd heard in the park that day. Uninvited. Unwanted. It felt . . . unedited was the only way he could think to describe it.

He had been the missing link in the circle. What would have happened to him if he'd stayed outside of it? Would he have died? Was *this* death?

He tried to quit thinking.

He tried to give himself to it.

But he just kept wondering if his world would ever come back to him.

BURY THE CHILDREN IN THE YARD

The Filthiest Thing He Had Ever Read

IT WAS THE filthiest thing he had ever read. Being an English professor, he'd read a lot. The students' final essays were a small stack on his desk. He had kept hers on top, reading it over and over. Now he moved it to the bottom of the stack and glanced up at the class. The room was too bright. The winter sky gray beyond the windows. Everyone in the room looked depressed. No one even paid attention to him. They just wanted to go home. All of their heads were bowed, texting, staring at whatever small screen they held in their hands. A few of them were hastily scrawling things or reading through some other text book. Probably preparing for another exam they were taking later in the day.

Except her. Ashley Burroughs. She stared right at him. He glanced back down at the stack of essays, caught his breath, pretended to scrawl something on one of them.

Her essay had come completely out of the blue. Even now, she sat in the middle of the class, wearing a skin tight white sweater, a plaid skirt, knee socks and, dear god, brown saddle shoes and pig tails. And she still managed to look innocent rather than trashy. Until last night, he had thought she was a post-secondary student. But he had looked her up in the student database. Nineteen. He couldn't believe he was thinking about going through with this.

Once he was sure his erection had subsided, he cleared his throat, took the essays in hand, and stood up.

"You're, um, free to go when you get your essay. And welcome to email me with any questions you might have."

He placed the essays on the students' desks. Most of them merely glanced at the final grade and either sighed with relief or grumbled with disappointment. Most of the grades were good to average. In the back left of the classroom sat Paul Skink. He had pulled a brilliant essay off the Internet and printed it out. Didn't bother typing it. Didn't bother reformatting it.

"Really, Paul . . . " He put the essay in front of the boy, an 'F' marked in red followed by a half-page diatribe. The kid guffawed, stood up, and walked slowly from the room.

Eventually, the only student left was Ashley. He had felt her eyes following him around the room. He wouldn't have thought anything of her essay if he hadn't been mentioned by name. Calling it an essay wasn't even accurate. It was really more like a pornographic story and again, if he, if they *both*, had not been mentioned by name, he would have just thought it was something written to grab attention with its offensive content. It was, however, remarkably free of typos and, at the end, she had written in pink ink: "I've wanted you to fuck me all year." Even if she had been a bad student or a different type of person, he would have just thought she was trying to lure him into something. Normally he wouldn't even contemplate something like this. But it had been a very long time since he'd had any kind of female contact. A long time since he'd seriously even considered it. It had been a long time for a lot of things.

"Ashley." He came up behind her and put the essay down on her desk.

"Yes, Mr. Brown?"

"That was, uh, quite a piece of writing."

She looked at the essay, noticed the 'A' written on it, and said, "Thank you."

"Did you, uh, *mean* what was written in there?"

"Yes, Mr. Brown."

"You mean . . . you would like to actually *do* that stuff?"

The tiniest of smiles curled her mouth. "Yes, Mr. Brown."

He glanced at the door to make sure no one within earshot was loitering there.

"I have a cabin out by the lake. Would you be interested in spending your winter break with me?" His heart pounded. He couldn't believe he just asked her that. He was a fifty-two-year-old man. He was this girl's professor. He knew he was completely out of line.

"I would like that very much, Mr. Brown."

"Please call me Steve."

"Okay."

"All right then. How bout we meet at Phuong's around noon tomorrow?"

She nodded. Her smile broadened.

"And wear your hair in pigtails again. I want something to hold onto when I fuck you from behind." His heart raced and he could feel his erection blossoming again. He walked back to the front of the room and began putting his papers and his laptop into his messenger bag. He watched her uncross her legs, catching just the briefest glimpse of white underwear. Her nipples stood against her sweater. She may have been blushing slightly. She swung her backpack over her shoulder, held her essay against her chest, and left the room. Steve exhaled a breath it felt like he'd been holding for the past five minutes.

He Was Content to Muddle Along in His Sad Existence

He got in his battered car and drove home through the gray Ohio evening. The college was not a city college. It was a small college in a small college town. He drove down Main Street, past all the historical homes, their windows glowing warmly. He imagined the happy families inside. Families gathering at home for the holidays over good food, strong drink, and warm fires. Many of the houses, he knew, were owned by professors just like him. Some of the more expensive homes were owned by the administrators and the department heads. He could have been one of them. It would have been so easy to become one of them. But a long time ago, something had derailed. He could pinpoint it but he didn't like to do that. At least not consciously. He was content to muddle along in his sad existence and didn't want to seem like the victim.

He turned off Main Street, into college housing now. Some of the houses were just as large but there was a generally squalid quality to most of them, owned by landlords who didn't really care and rented by people who would be living there for nine months at the most, sometimes two or three or more to a bedroom. Then he was away from the town and into the country, on his way to his shabby apartment in a trashy Dayton suburb.

He wondered when his heart was going to stop racing.

Neither Nabokov Nor Coltrane

It was dawn before he finally fell asleep. He kept thinking that what had happened in his classroom with Ashley couldn't have possibly happened. He was drawn tight with sexual tension and had to fight the urge to masturbate, a desire he gave into daily, sometimes more than once. It was a desire that made him feel invigorated and alive because he knew it wouldn't be around forever.

Nothing ever was.

He'd been reading Nabokov's *Invitation to a Beheading* and, by the time he decided to go to bed, realized he hadn't digested a word. The John Coltrane record he'd been listening to had stopped a while ago. Even the irritating sounds of the white trash neighborhood—arguing, drunken yelling, dogs barking, sirens, shitty cars with bad exhaust systems—had gone unnoticed. He couldn't stop thinking about Ashley. It was always the quiet ones. He knew she wouldn't expect anything more than a few days with him, but she hadn't seemed the type. Normally her hair was not worn in pigtails but down. It was a coppery brownish color and wildly curly. She was what most her age probably referred to as "cute" rather than "hot." Apparently cute was his type. While he made it a habit of covertly ogling students she was someone he found himself returning to. And sometimes he had even fantasized about her during his masturbation sessions. The word "ripe" often popped into his head when he looked at her. She was perfect, right now, at this age. She dressed mostly conservatively. Even what she wore today, if not such a cliché, would have been considered conservative. Hell, it was still the uniform at a lot of Catholic high schools. Sometimes he would play a game where he looked at his students and imagined the rest of their lives for them. He saw Ashley dating around in college. Mostly friends of friends. She wasn't a bar type. Not a hookup type. She would graduate college and maybe begin work on a master's degree, but her first priority would be to find some sort of boring, stable job. If she were lucky, it would even pay for her education. She would eventually meet someone she met at work or through a coworker. Someone who was verifiably economically stable and emotionally sound. By this time, she would be carrying a few extra pounds. Still cute but no longer ripe. The type of woman you *know* is going to get fat. She would eventually marry someone who was basically just like her and it wouldn't really matter anyway. At this point, both of their biological clocks would be ticking so loudly for them to both fall into their particular demographics they would appropriately mold and sacrifice parts of themselves to mesh perfectly. She would have a child and, if post-partum depression didn't fuck with her too much and jeopardize the marriage and if she were allowed to quit her job and stay home, another one. But then it would be time for the husband to get a vasectomy and, at this point, it would be her and her children with the husband as a minor accessory.

Dismal.

By the time he got into bed, his lustful thoughts had turned to guilt and he went to sleep thinking about the accident. Nothing turned dreams into nightmares more than that.

The Specific Reason Both of Them Were There

He awoke at ten, made some strong coffee, and watched CNN for about an hour before heading to the Vietnamese restaurant on the outskirts of campus. He thought that would be a safe spot since most of the other students would either be engaged in their last day of finals or on the way home. Phuong's was usually empty anyway.

Ashley wore a spring green wool peacoat, black snow boots, thick white leggings that stopped above her knees and, as requested, the skirt and pigtails. She waited in front of the restaurant. Steve did his best job of parallel parking, which was still laughable, and got out. He'd been trying to think of something to say and ended up managing only, "Hungry?"

"Starved," Ashley said.

They went inside to eat and make small talk. Comments about the weather. What the other one was going to order. Ashley stripped off her coat. She wore a simple white blouse unbuttoned to reveal just the slightest bit of her cleavage. It was enough for Steve. He tried not to stare at her breasts pressing against the shirt. Padded bras left so much to the imagination.

"So why aren't you going home over break?" He hesitated to ask this, thinking it might be something financial. At their school that wasn't usually much of a problem but there were still plenty of students there on financial aid. Financial aid didn't cover plane tickets.

She shrugged. "Mom and Dad travel. They're in Barbados until March. They offered to fly me out there but, I don't know, it seemed like a hassle."

So money definitely wasn't the problem. "Barbados in December sure beats the hell out of Ohio. Might be worth the hassle."

"Ah, yes, but you're not there."

And she had immediately drawn his attention to the specific reason both of them were there. He almost choked.

"Well, yes, um, I'm certainly glad you decided to stay behind."

"Have you ever fucked a student before?"

Jesus. He could feel himself blushing. Felt relieved when the waitress brought a plate of spring rolls. But he wasn't off the hook.

"So . . . have you?"

"Not, uh, not since I was one."

She laughed.

"Have you ever, uh, done something like this with a teacher?"

She picked up a spring roll, licked her lips, and said, "It's never been something I've wanted before."

He picked up a spring roll and took a bite, noting she didn't directly answer his question.

They both finished eating fairly quickly. He put her coat on for her, took a deep breath of her hair. He opened the car door for her, waited for her skirt to slide up as she sat in the seat. Then they were on their way to his modest cabin on Furnace Lake, the maintenance of which was the one indulgence he had ever allowed himself. It was one he thought he had paid for every day of his life but he couldn't seem to part with it. On the ride there, he kept wondering why he didn't just take her back to his apartment, bang the hell out of her, and be done with the whole sordid affair.

Maybe she deserved more than that but, in the end, he thought the result would be about the same.

The cabin was about an hour away in the opposite direction of the college. Otherwise, he wouldn't have bothered wasting the money to rent his shitty apartment and lived in the cabin year round. The radio was on NPR and he considered asking her what she planned on doing when she graduated just to make polite small talk. He stopped himself, cleared his throat, and said, "So I probably don't need to really bother with much conversation, huh?" He thought of that story she had written. Whoever she was on the outside was not reflected in that story. Maybe she had tried to show him what she really thought. How she wanted life to be. Who was he to argue with that?

"Not really. Unless you want to."

"Maybe later. But not so much right now. I *cannot* stop thinking about fucking you." He glanced over at her. Long enough to catch the smirk and the hint of color flushing her cheeks.

"I've been wet since meeting you at the restaurant."

He grabbed her hand and put it on his thigh. More female contact than he'd had in over a decade.

She scooted toward him in her seat and moved her hand up his thigh until she found his penis. It was hard and she began rubbing it lightly. It stiffened further. He looked down at her hand. Dull silver rings on her thumb and index finger.

Her thigh was warm on his free hand. He moved it up to her crotch. Even warmer. Her underwear were damp. He wanted to go inside them, but he also enjoyed torturing himself. He found the outline of her labia and began tracing it with his pinky.

"Are you thinking about my pussy?" Her whisper was full of warm moist breath that reached into his skull.

"Yes."

"You feel pretty hard. Are you thinking about being inside me . . . Steve?"

He continued to lightly rub her. "Actually, I'm just thinking of your pussy. What it looks like. What it tastes like."

"And you're so busy driving right now."

"A shame."

She unfastened her seatbelt, unbuttoned and unzipped his pants. He lifted his ass up off the seat and she tugged his jeans and underwear down past his scrotum, his penis springing free. She dipped her finger in the pre-come gathered at the tip and smeared it around.

"You have a fine looking cock."

"Thanks."

"Have you ever done something like this?"

"I was young once, too . . . and married. I've done just about everything. But that was a *very* long time ago."

"Whatever girls you've had, I'm not like them."

"No?"

"No."

"Show me."

"What are you going to do if I don't?"

He wanted to tell her that was okay. It would be all right if she just wanted to talk. But he thought she must be playing with him. Her story had them doing some pretty sick stuff.

He didn't say anything.

She rested her chin on his shoulder. "What if I didn't exist? I mean, like what if I didn't have any feelings? And what if no one was watching and you never had to answer for your actions? What if the only thing you had to worry about was your next orgasm? What if that was the only thing that existed?" She wrapped her hand around the length of his cock. "Boys my own age are kids. I get bored with them. I'm only doing this because I thought you might have enough experience and imagination to make it interesting. I'm a sick sick girl."

He took his hand from between her legs and grabbed one of her pigtails.

"Put it in your mouth."

She maneuvered around in her seat until sitting on her knees. She leaned over him. He focused on the road, feeling her tongue run up the length of his cock. She stuck the tip of her tongue against the opening of his penis. She opened her mouth and took the head of his penis in. He grabbed the back of her head, pushed it down until she gagged, then let go. He thought of his dick in her mouth, in her throat. She continued to bob her head up and down, slowly. He was almost shaking. He didn't think he could reach an orgasm while he was driving and still stay on the road. The next pull off he came to, he turned the car into it and put it into park. He let his seat back and used both of his hands to press her head down on his cock. He leaned back and began pumping his hips toward her face. She gagged but made no attempt to back off. He went faster and harder, feeling his penis in her spasming throat. Then he thrust and held it while he came. She backed off, coughed, retched, and wiped some come from her bottom lip. Her eyes were watery but she smiled at him.

"See. Not so hard." Her voice was raspy.

He grabbed her head and pulled her toward him, kissing her, tasting maybe a bit of himself on her tongue.

They both readjusted themselves and he pulled back onto the road. She asked him if it was okay if she smoked. He said sure. It really didn't bother him. If it had, he would have told her no. He almost told her no anyway.

There was a small carry-out a few miles from the cabin. He stopped there, told her to wait in the car, and went in for some fruit, wine, beer, lunch meat, and bread. It had been a while since he'd had to worry about feeding anyone. He also paid for a couple bundles of wood for the cabin's fireplace. Maybe it would be a good touch.

He Didn't Want to Tell Himself It Was Guilt

It was still light when they reached the cabin. Steve didn't think either of them had spoken since he'd come out of the carry-out. Ashley sat there beside him, and he was very aware of that, but he still felt a million miles away. There was something else inside of him too. He didn't want to tell himself it was guilt. Not after all these years. That would have been ridiculous. The cabin was one of many others surrounding the huge Furnace Lake. The spot was still heavily wooded and mostly invisible from the other cabins. Not that it mattered this time of year. It helped give him the illusion that Furnace Lake wasn't one of the biggest vacation destinations of the area in the summer. Not that that really meant much in Ohio. There were maybe a couple of boat and bike rental places, the carry-out, a tiny movie theater in what consisted of Furnace Lake's downtown. The theater, like most of the businesses in town, was only open Memorial Day through Labor Day.

He unlocked the door and opened it for Ashley. He flipped a light switch and turned the thermostat on the electric baseboard heat up. Soon the place would smell like burning dust, not a completely unpleasant smell. They put their bags on the kitchen counter and he plugged the refrigerator in and pushed it back against the wall.

"Nice," Ashley said. "Cozy."

"Thanks. It's not much. Been in the family for years."

He rinsed out a couple of coffee mugs, uncorked the wine, and poured a little in each glass. He handed her one of them. She took it with her free hand. The other hand held her phone. A slight smirk tilted her face.

"This probably isn't the best stuff in the world," Steve said. She dismissively nodded at him. "Uh, miss a lot of calls?"

She put the phone in a pocket in her skirt. "No one under thirty calls anyone anymore."

"Ah, yes, texting. An art that never found me."

"I've always found it interesting how reluctant bookish types are to take up texting. It seems like it was made for you."

"Maybe it's because of what it does to the English language. Or maybe it's because we're so quiet most of the time it's occasionally more exciting to open our mouths. Probably good you have that though. In case of emergencies. I don't have a cell phone or a land-line here. Keeps it peaceful."

She took a gulp of the wine. "I'm still kind of wet." She set the glass back on the counter.

He polished his wine off and put his hands around her upper arms, leading her to the one bedroom in the back of the house. This room was the smallest and was already pleasantly warm. He turned her to face him and leaned her toward the bed until she lay on her back. This was going to be like unwrapping a present. He wanted to do it a little at a time.

He parted her knees and lifted up her skirt. She wore boy brief underwear, black and trimmed in white. He slowly pulled them down. She had absolutely no pubic hair. He didn't mind this at all, although it was the first time he'd actually seen it in the flesh. He kneeled between her legs.

"So what do you think?" she asked. "It looks like a peach that's been sliced open, doesn't it?"

He looked at it and considered. Then he nodded. "But let's hope it tastes like you."

He kissed all around it, gently sucking and biting in certain places, before running his tongue along the labia, teasing the clitoris, and eventually plunging his tongue inside of her. Her moans seemed to come from very far away. She writhed her hips and he cupped her ass with his hands. He alternately tongued her and sucked away the excess come. Her hands were gripping the back of his head.

He pulled back and said, "I want to watch you play with yourself now."

He pulled her skirt the rest of the way off and moved one of her hands between her legs. She slowly began massaging herself with her fingertips. He stripped off his clothes and went to the head of the bed. He slowly unbuttoned her shirt and unfastened her bra. Her breasts were full and perfectly formed, the nipples an innocent shade of pink. He took one of them in his mouth, massaged the other one with one of his hands, and stroked himself with his remaining hand. She moaned and said his name. Eventually they got under the covers and he slid into her for the first time. They went slow. He was gentle at first. As he approached orgasm, he grabbed her behind the knees, forcing her legs to either side of her head while he pounded into her and she continued moaning that gradually escalated into screaming.

They lay in bed and held each other for a while before getting up to get something to eat. She checked her phone again and typed off a message in return. Before going back into the bedroom, he made her leave it in the kitchen.

"I notice you didn't bring any kind of bag," he asked.

"Well, I didn't think I'd really need the clothes and I wasn't sure how long we'd be here. I figure you have a shower."

"That I do."

"I'm a light packer. I don't like to be responsible for a lot of stuff."

When they went back into the bedroom, he spanked her until her skin was hot and red, and then he fucked her in the ass. Afterward, she went to the bathroom and he dozed off. Had the dream.

Obsession and Insanity

He woke up momentarily disoriented. Once he realized he was in the cabin and remembered *why* he was in the cabin, everything seemed to become even more of a dreamlike blur. His eyes were open but it was so dark they may as well have still been closed. He reached over to feel the other side of the bed. Ashley wasn't there.

He hadn't bothered setting the clock in the room, never wore a watch, and didn't have a cell phone so he had no idea what time it was. He was still completely naked. He swung his legs over the edge of the bed, felt around for his pants, and slid them on. He pulled on his sweater and socks, remembering it would be pretty chilly outside the room.

He went out to the main part of the cabin, expecting to find a light on, Ashley maybe sitting on the couch and reading or something. It was dark and he didn't see any sign of her.

The porch light shone in through the front door. He didn't remember turning it on so he opened the door and leaned out. Ashley sat in one of the wooden deck chairs, texting something and smoking.

"There you are," he said.

She looked at him. It looked like she'd been crying. "Yep."

He looked out over the dark lake. It had warmed considerably, not at all unusual for Ohio, and a fog was rolling in. There probably wouldn't be any visibility come dawn.

"You going to be out here a while?"

She held up her cigarette for an answer.

"Let me grab some shoes. Need anything?"

"I'm okay."

He slipped his shoes on, went to the kitchen to grab the bottle of wine, noting that it had been depleted considerably since their earlier glasses, and grabbed a fleece blanket off the back of the couch.

He set the blanket on Ashley's lap and said, "Thought you might be cold."

"Thanks."

He uncorked the bottle with his teeth and sat down in the chair beside hers. A chill went up his spine. This was too familiar. He wanted to tell her to go grab her things, they needed to go, and then he remembered she hadn't brought anything. He thought maybe that made it even weirder. Like she could just move right in and take Heidi's place. Like that was what he'd been waiting for for the past twenty years. The dream still rode his brain hard. He took a healthy slug of the wine. It would either help the dream fade or set the bear trap his mind had become, waiting to obsessively snap down on the littlest thought and stay clamped until it twitched its last.

But it would never twitch its last. Steve knew that.

"Couldn't sleep?" Steve asked.

"Didn't try."

"You're being very laconic."

"I don't know what that means."

He chuckled. "I'm not sure I do either." He took another swig of the wine and passed her the bottle. She took it without protest.

"How's your ass?"

"Sore." She smiled, but still looked like she was ready to cry.

"You look like you've been crying."

She looked out toward the fog gathered on the lake. "Why do they call this place Furnace Lake?"

"Obsession and insanity."

"What does that even mean?"

"Well, this is Ohio's idea of a resort town. Resort towns don't happen unless there are people to visit them and spend money there. As it happens, there's a town about twenty miles to the south called Milltown. Its main industry, at one point, was steel. So one of them came to this lake while the sun was setting and glowing orange like a blast furnace and they decided to name it Furnace Lake. It's a totally horrible, unromantic, disgusting name."

"I agree. It does sound warm though."

"But most people are only here in the summer. It seems like a furnace is the last thing you'd want to think about on a sweltering summer day."

"You might be right. Do you stay here in the summer?"

"Usually. Unless I'm teaching summer classes."

"Do you plan on doing that this year?"

"Probably not. I don't really need the money like I used to. That's really the only reason any professor gives up his or her summer."

"Doesn't sound fun."

"So, yeah, I'll probably head up here the week after finals. Would you be interested in joining me?" He didn't even know why he asked that.

She rolled her eyes. "That's a little too far in the future."

"I know. I don't even know why I asked. I've had a lot of fun today. I guess that's why. You've been very . . . kind to me."

"You act like that doesn't happen much."

"Well, not in that way. It's been over twenty years since I've had sex."

She reached out and patted his knee. "No it hasn't. It's only been like two hours."

"True. I guess I can't argue with that. Now the clock starts all over again."

"You did good after that long of a layoff."

"Thanks."

"Actually you did good period."

"Thanks more."

"Do you want to talk about it?"

"About what?"

"You fuck the same way you seem to live."

"What does that mean?"

"Like somebody who has something really wrong with them."

"Hm . . . what about you?"

"This isn't about me. Besides, I'm just a nineteen-year-old girl with a healthy sexual appetite. I could have landed some boy from the school and convinced him to come back to my parents' empty house for the weekend and fuck my brains out like a nineteen-year-old boy and it would have been like getting fucked by a nineteen-year-old boy. I like someone who's seen a little more. Thought about it a little more. *Planned* for it a little more. See, I didn't really have to tell you anything I wanted and you gave me a pretty nice day. So . . .

wanna talk about it or not?"

He took another drink from the bottle. Followed by another. And suddenly he was almost blubbering. It seemed difficult to draw his next breath. He'd spent so much time just trying not to think about it that it never really occurred to him that he might actually talk to someone else about it. There was a period of time when he felt like he should probably go see a psychiatrist but he thought he was coping with it well enough on his own.

"Maybe."

"It'll make you feel better."

"I doubt that."

"Then it'll make you feel something."

"Where do I start?"

"Start with where things started to go bad."

That Was the Beginning of Bad

The miscarriage or the accident. Where to begin?

Start with the miscarriage. That was the beginning of bad. The accident was more of a worsening.

Heidi was pregnant and they weren't ready for it but they were still happy. The doctor told them she was pregnant with twins—one girl and one boy—and they knew they definitely weren't ready for *that* but, in a way, they were even happier. They had talked about having children, although they thought it would be something that would happen around the time they turned thirty. When Heidi got pregnant, she was twenty-four and Steve was twenty-six. They'd only planned on having two children and, ideally, they would be a girl and a boy. This would, in a way, be like getting it over with in one fell swoop. Then they could focus on their academic careers and child raising. *Focus.* It was something they'd both been lacking. If they had kids, they could stop trying to figure out who it was they wanted to be. They would have it handed to them. They would be parents and everything else would be secondary.

She was seven months along when Steve took her to the emergency room with swollen feet and bleeding. She'd had a couple of scares earlier on and had always been told everything was just fine. They were just overreacting. Their doctor had assured him that was perfectly normal for first time parents. Steve wasn't very worried.

From the moment the doctor inspected Heidi's stomach for the heartbeats there was nothing but worry. The next several hours were a steady ratcheting of that worry until it escalated to panic and then soul crushing grief.

He supposed the acceptance never came for either of them.

Heidi was in the hospital for a couple more days to let her recover and make sure everything was physically okay with her. From the day they returned home, to the tiny apartment Steve still lived in, he felt like he was in the unique and terrible position of trying to make Heidi feel better while dealing with his own grief. Meaning he tried not to be very open with his grief. Maybe it would have been better if he had but there was part of trying to feign normalcy that he liked. If he hadn't been the one to do it, life would have become unbearable. To Heidi, this was seen as something cold and callous. He didn't care about her. He didn't care about anything.

They argued a lot. He tried not to. He did a lot of tongue biting. But there were only so many attacks he could take before breaking down and fighting back. And maybe, sometimes, his return attacks were overly vicious. He was doing everything he could.

Heidi dropped out of the master's program.

Not to worry. She needed a little more time before dealing with that kind of mental strain.

She stopped going to her job at the library.

Not to worry. He was an assistant professor so they had a steady income. It wasn't much but their living expenses were almost non-existent and their parents helped out, probably because they felt sorry for them.

She stopped getting out of bed. Stopped cleaning the house or herself. Steve suggested she see someone. She accused him of calling her crazy. Asked why he'd married her if he thought she was a psycho. Arguing was pointless. He would just leave. Go to a bar for a couple of hours while she cooled off or drive the half hour to his parents' and sleep in his childhood bedroom. Few things were more humiliating than that.

The next spring he returned home from his last class of the semester and it was like Heidi had become someone else. They had a good summer. She smiled more. Was completely manic, in a good way, on some days, and they had lots and lots of sex. There was an almost frenzied quality to it. Toward the end of the summer, he realized she wasn't her old self at all. She had merely filled herself with some kind of obsessive optimism. Many times she mentioned "trying again." Steve told her there wasn't anything wrong with him and she wasn't using any birth control so, as far he was concerned, every time he came they were "trying again."

But nothing happened.

He was secretly relieved by this. He felt like, if there was anything good that came from the miscarriage, it was that they weren't ready for one kid, let alone two. It was a reprieve. He wasn't really one to believe in signs. He knew it was just biology and rotten luck but if either of them was the type to believe in signs, that would have been their mantra: "It was probably for the best. Maybe we weren't ready anyway." And while that kind of belief was something Steve had always seen as a sign of mental weakness, he was starting to realize that was exactly *why* people believed in those sorts of things. To keep themselves sane. Shouldering all the knowledge, all the *burden* of something like that was maddening.

Once he realized she didn't see it as sex, just babymaking, he started to lose interest.

They started arguing again.

She started going out with friends, girls she'd gone to high school and college with.

Steve felt like things were falling apart all over again. He was going to work to fix the relationship but the miscarriage was a trauma he didn't want to have to go through ever again. He made an appointment with a urologist, lied and said he was ten years older, told him he already had three kids, and got a vasectomy. He wasn't going to tell Heidi about it. If he could get her through this "trying again" phase then maybe they'd go to a fertility doctor and, if she were able to have children, he would be sterile. Therefore he could be the one to feel guilty about it. Maybe talk her into adopting a child.

Who was he kidding? She had been staying out all night and he was pretty sure she was fucking at least one other person, possibly more. He wanted to either start over with the old Heidi or someone else completely. Or not at all.

Less than a week after getting the vasectomy she changed again. Less frenzied. Less manic. More like her old self. And affectionate. She stopped mentioning anything about trying again. Maybe Steve's plaintive attempts to wait had finally taken hold. He thought she had even started taking her birth control pills again.

That winter—Friday, December 7, specifically—they went to dinner in Cincinnati. On the way home they hit a patch of black ice and crashed into a tree. Steve remembered sliding off the road clearly, but everything that came after that was a combination of hazy memory, his police report, and the newspaper articles he'd read against his better judgment.

The car slid off the road and into a tree. The car was totaled. He and Heidi were nearly totaled. But conscious. The car's engine was completely silent, the interior awash with beeping sounds and flashing lights. He looked over at Heidi. Her head was covered in blood. Her breath was shallow. He kept asking if she was okay. And she kept looking in the back seat and saying they had to take care of the kids. Telling her she was delusional or crazy was the furthest thing from Steve's mind. Yes, yes, he said, we'll take care of the kids but we need to find someone. We need to get help. And she said that wasn't what they needed. They didn't need help. The children needed to be buried. They were beyond help. There was a brief moment where he wondered if she was talking about the miscarriage. Maybe she was confused. He told her that they had already buried the children, didn't she remember? She told him that wasn't right. They never saw what happened to them. Anything could have happened to them. And besides they weren't buried they were cremated. That's right, Steve remembered. They were cremated. We have the urn in a kitchen cabinet. Yes, she said and wiped blood out of her eyes. And we need to make sure these get taken care of by us. She told him to get the boy and she would get the girl. He was amazed they were able to get out of the car. Amazed they were able to move at all. Heidi opened the back door and feigned taking a child out of a car seat. Steve did the same. She took off walking through the woods, through the slushy mud that was winter in Ohio, and it occurred to Steve that they were much closer to the cabin than they were the apartment and that was quite likely where they were going. The coroner would later say he thought it was nearly impossible for them, especially her, to do what it was they had done. Even the police report was free of any description of them wandering through the woods, as though he had completely blacked out during that period. They arrived at the lake and continued to walk to their cabin. Once at the cabin Heidi demanded he go retrieve a shovel, two if they had them. He went to the small utility shed, unlocked it, and removed a shovel. There was another one in there, but the thought of Heidi digging anything made him nauseous. He returned with the shovel and she said they didn't need to dig two holes, they could just bury them together. He began digging. Told her she should go up to the porch and sit down. She said she was okay, she wanted to hold their babies. While he dug, she stood in the moonlight of the crystal clear night and stared out at the lake. What was she thinking? He knew she wasn't in her right mind, but what was going through her head at that moment? He dug quickly. The ground wasn't frozen and it was still damp, which made it that much easier. He dug down maybe a little more than a foot. His head was swimming and spinning and he felt like he could collapse at any moment. He told her he thought it was ready. She bent down on her knees and placed the imaginary children in the hole and said something that sounded like a prayer. Then she collapsed face first in the hole. He pulled her out, lay down beside the hole, and cradled her in his arm, her head resting on his shoulder. The way they used to sleep when they had first gotten married.

Just Gone

"Can I have one of those?" Steve pointed at Ashley's pack of cigarettes. She handed them to him. He lit one, fought back a cough, and said, "The next thing I remember was sitting in the back of an ambulance. I kept asking them what happened to Heidi and they wouldn't tell me. That's when I knew she was dead. By the time we got to the hospital, she wasn't even hooked up to anything. Just gone. She was probably gone before they even got there."

Steve thought he would cry if he ever told that story but he wasn't.

"Was that the first time you've ever told that to anyone . . . besides the police?"

He nodded slowly. "I think it felt good. I never realized how crazy it sounded."

She kind of laughed. "It did sound pretty crazy. And sad."

"Definitely sad."

"And your life just stopped then, huh?"

"Well, I didn't think it had at the time but now . . . I guess looking at all the wasted years, you could probably say that."

Then he did cry. She took the cigarette out of his hand and crushed it out on the arm of the chair. She placed a hand on the back of his head, pulled him up out of the chair, and walked him to bed.

When he woke up the next morning she was gone.

He Found Himself Completely Enervated

He went back home as soon as he looked around and waited long enough to know she wasn't there and wasn't coming back.

For the next four months, he divided his time between his apartment and the college, just like always. He pulled her file at school and noticed she hadn't enrolled for the second semester at all. He emailed her. He didn't feel comfortable calling the number he had for her and didn't know if she would really want him to call her anyway. The cynical thought would have been that she got what she wanted and then decided to disappear but what could she have possibly gained from their encounter? He had certainly had a good time but their last bout had nearly left her in tears. He hadn't given her any money or promises or anything. Maybe he'd just freaked her out. Or maybe she had realized she'd made a big mistake and decided to take off. She could have had someone come and pick her up or maybe she took a bus or something. He couldn't exactly ask around about her at school without looking like a creep. Maybe he would have approached one of her friends but he hadn't really paid attention to who she hung around with, if anyone. He was usually focused on her.

For the first month, the elation of their meeting and the hope she would contact *him* sustained him. In February and March—the last couple months of guaranteed cold weather—he found himself completely enervated. This was usually a bad time of year for him anyway. One can only take so many months of gray, miserable weather. He used to come home from class, make a small but tasty meal from scratch, and spend the evening reading and listening to music. If these things didn't make him authentically happy, they at least got him very close to the real thing. Representations of happiness. Then he would usually find some pornography on the internet or jerk off to the thought of one of his students before falling asleep. But now he didn't even feel like doing that.

He told himself he had had something and let it get away but he knew he was kidding himself. What did he have? Ashley was just a girl who wanted to sleep with one of her professors. They did that for a few hours, she probably realized it wasn't what she thought it would be, and decided to bolt. Probably even had her boyfriend from back home pick her up. In a way, it was hard not to be mad at her, but he knew if she called or contacted him, he wouldn't show her any trace of anger.

By the middle of April, a gorgeous spring had finally arrived. When classes ended at the end of May, Steve was looking forward to packing up and heading to the cabin for the summer. The week before he left, he had the dream every night. There were minor variations. In a couple of them, Heidi was Ashley. In one of them, Steve dug the grave and the grave became a bed and he fucked Ashley in it but halfway through she became Heidi and Heidi was rotting and wearing her bridal veil and ejaculating sperm from her nipples. Steve decided when he came back, if the dreams hadn't gotten any better, he would finally see a psychiatrist, to see if he could prescribe something to help him sleep more than anything else.

Most of the essentials were already at the cabin so all Steve had to pack were some clothes and groceries.

The Twin Dimples Just Above Her Waist

Steve opened the cabin door and stood there with a grocery bag in one hand and his keys in the other, thinking he hadn't had to unlock the door but also thinking maybe it was something he'd done so many times in the past he just didn't remember doing it. He pocketed the keys. The cabin didn't seem as stale as it usually did. Maybe that was because of his winter tryst. That was how he had decided to think of it. A "tryst." It made it sound more festive, which he guessed it was. It was the fallout that was depressing. Of course even that was relatively small compared to the fallout that had been the last twenty-plus years of his life. He'd decided to let the lease on his apartment go when it ran out this October. He had plenty of money to buy a house. Maybe he'd even join a dating site or go out to bars or something. Hell, maybe he'd even grow the balls to ask one of the several single female professors he knew out. Opportunities like Ashley were not going to come around every year. So far the odds, apparently, were more like once every twenty years. He didn't know if he'd be around when another presented itself.

He set the bag of groceries on the kitchen table and felt bad about having relegated Ashley to an "opportunity."

He heard footsteps and turned around quickly.

Ashley stood in the door of the bedroom.

"Don't be mad," she said.

Steve didn't know *what* to say. He felt like he was blushing, trying to find the right words before opening his mouth. He'd thought about Ashley so much over the past few months that his emotions had spanned the entire spectrum more than once.

He gripped the counter and looked away from her. "I'm not sure what to say. Why . . .?"

"Why am I here?"

"Um . . . yeah, I guess. And how?"

"I thought I would surprise you."

"I'm . . . definitely surprised."

"And happy?" She smiled and approached him.

Fuck it, he thought. He opened his arms and accepted her, pulled her into him and wrapped her tightly. "Very happy."

"We can pick up right where we left off."

He didn't waste any time. He walked her over to the couch, bent her over the arm, peeled down her jeans and underwear, and pushed himself in. It didn't last long. He tried to force all the questions out of his head. Looking down at her back muscles writhing under her skin tight t-shirt and the twin dimples just above her waist made it not that hard at all.

They Already Acted Married

When they finished, she stood up, pulled up her pants, and adjusted her bra. Steve went to the car to grab the rest of the stuff. Out by the car, he took a second to stop and look around. Summer was finally here. The woody smells and sounds immediately made him feel more restful. He saw other families in the distance, in the yards of their cabins, some of them barbecuing. There were even a couple of boats out on the lake. Steve liked it here. If he didn't he would have probably sold the place immediately after Heidi died.

He went back into the cabin and found that Ashley had already put the groceries in the refrigerator.

"Very domestic," he said.

She shrugged. "Well, you know . . ."

He looked at her for a second. "No. I really don't. I have a lot of questions for you."

"But you *are* glad I'm here, right? Even after shooting your wad in me? Which is running out even as we speak."

"Lovely."

"It's mostly your fault."

"Agreed. Hungry?"

"Starved."

Steve decided to save the questions for dinner. He didn't feel like dragging the grill out so he just decided to make something in the kitchen. Maybe some kind of chicken stir fry. He reached into the pantry and grabbed the bag of rice.

"What do you need from the fridge?"

"Maybe just the chicken. Unless you put the teriyaki sauce in there too."

She handed him the chicken. "The sauce should be in the cabinet."

Steve turned back to the cabinet and was overcome with a case of the shakes. It was eerie. They'd spent one day fucking and had now been together only a few minutes and they already acted married. He liked that feeling. It surprised him.

He poured some water in a pan, dumped in a couple handfuls of rice and a bit of olive oil, and set it on the stove. She put a bottle of beer in front of him.

He chopped the onions and the peppers and then didn't really have anything to do until the rice started boiling. He couldn't wait until they were sitting down. If he did, he wouldn't ask her at all. He'd just fall into whatever groove she wanted him to fall into.

"So how long have you been here?"

She was cutting the chicken and looked up. "Huh?"

He nodded at the bottle of beer. "That's a Budweiser. I brought Heineken. Also, the stuff I brought wouldn't have been this cold."

"Just since last night. I promise."

"What made you want to come back? I notice you dropped out of school."

"Yeah. I guess I was just thinking about you. Can we talk about it later, maybe?"

"Sure. I hope it's nothing too serious."

"Just family stuff."

"I might not be able to empathize."

She smiled and took a sip of his beer.

"How did you get in, anyway?"

"The window in the bathroom. I popped the screen out and the window was unlatched."

"That window's tiny."

"I'm not very big myself."

He still didn't see how it was possible. But maybe the window had become smaller in his mind. He told her he had to pee and she asked if he didn't believe her. He laughed and said of course he did but, once in the bathroom, he did find himself studying the tiny window. He still didn't see how it was possible but it would probably be rude to measure her.

Everything Was Made of Lead

A half hour later they sat at the small table in the kitchen, their dinners half eaten. They had made casual conversation. He'd asked her why she had dropped out of school and what she'd been up to and she gave him back a steady stream of what were probably lies. Then he asked her how long she'd really been staying here and she stammered and her eyes hardened somewhat. While he was in the bathroom, he'd noticed most of his supply of toilet paper was gone. So she'd either cleaned up well or not made much of a mess in the first place, but she'd definitely been here for more than a night.

"I never left."

"What?" As happy as he was to have her in front of him, he couldn't help but be a little angry with her.

"Yeah. That time this winter. I never left. I went for a walk and just kind of hid until I saw you leave."

"But why?"

"I told you. Family stuff."

"Fighting with your parents?"

"Something like that."

"You're going to have to stop being so cryptic."

"I don't know what that means."

"Maybe I should punish you."

"Oh. Are we still playing that game? I was going to humor you and let you play the husband and wife game but, to be honest, that was already getting a little boring."

"Get into the bedroom."

"But I'm not even finished eating."

"Now."

She stood up and made a mock pouting face.

"I really am mad at you, Ashley."

She stomped off into the bedroom. He tried to stand up to follow her but it felt like everything was made of lead. He forced himself to stand and was distantly aware of his body hitting the floor and then he wasn't aware of anything.

We Live Down Here Now

He dug the grave until it felt like every muscle had given out and he might fall down. He looked down at the grave and was pleased to see that it was as deep of one as any he'd remembered digging. The palms of his hands stung. He looked over his shoulder at the cabin. Expecting to see it darkened. But the lights were on and there were people inside. It was good that somebody still wanted it. He could hear distant laughter and music. See the silhouettes of people in the window.

He looked back at the grave. He couldn't see the bottom of it. A voice called from the grave but he couldn't see who it was coming from.

He got down on his hands and knees and then his stomach and leaned his head into the grave. It was Heidi, calling to him.

"What are you doing up there?"

"I had to dig the grave. We have to bury the children. What are you doing down there? How did you get down there?"

She laughed. "We live down here now. The kids are already down here. You should join us."

He pulled himself with his arms, feeling the moist grass on his stomach, before sliding down the side of the grave. He was afraid he'd just fall in head first but it was angled more than he thought it was. Like a slide. He slid to the bottom. The grave was quite roomy. He looked around but didn't see any sign of Heidi and the children. He stood up. The grave leveled off but continued into the distance. The narrow earthen corridor surrounded him as he walked deeper into it.

It curved to the right and when he made the turn he had to shield his eyes against the glow that met him. It was like a giant fire. He thought he could make out Heidi in the middle of the fire, a waist-high child to either side of her.

"I don't want to go any farther," he said.

"You have to. Your family's here."

He cautiously stepped toward them. Gradually his eyes adjusted to the light and he could begin to see the children as something other than black shapes. One was a girl and one was a boy. They looked happy and clear-eyed. Heidi wore her wedding veil. As he drew closer, he noticed her nipples had elongated and reached the mouth of each child.

Steve stopped.

"Come on," Heidi said.

"No. I can't."

Steve took off running in the opposite direction but the corridor was gone and he found himself running into loose dirt, trying to move his arms and legs to kick out of it, but nothing was moving and he was suffocating.

Slit Rider

"Finally," a male voice said.

Steve opened his eyes to see a hideously ugly guy taking his hand away from Steve's mouth. The first thing Steve thought was that he'd been holding his nose closed to try and get him to wake up. The guy might have been a teenager, or recently a teenager, but there was something a lot older looking about him. He had a tattoo on the front of his neck that said SLIT RIDER in vaguely gothic lettering.

"Who the fuck are you?" Steve asked.

The man stood up and said, "I'm Slit Rider, fucker."

Steve's heart raced. He looked down at himself. He was tied to a chair. He wasn't wearing any clothes.

"What the fuck is going on?" he asked. "Why are you in my house? Where's Ashley?"

The man laughed. "Ashley's dead, stooge. Ashley's been dead a long time and something. Reborn as Sharon X. Now she's here. Now she's mine. Two hands. Two feet. Electric brain."

Steve took a deep breath and closed his eyes. He didn't know what was going on. The only thing he could think was that this was maybe Ashley's boyfriend or something and he had apparently found out what he and Ashley had been doing and was upset. But Steve didn't know how to defend himself against that. He wasn't going to tell this jackass everything was Ashley's doing.

"Look," Steve said. "I don't know who you are or what you want but if you untie me now and just leave, I won't press any charges."

The man (Steve had a hard time thinking of him as Slit Rider) leaned into Steve. He reeked of whiskey, smoke, and maybe something else. Some foul underlying odor. "That's a good thought box, Steves. I don't know why I didn't think of that and everything else with the laughing. Horseplay." Now behind Steve, the man tugged on a couple of the ropes. Then Steve felt his hands around his neck. The man squeezed until Steve blacked out.

Almost Everything in the Cabin Was on the Verge of Falling Apart

This time when he came to there wasn't anyone in front of him. The room was dark. He heard loud music that sounded like clanging metal and a drum machine coming from the next room. It sounded like there were also a lot of people in there. Raucous shouts and laughter. Steve tried to rock the chair back and forth until he realized if he actually managed to tip it over he would probably still be tied to the chair, only on the floor and with the ropes quite possibly binding him in an even more uncomfortable position.

Unless he could get the chair to break. Almost everything in the cabin was on the verge of falling apart. If he could get the chair to break, it might create some slack in the rope and then he could get out through a window and go to one of the neighbor's houses. He needed to call the police. The people in the other room were making so much noise he was kind of surprised one of the neighbors hadn't called the police already.

He made a motion like standing up straight to see if he could weaken the chair at all. He heard it creak but it gave only fractionally. He might have been able to inflict more damage if he didn't feel so weak. He assumed Ashley or Sharon X or whoever had slipped something into his beer. Maybe even the food. But probably the beer. It was Bud so it pretty much tasted like shit anyway. He wouldn't have been able to tell.

He continued to slowly grind against the chair. Hoping it would give a little more before trying to drive himself into the ground with it. If he was going to do that, he wanted to be pretty sure it was going to break. He listened to the sounds coming from the other room. He was still trying to figure out why this was happening and was hoping they would be talking about it. Maybe give him some kind of clue that could become a psychological advantage.

The music *was* really loud and sounded intolerable. If they *were* having a party, he didn't know who partied to this kind of music. The only words he could make out were what sounded like a woman talking about "shoulder pads" and "conquering the moon." Not a lot of help. Those phrases were repeated over and over. There weren't any other discernible words. Someone else just shouted "Wheee!" continuously like they were on the world's longest slide or roller coaster or something. He guessed there were at least five or six people in the room. It was possible that Slit Rider and Ashley were the only people who knew he was in here. So he decided to see if he could go ahead and rock the chair onto the floor. If it broke then he'd be able to get out through the window. If it didn't then he would shout for help. He highly doubted it but supposed it was possible someone in the other room would help him. He thought about the gun he had hidden away in one of the kitchen cupboards. Wondered if they'd found it yet.

He didn't know how much real danger he was in anyway. So far, other than drugging him and choking him to the point of unconsciousness, nobody had done anything to seriously hurt him. Maybe they didn't *want* to hurt him. What kind of motive was there anyway? If Slit Rider really was Ashley's jealous boyfriend or ex-boyfriend or whatever, he would have probably just beaten the hell out of Steve and called it a day. Maybe taken Ashley with him. Ashley had been using Steve for a place to stay and, he supposed, it was entirely possible Slit Rider had been staying here with her. So maybe they wanted money. Steve had plenty of money. He had no problems with giving them whatever they asked for. Of course he would go immediately to the police once he was able.

He heard something that sounded like a window breaking and wondered, once again, what the fuck they were doing in there.

He gritted his teeth and began rocking the chair back and forth, more and more violently, until he hit the ground and was . . . lying on his side on the ground and tied to a chair.

Fuck.

It Seemed No One Heard Him Collapse

With all the commotion going on in the other room, it seemed no one heard him collapse. He thought once again about crying out but didn't see how that would help anything. It would probably just serve to infuriate Slit Rider even further. If he had been furious before. Steve wasn't really sure. It was kind of hard to gauge any type of feeling from the man. There was something off about him but Steve couldn't figure out what it was. It looked like he was missing something.

He continued to struggle against the chair and the rope.

At least an hour passed before anyone entered the room. Slit Rider was the first one in. He turned the lights on in the room.

"What the fucks!?" he shouted. He walked over to Steve and uprighted the chair. "You're going to want to sees this. Take a magic looks, astronaut."

Ashley was the next to enter the room, followed by two more men. One of them was missing an arm. The other one had an eyepatch. The one with the eyepatch said, "I am not ready yet." Then he vomited on the floor and said, "Now I am ready."

Ashley walked slowly toward Steve and sat on his lap. The three men stood in front of the bed, about a foot in front of Ashley, and began removing their clothes. Ashley was doing the same although in a much slower, more seductive manner.

"Ashley," Steve tried to whisper in her ear. At that point, the room was so quiet while the men waited for her to take her clothes off that they probably heard him. Maybe there was a lot of blood pounding in their ears or something.

Halfway through unbuttoning her shirt, Ashley turned so that her face was barely an inch from Steve's. "I am *not* Ashley. Not anymore. Ashley is dead. Now I am Sharon X. Slit Rider has baptized me and I was born again. Born from space, not a mother. Mothers are gross."

Steve tried to find whatever it was he'd seen in Ashley's eyes before. Maybe he hadn't seen anything. Maybe he'd been so blinded by the prospect and the actual act of sex that it didn't really matter what he'd seen in those eyes. Maybe she was really high on something.

"Come on," he said. "You're throwing your life away with these people."

"At least I had one to throw away."

That remark cut deeply. He felt like she'd listened to his story without any sympathy whatsoever. Listened to it for ammunition more than anything, possibly.

She stood up and turned fully in front of him. She finished unbuttoning her shirt and let it drop to the floor. She unbuttoned her jeans and peeled those down. She had an "X" tattooed on her bare pubis.

"Watch this if you doubt Slit Rider's space magic."

Steve had the feeling he was about ready to watch a whole lot of things he didn't really want to see so wasn't sure what Ashley was specifically talking about.

She lay on her back on the bed. Eyepatch and One Arm went to either side of the bed. Their cocks were large and erect. She took one in each hand. She spread her legs and Slit Rider lowered his head between them. He dived in like an animal, licking and slurping. Steve thought about the deposit he'd made there only a few hours ago and wasn't sure if he was satisfied or nauseous. One Arm leaned into Ashley and she took his penis into her mouth.

"Ashley. Sharon X. Whatever. Why are you doing this?"

She took her mouth away. "Why shouldn't I be? I've known these guys longer than I knew you when you did this to me."

Slit Rider hopped off the bed and pounced in front of Steve. He belched in his face and threw his arms up in the air like he'd achieved some victory.

"Now I've got your sperms in my belly! Dead sperms with nothing ever in them! Dead sperms! Dead sperms! Dead sperms!"

He was leaping up and down. Steve couldn't help but notice Slit Rider was erect also. And that his penis was huge. Slit Rider grabbed his penis and began slapping Steve's cheeks with it. Then he turned and leaped between Ashley's legs, thrusting quickly. She was now taking turns sucking Eyepatch and One Arm and, when she didn't have a penis in her mouth, grinning at Steve. A few seconds later, Slit Rider thrust harder and cried out. Steve thought he shouted "Rocket" but he might have misheard him. Everything the guy said seemed to be something like gibberish so he figured it probably didn't really matter anyway.

One Arm took his turn next.

Slit Rider left the bed to stand next to Steve and poke him in the face with his index finger, as though testing his reality. Steve fantasized about biting it off.

One Arm was finished even faster than Slit Rider and Eyepatch took his turn.

When he finished, Ashley pulled her knees up to her chest and rocked back slightly. That was the first indication Steve had of what he might be in for. Slit Rider was giggling. He searched around the clothes on the floor until he came up with a belt. He forced Steve's mouth open by poking him in the eye. Then he wrapped the belt around Steve's head. Steve closed his mouth as far as he could, teeth pressing into the leather, but he didn't get it closed all the way. Slit Rider and Eyepatch lowered the chair until Steve's back was on the ground. Ashley was suddenly above his head, lowering her glistening vagina to his mouth.

The semen came out in clumpy, warm drops. Steve closed his eyes, thinking that might help him to avoid throwing up. Not that throwing up the sperm of three men was unappealing, he just thought that, with the belt in his mouth, it might make things even worse.

"You like that?" Slit Rider was whispering into his ear. "All that sperm's filled with little space babies. You're going to be just like the Virgins Mary. Shooting out babies without us having to fuck you in the mouth hole."

They left him on his back and went back to their partying, music turned up, the smell of smoke wafting from the main room. Steve thought he was so tired and had released so much adrenaline that he might actually be able to go to sleep but they'd left the light on and it was shining right into his eyes. Maybe two hours later Ashley came back into the room and lay next to him on the floor. Her hand went to his penis and he told himself he wasn't going to get hard, that she repulsed him, but he got hard anyway.

"The problem with you is that you don't see anything."

"I don't see how you're in any condition to diagnose my problems. You're less than half my age and you might be insane."

"That's very hurtful. I indulged you, didn't I?"

He didn't say anything.

"That one night. I told you you could do anything you wanted to with me and I thought you did. I thought I let you. I thought I let you indulge. Maybe you should have killed me. Maybe that was really what I wanted. What would you have done if I'd told you that was what I wanted? That I had always felt dead inside and that I wanted you to kill me and fuck my corpse. That I didn't really have a family, no one to go back to, no one to miss me. That I'd already withdrawn from college. Would you have done it?"

He didn't answer. How could he? Of course he wouldn't have done it. But was that what she wanted to hear?

"You don't see anything that matters. You think women have to be brides or whores. You saw me as something innocent, didn't you? And then you saw me as a whore. But I bet you started thinking about something more than just fucking me that first time I gave you head in the car. Probably because you felt guilty. That's probably why you told me that story about your family."

"Not family. Wife."

"Oh, right, because the children didn't exist. They were imaginary. And you're wife was crazy. Did you know she *was* actually pregnant with twins?"

"Not mine. And good job. You looked it up. Thanks for believing me."

"Of course not. They couldn't have been, could they? Jesus, you're rock hard."

He didn't say anything.

"I met Slit Rider right before I came out here with you. That was one of the reasons I came with you. You were normalcy. I thought you were the most normal person I'd ever met. And I wanted to taste it. I wanted to see if that was something I could be."

"I'm not that normal."

"But you are. Don't you see that? Don't you realize that's what normal is? Everyone has problems. Everyone has a shitty life. But people who embrace that and do something with the misery are seen as the abnormal ones. And the people who apply normalcy like a camouflage suit are seen as the normal ones. And I figured out why this is. Because we're a democratic society, Steve. And when there are more fucked up people than not fucked up people, that becomes the status quo. The mentally healthy—people like Slit Rider—are outcast. That's why we have to make our own society."

She jerked him vigorously and he couldn't help coming. He didn't say anything else. He just closed his eyes and nearly wept. He was hoping they were just thieves but now he was starting to think they were some kind of death cult or just psychopathic or out of their heads on something and that scared him a lot more.

"Listen to Slit Rider. He'll teach you that everyone is a beautiful creature from space. There is no normal. There are no mothers, no whores, no men, no women. Wielders of cock and pussy. That's all we are."

She dipped her fingers in his semen and spent several minutes sliding them in and out of his nostrils.

Slayer

He must have fallen asleep or passed out eventually. He didn't remember her leaving the room. He didn't remember much of anything. There were the party sounds in the other room and he just tried to find a comfortable bass line and focus his attention on that and the next thing he knew the room was filled with morning sunlight and Slit Rider was jerking his chair up and throwing Steve's wallet at him and shouting "No pins. No pins. No pins."

Luckily, Ashley came in after him to translate.

"We need your PIN number, Steve."

He laughed.

Yesterday, before being forced to drink the semen of three men after watching them fuck a girl he'd become fond of, he would have given them the number easily. Hell, he probably would have driven them to the ATM just to avoid further trouble. Now they had put certain things into perspective. He'd been humiliated and terrified. But that wasn't it. He'd also had it made painfully clear to him that he had basically died a long time ago. If he got out of this, he would make some changes, sure, but he was finished emasculating himself. And he still wasn't sure if they were actually homicidal or just goofballs.

Steve laughed, he couldn't help it, and said, "I'm not giving you the number. It's private. It's personal. Feel free to steal anything that isn't nailed down. But I'm finished volunteering information." He looked at Ashley. "You've been irresponsible with it so far."

Something like wild rage shot through Slit Rider's eyes—shot through his whole face—before it returned to that creepy blank potato and he stood up straight.

"Bring in Slayer!" he shouted.

Steve didn't know what to expect. He thought maybe Slit Rider was talking about One Arm or Eyepatch, since Steve hadn't caught their names previously. Or maybe another man, large and brutish, someone fitting of the name Slayer.

In walked a very young girl. She couldn't have been more than twelve or thirteen.

"You know what to do, Slayer."

The girl walked in front of Steve and got down on her knees. He tried to cross his legs but he couldn't. At least he figured he wasn't going to get an erection. There was nothing about that particular age bracket that turned him on. But then the thought that he *shouldn't* be aroused was slightly arousing him so he had to focus on the other people in the room. How much he hated them. How awkward this whole situation was.

Slit Rider had some kind of smartphone in his hand, aiming it at Steve and the girl.

"We'll gets it all on camera. Big crime. This."

Steve looked at the girl and said, "Don't."

Her head paused in its descent to his crotch. At this point, he was just happy she understood a word he said.

"Is that all you want? The pin number to my debit card? I don't really have much in there."

"It's tip of the iceberg of dicks."

"Also, this would probably be more of a crime if I wasn't in restraints. I mean, what? She's going to give me head and I'm not going to be aroused and I'm not going to come and then you're going to show this video to somebody and prove to them that I was held against my will while somebody else forced this underage girl to perform oral sex on me. How is that a good idea?"

"He's got smart brains. Hold ons, Slayer. Don't move around on its."

Slit Rider left the room and came back with Steve's gun. He was hoping they hadn't found it. It was a fully loaded Glock. Steve kept it around the cabin only as a last ditch thing. Maybe at one point he'd bought it to convince himself he wasn't suicidal like some people keep a bottle of booze or a pack of cigarettes in their homes to prove to themselves they're no longer addicted. Slit Rider handed the gun to Ashley and started untying Steve.

"Now you will be criminal," Slit Rider said.

The ropes dropped and Steve immediately felt tingling in his arms and legs. He'd had a grand vision of the ropes dropping away and him springing into action but, if he tried to move now, he would just fall on his face.

At least he was able to twist his legs and penis away when the girl bent for it.

Ashley, possibly mistaking this for an escape attempt, pulled the trigger.

Part of the girl's face exploded outward and blood sprayed Steve's chest. If the bullet hit him, he was unaware. Now he had to move. He lunged for the door of the room and, as he feared, went sprawling face first. He was also aware that he was screaming. And maybe pissing.

"What do you want?! What do you want?!" He thought he said

this a hundred more times.

"Shit," Ashley said.

"No bigs," Slit Rider said.

Steve hoped maybe a neighbor had heard the gunshot. Maybe they thought he'd finally decided to off himself.

"We need to get out of here," Ashley said.

"Calm calm."

"Grab Parachute and Tram and let's get the *fuck* out of here."

Slit Rider slapped Ashley and she shot Steve in the back of his right leg. It felt like a lead weight and then nothing. Maybe that was the beauty of shock.

Slit Rider grabbed Steve around the wrist and dragged him into the main room. Ashley ran to the door and said, "Jesus, Slitty, they already took off. Fuckers probably left with the first shot."

The only thing Steve had the capacity to do in the way of self-defense was roll. He began rolling to his left, not really knowing where his ultimate goal was. His legs felt like sandbags attached to his body. Slit Rider leapt over him and placed a foot on his waist. Slit Rider threw his hands up in the air.

"Don't you sees, Sharon X? This is how it's meant. We are ready for space. Ready for space!"

"What the fuck are you talking about?"

"Shoot me in the face. Do it now!"

"I'm not going to shoot you in the face. We're not meant to die."

"Not die. Space!"

Slit Rider moved toward Ashley. With Slit Rider's foot gone, Steve began trying to army crawl. He thought he would try for the bathroom. See what happened then. At least there was a door with a lock on it. He didn't think he had any hope of making it out the window and knew there was no way he could make it past Slit Rider and Ashley to get to the front door. He stopped to look back at Slit Rider and Ashley. Slit Rider had his hands around Ashley's and the gun and then there was a loud crack and he hit the ground. Since Steve was the only person besides herself Ashley hadn't killed, he crawled for the bathroom even faster, almost expecting a bullet to find its way into his head. Before pulling himself into the bathroom, he looked back and saw Ashley standing over Slit Rider's body with something like reverence in her eyes. She wasn't crying anymore. She still held the gun in her hand.

Steve closed the door to the bathroom.

He heard another shot.

Bury the Children in the Yard

Steve didn't know how long he stayed in the bathroom. Didn't know what he was waiting for. Sirens maybe. He either dozed off or passed out from the pain. While he was out he had the dream. This time it was different only in that it didn't have any children in it. He and Heidi still wandered away from the car after the accident but when they got to the cabin she collapsed onto the ground and told him to bury her because she was killing him. She said she was already dead. Had been for a long time. He did what he was told and didn't wake up until he miscalculated with the shovel and brought it down on his foot. By the time he awoke, the pain had traveled all the way up his leg.

There still wasn't any sign of the police.

He tried to stand up and managed it with relative ease. He looked at his leg. The side of his leg had a line of flesh that had been torn away. The bullet must have only grazed him. He felt stupid and cowardly. Maybe his leg had still been asleep when Ashley shot at him. If so, that meant he might have been able to do something about the scene in the living room.

He walked out into the living room, the smell of blood and shit hitting his nostrils.

Slit Rider still lay on the floor. Ashley lay crosswise on top of him. The gun lay on the floor a few feet away.

He found one of Ashley's cigarettes, took it out to the front porch, and lit it.

The sun was just going down, the sky was clear, and the lake glowed a hellish orange.

He was surprisingly calm. This was the second most traumatic thing that had happened to him and, in a way, he didn't even feel a part of it. He owned the cabin where it took place. He'd had sex with Ashley but what did any of it have to do with him? What would happen if he *did* call the police? He would be questioned, for sure. But he was convinced he wouldn't be found guilty of anything. Which he wasn't. And then what? And then life would go on exactly as it had before.

He might as well be one of the corpses in the house.

He stayed on the porch until night bloomed, black and moonless.

He went into the house and cleaned his wound and bandaged his leg. He thought about burning down the cabin. But that didn't seem poetic enough. He went out to the tool shed and found his shovel, probably the same one he'd used to bury his imaginary children. He could now hear some of the families around the lake, kids shouting, adult conversations. Laughter. Full lives. Where were they earlier? Maybe they were so turned inward they didn't hear much of anything happening around them. And maybe that was only because they were on vacation. In Steve's experience it seemed like most people paid way too much attention to things that didn't really have anything to do with them. Maybe that was it. Maybe they turned away when it was anything that might demand some kind of involvement and chose only to focus on minutiae.

Who knew?

Who knew much of anything?

Steve was sure he didn't. He was going to dig a hole. The sun would be coming up in about seven hours so he thought he had some time. Then he would drag the corpses from the house and put them in the hole. Then he would fill the hole and go into the cabin and clean up as best he could, but not perfectly. He didn't think he wanted to remove all the evidence of what had happened. He would know *some*thing had happened. He wouldn't tell anyone about it no matter how much he might want to. It would be his.

He broke the ground with the shovel and some dark cloud broke within him, filling him with thunder and lightning and rain. He listened to the families around him play and continued to dig the hole.

Other Grindhouse Press Titles

#666__*Satanic Summer* by Andersen Prunty

#066__*Depraved* by Bryan Smith

#065__*Crazytimes* by Scott Cole

#064__*Blood Relations* by Kristopher Triana

#063__*The Perfectly Fine House* by Stephen Kozeniewski and Wile E. Young

#062__*Savage Mountain* by John Quick

#061__*Cocksucker* by Lucas Milliron

#060__*Luciferin* by J. Peter W.

#059__*The Fucking Zombie Apocalypse* by Bryan Smith

#058__*True Crime* by Samantha Kolesnik

#057__*The Cycle* by John Wayne Comunale

#056__*A Voice So Soft* by Patrick Lacey

#055__*Merciless* by Bryan Smith

#054__*The Long Shadows of October* by Kristopher Triana

#053__*House of Blood* by Bryan Smith

#052__*The Freakshow* by Bryan Smith

#051__*Dirty Rotten Hippies and Other Stories* by Bryan Smith

#050__*Rites of Extinction* by Matt Serafini

#049__*Saint Sadist* by Lucas Mangum

#048__*Neon Dies at Dawn* by Andersen Prunty

#047__*Halloween Fiend* by C.V. Hunt

#046__*Limbs: A Love Story* by Tim Meyer

#045__*As Seen On T.V.* by John Wayne Comunale

#044__*Where Stars Won't Shine* by Patrick Lacey

#043__*Kinfolk* by Matt Kurtz

#042__*Kill For Satan!* by Bryan Smith

#041__*Dead Stripper Storage* by Bryan Smith

#040__*Triple Axe* by Scott Cole

#039__*Scummer* by John Wayne Comunale

#038__*Cockblock* by C.V. Hunt

#037__*Irrationalia* by Andersen Prunty

#036__*Full Brutal* by Kristopher Triana

#035__*Office Mutant* by Pete Risley

#034__*Death Pacts and Left-Hand Paths* by John Wayne Comunale

#033__*Home Is Where the Horror Is* by C.V. Hunt

#032__*This Town Needs A Monster* by Andersen Prunty